About the Author

*V*ANINA MARSOT holds an MFA in literature and creative writing from the Bennington Writing Seminars. She has translated numerous television shows and feature film scripts. She divides her time between Paris and Los Angeles.

Foreign Tongue

Foreign Tongue

A Novel of Life and Love in Paris

VANINA MARSOT

HARPER

NEW YORK · LONDON · TORONTO · SYDNEY

HARPER

HarperCollins books may be purchased for
educational, business, or sales promotional use.
For information please write: Special Markets Department,
HarperCollins Publishers, 10 East 53rd Street, New York, NY 10022.

FIRST EDITION

Designed by Ruth Lee-Mui

Library of Congress Cataloging-in-Publication Data is available upon request.
ISBN 978-0-06-167366-5

09 10 11 12 13   OV/RRD   10 9 8 7 6 5 4 3 2 1

For my parents

I want to beg you, as much as I can, dear sir, to be patient toward all that is unsolved in your heart and to try to love the *questions themselves* like locked rooms and like books that are written in a very foreign tongue.

RAINER MARIA RILKE,
Letters to a Young Poet

L'histoire est entièrement vraie, puisque je l'ai imaginée d'un bout à l'autre.*

BORIS VIAN,
L'Écume des jours

*The story is entirely true, since I imagined it from start to finish.

Foreign Tongue

1

Il n'y a pas de malheur pire que celui qu'on a. *
—ARAB PROVERB

I could start like this, third-person omniscient: "She chucked it all and moved to Paris." I like "chucked it all," as if you could shove chunks of your life out the door of a moving vehicle, say a 1968 Chevrolet Camaro, newly restored on fat tires, vintage Beastie Boys playing in the background. Or how about "She picked up and left," with its faux-folksiness, a hair away from "she jes' plum picked up and left, Jed." As if one could pack one's possessions in a skirt and hoist it up, hoops and crinoline, and take off. Then there's that slightly perplexing "picked up." It reminds me of my childhood jackstraws game. All those plastic, bone-colored pieces. A hoe jimmied up by a rake or a sword or a trowel. The first few rounds are always carefree, reckless. It's only near the end when precision and silence rule the game. When everything hinges on the last move.

Or no dodge-and-weave, no embroidery, no third-person, no all-knowing voice: I left. It was easy for me to move to Paris, and I had to leave.

*There is no greater misfortune than one's own.

Like that. One day, my life became unbearable: straw, camel, back, and the unmistakable sound of splinters, or whatever a broken heart sounds like to the possessor (for the record: shattering glass, snapping tennis racket strings, the braying of world-weary donkeys, the high-pitched, internal bat-squeak of air being forced through congested sinuses, to name a few). I called my gabby travel agent. Many minutes and credit card numbers later, I had a ticket and a week to pack and get my life in order.

It wasn't as wacky as it sounds. I had dual citizenship and some mad money stashed away; my copywriting gig for an entertainment PR firm was portable; and, in a neat trick, I sublet my apartment to my landlady's son. I let my parents know I needed a change of pace. I knew better than to tell them the real reason I was leaving town. If I told my mother, she'd worry the entire time I was gone, and I couldn't tell my father. He was so unnerved by any display of emotional distress that he invariably shut down, his eyes either glazing over or darting back and forth in search of the nearest possible exit. All of my friends figured a change would do me good. Except Lindsay.

"Anna, you're running away," she said, point-blank on the phone. As if the accusation, like a bullet, would stop me in my tracks. I could picture her in her stainless-steel kitchen, baby Ethan balanced on her hip, while she edited a movie trailer on three iMacs and puréed organic bok choy. Ever since she'd become a mother, she'd had no time for anyone's bullshit, least of all mine.

Figuring there was no point in arguing, I trilled, "Yes, I am," nearly like a country singer. I felt giddy. "And righteous about it," I added. I emptied a box of chewy caramel calcium supplements into a Ziploc bag and listened to her exhale long and impatiently. Surveying the somber piles of clothing around me, I thought of something Hank Williams Jr. had said about black being good for funerals and everything else.

"Remember when I was having a rough time? How I wanted to get in a boat and take off? But I knew that once I got in the boat and put out to sea, all my problems would crawl out of the woodwork, I knew they'd find a way onboard as stowaways." She was relentless, a Sherman tank of run-on sentences. My nose twitched. There was a prettier way of telling it, and she'd butchered the metaphor. "You have obligations, responsibilities," she added.

"Actually, I don't," I uttered, a tad bit waspishly. "I don't have any commitments, and being in this city has become unbearable. *I can't stay here.*" The last sentence came out like a low howl, barely restrained from being frightening. I could have used the word "keening." It would have been right.

She was quiet. Remarshaling forces. "What, you think they don't have *People* magazine in Paris?" she countered.

"Don't."

"I bet they even have *Entertainment Tonight*. Dubbed, but still."

"Now you're being mean," I tried.

"Just move on! Deal with it!" she yelled. "You're not the first person in the world this has happened to!" Very, very gently, as if in slow motion, I put the phone back in its cradle and tiptoed away.

It was going to be a while before she forgave me; we weren't hang-up-acceptable sorts of friends. I was setting fire to lots of bridges. I mulled this over as I stuffed socks into shoes. It was probably simplistic, but I had a notion that the universe worked in a few key ways and I wasn't ready to give up on them. I believed most people were supposed to find each other and, if they were so inclined, have kids; that is, people who wanted to do that sort of thing. Not that it was supposed to be perfect. Sometimes it worked, sometimes it didn't. Sometimes someone died, or they broke up, or random tragedy struck (though I could get paranoid about driving on the freeway, I tended to confine this line of thinking to natural disasters and times of war). I was a late bloomer, but I'd finally figured out that I wanted to be part of that world.

So, when I met and fell in love with Timothy, I thought I was following the master plan, the great scheme. ("Yay!" the lemmings cry as they rush the cliff en masse.) And I fell hard: I thought Timothy was The One. But the relationship conjugated itself differently: I met Timothy, I fell in love with Timothy, I had my heart broken by Timothy. *Amo, amas,* amok. It took less than six months.

In the past, my former boyfriends had disappeared obligingly into the woodwork. Our paths didn't cross. It was as if we unconsciously divided up the city between us: you take Echo Park, Downtown, Culver City, and the South Bay, I'll take Santa Monica, Venice, and Hollywood; give my regards to Rajee, the chef at that Punjabi dive you love, and in return, I expect never to run into you renting movies at Vidiots.

Okay, not really. But L.A. was big enough that I never ran into Ned, Paul, or Phillip. Not even the crazy mime, whose name I can't remember. I could imagine them dead, though I mean that in a benign neglect/off-my-planet way, not in the blue/toe-tag way. Now, here's the kicker: Timothy became famous. Magazine-cover famous. Pop-culture famous.

With a mounting sense of panic crossed with nauseated curiosity, I listened as friends called to warn me about page 207 in this month's *Vanity Fair,* page 54 in *Entertainment Weekly,* and page blankety-blank in *Newsweek,* not to mention the various websites and blogs. It wasn't awful merely because he looked good on those pages but because he was photographed with beautiful, famous women, none of whom was me.

It started slowly—an article in the *Los Angeles Times*—and snowballed. After the two-page story in *Rolling Stone,* the interviews in both *Los Angeles* magazine and the *New York Times,* not to mention the appearance on E! Entertainment Television, I had a T-shirt printed up that said "Ionesco is my copilot." No one laughed, except for the goateed anarchist who pours java at my local coffeehouse, and that was more of a snigger.

This is how it happened that last night in his crumbling, rented, Mediterranean-style house in the hills. Something was off, had been off for a few weeks, but he'd been traveling, and I thought I was reading too much into the silences and awkward moments on the phone. But at dinner in a loud Italian restaurant shortly after he got back, I felt something funny in the way he kissed me. A kiss is almost like a person—it can be sly, guilty, and apologetic in the same mouthful. This one was also overconfident, like it had a couple of new tricks up its sleeve and was showing off. And yet, disguised as it was in the person of the man I thought I knew, I disregarded it.

Except, there it was again, later, in bed, that same guilty kiss. I pulled away from him and sat up. My grandmother's locket, a rose-gold heart with a smaller heart picked out in diamond chips, a piece of jewelry I almost never wore but had fastened around my neck on a whim that very afternoon, swung back and rapped me on the sternum like a knock on a hollow door. In the next moment, the words were out of my mouth.

"Are you sleeping with someone else?" I asked in a strangled voice.

I hadn't suspected anything. I'd never even thought it, but there it was, and as I asked it, I realized I knew the answer. Or knew that I'd asked because I knew the answer—or because my grandmother's locket, a gift from my grandfather ("For my dearest Ninon, with all my love, Aurélien"), heavy with symbolism, spoke to me. In that moment, I felt an eerie chill, a voodoo moment when time slowed down, and questions and their answers walked hand in hand up a garden path. I could hear the silent, yawning space between each heartbeat as I got smaller and smaller, fuzzier and fuzzier, Alice in Blunderland.

He kept talking, but I couldn't hear. I put on clothes and left, driving down the hill and across two freeways back home to Santa Monica, where I cried for the next month.

I did have some better days, when I heard a whisper of optimism, believed that finding real, lasting love was possible. But this is the twenty-first century, and I lived and worked in the entertainment capital of the world, and some weeks, the realest thing I felt was followed by a credit crawl and end-title music.

Timothy and I never talked again. It was shortly afterward, in some malevolent twist of fate designed to drive me batty, that he became It Boy in the media. Maybe I should have hung around, because no one stays It Boy forever. But three months was about all the stamina I had. You don't get over someone when you're constantly being reminded of him. The fact of his ubiquity made it impossible to pretend he was dead. I had no other coping maneuver, so I did what any sensible woman would do.

I ran away.

2

There is but one Paris and however hard living may be here,
and if it became worse and harder even—
the French air clears up the brain and does good—
a world of good.
—VINCENT VAN GOGH,
The Complete Letters of Vincent van Gogh

When running away, I recommend arriving with keys. Makes you feel like you're actually in control of the situation instead of on the lam from your life. When the immigration official at Roissy asked me where I'd learned to speak French so well, I slid out my *carte nationale d'identité,* revealing my dual citizenship. He smiled as if I'd shared an intimate secret and said, "Welcome home."

I took a taxi to Tante Isabelle's apartment in the Eleventh Arrondissement, sandwiched between the Bastille and the Canal Saint-Martin on one axis, République and Belleville on the other. My father's sister and my favorite aunt, she lived in San Francisco most of the year. Fed up with the rental agency she used to rent her pied-à-terre to tourists, she'd FedExed me the keys to her fourth-floor flat, no questions asked. I walked into the late-nineteenth-century limestone building, scrunched myself on top of my suitcases in the minuscule elevator (*capacité: trois midgets*), and rode up.

Inside, it was dark and smelled of old books, furniture polish, and mothballs. The French don't like to see front doors, maybe because they like to pretend the outside world is that much farther away, or to hide the sight of the inevitable electricity and gas meters. So they put up curtains or separate the entrance from the rest of the house by French doors, as Tante Isabelle had.

The doors opened onto the living room, a mix of antiques and IKEA. Under a rectangular, ormolu mirror was a black leather sofa, its stuffing flattened with use. A coffee table strewn with old issues of *Figaro Madame* and *Télérama* sat in front of it, flanked by a pink velvet bergère and a kilim footstool like an obedient pet. A floor-to-ceiling bookcase took up one wall, with a niche for the stereo and television. A leather-topped desk and chair stood on the other side of the room, in front of a bar trolley, and another large mirror stretched almost to the ceiling above the white marble fireplace mantel behind it.

Tante Isabelle's bookshelves contained a thorough collection of France's greatest hits of the nineteenth century, gold-tooled and bound in morocco leather: Balzac, Flaubert, Zola. I pulled *Madame Bovary* off the shelf and flipped through the thin, crisp pages, liver-spotted and dense with print. There were also art books, various Paris guides and maps, and paperback novels in English.

A worn Oriental rug covered the *point de Hongrie* wood floor. Two windows gave out onto balconies—ledges, really, with wrought-iron guardrails—above the busy street.

Off one side of the living room was the kitchen, well-equipped with gleaming appliances to attract renters, including a stainless-steel fridge (contents: one bottle of champagne, two frozen Weight Watchers dinners *au saumon*, crusty with ice), and a sturdy pine table that seated four. Down a small hallway was the remodeled bathroom, pristine and sparkly white (again, to attract renters), and a bedroom, dominated by a large bed with a fluffy white duvet and an armoire.

I fell backward onto the duvet and sank into goose down. Everything I needed.

Except Timothy.

There he was, just like Lindsay had warned me, a stowaway on the escape boat.

I rolled onto my side, clutching my knees to my chest. We'd talked about coming to Paris together. One of the many late-night conversations we'd had about the future by the aqua-blue light of the digital clock. Two weeks in September, my favorite month, *la rentrée*, when everyone returned from vacation and the city woke from the summer *sieste*. "I want to see Paris through your eyes," he'd said, his arms around me, his chin digging into my shoulder. "I want to know it the way you do."

I sat up. I didn't want to cry over Timothy in this bed; I'd cried enough in my own back home. I dragged my bags into the bedroom and thought about unpacking and heating a frozen meal for dinner. It wasn't anywhere near comforting enough.

I called Bunny. An elderly bachelor and former journalist I'd met years ago when I'd had a part-time research job at the *International Herald Tribune*, he'd settled down to a comfy editor's job at a publication division of UNESCO. I'd come up with his nickname after he drove me home one night in his VW Rabbit. Randolph, his real name, seemed too much of a mouthful, and he was not a Randy.

"H-e-e-e-y, it's you!" he said, making his familiar neighing sound. "Did you just get in? How was your flight?"

"Fine. The apartment is perfect except for food. Are you free for dinner?"

"I could be, if you're willing to meet me halfway," he said. "Le Soufflé, on the rue du Mont Thabor. They've got AC. Eight o'clock?"

"*Parfait,*" I said.

....

I unpacked, took a long bath, and walked over. I meandered through the Marais, up Etienne Marcel, and around place des Victoires. I felt like a proprietary hound, sniffing at sidewalks and corners, verifying all the landmarks of my favorite city were still where they were supposed to be.

It was hot out. The sun was still high in the sky; it wouldn't set for at least another couple of hours. I'd always resented being put to bed at eight o'clock on summer childhood trips to Paris. It had felt wrong to go to sleep when it was still sunny out.

"Ouf, if we let you stay up until night, you'll be up until ten-thirty," my grandmother had said, shutting the metal *volets.* I'd had trouble sleeping in that room, with the sunlight forcing its way like white knives through the lateral slits in the shutters.

As I walked, I heard smatterings of English, mostly in American accents. A lot of Parisians were already on vacation; in two weeks, the city would feel empty except for the tourists. Boutique windows were papered with end of season sale signs: SOLDES and 50% REDUCTION. I took off my sunglasses in the Palais Royal, and strolled under the arcades behind a group of teenagers with elaborate tattoos. I moved around them and passed an olive-skinned man in a safari jacket, smoking a thin cigar. He gave me one of those penetrating looks that seem to be a comment, an examination, and an invitation all at once. A look that took me in, as opposed to merely examining the scenery.

The effect was shocking, no less so than if he'd reached out and touched me. I'd forgotten that, the Parisian stare; in L.A. you look casually and either glance away or give a noncommittal smirk if you make eye contact with someone on the street, and most of the time, we're not on the street, we're in cars. It felt potent and provocative, a reminder to pay attention. I overshot the rue du Faubourg Saint-Honoré and had to backtrack to the restaurant.

Bunny was already there. He was an unusually tall man, six foot eight, which would have been intimidating except for his aging, freckled baby face, with kind brown eyes that turned down at the corners. He wore a striped oxford shirt and khaki pants. He pushed his reading glasses back up his snub nose, looking up from his newspaper.

"Jeepers, you're a sight for sore eyes," he remarked. I leaned over and kissed him on both cheeks.

"You, too," I said. He gave a smile disguised as a grimace. He'd aged since the last time I'd seen him, nearly two years ago: more of the freckles were age spots, and his hair was more salt than pepper.

"Une bouteille de Brouilly, s'il vous plaît," he told the waiter. I glanced at the menu. The restaurant did little else than soufflés and always seemed to be full of tourists, but Bunny liked it, and what they did, they did well. Over dinner, we talked about politics and movies, pop music and books, bringing each other up to speed.

"That Fergie is something," he said, eyeing a passing chocolate soufflé.

"Oh, good lord!" I made a face.

"I need something to get me going on the treadmill," he said. He cleaned his glasses with a napkin and then leaned in to examine me. "Tell me. What's the real story? Why the sudden trip?" he asked. "You thinking of moving back to 'Ris?"

I smiled. Bunny had abbreviations and nicknames for a host of things. Paris was 'Ris, the rue de Rivoli was Ravioli, and feet were dogs. Certain houseflies were Charlies, who spread illness and germs; others were Irwins, kind and innocuous. Alas, he'd tell you, there was no way to tell them apart.

Before I could answer, he asked, "Did I show you my new cards?" He placed a business card on the table. In an Art Deco font, it read, "Randolph Isaiah Pettigrew," and underneath it, "Urban Parasite." His number was printed at the bottom.

"Not bad," I said. "I liked the last one, 'Master at Nouns.'"

He shrugged and took out another one. "I'm saving this one for my retirement," he said. It said "R. I. Pettigrew, *Inspecteur des Parcs de Paris,*" and was printed in green.

"You're going to spend your retirement inspecting Parisian parks?" I asked.

"Keeping an eye out on the sparrows. See?" he asked, pointing to three little birds punctuating the upper left corner of the card. "Originally, I had *'Flâneur des Espaces Verts,'* but this is less pretentious. Keep it," he added. "You didn't answer my question."

I toyed with my wineglass. I felt bloated with Timothy, like the fact of him had taken over my life, as if talking about him now would perpetuate it.

"Hey," Bunny said, putting his hand on mine. My eyes welled up. I took a couple of deep breaths and told him the story as briefly as I could. He didn't judge, he didn't give advice, and for a while, he didn't say anything. He passed me his navy blue bandanna, scented with lily of the valley, to mop up.

"I hate those kinds of stories," he said, after a while, looking annoyed.

"Me too," I agreed.

....

I linked my arm in his as we strolled along Ravioli after dinner. At eleven, the sky was darkening to a velvety, royal blue with only a couple of stars.

"You going to stay for a while?" he asked. I shrugged; I hadn't thought that far in advance. "Why don't you get a job?" he suggested. "Keep you from thinking too much. Earn some money, have a regular schedule, meet some new people, stay busy . . ."

"But it's summer," I pointed out.

"It's not impossible to find a job, even now. Something part-time.

Volunteer. Teach English. I can ask if anyone needs a research assistant," he said.

"Maybe." I glanced at the Jardin des Tuileries, where a Ferris wheel, lit up with multicolored neon lights, towered over a summer amusement park. Bunny followed my sight line and gave me a questioning look.

I shook my head. "I'm scared of heights," I explained. We stopped in front of the Concorde métro.

"Think about it," he said, leaning down to kiss me good-bye. "A job may be just the ticket." He walked down the stairs and raised a hand to wave, not turning around.

3

*As far as modern writing is concerned,
it is rarely rewarding to translate it, although it might be easy . . .
Translation is very much like copying paintings.*

—BORIS PASTERNAK

Before they left on their respective summer vacations, Althea, Clara, and I met for dinner at Chez Omar, an old-time couscous place in the Marais. I'd met Clara years ago, when I'd studied in Paris for a year in college. A short, energetic *Parisienne de souche* with a face like a Botticelli cupid under a mop of red curls, she managed her jewelry design business out of an airy, luxurious apartment and conducted what seemed to be doomed, if long-term, love affairs with unavailable men. It was all very operatic.

Althea, on the other hand, was half-American, half-English, and still happily involved with Ivan, her half-English, half-French boyfriend of the past three years. She had pale, freckled skin, a firm jaw, and one of those easygoing manners that somehow managed to sway everyone into doing exactly what she wanted. A graphic designer with a penchant for dyeing her hair different colors, she was currently sporting purple and green tresses. After I gave my nutshell version of why I was in Paris, they exchanged a look.

"You should stay at least until Christmas," Althea announced.

"You've got an apartment, rent-free," Clara chimed in. "You should enjoy this freedom—not everyone can go live somewhere else so easily." She lifted the conical clay lid off her preserved-lemon *tagine* and breathed in the smell. "And you can't get this in Los Angeles. I know, I've been there."

I ladled vegetables over my couscous. "I'm thinking about it," I admitted, finally acknowledging an idea that had taken hold the second I'd landed, or the second I'd gotten out of the taxi to Tante Isabelle's and smelled the ripe peaches from the *primeur* and fresh bread from the *boulangerie*, albeit mixed in with bus exhaust: I wanted to stay.

"You need a break from Los Angeles. Longer than a vacation," Althea said. "*En plus*, we want you here."

....

I threw myself into life in Paris. Just because almost everyone I knew had gone on vacation didn't mean there weren't lots of things to do. Besides, keeping busy seemed to be the best cure for what ailed me. I went to a Rohmer festival at the Action Ecoles, briefly took up running until the weather got too hot, bought some clothes and shoes in the sales, and discovered a number of excellent cafés in Tante Isabelle's neighborhood. My favorite, Le Schtarbé, which had a toy model of an Airstream trailer hanging outside instead of a shingle, became my hang for a late-morning breakfast of *tartine au beurre* and *café crème*.

I made gleeful trips to my neighborhood Monoprix, loading up my shopping cart with my favorite foods: *fromage blanc, crème de marrons*, every variety of cookie made by LU and Bahlsen, green olive tapenade, *pain Poilâne*, butter from Normandy, and various cheeses and yogurts. I bought a DVD player, thinking it would make a good present for my aunt, and rented French films that hadn't gotten U.S. releases.

Still, there were too many times when I was alone with my thoughts, and my thoughts turned to Timothy. He was there, in my head, as if lying in wait, when I came home. Sometimes I dreaded going to bed: in the dark, my loneliness for him felt like a bottomless chasm I fell into, over and over again.

And then there were the dreams. I dreamed about him less than I did in Los Angeles, but there were still nights when I dreamed Timothy and I were walking around the reservoir or chopping vegetables for a meal; when I dreamed we were in bed, filling out the *New York Times* Sunday crossword puzzle; and worst, when I dreamed I'd woken up and he was there, next to me.

When my bedtime anxiety got too bad, I went out to Le Schtarbé or Le Zorba for a glass of wine, but it was hard to tell what was worse: talking to strangers, or putting on my leave-me-alone face and actually being left alone in a crowd. Sometimes it was easier to take a sleeping pill and turn the long *traversin* pillow sideways in bed. Curling my back against it, I almost felt like I wasn't sleeping alone. When both cafés closed for the summer vacation, the decision was made for me.

A couple of weeks into my stay, I found an unpleasant surprise in my e-mail. George, my boss at the PR firm, had been fired, and his replacement, one Everett Lewicki, didn't seem at all inclined to throw me any work, especially as I was out of the country. George wrote that he was volunteering for Habitat for Humanity in Madagascar and wasn't at all sure he'd want to go back to the rat race after seeing the lemurs.

I took out my credit card receipts and looked at my bank account online. If I wanted to stay awhile, I'd have to dip into my savings. Despite what Bunny said, Paris in August was no time to be looking for work. I shoved the receipts from my shopping sprees into an envelope and got up. Maybe this was the time to finally read *Du côté de chez Swann* in French. I reached for the leather-bound volume and fell asleep reading it on the sofa.

. . . .

It was muggy in the morning. The sun poked through fluffy white clouds in the west as I walked through the park behind Notre Dame. The cathedral looked like an old Yvon postcard: biblical clouds surrounding iconic edifice. I half-expected a dimpled cherub diapered in blue to float above it.

A group of small boys played soccer between the trees, kicking up clouds of dust and shouting. One kid yelled, *"C'est chanmé!"* and another shouted back, *"Portenawaque!"* They gathered in a circle to settle the dispute. It took me a few minutes to figure out what they were saying: in *verlan,* the slang that reversed syllables, it was *"méchant,"* or mean, and *"n'importe quoi,"* the polite phrase for bullshit. Every time I came to Paris, there was new slang—or old slang that was new to me: on my last trip, I'd learned that *"ʒarbi"* was *verlan* for bizarre, and that *"ouf,"* usually an expression for exhaustion, was also *verlan* for *fou,* or crazy.

A crowd of people leaned over the ledge by the river. Down below, a horse-drawn carriage, festooned with roses and feathers like Cinderella's coach-and-four, idled on the riverbank while a film crew tinkered with lights and cables. A gloved hand appeared through the carriage window and dropped an empty Evian bottle to a waiting PA.

I crossed the river to Shakespeare & Company and combed through the used books, hoping to find a vintage pulp novel with a lurid cover, or one of the Mary Stewart mysteries I used to read as a kid. A stocky blond woman with a limp, hand-rolled cigarette dangling from the corner of her mouth, *une clope au bec,* added job postings to the blackboard by the entrance.

"Any of these jobs worth checking out?" I asked.

"Depends," she said and shrugged, pushing hair out of her eyes. "Do you speak French?" I nodded. She looked at a card in her hand, and I noticed her nails were bitten down to the pink. "This guy always needs translators," she said. "Pays pretty well." She handed me an index card from the stack she was transcribing onto the blackboard. Editions

Laveau, on the rue de Condé, needed a translator, "English mother tongue."

"Thanks," I said.

"I'd go now. By this afternoon, you'll be too late," she said and clicked at me, like a gunslinger to a horse.

Pocketing the card, I sped over to the Sixth and up the rue de Condé. I knew a bar there, little more than a black tunnel lined with leather seats and a glittery white gravel floor. The décor consisted of spotlit stone statues of Buddha and Ganesha. Back when I'd lived in Paris after college, Clara and her then-boyfriend had taken me there for swimming pool blue cocktails and killer rounds of backgammon. Another time, I'd taken a date, a redheaded rock-climber, there. When he'd told me I was mysterious and beautiful, I'd kissed him, because he'd made me feel like I was. We'd strolled along the banks of the Seine, making out under bridges until early in the morning.

At number seventeen, I found Editions Laveau, a small bookstore with yellow anti-glare film on the glass. As I walked in, a cowbell affixed to the door pealed, rattling my teeth. There were antique books everywhere: leather-bound, crumbling, piled waist high on the floor, displayed on mismatched tables. A tall, pointy-faced man who looked like Jean Rochefort's mean older brother emerged from a back room.

"Puis-je vous aider, mademoiselle?"

"Vous êtes Monsieur Laveau?" I asked.

"Lui-même." He inclined his head, an owl at a dinner party.

"Je suis venue à cause de l'annonce."

"Je regrette, mademoiselle, mais je cherche quelqu'un qui parle anglais comme sa langue maternelle. Bonne journée." He was looking for a native English speaker. With that, he dismissed me and turned on his heel.

I squawked in protest. "Excuse me, I don't think I made myself clear," I said, switching to English. He turned around. "While I'm flattered that you consider my French good, English is my native tongue." He knit overgrown eyebrows and looked me up and down. Feeling less than fashionably Parisian in my slightly sweaty T-shirt and jeans, I raised a defiant eyebrow in response.

"You read the announcement, did you not, *mademoiselle*?"

"Of course." I pulled the index card out of my back pocket and re-read it. "Serious French author requires excellent translator for"—My face grew hot. I'd mistaken an "r" for an "x."—"erotic novel. Discretion, humor, and a refined sense of nuance required."

On how many levels can you blush, and are they discernible? What did that blush give away? That I hadn't read the ad carefully? The fact that the translation was for an erotic novel? The fact that, when I was twelve, I'd found a paperback copy of *Emmanuelle* in the garage, among a pile of old *Newsweek*s, and had read it in secret? Monsieur Laveau looked at me with a superior, half-amused expression, as if he'd read my mind. I tried to compose myself, making my face blank, expressionless.

He looked disappointed. I had a sensation I'd had before in France, that not everyone finds a blank slate charming and guileless, the way we do back home. Here, they prefer complexity: an acknowledgment that we are all guilty; or at least, no one is innocent. Nevertheless, he gestured toward the back, and I followed him into a book-lined study with an espresso machine, a large desk, and two windows looking out onto a leafy courtyard.

He offered me coffee in thickly accented English. I sat on a worn leather club chair, the kind chic American bistros buy by the truckload at French flea markets. Only this one hadn't been reupholstered since Vichy, and I sank into a deep, lumpy hole, inches off the ground. Impervious to my discomfort, Monsieur Laveau handed me a cup of coffee with an acorn of brown sugar and sat behind his mahogany desk.

"Tell me about yourself."

"You know, that's actually pretty boring," I said and laughed, a bit coquettishly.

He looked baffled. "Nevertheless, I'd like to hear your English a bit more." Oh, right, this wasn't about me. I explained that I was raised more or less bilingual in Los Angeles, because my father was French, and I'd lived in Paris at various times. I mentioned that while I'd never done literary translation, I'd done translations of PR copy for several French and French-Canadian film releases. At the mention of film, his eyebrows shot up, and he scribbled a note with a fountain pen.

As I spoke, lifting my chin so I could see more of him over the desk, I took in more details about Monsieur Laveau: well-preserved, maybe late sixties but looked younger, with blue eyes, a lined face, and high, almost Slavic cheekbones. He wore a *chevalière,* a ring with a family crest, an accessory with a certain amount of snob appeal. Nestled inside his white shirt was a loosely knotted cravat, and though his cuffs were frayed, he had a certain shabby style. A few wiry white hairs stuck out from his neat gray head, and his mustache limped at the corners like Droopy Dog's jowls.

"Can you be discreet?" he asked, cutting me off as I rambled on about my English major in college, my love of nineteenth-century literature, and how that had led to my stint with a big entertainment public relations firm and subsequent freelance PR work.

"Sure. Why?" I asked.

He sat back in his chair and frowned. It was a powerful frown, emanating disapproval and deepening the furrows all over his face.

"My client is quite well-known," he said. He ran his fingers along the edge of his desk. "He has published very serious books about politics and sociology. But recently, he has written a novel, his second, very loosely inspired by *le grand amour de sa vie.* It is this erotic novel we are talking about. I do not know the extent of your familiarity with contemporary French writing, but it is not inconceivable that you might imagine you know who the writer is."

I squirmed. His manner was condescending, borderline insulting.

"Thus," he continued, "he wishes to remain anonymous. The book will be published at next year's *rentrée,* but he wants it translated into English. I don't know whether this is because of some clause with his publisher, or something to do with the foreign rights. I simply said I would be of help in finding a translator. A woman, of course—"

"Why a woman?" I interrupted.

"*Mais enfin, mademoiselle,* this is the story of his great love," he said reproachfully, as if I'd asked a crazy question.

"I'm sorry, *monsieur,* I don't understand."

"It is of no importance." Waving his hand in the air, he droned on at length about nuance and translation. A chair spring dug into my rear. The book was probably some ghastly novelette full of details the rest of humanity should be spared, but that might be good for laughs, and it would beat teaching English or waitressing.

"As I have had a hard time finding good translators, I will ask you to take this first chapter home with you and give me your best effort by, shall we say, next Monday."

"Like homework?" I smirked.

"Precisely. If he likes your work, you will be hired. If he doesn't like it, I will write you a check for two hundred euros and we will go our separate ways." He gave me a large envelope. I shook his hand and walked outside. Half my rear had fallen asleep. Pins and needles poked at me all the way to the place Edmond Rostand, where I knew I'd find Bunny upstairs at Dalloyau.

Stirring his *crème, The Economist* open in front of him, he neighed when he saw me. "He-e-e-y! How the hell are you?"

"Pretty good." I kissed him on the cheek and sat. "I took your advice. I may have a translating job."

"Let's celebrate! What is it?" he asked, ordering his two favorite pastries, which also happened to be mine: an *éclair au chocolat* and an *opéra.*

"An erotic novel, written by some anonymous guy," I said, grinning.

"Even better!" he said, rubbing his hands together with a leer. "Seriously, I'm pleased. You need something to keep your brain busy. It's the only remedy," he said.

We split the pastries and ate them while Bunny told me about his day. He'd been to one of the *trois-fois-rien* discount stores and laid out his finds on the table: an Astérix coffee mug, a pocketknife, and glow-in-the-dark lip gloss.

"What are you going to do with this?" I asked, pointing to the last item.

"Use it. I have chapped lips."

"It's lip gloss, Bunny, not lip balm."

"You still can't have it," he said, wanting me to argue with him.

"I bet it smells girlie, like bubble gum or something," I said.

"I like bubble gum."

"It's shiny. Shiny is not a good fashion statement for a man your age." I picked it up. "Shiny with *glitter?*"

He let me have it, conceding with a loud sneeze. Afterward, I walked to Gibert Jeune, the student bookstore, to buy a dictionary of slang, or at least obscenities. I'd wanted one for a long time, and I was sure I'd need it for my translation, which I'd decided was going to be flowery and rude, and would probably reduce me to fits of giggles. I wanted to be prepared to understand every single thing.

4

*Pourquoi vos genoux me donnent-ils envie
d'inventer des verbes transitifs?*[*]
—FRÉDÉRIC BEIGBEDER,
"Spleen à l'aéroport de
Roissy-Charles-de-Gaulle"

How I loved reference books: their heft, the joy of randomly opening them up and finding some interesting morsel of knowledge. In L.A., a collection of them edged the far side of my desk, my first line of defense, but the only thing I'd seen in Tante Isabelle's apartment was a dilapidated paperback dictionary, brown with half a century's age. I'd need more to do any translation justice.

Or rather, that's how I justified springing for some major reference book booty: the indispensable Larousse *Dictionnaire de l'argot,* a Harrap's French–English/Anglais–Français two-volume set, a paperback *Dictionnaire des synonymes,* and a *Petit Robert*—a pricey dictionary at sixty-seven euros. In the métro, I ripped the cellophane off the dictionary of slang and flipped through it like a sweaty-palmed kid.

On a graph-paper pad, I scribbled some notes on rude language, try-

*Why do your knees make me want to invent transitive verbs?

ing not to laugh. Some words I already knew, like the fact that "pussy" in English is the same as *"la chatte"* in French, meaning both a cat and women's genitals. But I hadn't known that *"une moule,"* a mussel, could also mean pussy (genitalia, not feline), or that *"un ʒiʒi"* could be both *"pénis ou vulve."* Or that *"un papillon du Sénégal,"* a butterfly from that country, was slang for penis.

I flipped to *"baiser."* As a noun, it means kiss, as in to give someone *"un baiser."* But in the verb form, to *"baiser"* someone means to fuck someone. You've got to wonder about a language that uses the same word for both "fuck" and "kiss."

Or not. I remembered a conversation I'd had at a party in Venice. As usual, I was nursing a bottle of beer and trying to figure out how soon I could leave, when the man sitting next to me said, out of the blue, "You know, I would never kiss someone I wouldn't fuck." I nodded halfheartedly, trying to remember where I'd parked.

"Ah, you, too." He'd looked impressed, as if this meant we had something important in common. "Kissing is just as intimate as fucking. More, maybe."

I'd thought it over as I drove home. I'd thought about how dogs' mouths were supposedly more hygienic than humans'. I'd thought about the dog lovers I knew who let their dogs lick them on the lips and how it made me appreciate cats. I'd thought about the bad kissers I'd kissed and the ones who made my knees weak—Timothy, of course, but also Robin, a fireman I'd dated for a month. It was true I'd kissed men I wouldn't sleep with, partly because I didn't like the way they kissed. But he'd been right about the intimate part.

I flipped to the ubiquitous *"con."* It always puzzled me how cavalierly the French threw around a word which literally meant cunt but was used to mean dumb, stupid, or useless. They use it everywhere, and while it's nowhere near as strong or offensive as it is in English, at least American English, it wasn't the sort of word I'd have used in front of my proper French grandmother. Harrap's entry showed: "con, conne.

n 1. *a F*: bloody stupid 2. *F*: bloody idiot; cretin; faire le c., to fool about 3. *nm V*: cunt."

On the other hand, the dictionary of slang said: *"con n,m. Sexe de la femme (vulve et vagin): . . . se dit d'un homme stupide . . ."* is used for a stupid man, and listed other uses: *"faire le con,"* to play at being an imbecile; *"à la con,"* meaning ridiculous, without interest; *"se retrouver comme un con,"* to find oneself alone and in a grotesque situation; *"si les cons volaient, tu serais chef d'escadrille,"* if idiots flew, you'd be squadron leader, et cetera.

As the train lurched into Châtelet, I remembered the famous feminist critic I'd heard lecture years ago. She'd worn a skirt made of men's ties and transformed all words with "con" into "cunt." It was both disturbing and hilarious to hear her speak matter-of-factly about things cuntentious, cuntemplative, and cuntroversial. Her point was that women's sexuality existed in the English language; it had just been subsumed into the structure and made invisible. It's not invisible in France.

I flipped back through the pages, looking for a definition of *"la chute des reins,"* a phrase I'd always wondered about. It was intriguing to me that this particular part of a woman's anatomy had a name in French. It's the place on a woman's back that begins where the waist starts to flare out. The literal translation is the fall, or slope, of the kidneys, which doesn't sound pretty, but in French, it's poetic. To me, it meant that the French language had mapped out this part of a woman's body; it wasn't undiscovered territory, semantically speaking: it had a name, a location.

On the other hand, maybe it was just a fancy phrase for "ass."

I nearly missed my stop, rushing out as the buzzer sounded at République. A newsmagazine headline at the corner kiosk read, *"Qu'avez vous fait pour les seins?"* What have you done for the breasts? I did a double take. Peering closer, I saw the word was *"siens,"* meaning your close ones or family.

Did merely looking up naughty words in a dictionary make me feel like everything in the world was about sex? Had I regressed to adolescence? Did the words have some kind of effect, or was it merely the suggestion of the erotic, emanating from the shapeless, anonymous text in the brown envelope in my bag? Was it awful? Was it brilliant? Was it hot? It was titillating, not knowing.

....

I raced up the hill and picked up some Chinese takeout in Belleville. At home, I took out the manuscript and squinted at the poorly photocopied pages.

Chapter One, I translated in my head. *The last time I saw Eve, she was laughing and dancing on a table.*

Of course she was. I put my feet up on the coffee table and read on.

She was the kind of woman who would have you believe she danced on tables every night, but I knew she'd come a long way from the affluent suburbs of Alexandria, Egypt, where no one dared do such things.

I have often wondered about that last time, where she might be now, if she knows I still think about her with a combination of pain and longing that is violent in its intensity, while at the same time soothing in its reminder of my past, of who I once was, and who I became, thanks to her.

Wow, that was clumsy. "Thanks to her" sounded awkward, even resentful. *"Grace à elle,"* by her grace, literally, was more delicate.

Just the first two paragraphs were going to be harder than I'd thought. There were intricacies in French that didn't translate easily into English. There was also the notion of feelings being violent, which was commonplace in French and seemed rarer in English.

The next two pages described her face (*of a purity of line like that of an ancient Egyptian princess*—sheesh) and her body (*long limbs, an exaggerated curve in the lower spine, a swan's neck, a softly rounded belly*).

Yada, yada, yada. It was a tedious catalog of this woman Eve's physical attributes: *caressing her skin was one of my greatest pleasures . . . it was smooth and soft, a warm golden brown with the scent of delicate flowers. I lost myself in the contours of her spine, the curve of her hip*—aha! *"La chute des reins."* I would have to find a better phrase than "her kidneys." Maybe "the small of her back."

I could do this. It would be a challenge, figuring out how to shape the text and convey the nuances of the prose while watching out for the tricky *faux amis*: false cognates that mean different things in each language. Spotting the obvious ones—like *entrée*, which means appetizer, not main course; *comédien*, which means actor, not comedian; and *phrase*, which means sentence—was second nature. But others were sneakier: *actuellement* means at the present time, not in fact; *éxperience* means both experience and experiment; and *une déception* is a letdown, not a lie. Some are sly on spelling: *le moral* means morale, versus *la morale*, which means morals. Even the alphabet could trip me up on one letter: the French "g" is pronounced like an English "j," and vice versa.

I skimmed the next few pages, translating in my head and looking up a few words before eating dinner in front of the evening news. I missed PPDA, the nickname by which TF1's former news anchor, Patrick Poivre d'Arvor, was known. Then I went to bed.

In the dark, I thought about the chapter, wondering if anyone would ever think about my skin like that. I ran my fingers along my body. The knob of my hip bone always reminded me of cows in European landscape paintings. I traced random patterns on my thigh, figure eights and stars.

I remembered the summer I'd spent in Paris with my grandmother when I was ten. I'd never been away from my parents for so long, and I was shy and lonely. But I made a friend or two in the parks before they went away for summer vacation, accepted the Jardin d'Acclimatation as a respectable alternative to Disneyland, and watched *Des chiffres et des lettres* and Japanese cartoons on TV before bedtime. But sometimes, clutching my Snoopy at night, I'd sing commercial jingles and the TV theme songs from *Gilligan's Island* and *The Brady Bunch*. Home seemed far away and confusing, and I was no longer sure where it was.

I punched the pillow into shape. A police siren Klaxoned its two-note call in the distance, the Doppler effect changing keys as it raced by. I could live here again.

5

La queue c'est féminin. Le con masculin. Question de chance.*
—SERGE GAINSBOURG

When Pascal, an old friend I'd met during an internship I'd had at a cosmetics company, came back from Greece, we met up for lunch near his office, at a glitzy bistro catering to the fashion industry, modeling agencies, and wealthy foreigners shopping on the avenue Montaigne. After two weeks in July on a beach in Páros with his boyfriend, Florian, he was dark brown and sported a neatly trimmed goatee. In a linen suit over a vintage metal concert T-shirt, he looked like a well-dressed pirate, as befitted the fashion editor for a men's magazine. I kissed his cheek and rubbed his shiny, shaved head.

We sat at a corner table. Pascal waved to the other diners, texted and talked to his office on his cell phone, and threw me apologetic glances. I ordered an overpriced *salade Californienne,* with avocados and shrimp, because that's precisely the kind of food I flew six thousand miles for, and watched a group of well-dressed Middle Eastern women with perfect eyebrows stroll by, laden with Chanel and Ungaro shopping bags.

---

*The cock is feminine. The cunt is masculine. A matter of luck.

"Alors. Raconte-moi tout," Pascal demanded, hanging up the phone.

"There's nothing to tell. I missed Paris, so I found a way to come back." I attempted a Gallic shrug. He looked at me, narrowing his eyes.

"Je ne te crois pas," he said. "Did you win the lottery? Did someone die?"

Heartbreak in French is *chagrin d'amour.* It means a disappointment in love, and it's like food poisoning: everyone knows what it is and sympathizes. It's probably covered under the state's socialized medicine umbrella. *Arrêt de travail pour cause de chagrin d'amour.* I told him about Timothy.

"C'est très people!" he exclaimed. The word "people," pronounced "pipeul" *à la française,* had become the term for celebrity or worldly gossip. Trendy places were described as *hyper-people,* celebrity sightings photographed in the paper came under the rubric *"le monde des people,"* chic nightclubs were where the *"nice people"* hung out. Pascal flipped open his phone and scrolled through the display.

"What is his name? Timothy *comment?"* he asked. "I have to tell Florian. *Il adore les potins!"* he said, pressing the speed dial.

"It's not gossip and that's not funny!" I said, snatching the phone out of his hand. "I'm telling you in confidence. Besides, I'm still getting over it."

"I am sorry, *chérie,"* he said, clucking sympathetically. "Can I tell him when you're over it?" he asked.

"No!" I glared at him. He picked at his smoked salmon and blinis.

"De toute façon, you shouldn't date well-known people," he remarked, watching a plate of fried calamari go by. "I should've ordered that." Turning back to me, he added, "It's always a disaster." He frowned and picked at the knife pleat in his trousers.

"He wasn't well-known when I met him," I said.

"Still. It's a rule. In any case, you shouldn't fall in love with them."

"How are you supposed to stop yourself from falling in love with someone?"

"You can't. But it doesn't matter; now you're in Paris. *Eventuelle-ment*, you will get over it," he said, waving to someone at the other end of the restaurant.

It wasn't comforting. *Eventuellement*, the mother of *faux amis*, means possibly.

We ordered dessert, but he got another call and had to rush back to the office. I took the manuscript out of my bag and ate my *mousse au chocolat* alone.

My education at the hands of women had been thorough. I felt confi-dent in my appeal, I had never wanted for partners. My current girl-friend, Daphne, was a striking, thin blonde with pouty—

I made a note to look up *pulpeuse*—does it mean voluptuous or fleshy?

—lips and heavy eyelids. A former model, she was now studying for an advanced degree in political philosophy. She'd begged off coming to dinner that evening, claiming her essay on Machiavelli and Han Fei was too pressing.

I went to Robert's birthday celebration alone, so it was with an unhampered and luxurious curiosity that I observed Eve, seated next to me.

"Would you prefer white or red?" I asked, offering to pour her a glass of wine. She mistook my stilted gesture for withering irony, considering the casual tavern we sat in. It was Robert's favorite dive. He was a writer who hobnobbed with the police investigators he wrote fat thrillers about.

"White. I prefer a headache to indigestion," she said in a snooty, languid voice.

"You're really a bitch with expensive tastes, aren't you?"

No, that wasn't right. The phrase was *"une poule de luxe,"* a female chicken with high-class tastes. *"Poule"* was also old-fashioned slang for a prostitute. In any case, the implication was insulting, but not as sledge-hammer dull as "bitch."

She turned to face me, an impassive sphinx look in her eye, and casu-ally backhanded the bottle onto my lap. . .

Oy vey. I counted the many ways in which I already disliked the writer. One, he sounded like a prick. Two, he sounded like a prick. Three, he dated models and bragged about it. Four, she's Egyptian, and in the first chapter, he'd already referred to her "sphinxlike" gaze. Five, he insults her and she spills wine on him: it was exactly how Americans imagine over-the-top French people behaving. Pretty soon, there'd be slaps in public places, screaming matches, loud arguments, a woman crying and wrenching open the door of a taxi in the middle of the street in the pouring rain, mascara running down her face. It was a bad French movie, all right. Or a Chanel commercial.

Four pages later, I stopped to shake my wrist and change the car-tridge in my fountain pen. I've always liked fountain pens. I'd started using them when I was a student here. Clara and I had taken a course on Marivaux at the Sorbonne. It met in a large amphitheater, and everyone smoked, which felt sophisticated in a bad way, exactly what I wanted in life when I was nineteen. The only thing I remember from the class now is the term *"marivaudage,"* a specific kind of courtly banter, light in tone, heavy on meaning(s). Which basically describes a lot of French conversation.

Back then, Clara took notes with an antique Waterman her father had given her. When I'd mentioned this to my grandmother, she'd re-marked that the only acceptable way to write letters was with a fountain pen. Years of thank-you notes and Christmas cards I'd written her with crayons, pencils, and ballpoints went down the drain: I was the bar-

baric, American grandchild in refined, old-world France. But she'd unlocked her Second Empire *secrétaire* and taken out a gold and burgundy Sheaffer.

"It belonged to your grandfather. You must fill it from a bottle." She'd demonstrated, twisting the top until a narrow metal tube protruded from behind the nib, lapped up ink from a glass inkwell, and retracted. I'd used the pen for years, filling it with violet ink and delighting in the scratch of the nib against paper. That same crisp rasp, as distinct as the sound of fingertips across razor stubble, always made me happy.

I scarfed down my *mousse* and looked back at the manuscript, thinking about the characters. There was no hesitating, no dawdling between them. Was this akin to the French aversion to snacking between meals? They went straight to her apartment, and boom, she already had her clothes off: *She stepped out of a pool of her clothes, dripping nakedness.*

I groaned. They'd spent the past few pages expressing dislike for each other, which would have been enough to discourage me, but no, now they were staring at each other like *ferocious animals* across an expanse of ironed sheets.

I read on and felt my face flush as I came to a vivid description of a certain sexual act. I put down my pen. This thing was going to flay me alive with mortification.

I picked it up again and doodled in the margin. This wasn't going to work if I got prim. I reread it and got back to work.

I eased her down to the edge of the bed and gently spread her legs, caressing the damp, warm silk of her skin. I knelt forward and ran my lips along her inner thigh, letting my hair brush up against her, feeling her muscles tense, then tremble. I pressed my ear to her flesh, then my cheek. She smelled of ripe, sweaty oranges—

I was going to have to work on that. I shook my hand out and continued.

—and had a beautiful, round ass. I plunged my hands underneath her to grab her buttocks and lift her to me, opening her up like a split fruit in late summer. Her sex was a rainbow of pinks, glistening and wet. I ran my tongue along the delicate fissure, slowly tracing every inch of her most intimate geography, lingering when I heard her breath catch. I pulled her into my mouth and slid a finger inside her swollen sex. Her back arched, hips rolling. A low moan escaped her lips and she thrust herself toward me, her hands clenched, bunching fistfuls of bedsheet—

"Vous aurez besoin d'autre chose, mademoiselle?" a waiter asked.

"Huh?" I said, stupidly. I looked around: the restaurant was empty. He probably wanted to go home. I gathered my papers and left.

I strolled down the sidewalk, gazing in boutique windows: pinstripes and organza at Dior, open-toed platforms and capes at Chloé, black and pink chiffon at Chanel. The sun broke through the clouds, dappling the street. The air was thick and still.

I stopped at a crosswalk. My legs felt funny, and my skin was a little clammy. A bus went by, ruffling my skirt and filling the air with warm, sooty exhaust. When I crossed the street, I noticed another, heavier dampness. Son of a bitch, I thought. That odious, pompous, self-satisfied, self-congratulatory idiot of a writer, whoever the hell he was—

He'd managed to turn me on.

6

*Paris has the reputation of being the naughtiest city in the world
and it is true. Paris is Naughty. Naughty if you want to look for it.
The American Tourist goes back home and whispers sly tales
about Purplish nights in Paris.*

— BRUCE REYNOLDS, *Paris with the Lid Lifted* (1927)

There was a message from Francis, an entertainment lawyer, on the machine. He represented a French band called Chronopop, and I'd done some translation work and writing for their electronic press kit and U.S. label launch. We'd never met, but from our numerous phone flirtations in L.A., I knew he was Irish, divorced, older. He was in Paris and wanted to take me out for dinner.

A date. My first date since Timothy. I mulled it over. I'd lost weight, and I had a silk dress I'd bought in the summer sales. I called him back. His voice, thick with that familiar brogue, barked a time into my ear.

"See you soon, you gorgeous thing," he added.

"How do you know I'm a gorgeous thing?"

"You American girls. *Not* good at compliments. Fuck, should I have said 'women'? Are you mortally offended now?" He barked with laughter and hung up.

I didn't feel like a gorgeous thing, but being called one nudged me in the right direction. A date, after all. Dinner with a man I'd never met. Anything could happen.

I put on stockings and high heels, sprayed myself with scent, and spent twenty minutes on my face. Two coats of rarely used but very effective curling mascara *plus* use of the eyelash curler that Timothy used to pretend to be afraid of. By the time I was done, I looked a little *fatale*, almost feverish—dark eyes, shiny lips, and hollow cheekbones. I powdered my long, thin nose as I listened to oldies on *Radio Nostalgie* and sang along: *"Je serai la plus belle pour aller danser."*

I shimmied into the dress. It was a slip of a thing, with tiny straps and a ruffled, flamenco-style hem that swooped up in front to midthigh. I scraped my brown hair back into a tight chignon. I looked more theatrical than I was used to: somewhat Carmen Miranda, sans fruit; a bit, as the French say, *olé-olé*.

"What the hell," I said to the mirror.

Francis was pretty much the way I'd imagined him: about fifteen years my senior, navy blazer, gold chain, tanned skin, and bulging eyes with deeply etched laugh lines. His face lit up when he saw me, and he pushed a man purse off the passenger seat as I got in. I suddenly wished my dress wasn't quite so insubstantial.

"Look at you," he said, whistling. "Snow White with cleavage."

Over a pleasant meal at a fancy Italian restaurant near l'Opéra, he told me about himself, how he'd piloted planes in the Caribbean, run a nightclub in Zagreb, and produced a few Spanish films in the nineties. He'd been divorced three times, no children, and now poured most of his money into a rhinoceros preserve in South Africa. "I'll tell you, Anna, being there," he said, "is the most fun you can have with your clothes on."

"I'll bite," I said. "Where's the most fun you can have with your clothes off?"

"Thailand." He grinned. "But Claude, my partner, keeps raving about this insane French dominatrix."

"You're kidding," I said, for lack of anything better.

"Honest injun," he said, holding up his palm. I may have winced. "Hold on, I think I even have—" His phone rang as he searched his wallet. "Bloody hell. I'll be right back." He pushed a card across the table and went outside to take the call.

Francis was a character, it had been an interesting evening, but I was done. I slouched back in my chair, contemplating my after-dinner options: face mask, mint-verbena tea, maybe crack open the Flaubert.

I slid the black and gold business card toward me. It read: *"Madame Véronique: bondage, sado-masochisme, domination, soumission, fétichisme, spécialiste en accrochage. Donjon disponible. Attention, âmes sensibles s'abstenir."* Dungeon available. Hey, not everyone has a dungeon. I wondered about the phrase "specializes in hanging." There was a phone number printed in Gothic gold type.

I could see Francis pacing up and down the sidewalk, gesticulating as he talked on his cell. I looked around the restaurant: a mostly older crowd, lots of couples, and a corner table of youngish businessmen in suits and ties who were all staring at me. Granted, I had paranoid tendencies, but this was unmistakable. Had I spilled something? Had my dress shifted? I glanced down, but the dress was fine. A little revealing but fine. Actually, very revealing. I looked up again, feeling a rush of blood to my face.

They thought I was a call girl. I felt it in the knowing, haughty glances of the women, the calculating looks from the table in the corner. The waiters, in their *smokings*, remained icily polite. They called me *"Madame"* and didn't make eye contact; they'd seen it all before. It wasn't my imagination: a waiter placed a snifter of cognac and a business card on the table in front of me, murmuring, *"De la part de monsieur,"* as he cocked his head toward the businessmen. One of them, a florid, beefy type with slicked-back hair, grinned. I thought I could hear the snap of his lips on his teeth.

He looked like one of my former students, from my days teaching

English to a senior manager at a telecom company. He'd hated lessons, resented my presence, and warmed up only when we talked about cars. He'd had shiny black hair parted on the side, worn tight suits around his barrel-like midsection, and bathed in cologne.

"I like, *comment dit-t-on,* difficult cars," he'd said.

"Sports cars?" I'd ventured.

"*Non, non, des voitures nerveuses.* I like to dominate them." He'd shot his cuffs as he said it, and admired his pudgy, manicured fingers. I'd been seized with a violent feeling of sexual repulsion.

I stared at my wineglass, frozen with embarrassment. I could feel my face turn red. I heard a low chuckle. I looked up, narrowing my eyes, and thought, You have no idea who I am. The gold print on the card twinkled at me.

And you never will. I fumbled in my evening bag for a pen. Not finding one, I pulled out a tiny stub of lip liner.

I flipped over Madame Véronique's card and scribbled *"Appelle-moi"* in waxy red. Then I drew a heart around it and motioned to the waiter to take it to my admirer.

I bit the inside of my cheek, took a deep breath, and looked up coolly. They passed the card around, and one of them gave a low whistle. Another said, *"Excellent,"* and snickered. They watched, silent, as Francis came back and sat down. When they left, I waved good-bye. Madame Véronique owed me big time: I had a hunch some bad boys needed spanking.

. . . .

We left after a round of espresso. In the car, Francis asked, "Shall I drive you home?"

"Yes, please. Unless you want to go out clubbing," I joked. He maneuvered out of the parking spot and slid his eyes over to me.

"Depends on what kind," he said. "I know a sex club nearby."

I felt a slight shock, a rattle, like when you hit your funny bone. I didn't say anything, wondering if he was putting me on.

He wasn't. "It's in a medieval building in the Marais. Very posh, with a restaurant, disco, and a few orgy rooms," he continued. Now I was perturbed. "You can watch," he added. "You don't have to do anything."

"So, it's like a porn movie but more erotic?" I asked.

"Sometimes less erotic. If the people aren't particularly attractive, for instance," he said, shifting gears.

"Ah," I said, studying his profile. I'd heard about these sex clubs, or private libertine clubs, as they were sometimes referred to, but I'd never been invited to one. It sounded so much better in French, *libertinage*—like it has a philosophical or political element, something that links it more to the racy eighteenth century rather than the seamy 1970s. No way in hell was I going, but it occurred to me Francis had some interesting knowledge. "How does it work?"

"The women rule. It only happens if a woman wants it to happen. For instance, someone—a man, or a woman—might make a gesture, and depending on your reaction, things would go from there. Like this." He ran his thumb down my bare arm. It was casual and insinuating at the same time, as if he'd licked me instead of touched me.

"I have a girlfriend in Paris, Ariane. She and I almost never have sex, but she loves going to this place, it turns her on. The last time we went, she ended up in a ménage à trois with an Italian stud and his girlfriend. I can tell you one thing, whether you have an orgasm at the club, or with me, or by yourself later on, it *will* blow your mind," he said. Then he giggled. He was like a horny bulldog puppy, happy and ready to hump furniture.

"I don't think so," I said.

"You're curious, admit it."

"No one's ever invited me to a sex club before," I confessed, wavering. Hell, I didn't know ordinary folks could go—I thought they were reserved for card-carrying denizens of some secret underworld. I could actually go to a sex club this evening, I thought, toying with the idea. I was curious. I could just watch.

"It's right there," he said, pulling over and pointing to a building with a valet parking attendant.

I laughed. It was a fake, tinsel laugh like, Oh, aren't I sophisticated? It was a laugh like, Isn't it interesting to imagine that I might actually contemplate going to a sex club in Paris? Francis turned to look at me. I opened my mouth to say no.

"When was the last time you surprised yourself? Did something wildly out of character, just for the hell of it?" he asked.

There it was: *la phrase qui tue*, literally, the sentence that kills, an arrow to the heart or, more likely, my self-image.

"I can't remember," I said, answering truthfully. I didn't often do unpredictable things: I'd gotten on a plane to Paris, after all, not Ushuaia or Ulaanbaatar. I looked down and traced a pattern in the thin silk of my dress, trying to conjure up another version of myself, someone adventurous and fearless, even reckless. It was seductive, this flirtation with another me. Before I could think it through any further, out rushed "One drink, and we leave the second I feel freaked out."

"Done," he said.

....

Inside, Francis shook hands with a doorman in a long black coat, then paid an entrance fee at the counter and took my elbow. We went down a stone stairwell, the rock cold and slightly moist to the touch, to a large room. I eyed the buffet, with an enormous cheese plate and trays of cakes and pastries, and wondered who came to a sex club for food. There was a strong smell of eucalyptus in the air. Between several low sofas, upholstered in an unfortunate airline-seat print, were shiny white ceramic statues of life-size naked women in suggestive poses. Ropes of fairy lights hung in swags along the walls. So far, it seemed almost ordinary.

At the bar, Francis greeted the owner, a petite woman in a tailored lace suit named Ginette. He explained that it was my first time. She smiled and told me not to be nervous. As they continued talking, I watched the bartender pour my drink, making sure he didn't slip some mysterious drug into my gimlet. I poked my head in the disco, where one couple slow-danced alone while an older man sat between two women wearing skimpy dresses on a leather sofa. As he rested his head against the wall, the two women leaned across him and started kissing. I watched for a moment, trying to look nonchalant, until the man unzipped his pants and waved me over. I backed up into Francis, who danced out of the way of his splashing whiskey.

"Ahoy, matey," he said. "How is our stranger in a strange land?"

"Observing the mating habits of the natives," I said, a little prim.

"Come along, Little Bo Peep." I followed him down another set of stairs to a *salon*. Through the somewhat low light, I could make out a wall with a giant "X," against which a naked man stood blindfolded, his arms and legs attached to leather restraints. A woman bent over him, her head bobbing up and down, while another man stood behind her, thrusting. I blinked and looked away, then looked back. Francis laughed.

In another dimly lit room, I squinted at various groupings of writhing bodies and tried to figure out who was doing what to whom, while a lot of squishy, slapping sounds made me think of cake batter and spatulas. There were men and women of all different ages and sizes, and most of them were tan and trim.

There was something both weirdly erotic—the strangeness of the situation, the sheer proximity—and weirdly mechanical about it. As I wandered about, I felt like I'd ventured into the kind of situation you don't necessarily enjoy but might look forward to telling people about later. I didn't stay too long in any one place and avoided eye contact as I watched people have sex.

I noticed that here, either you got off or you got off watching. The former was out, as I didn't go for sex with strangers and I wasn't attracted to Francis; and the latter didn't work for me either, as it turned out to be strangely bereft of the thing that could make it engaging: a story, a sense of who these people were. I began to feel more and more out of place.

A pair of lips grazed the back of my neck as a hand cupped my buttocks.

"Cut it out, Francis," I said. When the fondling didn't stop, I turned around. It wasn't Francis but a tall, thin woman about my age, with an asymmetrical haircut in a cut-out leather dress. She gave me a friendly smile. Behind her stood a tan man with full lips, fondling her through the slits in the leather. She was all bones and angles, like an Italian greyhound, and as I gave them an apologetic look, I had an absurd, vain thought: Was I her type? If I were gay, would she be mine? *"Excusez moi,"* I said, and went to find Francis. He was at the bar, talking to the bartender. I tapped him on the shoulder.

"I'm pulling the rip cord," I announced. He shrugged and drained his glass. We went upstairs and down the street to the car.

"Well?" he asked, hands shoved in his pockets.

"I get it, but I don't get it," I said. "It's funny, I kept wondering what all those people wanted, aside from the obvious. A connection? A thrill, something different? Who are they? What are they looking for?"

Francis shrugged. "It's not that complicated. I was looking for a girl I met the last time. She was beautiful. From Cameroon," he said, wistful. "Shall I take you home?" he asked. I nodded. It was a short drive. I gave him a kiss on the cheek and went inside.

I got morose in the elevator. Was this what my life was going to be like? Being taken to sex clubs by kinky, aging lawyers? I wasn't that sort of person; in fact, I was actually kind of prudish, even though I didn't like to admit it . . . and . . . and . . . somehow, this was all Timothy's fault. Yes, I was going to go down that path. I was going to sit in the dark and contemplate my sorry life.

The dress saved me. Inside the apartment, I caught a glimpse of myself in the hall mirror. The dress still looked good, and it wanted to party. It was barely past one-thirty, early for Paris. Before I could

change my mind, I called Pascal. Sure enough, he was at a nightclub
with a bunch of fashionisti and invited me along. I changed into a pair of
lower heels and caught a taxi.

....

Castel was an old-fashioned yet perpetually chic private club crowded
with hipsters, a smattering of aristos and intellos, and just enough local
color to keep it from becoming boring. A brass slat in the door slid open,
and a pair of eyes scrutinized my appearance before letting me in. I found
Pascal holding court with a few friends. My dress perked up.

"Darling!" he shouted and got up to kiss me. *"En robe du soir! Quelle
surprise!"*

I grinned and kissed him back. I sat next to Céline, an old friend of
Pascal's and a booker at a modeling agency.

"Where have you been?" she asked. All the other women were
wearing jeans, tank tops, and high heels, just like everyone in L.A. She
handed me a glass of champagne.

"Out to dinner with a lawyer," I said. "He took me to a *club libertin*."

"Tu plaisantes! Really?" she asked. I nodded. "I've always wanted to
know what really goes on in those places," she mused.

"I know, that's why I went," I said. Three women leaned in to hear
more.

"What really goes on where?" asked Pascal.

"Des clubs échangistes," Céline said.

"People fucking," he said drily. They all looked at me. I nodded in
agreement. *"On y* go?" he asked. We trooped downstairs to the small
dance floor. I hadn't danced in a long time. Only teenagers go dancing
in L.A. I danced to music I didn't recognize, sweating through my dress
and not caring. In the mirrored column, I could see my makeup had
melted away and my hair, loosened from its tight bun, hung in limp,
gel-soaked rattails, but it felt good to dance in a crowd, with music too
loud to think.

At four, we went to a bar in the Tenth with purple leather poufs to drink mint cocktails, smoke water pipes, and listen to Arab lounge music. I left sometime after five.

The rue de Paradis was empty. Not a taxi in sight, which was just as well: I needed to walk off the alcohol. I tallied up my intake: champagne and wine with dinner, vodka at the sex club, more champagne at Castel, and mint cocktails at Le Sultan.

Drunk off my ass, I concluded scientifically. My heels clattered on the pavement, and I veered to avoid a long smear of dog shit. It was quiet. My dress was damp against my back. My footsteps rang out, echoing against the buildings. I debated whether walking home drunk was stupid or reasonable. A homeless man sat on the sidewalk, burping loudly and waving his hands in the air like a conductor. He looked a little scary, muttering to himself in a gravelly baritone, but crossing the street to avoid him seemed unnecessary and rude.

As I passed him, he asked for a light. I kept walking. He shouted, *"L'amour n'est pas une pomme de terre!"* Love is not a potato. I doubled back and gave him a purple matchbox from the lounge place. He looked at me with rheumy, clever eyes.

"Merci, chérie," he said.

"Bonne nuit," I said.

As I wove through narrow streets, I saw lights on in a few apartments, illuminating beamed ceilings, crystal chandeliers, marble mantels, and the spiky shadows of potted palms. Paris by night, a tour of apartment ceilings. *La promenade des plafonds la nuit,* I mused, pleased with my phrasing until I realized it sounded like the ceilings were going for a walk at night instead of me.

A bird sang. The black sky was beautiful, the air smelled of woodsmoke, and I soaked up the city like a sponge. It was magic—the past, present, and future all in one place. Other centuries' footsteps whispered next to the slap of my own.

Crossing the canal, past thin trees like shocked paintbrushes, I heard a low, mournful moan, coming from close by. I looked around, but there was no one there. I heard it again: a human moan, not an animal one. I pulled my wrap tighter around me. The sound became a chorus of moans. I broke into a run. A taxi zoomed up the street, diesel engine clanking, and then it was quiet again.

I passed a faded Pernod billboard on the side of a wall. It reminded me of the old signs in the métro, pasted on the tunnels between stops. I remembered cupping my hands around my eyes and looking for the Dubonnet ads when I was a child. First there was a chorus line of Belle Epoque can-can girls, beneath the word "Dubo." Several yards later was the same image, but with "Dubon." The last poster said "Dubonnet." I liked those old ads, and the faded ones on the sides of buildings, the semihidden traces of the past.

My thoughts went to Timothy, the way a tongue searches out a painful tooth, stupidly and relentlessly. I thought about his habit of making up song lyrics in the car and how sweet he'd been when my cat died, how he liked to invent stories about other shoppers in the supermarket, and how deeply, profoundly awful his cooking was. How he told me I was beautiful and I believed him.

I felt in my purse for my phone. I thought about calling him, but I knew it was the kind of thing I would justify in my alcoholic stupor and then regret in the morning.

Was it regret or remorse? In French, they mean different things. Regret is for things you haven't done, remorse is for the things you have. Hence the saying *"Vaut mieux avoir des remords que des regrets"*: It is better to have remorse than regret. The French think you should do stupid, emotional things that you'll feel horrible about in the morning rather than wondering—*for the rest of your life*—what would've happened if you'd done stupid, emotional things that you would've felt horrible about in the morning.

At the square by the boulevard Jules Ferry, I stopped in front of the statue of *La Grisette*. She was heartbreaking, a flower girl in an 1840s gown and an absurd hairdo, her thin arms holding a basket of flowers for sale, ignored by the pigeons and passersby. She'd wanted so much and gotten so little. That's when I gave in. I sat on a damp bench and cried. I was pitiful and pathetic; digging myself out of my own bottomless pit would take more than a spoon.

7

I am so glad you have been able to preserve
the text in all of its impurity.
—SAMUEL BECKETT of *Endgame*,
in a letter to Alan Schneider dated 1957

I fought through layers of consciousness to wake up. It was like paddling through mud with ineffectual limbs and an anvil for a head. When I surfaced, I had a stuffed nose and my tongue tasted like a brown chenille bedspread in an ugly motel, but I had to get up: I had brunch plans with Bunny at a *salon de thé* near WHSmith. I took a shower and threw on clothes, nagged by an unsettled feeling, like I'd had a dream in which I'd wanted to remember something but I couldn't remember what the something was.

I gulped down my first *café Viennois* in silence, appreciating Bunny's strict brunch rule about not engaging in conversation until you'd ingested coffee, a gallantry left over from his days as a hard-drinking newspaperman. We were at L'Auberge Viennoise, a place I referred to as Heidi's House, for its gemütlich, Alpine dollhouse atmosphere. A collection of yellow-yarn-haired dolls in lederhosen sat on a china cabinet, and a parade of hand-carved wooden toys decorated the window ledge.

Our table groaned under the weight of a silver coffee urn, a pitcher of steamed milk, a basket of *pains au chocolat, pains aux raisins,* croissants, and brioches as well as *tartines,* a crated tub of creamy *beurre d'Echiré,* and jars of jam—*figue, cerise,* and *abricot,* all *fait maison.*

"I had a weird experience last night," I said.

"Drinking'll do that." He sank his chin into his neck, giving me a knowing look.

"No, I mean really weird. I was walking home about, I don't know, four in the morning, and I heard moaning by the canal. I looked around, but there was no one there." I pulled the top off a brioche.

"Where?"

"Not far from my place. Near Saint-Louis," I said, referring to the hospital.

"Moaning, huh?" Bunny asked, with sudden interest.

"You've got an archaeological gleam in your eye," I remarked.

"It's not far from Montfaucon," he said. "Site of medieval Paris's infamous gallows. The hanged bodies were left dangling in the air for everyone to see."

I put down the brioche. "Very funny. Like hanged people moan."

"Maybe the ghosts of their relatives do," he said. I made a face. "I'm just trying to give you a rational explanation—"

"Ghosts," I interrupted. "Of gallows hangings. That's supposed to be rational?"

"You're the one hearing things," he said, biting into a *tartine* slathered with butter and marmalade. "How's the translation?" he asked.

I grimaced. "I don't know how you can eat that stuff, it's orange *and* bitter."

"The subtle joy of bitter fruit is an acquired taste, my young friend," he explained, wiping his mouth with a corner of white napkin. "Like so many things in life. So?"

I poured more coffee into my cup and stirred in two heart-shaped sugar cubes. "You know, it's an erotic novel," I said.

"I remember. Have you gotten to the dirty bits?" he asked, eyes twinkling. "Don't make me beg."

"I guess. They're mostly embarrassing," I said. Bunny's playful look made me squirm. We'd never talked about sex, and I didn't know that I wanted to start. "I mean," I tried to explain, "everyone probably has their own combination of spices in their sexual cooking cabinet, but revealing them makes them seem, I don't know, absurd. Distasteful, even." I winced, sounding more judgmental than I felt.

He sat back, looking disappointed, but in me, not the translation.

"For example," I fumbled, "what is it with this femme fatale fantasy? This fantasy of a woman who waltzes into his life, and boom, they're a perfect fit, the sex is great—"

"Doesn't everyone have that fantasy?" he asked. "The right person at the right time?"

"I guess, but the way he describes it . . ." I trailed off. Bunny was elsewhere, slowly slathering marmalade on another *tartine*. "What?"

He looked up, dreamy-eyed. "There was this thing Diana and I talked about a long time ago," he said, mentioning an old girlfriend. "A spinning basket," he explained. "The woman would sit in a basket suspended from the ceiling. It had an opening in the bottom so you could penetrate her from below while the basket spun around."

I choked on my coffee. "Did you ever do it?" I asked.

"No, but it was wonderful to think about." He pulled an ear off a baby croissant, scattering a flurry of flakes on the tablecloth, and ate it.

"I've never thought of twisting as particularly erotic," I said. Bunny shrugged and bit off the other croissant ear. He handed me the book review section of *The New York Times* while he scanned the front page, humming.

I stared at the paper, not reading it. I was a little freaked out by the thought of this sixty-three-year-old man and his *Playboy* magazine of the seventies fantasies. Not that he wasn't allowed to have them, but I didn't want to hear about them—the same way I didn't want to know anything about my parents' sex life. Bunny was like my wise, indulgent uncle, and I liked being his favorite protégée. I didn't want any messy bits.

My eyes drifted across a headline. At the same time, wanting everyone to stay in their prescribed roles made me feel like a fascist. I sighed.

"Now what?" he asked, not looking up from the *Times*. I shook my head. "I shouldn't have said anything," he said, folding the paper.

"No, I'm glad you told me," I said, trying to sound sincere. I rolled pieces of bread into little pellets.

"You are not!" He smacked the table with the newspaper. "Maybe you shouldn't be translating a sex book if talking about sex makes you so uncomfortable," he said.

"I'm not uncomfortable! I just want you to keep it to yourself!" It was out before I could pull it back. He picked up the Op-Ed section and ignored me. We sat in uncompanionable silence while I tried to figure out how to make amends. A polka played in the background.

"Bunny?" I asked. I pulled the translation out of my bag and put it on the table. He didn't answer. "Bunny." He lowered his newspaper. "Would you read it? I want to know what you think." He gave me a baleful look, but he picked up the pages.

. . . .

Eve, Eve, the name haunted me like the first woman who ever haunted man. She was the first woman to me. She virtually erased everyone else, reduced my past to a collection of half-forgotten dreams, memorable as cold coffee. The phoenix of my destiny. There was no one else. Even now, I can still remember the sound of her laughter, the smell of her neck, the shape of her breasts, the texture of her skin, her tender look, as precious as a secret a child shares with you.

She ignored me for the rest of the evening, after knocking the wine into my lap. I ignored her back, but I could sense her next to me, an irritant, an intoxicant. I laughed, told crass jokes, entertained myself hugely, all the time hoping she was wondering who I was, this man who sat next to her with his back turned, immune to her charms. I have found that nothing intrigues a beautiful woman more than a man who ignores her.

At the end of the evening, I gave her the most perfunctory of good-byes. In the crisp night air, I stumbled toward my car, regretting the two cognacs.

Her voice rang out in the night. "Where are you going?" she asked. I squinted. A dark shadow in a coat, she was there, waiting for me. Even in my stupor, I felt triumphant.

"Home, if I can find my bloody keys."

She stepped closer. I could see her lips, shiny in the dim light. "Here." She put a hand on my waist, the way a man holds a woman. With her other hand, she searched my pockets.

"Find what you're looking for?" I drawled. She shoved the keys at my chest. They fell on the pavement. I looked down in stupefaction as she walked away. I ran after her, grabbing her arm.

"Don't! You're too rough!" she said. I moved closer, putting my arm around her waist, and pressed myself into her back.

"There's something I have to do or I won't be able to sleep," I said, speaking into her hair.

"I don't care about your sleep, Jean-Marc. Leave me alone."

"But I do. Turn around." She didn't move, so I walked around to face her. I trailed my hand down the nape of her neck, her spine, the curve of her ass. She still didn't move. I could hear her breathing, calm, deep.

"Why do you stand there like a statue?" I asked.

"You're like a drunken bear at a circus. There's something cruel and fascinating about watching. I wonder what will happen next." She smiled, mocking me. I wanted to shatter her complacency, her superior taunting. I lunged forward, took her face in my hands, and kissed her.

"Enough," she said, pushing me away.

"Too bearlike for you?"

"Go home." She tightened her trench coat belt with two hands.

"I'll kill someone." I stumbled and laughed.

She looked at me, then tossed her head. "I'll drive."

She walked back and swept up the keys with a fluid movement. I don't remember how she found my car or how she got me into it. I tried to kiss her neck, but she pushed me aside.

"But it's an automatic," I blathered.

"I know what it is, you fool." She drove quickly through the empty streets. At the place de Clichy, I realized we weren't going to my place. I followed her up six flights of stairs to a sparsely furnished apartment under the eaves. She threw me a blanket, pointed to the sofa, and went into her bedroom, closing the door behind her.

I drank a large glass of water. I waited, then knocked on her door. There was no answer. I knocked again.

She opened the door and looked at me, her eyes glittering. She slid her dress strap off one shoulder. The fabric fell to a puddle at her feet. She stepped out of it, dripping nakedness. I loosened my tie. She stepped away, removing the pins in her hair. As we stared at each other across the bed, the air became charged, almost too thick to breathe . . .

As he read, Bunny's reactions flitted across his face: a frown, a smirk, raised eyebrows, pursed lips. He turned the page. His hands were large, with thick knuckles and neat, broad fingernails. I knew how the skin on his cheek felt, I'd kissed it often enough: soft and papery. Perhaps to compensate for his height, he tended to stoop, but he moved gracefully. Just because he was old enough to be my father and I didn't want to sleep with him didn't mean he didn't have a sex life. Despite myself, I wondered what he was like in bed, and suddenly sensed he'd be nervous and kind and surprisingly adept. I shook the thought away.

Bunny shifted in his seat, and the corners of his mouth twitched.

He'd gotten to *that* part: the short but graphic sex scene. He put the pages down, nodding.

"Is there more?"

"Nope. That's chapter one." I felt pretty pleased with myself and reached over to nab the square of dark chocolate off his saucer. He finished his coffee.

"It's a bit clinical——" he began.

"Believe me, the original is worse," I said.

Nodding again, he looked at his coffee cup, then put it down, squaring his shoulders. "You're going to have to do better if you want the job. The language is stiff and stilted. He doesn't sound at all likable—in fact, you make him sound like a pompous——"

"He *is* pompous!" I exclaimed.

"——horse's ass. Which may be the case, but he isn't going to hire you for pointing it out."

"Wait. I'm supposed to pretty it up?"

"Not the way you've done it. The way you've written it, it's like a Harlequin romance. I hear they're sexing those up." His mouth twitched again as he tried not to laugh. Furious, I fumbled in my bag and shoved the original at him.

"Read the French!" I said.

"Look, I'm just saying——"

"Read the original, goddammit!" He read the manuscript while I fumed.

He finished reading and put it down. "I apologize," he said. "It's a brilliant translation." He signaled for the bill.

"And?" I asked.

"And nothing."

"Don't play around, Bunny. It's not nice."

He sighed. "Either you want to know what I think or you don't."

"I want to know what you think. I respect your opinion," I said, small-voiced.

"Then stop biting my head off," he said, glaring at me. "You're not going to get the job if you turn that in," he repeated, jabbing a finger at my draft. "It shows up every single pretension in his stupid prose and makes him sound like more of an imbecile than in the original, where a certain flowery elegance buys him some leeway, if not credibility. Here, it's stripped down, literal, and"—he paused to push up his sleeves—"dreadful. I wouldn't read any more unless I was being paid or had nothing else to do."

Stung and embarrassed, I looked down at my translation and the French original, trying to see what he saw, but the words blurred in front of me.

"He-e-e-y," Bunny neighed. "It's not that bad."

I picked at a ragged cuticle. "What do I do?"

"Do you want the job?"

"Mmm-yeah. No." I sounded sulky. "Maybe."

"Jesus, I hate it when women act like cats in front of an open door. In or out. Yes or no. Fish or cut bai—"

"Oh, shut up! Yes, I want the job."

"Then you have to write it well. Not a literal translation," he said. I shook my head, not understanding. Bunny cupped his fingers like he was holding a fruit. "If you translate literally, he sounds like a jerk, but he doesn't sound like one in French. Maybe he's not likable, but he's not a jerk. Jesus, Anna, you speak both languages, you know you can't do it literally—the aesthetics are different. Do a translation of what you could imagine it to be if it lost its pretensions and grew up one day to be a solid and intelligent citizen."

8

Le français ne fut pas pendant plusieurs siècles la langue des cours d'Europe parce que ce serait la langue la plus précise, comme on a voulu le faire accroire, mais parce que c'est la langue qui permet d'être le plus précisément imprécis.[*]

—PASCAL BAUDRY, *Français et Américains: L'autre rive*

The day I printed out my much-revised translation of chapter one was sunny and cool, so I put on jeans and a sweater and walked to Editions Laveau. The cowbell clanged as I walked in. Monsieur Laveau, phone glued to ear, poked his head out of his office, scowled at me, and ducked back in. He raised his voice and slammed the door.

The bookstore smelled musty and humid, old leather mixed with damp. I paged through a handsomely bound George Sand and ran my fingers over a twenty-volume set of Saint-Simon's memoirs. I sat on a stack of dusty *Revue des etudes napoléoniennes* and took out the envelope.

Laveau opened the door, plucked the envelope from my lap, gave me a five-euro note, and shut the door. I looked down at the bill. Was it a

---

[*]French was not the language of European courts for several centuries because, as popular wisdom would have it, it is the most precise language, but because it is the language in which one can be most precisely imprecise.

tip? Did he think I was a messenger? I turned it over in my hand.

"*Mais alors,*" he scolded, coming out of his office two minutes later. "*Vous êtes toujours là?*" He fixed me with a pained look. He had no idea who I was.

"Yup, still here," I said, hoping English would jog his memory. He continued to stare at me. "*Il me semble que vous me devez une petite somme d'argent,*" I prodded, my voice squeaking. "*La traduction.*" Enlightenment dawned.

"*Ah, oui, c'est vrai. Entrez, mademoiselle, je vous en prie,*" he said. I followed him into the office and stood, avoiding the evil club chair. I spotted my translation on the floor, on top of a pile of papers. In fact, the whole office was littered with small mountains of manuscripts and papers. It occurred to me that there were probably lots of us bilingual women running around Paris, looking to make some extra cash doing translation. I was probably one of many he'd hired on spec. "*Tenez,*" he said, handing me a check. It was for three hundred euros, more than the amount he'd said, and it was blank. So, he'd forgotten my name as well.

I eyed the piles of paper again. His author probably didn't read more than a page or two of our translations before he tossed them into the *poubelle* with a weary sigh. Monsieur Laveau ignored me, rifling through a file folder while I stood there, shifting my weight from foot to foot. I'd worked hard on that translation, and it didn't matter.

"*Au revoir, monsieur,*" I said. He nodded, not looking up. Because I figured it was the last time I'd have to deal with him, I added, "*C'est bien dommage.*" It's a pity.

That got his attention. "*Pardon?*" he asked.

"*Non, rien.*" I shrugged. "*Enfin, c'est dommage que personne ne lira ce que j'ai traduit. Le chapitre est nul, mais pas si nul que ça.*" It's a pity no one will read what I translated. The chapter is bad, but not that bad. I said it breezily, offhand.

"*Mais voyons, mademoiselle*—" he began, his voice deep with reproach. The phone rang, and he waved at me to stay, but I didn't feel like it. I didn't want to wait obediently while he talked, I didn't like being waved at, and I didn't want to be polite.

I yanked open the door and walked outside. On the sidewalk, I felt like a rebel, walking out on someone who reminded me of my disapproving French grandfather. The 96 bus approached the carrefour, and I chased it down, running like it was the last bus out of the Sixth ever.

....

Even though the French claimed the summer exodus wasn't as extreme as it used to be, by mid-August, Paris felt emptied of Parisians. Restaurants and stores closed, leaving hastily scribbled signs taped to their doors notifying customers of the *fermeture annuelle*. There were lines at the big museums, with double-parked tourist buses, their engines running to keep the AC on for one white-shirted driver. In less touristy neighborhoods, nearly all of the *commerçants*, including my *boulangerie* across the street, closed, and some drivers didn't deign to stop at red lights.

Bunny went to Lake Constance, somewhere in Austria, where friends of his had a chalet. Pascal went away again, to join Florian on the île de Porquerolles. Clara called from her sister's place in Corsica, repeating her invitation for me to join her. Althea and Ivan sent me a postcard from the Dordogne, where, she wrote in green crayon, they were eating and drinking too much.

I visited the smaller museums—the Jacquemart-André, Nissim de Camondo, Cernuschi, even the Musée de la Chasse, with its stuffed deer heads. At the Fondation Cartier, I toured a room with nine oversize black-and-white photographs of the Namibian desert. The shadows of the sand looked like flesh: the dip of a belly button, the back of a knee, the hollow of a neck. I thought of Eve, the author's description of her skin. After ten days of no real conversation beyond slip-thin exchanges of pleasantries, I was a little bored and counting the days until *la rentrée*, at the beginning of September.

Another day, after holing up at the Action Christine for a Jean Gabin double feature, I went to the Musée de Cluny to visit the Lady and the Unicorn tapestries, which I hadn't seen since I was a kid. I wandered through the medieval garden and followed an elderly couple with matching gray haircuts and tracksuits down a flight of stairs to the ruins of the Roman thermal baths.

It was cold and quiet in the *frigidarium*, and I looked for the mosaic mentioned in the information pamphlet. It was eerily quiet, and the city seemed far away. I scraped my feet against the stone floor and admired the carved arches. There was something intriguing about the place. In the stillness, I could feel, well, if not an ancient hush, a respectable age.

The elderly couple spoke, and the sound bounced off the walls. I couldn't tell where they were, but they had English accents.

"You know, I'd rather like to get back," she said, playfully.

"Hungry already? We've only just had tea."

"Richard. *Think*." Then a shuffling sound.

They were in their seventies, and they were kissing behind a wall when I bumped into them. A flurry of embarrassed apologies ensued. We flew in opposite directions, like repelling magnets.

I kept seeing them kissing, eager to get back to their hotel: her hand, grasping the shiny, nylon waistband of his pants, his arm around her shoulders, nose pressed into her cheek, awkward and hungry. Timothy and I had kissed under an archway in Venice, as passing car headlights striped us with light.

I stood in the Roman bathhouse. I was a lonely person in an empty town.

I walked back through the winding streets of the Fifth, away from the bustle of tourists in the Quartier Latin. I walked around the Arènes de Lutèce, down behind the Jardin des Plantes, and I had no context and no contact. I might as well have been a ghost, wandering through streets where real people lived. I felt immaterial, disembodied, incapable of making an impression: if I'd walked through mud, I wouldn't have left prints.

At home, I ran a bath with water so hot I had to ease into it. A thin line between bathing and braising. The air was steamy, and my toes turned red in the water. I bent down, reached my hands in for balance, and lowered myself into a sitting position. The contrast between hot water and cool air made me want to scratch my skin, and I watched the waterline itch its way up my knees as I straightened them. Tiny bubbles clung to my stomach. I gave them a nudge and they floated away. My breasts floated on the surface like buoys, the nipples puckered and pink. Heat licked off the water, and I felt groggy and still, suspended.

The phone rang, and I had to duck the stupid and impossible hope that it was Timothy, but it was just Pascal and Florian, back in town and asking me over for dinner.

I got dressed and walked across the *grands boulevards* to their little two-floor courtyard house in the garment district, *le sentier*. A set decorator, Florian had created a jungle of greenery with potted plants around the front door. Inside, Pascal was cutting up a melon when I kissed him hello. The décor had changed since the last time I'd been there, two years ago, the old zebra stripes replaced by sage green suede furniture with brown leather pillows.

Florian came downstairs as I was wrestling with their ancient sharpei, Butch. Except for the tan, he looked the same: ruddy skin stretched across sharp, raw-boned features, long, thin nose, big ears. We sat down to a dinner of *melon de Cavaillon* with *jambon de parme*, followed by pasta primavera and a big green salad, all of it washed down with rosé. Florian, eyes twinkling with an almost malevolent delight, wasted no time in firing the opening salvo in that national sport, the argument.

"There is no such thing as good American television," he declared.

"That's not true. There are lots of good shows on American TV," I said, finding myself in the dubious position of defending something I rarely watched.

"*Oui. Alerte à Malibu,*" he scoffed, using the French title for *Baywatch*.

"Give me a break," I scoffed back, helping myself to more salad. "That's like me saying there's no good French music and backing it up by citing Johnny Hallyday."

"Name one good TV program," he said. Before I could, he added, "It's all crap, designed to pander to the lowest common denominator and sell useless products to your consumer culture while the masses starve."

"What masses? We have poverty, no doubt, but no starving masses," I protested.

"Of course you do. As does the rest of the world."

"But that's not what we're talking about. We're talking about TV, and there *are* good shows, you just don't know about them because they're not on French TV—"

"*Laisse tomber,*" Pascal murmured, urging me to let it go. I ignored him.

"Like *The Office*, or *Lost*, or *The Daily Show*," I continued.

"Paid for by powerful media conglomerates whose only real interest is making money," Florian retorted. "What do you have, six media companies? Six?"

"But that doesn't mean the shows aren't good!" I said. "Stop changing the subject!"

"That *is* the subject," he said.

"No, it isn't. The subject is whether there's anything good on TV," I said.

"*Oh, les Américains,*" he sighed. "*Toujours premier degré.* So literal."

I turned to Pascal. "*Aide moi!*" I pleaded, but he shook his head and took a drag off his cigarette.

"He pisses me off!" I exclaimed. Florian smiled, little shark teeth gleaming. "Yes, you," I said, glaring at him. The French consider a meaty, messy argument good, clean fun for the whole family; moreover, they like to go off on tangents and dart around the issue like it's a soccer ball to be kicked around a field. Florian dropped a kiss on the top of my head.

"*Allons,* I'll buy you an ice cream," he said. "It's my turn to walk the dog." I kissed Pascal good night, and Florian, Butch, and I walked down the rue Montorgueil to Amorino, the gelateria, where we stood in a line stretching out onto the sidewalk.

"*Alors, dis-moi.* Pascal told me a little bit. *Comment vas tu?*" Florian asked.

"So-so," I said. "Some days are better than others. Today wasn't one of them."

"It is very important to be faceful," he said. His English was good, but sometimes he struggled with the "th" sound, especially when he was tired. "You know, I am in love with Pascal, and Pascal is in love with me. It is the most beautiful thing: the man I love loves me." I bit my lip as he spoke. "And in the gay community, it is much harder to be faceful," he added, his big, round eyes solemn. "*Alors,* this Tom—"

"Timothy," I corrected.

"Bah, Tom, Tim, it's a name for a pet. A black Labrador. *N'est-ce pas,* Butch?" He bent and scooped the dog up in his arms. "He was no good," he concluded. I leaned over and kissed him on the cheek. "It's the truce," he protested.

We got our cones and walked outside. Half a dozen American senior citizens, all wearing flag pins, stood on the sidewalk, comparing flavors. Florian grinned and shouted, "God bless America, and vote Democrat!" He'd started saying it after 9/11 and hadn't stopped.

9

The novelty of *la rentrée* faded, and by the end of the first week in September, the city shifted into regular speed. Despite the fact that I'd had to transfer more money out of my savings, I continued to live as if I were carefree, on vacation. I woke up late, lounged around, checked e-mail, saw friends, explored the city, and shopped for food, one of my favorite activities.

On my way to the rue de Buci market street across the river, the smell of charred sweet corn wafted over from a makeshift brazier fitted into a supermarket shopping cart on the corner. I bought my weekly *Pariscope* at the kiosk, and the elderly man with gold-rimmed glasses who'd never acknowledged my existence beyond returning change smiled and wished me good day.

Startled, I felt my dry lips stick to my teeth as my voice hiccuped over the polite *"Vous aussi."* It was the first time my larynx had formed

---

*Nothing is more irresistible than a stranger. A man who walks into a bar is worth all the men one has lived with for twenty years.

sounds that day. I had to remember to talk to myself over breakfast in the future; I smiled at the thought of behaving like a crazy person in private in order to prevent the appearance of such in public.

A hefty butcher in a bloody apron, unloading large pieces of beef from a van, roared, *"Vous voyez? C'est beaucoup mieux quand vous souriez!"* You see? It's much better when you smile. He slid mottled, pudgy fingers down his chest, as if he were looking for suspenders to tuck his thumbs into.

The French have an expression for a surly face: *"aimable comme une porte de prison,"* as friendly as a prison door. Apparently, it was the face I usually wore, but for some reason, I didn't have it on today, and people noticed.

I crossed the river at the Pont Neuf. There was a furniture store on the other side that always made me happy, partly because each of its picture windows exhibited a single chair, angled just so and lit like a Hurrell model, and partly because of its name, Etat de Siège, which means state of siege, but *"siège"* in French also means seat, armchair. It wasn't a translatable pun, though I'd toyed with "seat of power."

There were lots of people milling about when I got to the market. I stood for a moment, watching the passersby. I've always loved French market streets. You can eavesdrop on conversations about recipes, see what fruits and vegetables are in season, and learn about the things people eat. At the *poissonnerie,* I'd learned that the orange sac attached to a scallop, *le corail,* is considered a delicacy. The secret to a velvety spinach velouté is to purée one whole ripe pear into it, a bourgeoise in a Burberry and an Hermès scarf told her friend at the vegetable stand.

I stopped in front of the *traiteur,* gazing at eggs in clear jelly like resin paperweights, various salads, quiches with golden brown *pâte brisée* crusts, and glazed tarts paved with mosaics of sliced fruit. A woman behind the counter moved a *tourte provençale* aside to give the *place d'honneur* to a whole poached salmon, covered in translucent cucumber scales. A black olive eye glistened at the head.

Across the street, a tourist shop sold polyester print scarves of the Arc de Triomphe, Eiffel Tower key chains, and reproduction street signs. There were also baskets filled with seashells, iridescent with mother-of-pearl or shiny with a genital pink. I picked up a spiky conch and held it to my ear. A brown stream of cold liquid raced down my forearm to the elbow. I gave a yelp and thrust the shell back. I mopped my arm with a tissue, but it had a shockingly foul and persistent odor, the smell of rotting seaweed, or rotting sea creature. In my bag, I found an old Air France towelette and scrubbed my arm, but I could still smell the stink beneath the artificial lemon scent.

I dumped the towelette in the trash and walked into a patisserie. An idea of dinner took the shape of a couple of chocolate éclairs, but then I saw the almond croissants, *fourré à la frangipane et au chocolat*. They were limp with filling, as if exhausted by their own excess, and decorated with piped chocolate and a dusting of powdered sugar. I stared, rapt, until the person behind me coughed.

"Pardonnez-moi, monsieur," I said, stepping aside to let a beige trench coat go by.

"Ah, Monsieur Laveau! J'ai votre tarte aux pommes ici," said the woman behind the counter. I looked up: it was the same Monsieur Laveau. I ducked my head, debating whether to say hello or bolt. He walked past me, dangling a medium-size cake box by its ribbon, and I blurted out his name.

"Monsieur Laveau?" I asked.

"Oui?" He looked at me blankly. I felt a flush of anger. Was I invisible? Was there no way to make an impression on this man?

"Je ne sais pas si vous vous souvenez de moi, mais je vous ai fait une traduction il y quelque temps?" As I reminded him of who I was, I started out okay, but then I made my statement a question, a nervous, adolescent tic. He studied me for a moment, then exclaimed:

"Ah, mais c'est vous! Mademoiselle, on vous cherchait! Vous n'avez pas laissé vos coordonnées, ni votre nom sur le dossier! Nous étions convaincus

qu'on ne vous trouvera jamais!" It's you! We were looking for you, but you didn't leave your name or phone number. We thought we'd never find you.

I didn't know who the "we" was, and his answer threw me. I knew I'd included my name and number on the manuscript, and I rushed to say so. *"Mais, monsieur, je suis certaine que j'ai—"*

"Venez, j'ai un autre chapitre pour vous, j'aurais besoin de la traduction la semaine prochaine, assez rapidement si possible," he interrupted. *"Trois cents euros par chapitre, ça vous va?"* he asked, taking my elbow and wheeling me around, presumably to the bookstore. Now I was even more convinced he'd mixed me up with someone else—I distinctly remembered him originally quoting two hundred euros per chapter, but I wasn't going to argue with more money.

"Vous avez bien deux minutes?" he asked, looking at his watch.

"Oui, mais, peut-être vous faites confusion avec quelqu'un d'autre?" Maybe you're confusing me with someone else?

"Mais non, mais non, mais non," he muttered, pulling me across the boulevard Saint-Germain. His nose twitched, and he let go of my elbow. I wondered if my arm still smelled of decaying sea creature. We walked up the street and into his store, and yet again, I stood alone among the piles of books as Monsieur Laveau leaped to answer the phone in his office, slamming the door behind him. I picked up a collection of short stories and sat down on a rickety chair in the corner. The cowbell pealed, and a tall man came in and said, *"Bonjour."*

"Bonjour," I answered politely, not looking up from the book.

"Vous attendez Bernard?" he asked, gesturing at the closed door.

"Oui," I said, glancing at him. He looked familiar, with a rugged, handsome face: olive skin under a mop of brown hair, beaky nose, square jaw, and hooded, brown eyes. Around forty, he wore jeans, a T-shirt, and a velvet jacket, an old leather portfolio tucked under his arm.

"Il nous fait toujours attendre, ce sacré Bernard," he said with a rueful, dimpled smile. He always makes us wait. I gave a quick smile and looked

away, feeling shy. *"Qu'est ce que vous lisez?"* he asked, tucking sunglasses into his pocket. I held up the book and read the spine.

"Stendhal, *Chroniques italiennes,*" I said.

" *'C'est la cristallisation, comme dit Stendhal,'* " he said, sounding like he was quoting someone. I squinted at him, puzzled.

"Une chanson de Gainsbourg cite la fameuse théorie de Stendhal sur la cristallisation de l'amour," he said, explaining that a Gainsbourg song referenced some theory Stendhal had. I shook my head: I didn't know it, either the theory or the song. He studied me for a moment.

"Ah, vous n'êtes pas française," he observed. *"Italienne?"* I shook my head. *"Espagnole?"* I shook my head again. *"Je sais,"* he said, tapping the side of his nose. *"Grecque."* I shook my head again. *"Dites-moi, alors,"* he asked, giving up.

"Américaine."

"Really? You don't sound American. You don't look American, either," he said, switching into accented but fluent English. "How do you know Bernard?"

"I'm doing some work for him. Translation."

"Ah." His speculative look said, So, it's you. I wondered if he was Monsieur Laveau's famous secretive writer.

"What's *cristallisation?*" I asked.

"It's a theory Stendhal came up with to describe the process of falling in love. There's a delightful drawing he made, comparing it to a journey from Bologna to Rome."

His phone beeped, and as he studied the screen, I realized where I'd seen his face: he was an actor. I'd seen him in a TV movie about police corruption, where he'd played an Algerian cop with a heroin problem. He caught me staring and held the look. A warm liquid pooled in my stomach.

"Olivier! Navré de vous avoir fait attendre," Monsieur Laveau apologized, emerging from his den.

"Mais pas du tout, mon ami. Je parlais avec cette charmante demoi-

selle—" Olivier said, still looking at me and leaving a silence open for my name. Monsieur Laveau's head swiveled around in alarm. He placed his hands on his hips, the picture of arms-akimbo vexation.

"Vous êtes toujours là?" You're still here? My jaw dropped open. It was pathological, the way he always forgot about me. Olivier folded his arms and grinned, finding this hugely entertaining. Monsieur Laveau muttered something unintelligible, took an envelope from his office, and thrust it at me.

"Tenez, mademoiselle. A bientôt," he said. He took my arm and hustled me outside. On the sidewalk, he apologized for being brusque and explained that he had a meeting with an important client. Then he reminded me that the translation was confidential. I nodded, bewildered.

"Bien. Vous n'avez rien dit?" You didn't say anything? he asked, cocking his head toward the store.

"Non," I said, wondering if telling Olivier I was translating counted.

"Bien. Bien, bien." He rubbed his hands together. *"A mercredi prochain,"* he added, reminding me to come back next Wednesday, and went back in. I walked away, turning over pieces of information like Scrabble tiles, wondering if I could arrange them to make sense. Was Olivier the writer? He couldn't be: Monsieur Laveau had described a famous intellectual, not an actor. Though the French did consider some actors intellectuals. Maybe Olivier knew the writer. Or maybe Olivier was his important client? Nothing fit together in any illuminating way.

On the other hand, three hundred euros a week under the table wasn't a bad income for someone who wasn't paying rent. I stopped in front of a boutique window and stared at my shadowy outline in the glass as I twisted my neck to unkink it.

"Puis-je vous aider?" asked the store clerk, a young woman in a miniskirt and high heels standing in the doorway. Startled, I realized I'd been standing in front of a window display of silk and lace lingerie, all the time wondering what the hollow at the base of Olivier's neck tasted like.

10

Je t'aimais inconstant,
*qu'aurais-je fait, fidèle?**
—JEAN RACINE, *Andromaque*

A few pages into *chapitre deux*, I came to the conclusion that I hadn't needed to buy a dictionary of slang for this project. I needed a medical textbook. For every word I knew (*"frenulum," "vagin"*), there were others I hadn't heard before, accompanied by descriptions of such scientific rigor that I began to wonder if the author wasn't either a doctor or a humorless obsessive-compulsive.

"Why settle for one?" Bunny asked when I told him on the phone. "Let's assume he's a humorless, obsessive-compulsive oncologist, specializing in colorectal cancer. And let's call him Heinz. I once had a terrible doctor in Munich named Heinz. Never get a colonoscopy. I'm sure dying is better."

"But he's French," I protested. "What are you up to?"

"Waiting for pizza from Speed Rabbit. They deliver it on farty little mopeds," he said. "You gonna read me something, or do I have to watch the porn channel to get a thrill tonight?"

*I loved you unfaithful, what would I have done if you were true?

I gave a long-suffering sigh.

"And don't take that long-suffering tone with me, young lady. Canal Hot is showing *Paula and the Randy Martians* in half an hour," he added.

"Okay, okay." I skimmed the next page. "Oh," I said.

"What?"

"It turns into a childhood memory. Apparently his father was a gynecologist, and he used to sneak into his office and pore over his medical textbooks, copy out the racy words. It's kind of sweet," I admitted. Bunny's intercom honked.

"That's the door," he said. "Call me later."

I found a website with a medical dictionary, looked up the words, and typed.

I copied the terms into a notebook, as if having them in my own hand was some kind of erotic communion. Ah, the pleasure of words! They were magic, conjurations and conjugations from the mysterious world of adults. Of course, the pictures helped. There was one book in particular, from the nineteenth century, with detailed engravings and faded colors. Multichambered, more intricate than a nautilus, a woman's anatomy was so complex. It was hard to imagine how everything fit inside. . .

A couple of pages on the vagina, uterus, fallopian tubes, and ovaries (*like flowers on stalks of fallopian tubes*—ugh) followed. I skipped ahead.

My first great love was Madame Ronet. She looked like the angel in my catechism book. My schoolmate Raymond's mother, she wore her thin platinum blond hair in a small chignon and painted her lips a bright red. Her curvaceous body and tiny waist, wrapped in tight-fitting suits, made me think of a fist squeezing a tube of toothpaste. When she ruffled my hair, I suffered alarming aches. The fact that she was one of my father's patients gave us a special bond, I felt. Once I stayed home from school feigning illness because I knew she had an appointment. After she left, I crept into the downstairs examination room and pressed the used cotton sheet to my face before Martine, my father's nurse, could clean up. It smelled of tuberose and sweat.

"You must watch out for my little Raymond," Madame Ronet told me. "He's not as clever as you."

It was true: Raymond was a boring little runt, whose principal interests were burning bugs with his magnifying glass and knowing facts about dinosaurs. But I did keep an eye out for him, even befriending him, because she'd asked me to. For my trouble, I was invited to the Ronets' country house for a weekend.

It was a damp, miserable cottage in Normandy, set on a grim stretch of local highway. Monsieur Ronet, a tense, burly fellow with a handlebar mustache, took us out for a long walk—"an airing," he said—then put us to work repairing a stone wall. At dinner, Madame Ronet served pumpkin soup and a gristly beef stew. We listened to a giant radio, shaped like a church window, while Madame mended socks with a darning egg. Later, she tucked us in bed.

The distinct crawl of insect feet across my forehead woke me up at night. Without thinking, I smacked my hand down, killing it with an audible crunch. I panicked when I felt a sticky pulp on my hand, and I ran down the hallway, colliding with Madame. She was dressed for bed, in a clingy nightgown under her open dressing gown, her hair in curlers under a threadbare red scarf.

"How horrible!" she exclaimed, blanching at the squashed insect carapace stuck to my forehead. She led me into the bathroom and cleaned my face. Afterward, while she heated a saucepan of milk and vanilla, I sat at the kitchen table, dangling my feet, mute with joy at being alone with her at last.

"There," she said, placing a cup in front of me. I blew on the surface, a fine pucker of milk skin already beginning to form. "My poor

little man," she said, stroking my face, "poor little Jean-Marc." I gave a theatrical sob, biting my lip to keep from laughing. It had the desired effect. She pulled me onto her lap and held me close to her chest. My nose was squashed flat against her nightgown, pressed right into the hollow between her breasts. "There, there. You'll be able to sleep now."

Not likely. I couldn't breathe.

It was the happiest memory of my childhood.

I was eleven.

The next few pages covered the author's adolescence, including a high school sweetheart and a brief affair with one of his father's nurses. The language was straightforward, factual. Then the narrative returned to its main subject.

Is there anything more compelling than the pursuit of a woman? All I could think of was Eve. The facts and routine of daily life were just a stopgap, a bookmark, a pause between notes, background noise. I lived through my senses. Information did not get processed through my brain; instead, I felt it on my skin, tasted it with my tongue, and caressed it with my fingertips. After an escalating campaign of phone calls, flowers, and lunches, Eve and I began an affair.

We met at noon, in the late afternoon, sometimes on weekends, but always at the same sparsely furnished apartment near the place de Clichy. We made love, ate, made love again. We didn't discuss jobs or friends or obligations, how we filled up the day until we saw each other. We kept ourselves free from the mundane details that dull most affairs. Instead, we talked about our childhoods, favorite books, memories. The time I spent with her was enchanted, and she'd agreed to a weekend in Venice with me later that month.

The first weekend in October hosted the most important horse race in France, the Prix de l'Arc de Triomphe. Daphne and I went with my cousin Yves, a sports journalist. He'd finagled us an invitation to a cocktail party at the loge of a wealthy Brit. Neither Daphne nor I knew anything about racing, so we drank champagne and soaked up information from the horse world cognoscenti.

Extravagant hats were traditional, so Daphne wore a wide-brimmed straw confection covered in plumage. It resembled nothing so much as an unidentified flying object after an infelicitous encounter with a chicken coop. She was more interested in examining other hats through her mother-of-pearl opera glasses than the horses.

Between races, we visited the paddock. The horses were magnificent, glossy, high-strung creatures. They knew they were about to run, and they twitched and pranced with anticipation. I angled my face beneath her hat and nuzzled Daphne's neck. Her skin was cloying and sweet with tea roses. A chestnut stallion picked his way around the ring, placing each hoof as if he were tracing a dance step. A tremor of excitement rippled through the spectators. I placed a hand on Daphne's hip and scanned the crowd, idly wondering if a familiar face would emerge.

It was Daphne who spotted her. "That woman is very elegant," she said, nudging me. I followed her gaze.

Eve wore dark glasses and an ivory suit, a black fox wrap draped over her shoulder. A small, veiled hat sat on her head at an angle. She stood next to a gray-haired man, her arm linked through his. My cousin mistook the object of my scrutiny.

"Not as old as he looks in the papers," Yves commented, tilting his head toward Eve's companion. It was Eric Beaufort de Blois, an industrialist who'd made a fortune in petrochemicals. "He got into horses about five years ago. Partnered with a Saudi prince and an Indian pharmaceuticals magnate. That's their horse in the next race."

"Who's the woman?" I muttered, trying to catch Eve's eye.

"Girlfriend, mistress, whore." He shrugged. "He's always photographed with different women."

So this was why she never mentioned a job, why she never went elsewhere, why there were never any questions about Daphne.

"Why are you staring at her?" Daphne hissed. At that moment, Eve saw me, and widened her eyes at the sight of Daphne's hat. She slid her sunglasses back on her face, a small smile playing on her lips. Beaufort caressed her cheek.

"I'm not staring at her," I said, turning to face Daphne.

"You were," she retorted.

"You're paranoid. I was staring at him," I lied. "He turned me down for an interview two years ago. Around the time the oil refinery scandal broke." Daphne looked uncertain. "You're jealous?" I asked, bending under the hat to kiss her. I kissed her again until she kissed me back, hoping Eve could see. I gave Daphne a meaningful look. She darted a glance around, understanding. "Come on," I murmured.

We sped back to the loges, and I pulled Daphne inside a private bathroom and locked the door. She laughed, breathless and dizzy on her heels. She undid my fly as I hiked up her skirt and lifted her, placing her ass on the edge of the sink. She wore a lace-edged garter belt and stockings, and it was easy to rip off her panties. She wrapped her legs around my hips as I plunged into her. Daphne was wet and she was hot, but as I thrust into her, I thought of Eve, the fur draped over her shoulder, the sly smile on her face. She moaned and I slid my tongue into her mouth—it was Daphne's mouth, I insisted to myself, it was Daphne I was fucking—but I could see only Eve's face as I came . . .

Asshole! Bastard! My fingernails clacked across the keyboard as I translated, despising the man who seemed to revel in his infidelity to the hapless Daphne even as he was fucking her. Granted, Daphne was about as perceptive as a veal, but this only made me dislike him more. I was, perhaps, just maybe, overidentifying with the veal, but that was beside the point. I called Bunny back.

"It's me. Why do men cheat?" I asked, terse.

"Why are you asking me?"

"'Cause you're a man. Give me a reason." There was a loud yawn, then silence on the other end. "Are you stalling?" I asked.

"Jesus, you're serious! Let me guess, you've been thinking about what's-his-face again. Let it go." His voice was scratchy.

"No, I'm translating this stupid chapter, and he's cheating on the veal with the femme fatale while still sleeping with the veal, and it's got disaster written all over it, and I just want to know *why*!"

"I'm not going to defend my whole gender—"

"Did you? I mean, did you ever—"

"I know what you mean, and that's none of your business. You might consider whether life with the veal isn't making him miserable and if the femme fatale isn't adding some excitement to his stagnant existence. We can continue this conversation when you dismount the high horse," he said.

"Damn it, whose side are you on?" I yelled, but he hung up. I stared at the receiver, bleating in frustration. Sheep, not veal, but close enough.

Of course, Bunny had a point. Bunny always had a point, but like a lot of points, sometimes it hurt when he used it. It would be easier to translate if I kept myself out of it, but it was hard to keep myself out of it since I was doing the translating. It seemed an unfair metaphysical joke that *this* story would be the one I got to translate.

I put water on to boil and searched the kitchen cupboards for something sweet. I found an open package of petit-beurre biscuits and pressed a soft, stale cookie to the roof of my mouth. Maybe Bunny was right. Maybe the narrator's relationship with Daphne was over. Maybe this was his way of getting out of it. Maybe there was always someone else. Maybe, as the cynical saying went, it took three to make a perfect relationship.

Or maybe there wasn't a reason. Maybe the world was random and mean and hurtful, and maybe sometimes people were, too. Maybe there wasn't a *reason* Timothy had cheated on me. Maybe someone he couldn't resist had come along. Someone like Eve.

Maybe I could be more like Eve, I mused, peering out the window and trying to picture myself as the exotic, mysterious, sexy woman. I thought about Olivier, then shook my head. I'd probably never see him again. I poured myself a mug of tea and retreated under the duvet.

I woke up later that night thinking about clothes: Eve's fur, Daphne's hat and lingerie, Madame Ronet's tight-fitting navy suits. There was an awful lot of attention to detail. The kind of detail women tended to notice more than men.

Could the author be a woman?

11

*I*toyed with the idea over the next few days, but by Wednesday morning, as I reread the chapter, I decided it didn't read as particularly female, though the descriptions of the clothes struck me as feminine. But maybe that was because I paid more attention to them. Besides, observing sartorial details was normal for a French man. A woman author was a nice theory, but I let it go. I'd heard a rumor once about *Story of O*: that Pauline Réage had written it to win back a lover who'd left her. Appar-

---

*Irène: I'm hesitating between a sugar waffle and a love affair.
Old lady: Well, have the waffle!
Irène: Okay, a sugar waffle.
Cook: With lots of sugar?
Irène (sighing): Oh, yes.

ently, it had worked: he came back, and she never wrote another piece of fiction. Which was one definition of a happy ending.

I fiddled around with the passage:

There was a private bathroom by the loges. I pulled Daphne inside and fumbled with the lock as she laughed, the porcelain perfection of her face creased with mirth. She grabbed my belt and deftly undid the fly, her fingers reaching for me as she sucked my lips. I grabbed handfuls of her silk skirt and lifted her onto the edge of the sink. Daphne spent a fortune on expensive lingerie; today she was wearing a pale pink lace garter belt and sheer black stockings. I ran my fingers over the short expanse of exposed bare thigh and hooked a thumb under the thin waistband of the lace panties. She gasped when I ripped them off, and wrapped her legs around my hips. I plunged into her. Daphne was wet and she was hot, but as I thrust into her, I thought of Eve, the thick, lush fur draped over her shoulder, the sly smile on her face. I howled and slid my tongue into Daphne's mouth—it was Daphne's mouth, I insisted to myself, it was Daphne's cunt—but it was Eve's face I saw as I came . . .

I went back and forth over "cunt," leaving it out, putting it back in, considering "pussy," trying out the more genteel "fucking," dithering over degrees. The irony of considering "fucking" more genteel than "cunt" wasn't lost on me. It was tricky territory, trying to figure out which words were more accurate. Err on the side of accuracy or mood? I couldn't get both to work. Today, translating felt like endless compromise, each version tipping the scales in a different, wrong direction.

Perhaps I was overthinking the nuances of profanity. I'd learned most of my French swearwords from my roommate, back when I'd lived in Paris after college. A lesbian with a Tintin haircut, she wore steel-toed boots, smoked three packs of Marlboro Reds a day, and had the foulest mouth I'd ever heard in French. She'd told me the hardness of words in French didn't translate directly to a similar hardness in English. "Asshole" is a fairly strong insult; *"trou du cul"* is something one eight-year-old calls another for knocking over his sand castle.

I left "cunt" in and printed the chapter out. On the radio, the news predicted clouds. I picked at the loose threads of my bathrobe and looked at my underwear drawer. It was a sea of sensible white cotton, most of it gone gray, plus some beige and black. Nothing that could be ripped off without causing severe friction burns; ergo, nothing conducive to quickies in bathrooms. I called Laveau and left a message that I'd bring the translation later that afternoon. Then I called Clara. After her summer vacation in Corsica, she'd gone on a quick buying trip to India to source precious stones for her jewelry collection. I invited myself over.

I walked to her place in the Ninth, a high-ceilinged apartment with plump sofas and damask walls covered in artwork she'd collected from around the world. A gilt Buddha looked down on the living room from its elevated perch.

"Ça tombe bien," she said when I got there. "I need you to try on some rings so I can see how they look like on another pair of hands. Would you like some mint tea?"

"Yes, please," I said. Her apartment smelled of beeswax and flowers. "Nice," I said, stopping to sniff a bouquet of peach and pink roses.

"Mmm," she hummed in a happy voice. "He knows how to apologize."

I followed her down the hallway to her workroom and stopped in front of a drying rack laden with lingerie. "Don't look!" she exclaimed. "It's such a mess, but there's nowhere else to put them!"

"No, this is an excellent coincidence. I was going to ask you where to buy nice underwear. Do you mind?" I asked. She shook her head. I looked at a pale green silk chiffon *balconnet* bra overlaid with red and pink lace and a matching G-string; a boned blue satin and lace bra with cups shaped like shells and attached with thin ribbons; even her plainest beige bra was draped in eggshell soutache embroidery.

"These are beautiful," I said, impressed and seized with a sudden desire for my own collection of extravagant underthings.

"It's an addiction, *lingerie*," Clara admitted. I fingered a pair of yellow silk panties with red tulips, then put them down.

"Wait, you have to hand-wash all this, don't you?" I asked.

"*Bien sûr!* You can't throw lace and silk into a washing machine," she said, adamant. This was a big strike against a potential purchase. Hand-washing was way too labor-intensive.

Another thought occurred to me. "Do you always match? I mean," I said, looking at a white eyelet ensemble, "what do you do if you're wearing a white top and black pants?" It was a serious question, but she thought I was poking fun.

"Ah, the metaphysical problems of the world," she mocked.

"Clara, I'm serious."

"You're impossible." She repositioned a black and lilac bra on the rack.

"No, really. All my underwear is white, beige, or black. None of it matches, except by accident. What do you do?"

Clara cocked her head. "You can always wear beige, though sometimes, *ce n'est pas evident*," she said. Even though I know the phrase means "it's not easy," I always hear "there is no obvious solution."

"How much does this stuff cost?" I knew it was a gauche question on two counts, direct and about money, but I needed to be fully informed before I decided to be a total cheapskate.

"*Ouf! Une fortune,*" she exclaimed, puffing her cheeks and letting out an airy raspberry of exasperation. It made her look like a disgruntled chipmunk.

"Humor me," I cajoled.

"About two hundred euros for a nice set," she admitted. I did the math.

"You have over three thousand dollars' worth of lingerie drying on this rack!" I squealed.

"Do I ask how you spend your money?" She raised an eyebrow.

"No, but—"

"It's tough being a woman, no?"

....

Clara opened intricately folded pieces of paper, showing me the spoils of her trip: pink citrines, yellow diamonds, magenta rubies, and multicolored tourmalines. I modeled rings for her, and she took pictures of my hands with her digital camera. When the sun came out, we went for a walk on the rue des Martyrs.

"You surround yourself with beauty," I remarked, thinking of her lingerie but also her jewelry, her furniture, the framed watercolors and engravings on the walls.

"Don't you?" she asked.

"I used to acquire a lot of things, but I don't actually live in them. I bring them out for special occasions," I said, thinking of my closet in L.A., crammed with dressy clothes and expensive shoes I rarely wore, and the trunk with my grandmother's monogrammed linen sheets and embroidered tablecloths, which I never used.

"That's stupid. Why do you buy things if you don't enjoy them?"

"You're right, it's stupid. But I keep thinking my life is on hold. One day, I'll have a use for those things when I hit the Play button again," I said, musing out loud.

"But then you would have to put Timothy behind you, and you're not done suffering over him," she remarked.

"Ouch," I said, frowning at her.

"I'm sorry. *Ne m'en veux pas,*" she apologized.

"Do you really think that's what I'm doing?" I asked, suspecting she was right and embarrassed that she knew.

"I shouldn't have said anything." She looked pained. "But—it's been a couple of months. How are you supposed to get on with your life unless you get on with it?" Clara said it kindly, but it stung. We walked in silence for a moment.

"I'd forgotten how direct you can be," I said lightly, tucking my arm in hers to let her know I wasn't offended. If I was honest, I could admit it felt like I'd been carrying my grief for Timothy around like a weight on my shoulders.

We walked into a park and sat on a bench. A group of chubby-cheeked children sat in a circle playing *le facteur,* the postman, the French version of duck, duck, goose, but instead of a head tap, it was played with a dropped handkerchief. One little boy started wailing, for no apparent reason, and his mother spoke to him sharply: *"Cyril! Arrête ton cinéma!"* Stop your cinema.

I love that expression. The closest equivalent in English is "drama queen," but it doesn't quite convey the connection to both film and illusion. Or the futile grandstanding.

"I'd been single for a long time before Timothy," I said, thinking out loud. "And even though there were lots of things wrong with the relationship—"

"There were?" Clara interrupted. "You never talk about *that.*"

"Sure. I can see that now: I made a lot of assumptions because I was totally infatuated. I misread him, I never called him on anything because I was scared that if I did, it would end . . ." I trailed off. "But I can't shake the feeling that that was it. Like now I should devote my life to saving the whales or ending child hunger."

"You're being ridiculous," she said with a disapproving look.

"Maybe, but sometimes, that's what it feels like. Other times, I think I just have to look harder."

"Look harder, but let him come to you this time. Don't do all the work."

"What do you mean?"

"Cours après moi pour que je t'attrape," Clara said, citing an old French

proverb. Chase after me so I can catch you. "No, don't ask me what it means." She shook her head. "Just think about it. Come on." We left the park and went down a narrow street.

"This will take your mind off things," she said, stopping in front of a lingerie boutique.

"I'm not buying anything," I said, gazing at an icy blue silk negligee.

"It's just what you need. *Une intervention*," she said.

"A what?"

"That's what they called it on *Les Sopranos*."

Clara pushed me inside and introduced me to Madame Laserre, the owner, a stick-thin woman in her fifties with a sharp nose and glossy black pageboy. Clara pointed out artful displays of bras, panties, teddies, and nightgowns, but I didn't feel like spending money on something no one would see.

"Why are you being so puritanical?" Clara asked.

"I feel fat," I said. Back home, this would make anyone back off.

"*Et alors?* Don't you think the fat would look better in this?" She waved an ecru silk camisole under my nose.

"Fine. But I'm just trying it on," I said and threw my bag into the small *cabine*. Madame Laserre took one look at my bra (shapeless, a little dingy, with wide, comfortably padded straps) and triumphantly informed me I was wearing the wrong cup size. She took my measurements and came back with a taupe and cream *balconnet* bra, and insisted I bend forward and wiggle to get the breasts to settle in the cups. Performing this action under the watchful gaze of this bird-like creature made me feel about as graceful as a beached aquatic mammalian, say a walrus or a manatee. I was relieved when she left to answer the phone.

"*Alors?*" asked Clara from behind the curtain. "*Puis-je voir?*"

"No, you can't. Go away," I said. I looked in the mirror. It was the prettiest bra I'd ever worn—even the straps were gorgeous, taupe tulle shot through with satin ribbon. The *balconnet* pushed my breasts up into a round, full shape, like in eighteenth-century paintings.

Clara poked her head in anyway. "It's so pretty!" she exclaimed. "It's just what you need."

"Yes, but lots of things are really pretty. It doesn't mean I have to buy them."

"*Et ça? T'as vu le slip?*" She held up a matching panty and garter belt. "You can choose a bikini or thong or the little boy shorts, or, *tiens,* these boring ones, what are they called?" she asked, holding them up.

"Briefs," I said sourly. She rolled her eyes.

"Fine. Go on, be sad, you can console yourself with all those nice things tucked away in Los Angeles. No, even better, you can donate them to the hungry children."

She let the curtain drop. I looked at myself in the mirror again and caved.

I forked over my credit card for the bra, boy shorts, and, what the hell, garter belt, and tried not to wince at the amount. Outside, Clara pinched me.

"Okay, I'm happy I bought it," I grumbled.

"Good," she said.

I looked at my watch. "I should run. I have to drop off the translation."

We kissed good-bye, and I walked toward the métro. "By the way, don't expect him to notice. They never notice," she called out over her shoulder.

"Him? Him who?" I asked.

"Him whoever. At least you're prepared."

12

Certaines femmes timides et tristes s'épanouissent à la chaleur de
l'admiration, comme des fleurs au soleil.*
—ANDRÉ MAUROIS

At Odéon, the late-afternoon light burnished the limestone buildings a pinkish gold and cast spindly Giacometti shadows behind
the pedestrians. I ran up the street to the bookstore, arriving just as
Monsieur Laveau lowered the Venetian blinds. His face twitched in pain
when he saw me. Maybe I was spoiled, maybe my friendship with Bunny
made me arrogant, but I was used to winning over older men. It was a
constant blow to my ego that he seemed to find no pleasure whatsoever
in my company.

"*Finalement,*" he said pointedly, opening the door.

"*Monsieur Laveau! Quel plaisir de vous voir!*" I exclaimed, pasting a
sunny smile on my face. My attempt to kill him with kindness elicited
nothing more than a lukewarm harrumphing sound. I handed over the
envelope and watched as he leafed through the pages. He looked jowly,
and the bushy eyebrows seemed to radiate out from his forehead like

*Certain sad and timid women blossom in the warmth of an admiring gaze, like flowers in
sunlight.

angry antennae. *"Vous n'avez pas bonne mine, monsieur,"* I observed in a solicitous voice. *"Est-ce que vous dormez assez?"* He didn't look up. Criticizing his appearance and asking if he was getting enough sleep might have been overdoing it.

I cleared my throat. At this, he remembered my existence, muttered something incomprehensible, and retreated to his office. I heard foraging sounds, the rustling of papers, and then he emerged, brandishing a check and another envelope.

"Tenez. Et voilà le troisième chapitre," he said, handing them to me. I opened the envelope and skimmed the first page. He jangled his keys in his pocket when I didn't leave immediately. *"Bon, à la semaine prochaine,"* he said, trying to send me on my way. I switched to English, a language where I had a far better command than he did.

"Monsieur, I'd like to know something. Do you have a sense of whether the author is pleased with my work, or if he has any specific instructions for me? Notes? Comments?" I was pretty sure he didn't because I'd have heard by now, but Monsieur Laveau wanted to leave, and I wanted to inconvenience him.

"He hasn't discussed it with me, *mademoiselle*. Now, if you'll excuse—"

"I see. Does that mean you have no idea how he feels about it?" I interrupted, a honeyed note in my voice.

"Of course I know how he feels about it, but he hasn't given me any comments for you," he said, irritated.

"He must be very, very busy, that he doesn't have time to discuss this with you. Or maybe he doesn't care what you think?" It was hard not to grin as I said it.

"Mademoiselle, je suis en retard," he said, tapping his watch.

"Oui, monsieur. But you don't know?"

He folded his arms and gave me a long, hard look, exhaling at length. Others had fallen before such intimidation, but I didn't budge. We locked eyes.

"*Mademoiselle, vous êtes une emmerdeuse,*" he said, breaking the standoff.

"*Oui, monsieur.* In English, the term you're looking for is 'pain in the ass.'" I turned on my heel. "Oh, and it's unisex, you can use it for both genders. *Bonne soirée,*" I added, over my shoulder.

I could almost swear I heard a muffled laugh as I walked out the door, but maybe I misheard the cowbell. In any case, it was the first time I'd managed to best Monsieur Laveau.

....

I waltzed down rue de Condé, crossed Saint-Germain, and wound my way toward the river. I stopped off at La Palette, one of Pascal's hangs. There was no sign of him, but there was an empty table on the sidewalk next to a potted tree. I squeezed myself into it, banging my hip as I sat. A tall, portly, irascible waiter I recognized from previous visits stood guard at the entrance. Fat fingers, bushy mustache and long sideburns, black waistcoat, long, stained apron: he looked right out of a Toulouse-Lautrec painting.

He planted himself in front of me. "*J'écoute,*" he said, succinctly.

"*Un verre de rouge, s'il vous plaît,*" I said, smiling up at him. "*Merci, Bruno,*" I added, remembering his name. He grunted but came back with a glass of red wine and a small dish of black olives.

"*Comme c'est gentil!*" I exclaimed, piercing one with a toothpick, trying to remember if they always gave dishes of olives or if this was just my lucky day. Bruno snorted, but it seemed like a friendly snort. Maybe this was the trick. Maybe being sort of deviously nice and semiflirtatious was what it took to avoid being ignored.

A familiar face approached another outdoor table. With an elated internal leap, I recognized Olivier as he sat down, his back to me, and lit a cigarette. He glanced around but didn't see me. He ran an impatient hand through his already disheveled hair and answered his phone. I sat there, trying to think up something clever to say, but then he stood up to greet a brunette valkyrie.

She looked about six feet tall, with full lips, high cheekbones, and the kind of thick, black, nerdy glasses that seem to make beautiful women look even more beautiful for not trying. She was probably an actress. Or a model. Olivier gave a strand of her hair an affectionate tug. I looked away. I didn't need to see the inevitable kiss.

The French do that. They have no compunction about it whatsoever. They kiss in public, and I mean big, wet, sexy kisses. People of all ages do it, and no one yells "Get a room!" If you don't like it, you can lump it, or look the other way, but most Parisians shake their heads indulgently, as if to say, "Ah, love," or something equally sappy. I didn't know why it was so aggravating, except that I was in Paris and no one was kissing me in a smart Left Bank café.

They probably had impossibly beautiful children. I sipped my wine, picturing their kids in Petit Bateau T-shirts and baby Dior overalls, pushing toy sailboats around the fountain at the Jardin du Luxembourg on a Sunday afternoon. No, they were cooler than that; I revised the image: they probably dressed their kids in mud-cloth ensembles hand-sewn by a Senegalese feminist collective in Barbès. They went to family tabla drumming classes.

The brunette caught me staring. Olivier turned to look at me at the precise moment when I did that extremely attractive thing whereby the lips miss the edge of the wineglass. Red wine dribbled down the front of my beige sweater. He waved. I grimaced and dabbed at my chest with a napkin, knocking my bag to the ground. Ducking my head, I scraped my knuckles as I retrieved my keys, wallet, and cell phone. I straightened up, bumping my head on the side of the table. Olivier stood in front of me.

"It's you!" he said with a smile.

"Ow. Hello," I said, rubbing my head. "Yup, it's me."

"What are you doing?" he asked. I hunched over, folding one arm across my chest to hide the stain.

"Wearing my drink. Well, isn't it a nice night? Don't let me keep you," I babbled. He cocked his head, looking bemused.

"May we join you?" he asked. I was speechless in the face of this near-perfect definition of hell. "Sandrine!" he called, waving his hand. The beautiful brunette walked over. "This is Sandrine," Olivier said.

"Anna," I said. She bent to kiss me on both cheeks.

"*C'est elle qui fait la traduction pour Bernard,*" he explained as she sat. "And how is the translation going?" he asked, in English.

"As well as can be expected," I answered.

"That doesn't sound very promising," he said.

"No, it's fine. I just can't talk about it. Monsieur Laveau wants me to keep it confidential."

"But I already know about it. The cat has left the baggie," he said.

"Bag," I said and bit down on the inside of my mouth, charmed despite my discomfort. I calculated I could leave Perfect Couple in ten minutes. Her cell phone rang.

"*Oui, maman, oui.*" Sandrine made an apologetic face. "*Bien sûr. Non, en fait, il est là,*" she said. "*D'accord,*" she answered and passed him the phone. He took it and got up to speak. "Our mother wants us to go to a cousin's wedding in the south," she explained, switching back into French. "We don't like this cousin, she's awful, but it's a delicate situation," she confided.

"Is it very soon?" I asked, merely to make conversation. Maybe I'd walk home.

"Next month."

"And is it a big family wedding?" I asked. I could catch the 96, or cross the river to Châtelet. I wondered if Monoprix had avocados; I was in the mood for guacamole.

"*Enorme!*" she said, laughing. Olivier hung up, passed her the phone, and looked at me. Suddenly, the full, potential meaning of the phrase "our mother" clicked into place like a roulette ball in a numbered slot.

"I'm sorry, did you say that was your mother?" I asked, using the handy-dandy French second-person plural. It came out overly dramatic, as if the question was of vital importance to national security, but I went with it.

"Yes," she said. She waved at Bruno and signaled for another glass of wine.

"Aha," I stalled, trying to find an elegant way of confirming this information. "Is it just the two of you, or do you have other brothers or sisters?"

"We have an older sister, Gisèle, but she lives in Milan," Sandrine said. I nodded sagely, as if this was the crucial piece of information I was looking for. Olivier half-smiled, as if he knew what I was up to and liked it. Feeling a wild urge to stroke his cheek, I sat on my hands. It was hard to control the insane internal bubble of euphoria I felt. *She's your sister! Yay! Are you single?* I asked Sandrine if she spoke English.

"Very little, though I must learn. It would be useful for work. I'm in advertising," she confessed. She really was very, very beautiful. Absolutely stunning. *And his sister!* I ordered another glass of wine as well. We chatted about movies and art exhibits, her summer trip to Croatia, his trip to New York, and places to see in Los Angeles. They were smart and playful, with a gentle way of ribbing each other that seemed to include me. I liked her tremendously, not just because she was his sister. I more than liked him.

The air did seem to sparkle between us. After a while, even my pessimistic side wasn't buying that this was merely wishful thinking on my part. He was warm and engaging, and when I looked at him, he held my gaze. Sandrine got up to take another call. Olivier switched back into English.

"Do you mind? I need to practice," he said.

"No, but I won't correct any grammatical mistakes. I hate it when anyone does it to me. I'm just warning you," I said. Somehow, it came out flirty.

"That's fair," he said and leaned closer to me. My brain froze. I tried to think of something intelligent to say, but speech seemed either superfluous or loaded with innuendo when all I could think about was the shape of his mouth and the slingshot tension in my stomach. He stroked the inside of my wrist. "I must confess. I have ulterior motives for wanting to talk to you."

"Oh?" I answered dreamily. His finger was making figure eights on the clustered network of veins. It felt like a cross between a caress and a hundred mosquito bites, lovely and unbearable. I wanted to scratch my wrist, but I didn't want it to end.

"I'm trying to get to one of Bernard's authors, and I think he may be the one whose work you're translating," he said. "I want to adapt one of his books for the screen," he clarified.

The thing in my stomach snapped, and something went thud, a boulder landing in soft dirt.

"I can't help you." I pulled my hand away. "I don't know who he is." I couldn't keep a note of *froideur* out of my voice.

"What's wrong?"

"I just remembered I said I'd meet a friend this evening," I lied, looking at my watch. I wasn't a very good liar. Embroidery, yes, outright lies, no. By the skeptical look on his face, I knew he could tell, but I stood up.

Sandrine came back. *"Mais, tu t'en vas?"* she asked, surprised.

"Oui," I said and described a fictional friend. The fictional friend was having a hard time getting over a breakup, and I'd promised to visit. And what a coincidence, fictional friend lived in the Eleventh, near me.

"I can drive you, I have my car," Olivier suggested.

"No, no, I'm already late, I'll pop in the métro," I said, waving him off, my voice high-pitched and cheery with insincerity.

I sped away, darting in and out of the throng on Saint-André des Arts, past the crepe places and postcard stands. So that was why Olivier was being so friendly. He wanted to get to the author, my author. I was a fool for thinking he was interested in me.

I crossed the Seine. The reflections of streetlamps bobbed on the surface of the water below. In the métro, someone played a mournful Air on the G String, the notes bouncing against the tiled walls. I sat on an orange plastic seat that looked like unsafe playground furniture and shook my head. He was a nice man, a nice, attractive man who was flirting with me, and I'd flown out of there like a crazy person. A complete overreaction.

The station was nearly empty. I walked to the edge of the platform, feeling the cold, damp air above the track. On the opposite *quai* was a billboard advertising a three-day sale at one of the big department stores. *"Les Trois J,"* said the caption, underneath a giant image of a woman sprawled on a red sofa, kicking her feet up in a pink lace negligee. The train came in. As we pulled out of the station, I glanced at the ad again, and a burst of heat flooded my face.

I'd left my shopping bag of new lingerie at the café.

13

Le désir possède une persistance indestructible.*

—JACQUES LACAN, *Ecrits*

I pondered my plight as I walked home from the station, hoping the bag of lingerie was still under the table at the café. A mass of pale-faced teenagers with piercings and spiked hair swarmed the sidewalk, Goth night at the Gibus. I'd forked over a lot of money for that lingerie. All for naught.

On the ground, I spotted a witch doctor card. I'd started a collection of them years ago, when I was a student in Paris. I wasn't the only one: there were websites devoted to collectors of *des cartes de marabouts africains,* and I'd even found a witch doctor card generator online. Catering to the African community, they were business cards advertising the various services of witch doctors, seers, or mediums. This one was dingy beige, with green lettering. *Grand Mage Mamadou* promised to cure all problems, including those related to "love, job, work, family, desire, and lack of desire." Results were guaranteed within twenty-four hours or your money back, and an address in the Nineteenth was listed. I put the card in my pocket. Maybe Mamadou knew where my lingerie was.

*Desire possesses an indestructible persistence.

I looked up the café in the phone book and called them. No, no one had found a shopping bag, a woman assured me. I explained I'd been there with two people, described the location of the table, and asked if "someone" might possibly be kind enough to go outside and check. She put the phone down. I heard clattering cups and the screaming milk steamer.

"*Ecoutez, il n'y pas de sac. Peut-être vos amis sont partis avec votre paquet,*" she suggested when she came back, done with her good deed for the day. It occurred to me that even if Olivier and Sandrine had taken my shopping bag, I didn't know how to get in touch with them, nor did they know how to reach me. Except through Bernard. Now there was an embarrassing scenario. The whole situation was maddening: overreacting, forgetting the shopping bag. I groaned and turned on the TV, trying not to think about it.

Later, when I climbed into bed, I couldn't sleep. I readjusted the pillow, turning it over, then turning it over again. Just when I got comfortable, my nose started itching. Then my ear. Then a spot behind my ear. My shoulder blade, thighs, calves, the small of my back. Itching led to thinking about itching. I flung off the covers, stomped into the bathroom, and popped half a sleeping pill. I burrowed underneath the duvet, scratched my chin and my cheek, and closed my eyes.

I dreamed the doorbell rang, and I stumbled out of bed, sleepy and discombobulated. It was Timothy. He was wearing a trench coat, and his hair was long and shaggy. He shoved a cardboard box into my arms. "Here," he said. "You left these at my place." He turned and walked into an old-fashioned cage elevator, slamming the iron door behind him with a clang. The box was full of things I didn't recognize: a collection of Chinese poetry, a Lonely Planet guide to South America, and a crocheted afghan. These aren't mine, I thought. Then: Oh, they belong to the other woman. I ran out of the building, chasing after him. His trench coat flapped open, whipping in the wind.

"Wait!" I yelled. "Why did you come all this way?" He turned around, and it wasn't Timothy, it was Olivier. He looked at me like I was a stranger.

....

In the morning, I spread a slab of churned butter on toasted *pain Poilâne*. The butter came from the open market, where they cut it with a garrote-like length of wire. It tasted of cream and salt, and I spread it in a thick, voluptuous layer.

I poured another cup of coffee and got out the chapter. I skimmed the pages: narrator and Eve finally go to Venice. The chapter was longer than the last one and contained at least a couple of sex scenes. I thought about turning on the computer and powering through a first draft, but it wasn't due for another six days, and it wasn't like me to get something done in an efficient and timely manner. I called Clara.

"Buyer's remorse?" she asked.

"Not quite." I told her what had happened. As she burst into cackles of hysterical laughter, I mused on the fact that Clara, like many French people, had a cruel sense of humor. My observation fell on deaf ears. She was too busy laughing.

"After all that trouble! *L'ironie est extra!*" she exclaimed between giggles.

"Yeah, yeah. Do you think Olivier has my lingerie?"

"I don't know, *ma chère*. Why not ask Monsieur Laveau for Olivier's number?"

"I can't. He wigged when he thought I was discussing the translation with him."

"*C'est quoi,* 'wigged'?"

"Flipped out—*il a flippé,*" I explained.

"I still don't understand 'wigged.'"

"'Wigged,' the past simple of the verb 'to wig,' derived from the noun 'wig,' like *perruque*. I'm assuming it's slang and that the etymology comes from slapstick comedy, a genre which could easily feature the loss of or a droll mishap with a wig, either worn by a woman or, when worn by a man, usually referred to as a toupee or rug, like *tapis*." I caught my breath. "Or it's from the expression 'to flip your wig.' Or lid. Not sure."

"*Ah, bon,*" Clara said. "But this means he can't ask Laveau for your number, either. You must sit at La Palette every day for the next week," she said.

I hadn't thought of that. "Really?"

"I don't have another solution, unless you want to research the name of his agent. He's an actor, no? I have to go, but I'll call if I think of anything brilliant," she promised.

I had hours to kill before I could go to La Palette. I sat at the computer and cranked out a rough translation, wrote e-mails, including a long, newsy one to my parents, and surfed, catching up on world events. I even checked out a couple of fancy lingerie websites, La Perla and Eres. Through some clever IMDb-ing, I found Olivier's credits, which were mostly French and Italian TV movies.

By late afternoon, my insides were doing flapjack somersaults at the thought of seeing him again. Anxiety built a nest in my stomach and settled in to roost.

I flipped through Tante Isabelle's music and put on a collection of Argentine tangos. A raspy, mournful voice filled the apartment, accompanied by a dramatic contrabass and a lilting *bandonéon*. I remembered the night Timothy and I had danced around the floor in socks as he tried to teach me to tango. I'd kept stepping on his toes and apologizing for my clumsiness. He'd taken my chin in his hand and spoken in a fake Spanish accent: "Never apologize to Timoteo for such things, *querida*." He'd been joking, but there was something in his look that I didn't understand.

I pulled on jeans and a pretty cashmere cardigan edged with lace. I swiped on some eyeliner and left it at that, not wanting to look like I was trying too hard. The tango played in my head as I strolled down the hill.

It was *l'heure de l'apéritif,* and the cafés were packed. Behind the BHV, the big department store, someone had stencil spray-painted two lines: REDOUTER CE QU'ON SOUHAITE, and below it, SOUHAITER CE QU'ON REDOUTE. To fear what you wish for, and to wish for what you fear.

The creature in my stomach ruffled its feathers in agitation. What did I fear most: Olivier being there or not being there? Did I wish for his presence or his absence? In front of the Hôtel de Ville, a teenager in aviator sunglasses passed out flyers for a theme night at a trendy gay *boîte* off the Champs-Elysées. A Queen Elizabeth impersonator with pink hair and a tiara held an enormous phallus like a microphone. Glitter script announced this weekend's "Gode Save The Gouine" party.

It wasn't a case of quaintly mistaken orthography. *"Gode,"* I'd learned from my dictionary of slang, was a dildo. A *"gouine"* was a lesbian. It was a bilingual pun. I crossed the Seine to La Palette, immediately finding an empty table, a sign that luck was on my side. The familiar mustache appeared in front of me.

"Bonsoir, Bruno. Vous allez bien?" I asked, risking an impish tone but sticking to the second-person plural.

"Pffft," he replied, letting air out through compressed lips. He rattled the coins in his waistcoat. I wasn't sure if it was an impatient gesture or a tic.

"Une tasse de thé, s'il vous plaît," I said, making up my mind. "Earl Grey."

"Je ne vous emmène pas les olives, alors," he grumbled.

"Pourquoi?" Just because I wasn't having wine didn't mean I didn't want the little dish of olives.

"Ça ne se mange pas avec le thé, voyons," he said reprovingly, playfulness in the guise of deadpan disapproval. I felt like a member of the club, especially when he brought a little plate of brown-edged *langue de chat* cookies with my tea. As I gave him my most winning smile, Olivier sauntered up. He shook hands with Bruno.

"Mais tu la gâtes, Bruno! Et puis quoi encore?" Olivier accused Bruno

of spoiling me, then ordered a coffee. *"Je peux?"* he asked, pointing to the chair across from me. I nodded, trying to look cool and wishing I'd worn something more feminine: a skirt, heels. Olivier's hair was an unruly mess, and he wore a gray, cable-knit wool sweater, bisected diagonally by the black strap of his messenger bag. I wanted to bury myself in it and gnaw on the yarn.

"You know Bruno?" I asked.

"I live nearby." He shrugged.

I nodded, stirred sugar into my tea, and thought, Your turn. He had a serious look on his face. I let the silence stretch out, even though the creature in my stomach squawked in protest. He leaned forward and looked deep into my eyes.

"I want one of your cookies," he growled. I moved to offer him one but caught myself. I could play, too. I pretended to think it over.

"Je regrette. That will not be possible." I took a careful sip of tea.

"Then you can't have your shopping bag," he shot back, folding his arms.

"It's of no use to you," I pointed out.

"What do you know? I may have many uses for such pretty *lingerie.*"

"You looked inside. Very bad form." I shook my head.

"I was curious. Why does she leave so abruptly? Where is she really going?" he asked, leaning forward. "What is in the bag she left behind? It was my only clue."

"Curiosity killed the cat."

"Et alors? Cats have nine lives. I must have at least one or two left. Cookie?"

"No." I bit down on my lower lip to keep from smiling, now a different kind of nervous: Olivier was fun.

"You're very ungrateful. I didn't have to take your *lingerie.* I could have left it with Bruno or Madame Sollers, and then you would have had to ask them. It would have been very embarrassing," he said, leaning back so Bruno could deposit his *express* on the table. I watched him unwrap a sugar cube and dip it into his coffee. The brown liquid leached into the crystals.

"It's called a *canard*, like a duck, when you do this," he explained and ate it.

"I know."

"Bien sûr."

"'Canard' in English means a false story. Not a duck," I offered. There was a small silence, and loud laughter from the table next to us. Olivier stirred his coffee.

"In French, *'canard'* also means newspaper, like *Le Canard enchaîné,"* he said.

"That I didn't know," I admitted.

"Hah! Cookie!" he demanded.

"If I give you a cookie, will you give me my bag?"

"If I give you your bag, will you stay instead of inventing an excuse to leave?" His tone was light, but the question brought me up short. It was strangely intimate, that he knew I'd lied and said so, and in the same sentence told me he wanted me to stay. It made me feel like I'd been found out, as if some shameful thing I'd been trying to hide, like a four-foot-long bushy tail or cloven feet, was both obvious and somehow beside the point. Or that my embarrassment should have been about the act of hiding something, and not about having something to hide.

I looked down at my lap, at the people at the next table, anywhere but at Olivier. *Redouter ce qu'on souhaite. Souhaiter ce qu'on redoute.* My face grew hot. I didn't know what to say. It was a relief when he spoke.

"Remind me. What does the duck say in English?" he asked gently, like he was letting me off the hook.

"Quack quack," I answered.

"Comme c'est débile. A duck says *'coin coin.'"*

"Oh, shush. Have a cookie," I said, offering him the plate.

"I am not so easily bought off." He bit into a cookie. "Or distracted.

What happened last night? Did I say something wrong?" He rubbed his fingers together, shaking off crumbs, looking at me.

Timothy had accused me once of being too good a poker player, of never showing my hand. "Half the time, I have no idea what's going on with you," he'd said.

"Okay," I said, taking a leap. "I had a great time with you and your sister. But I don't know how much of this"—I waved my hands in the air—"is about trying to get information about Monsieur Laveau's writer." He stiffened, like I'd insulted him. I felt my face redden, but I pressed on, explaining, "I'm a little self-protective these days."

"*Et?*"

"*C'est tout,*" I said.

He nodded. "It is disarming, when you speak directly," he said, but his voice had taken on a formal, almost distant tone.

"I wish I did it more." I grimaced. He looked away, then back at me.

"Listen, it's not sinister," he said, running a hand through his hair. "I'm interested in Bernard's writer, but I'm working on him. I don't even know for sure that he's the person you're translating. *C'est compliqué.* Can we have dinner soon, and I'll tell you about it?" It wasn't the best answer in the world, but I could live with it. I nodded.

He looked at his watch. "I must go," he said and tapped the table. "*Je peux t'appeler?*"

I gave him my phone numbers and watched as he programmed them into his cell phone. He opened his bag and pulled out my rumpled shopping bag.

"Thank you," I said. "I'm very glad I didn't lose it."

He leaned over the table. "I'll call you," he said and kissed me on the mouth, hard. He walked away, and I sat there, running my fingers over my lips.

Someone said something, but I wasn't listening. It became more insistent, until finally, Pascal put a hand on my shoulder, shaking me out of my reverie.

"*Oh, là, tu dors?*" he asked. "What are you doing in the 'hood?" I squinted up at him, wondering where he was learning all his American slang. He waved at Bruno and signaled for two glasses of wine. "*Eh, oh!* You're not sleeping, you're dreaming," he said, snapping his fingers in front of my face. "What's his name?" he asked, guessing.

"I'm not telling you. You'll only make fun of me," I said.

"Why, is he famous?" he asked, joking.

"No, not really," I said, but I must've looked guilty. He gave me a sharp look. "An actor," I confessed.

"*Ah, non! Mais ça ne va pas la tête?*" he asked, rapidly tapping his temple with his index finger, the French national gesture for "What the hell is wrong with you?" or "Are you insane?" With minor variations in tapping speed and facial expression, it's employed for everything from mild insanity to the ultimate outrage, bad driving. They go wild with the temple tap at l'Etoile.

"Didn't you say you were never getting involved with another man in the entertainment industry?" His mouth set in a thin horizontal line of disapproval.

"But that was in Los Angeles!" I protested.

"It was not. You said it here. I heard you. You said it to me," he said.

"Well, I meant it about Los Angeles," I muttered.

He slapped his pack of cigarettes against his palm, then took one out and lit it. "I'm meeting Florian for dinner. You want to join us?" he asked, exhaling smoke.

I shook my head and kissed him good-bye. I swung my shopping bag as I floated home through the Marais.

14

Il y a deux histoires: l'histoire officielle, menteuse,
puis l'histoire secrète, où sont les véritables causes des événements.*
—HONORÉ DE BALZAC

The sheets were cold and the memory came to me before I could
stop myself. One of the things I missed most about Timothy was
how warm he was. His body was like a furnace, it heated the whole bed.
He didn't mind my cold hands and feet. "Wrap yourself around me,"
he'd say, and I'd twine around him like a vine, *comme une liane*, finding a
nook in his neck for my nose. I thought that was what love was, someone
who warmed you up when you were cold.

I felt a sharp pang, half longing, half loss. I rubbed my feet against
each other to warm them up, and thought about Los Angeles. One of
my favorite things about living in California was getting in a hot car on
a cold day. The heat enveloped you, seeping into your pores like a sauna
until it got unbearable and you had to open the window because even
your teeth were hot. I burrowed under the duvet and forced my thoughts

---

*There are two histories: the official, dissembling one, and the secret one, where the true
causes of events are to be found.

away from Timothy, imagining instead what warming myself up with Olivier would feel like.

I looked over the manuscript in the morning, but it didn't read the way I'd remembered. Sure, they went to Venice and had a big fight, but now it seemed poignant, even charming. Was I half-asleep when I read it the first time? Feeling bitter and jaded? Was my mood so different now? Puzzled, I sat in front of the computer and rewrote the second half of the chapter.

We ate in a restaurant under a ceiling made from the ribs of an old sailing ship. We had tagliarini alla granseola, pasta with Adriatic sea crab, a Venetian specialty. I told her about the sea creatures that lived in the canals, the odd crayfish and fleshy eels. I told her about the Mariana Trench, the deepest point on the earth, and the fish that lived at the bottom of the ocean. Strange fish, with sharp, glassine teeth; fish with hanging lanterns above their heads so they could see in the abysmal dark; fish who lived their lives in a permanent night under the terrible pressure of the water.

Fish tales, she said.

I made a note to find out if the expression "fish tales" means the same thing in French as it does in English.

It is only fitting, she said. I caught her hand across the table, holding the fingers captive. I turned it over and stroked the inside of her arm. The soft skin was like a secret revealed, translucent, traced with a fine blue-green network of veins. The skin on her breasts was nearly transparent as well, revealing her bloodstream as plainly as the lacy veining on a leaf. I thought of an old lover, Fimi: a white-blond Finnish girl with pale lashes and brows. Her skin was white, with a bluish tint, like a water creature: a sprite.

We strolled away from San Marco after dinner, walking in the cold, damp air. The crowds thinned and dwindled, until it seemed we were alone in the city. At night, La Serenissima had an air at once enchanting and perilous, as if angels and monsters lurked around each corner.

"It's a city of stories," Eve remarked, as we stopped to look out over a canal. "I read one in an English book once," she said. "An old lady, a French grandmother, goes to visit Venice. She'd been famous in her youth for her beauty, and had had many lovers. She'd married well, had children and several grandchildren. When her husband died, she decided to travel, revisit the cities of the classic Grand Tour with her favorite cousin.

"In Venice, on a small canal, they came upon an exquisite, Moorish-style, pink house. Mysteriously drawn to it, they rang the doorbell and asked to visit. A caretaker told them the house had been uninhabited for years, but he would show them around.

"They toured the drawing rooms, with furniture covered in white sheets. There were elaborate ceiling frescoes and tall windows hung with faded silk. The caretaker pointed out various features of the house, and the grandmother became distant and odd, as if she were warding off a chill, or an illness. When at last they were shown the master bedroom, her face cleared. She walked into the center of the room and announced, 'If, on the night table, there is a box with a key on a black ribbon, this house belongs to me.'

"There was, as well as a letter addressed to her. A former lover had given her the house decades ago, and she'd forgotten about it until being there triggered the memory."

Eve looked out over the water and smiled. "How I'd love to be like her when I'm eighty," she said. "To have lived so much! Imagine traveling through Italy and discovering a Venetian palazzo a former lover had left you."

"Do you want a Venetian palazzo?" I asked.

"No!" she exclaimed. "I want to be a respectable grandmother who

had a scandalous youth. Don't you understand?" Eve pulled her shawl around her shoulders.

I thought I recognized the story but couldn't place it. Maybe I'd read the same book. I knew what she meant, though: I understood yearning for a rich, adventurous life to look back on.

"Now, I've a Venetian story for you," I said. "A foreign businessman came to Venice. His meetings finished late, and he found himself stuck in town, as there was no train home that night. Since he was in a city fabled for its beauty, he decided to treat himself to an expensive dinner and an expensive companion. The concierge was unable to help him with the latter. 'Signore, I regret to inform you there is no red-light district in Venice,' he said. But the concierge's assistant chased after him. 'My uncle may be able to help,' he said. 'If anyone knows, he does.'

"The foreigner was directed through a maze of streets to the uncle's antiques shop. Dark and nondescript from the exterior, inside it was an Ali Baba's cavern of treasures: Moroccan lanterns, Persian ceramics, Indian beds, and Turkish kilims. There were chairs inlaid with mother-of-pearl, mosaic tables, tapestries, and blown-glass vases and lamps. In the back, the foreigner found a wizened man with old-fashioned spectacles and a crafty demeanor. He explained his problem.

"'I have the solution,' said the old man. 'I have a book I will sell you. Oh! A rare book, the only one of its kind. Inside, there is a name and an address. You may have it for this sum,' he said, naming a figure and placing the book in front of the foreigner. It was bound in gold-stamped leather, a handsome artifact. Having come this far, the foreigner pulled out his wallet and paid him.

"Inside the book he found a name and an address. He studied his map and, after losing his way several times, found his way to the address indicated. He rang the doorbell of a crumbling palazzo. A man answered the door. The foreigner asked for the woman whose name

*he'd found in the book. 'Well, she lived here,' said the man, startled.
'But signore, that was over sixty years ago. She was the last prostitute
in Venice.'"*

I liked that they were telling each other stories, though I liked hers
better. I saved the draft. The phone rang. It was Olivier.

"What are you doing?" he asked.

"Working on the translation," I said, happy to hear his voice.

"You say these things just to provoke me."

"Yes." I smiled. I could hear the way it changed my voice.

"I know it's the last minute, but would you like to come to a cocktail
party tonight? There will be some interesting people. You might enjoy
it," he said. His voice was smooth, nearly viscous. It poured into my
ear. Silver-tongued, the Greeks used to say. *Mielleux,* the French say:
honeylike.

"I'd love to," I said, pressing my ear into the receiver.

"Can I meet you there? I have to be at the theater before."

"Are you in a play?"

"I'm directing something. I'll tell you about it."

"Do I need to dress up?" I asked hopefully.

"Not so much. It's at a friend's house, Laure de Saligny and her husband. Meet me there around seven-thirty?" he asked. "We could have
dinner afterward."

I wrote down the directions and hung up. I slid over the wood floor
in my socks and bounced from one foot to the other while I searched the
closet for something to wear and speed-dialed Clara.

"It's me, it's me, why aren't you there? Not only did I get the lingerie
back, but I think I'm going to wear it!" I babbled into her voice mail.

....

The rest of the afternoon, I was useless. I tried to distract myself by
doing one of Tante Isabelle's yoga DVDs, but I knocked the back of my

head on the coffee table doing downward dog. I ran out to Monoprix and bought two pairs of black stockings and the wrong batteries for the TV remote. I painted my toenails, then spent half an hour fixing the smudges. I had to force myself to put down the eyebrow tweezers before I plucked myself into the silent film era.

I propped my feet on the coffee table to let the polish dry and caught the end of one of the literary talk shows. The episode was devoted to the fall book releases, and a wraithlike man with spiky, gelled hair delivered an impassioned monologue decrying the amount of attention devoted to the highly overrated Rémi Le Jaa, an opinion unpopular with the studio audience, who booed him.

It was a name I hadn't heard before. I turned off the TV and studied Tante Isabelle's bookshelves: nothing by Le Jaa.

I wiggled into my new lingerie, sucked in my stomach, and pranced around the bedroom. Leaning back on the bed, I lifted one leg, pointed my toes, and pulled on the stockings. Stockings always made me feel glamorous, a little retro, like Monica Vitti in smudgy black eye shadow. My mother wore stockings. I remembered watching her fasten them with nublike clips that didn't exist on any other piece of clothing.

I slipped my feet into a pair of high-heeled, black silk pumps with velvet bows and pink flowers embroidered on the heels, one of my expensive summer sale purchases, and shimmied into a tight but slimming, sleeveless black turtleneck dress. I sucked in my cheeks, turned three-quarters, and did my best Faye Dunaway in front of the mirror.

I looked like a slut. I changed a half dozen times before returning to the black turtleneck dress. As I struggled back into it, I broke out in a sweat. It was oddly muggy for mid-September. Little bits of black dress lint stuck to my face. I rubbed them off with a towel.

I still looked like a slut. I covered up with a fitted jacket. Now I looked like an undertaker. I put a run in my stocking when I bumped into the desk rushing to answer the phone. It was Bunny.

"*Under the Volcano* is on cable. Wanna join me for Mexican food and a cocktail I call Lighter Fluid Surprise? My own invention," he said.

"Raincheck? I've got a date," I said. "And there is no good Mexican food here."

"You are so wrong, my young friend. I got an Algerian guy in Boulogne who makes carne asada like you would not believe," he said. "Are you in the freak-out about what to wear stage?" he asked. I cradled the phone between my shoulder and ear and ripped open another package of stockings.

"Yeah. What do you think, slut or mortician?"

"Mortician. That's the look that always does it for me. In fact, I dated a mortician. New York, 1967—"

"Bunny!"

"Okay, okay. Mortician. It's less obvious. Have fun."

I pulled on a fresh black stocking, hoping both legs matched. All this dithering was very time-consuming: it was already seven-twenty. I rushed through my makeup, swiping on a couple of coats of mascara at the last minute. It was seven-thirty. I put my hair up with a barrette, stuffed my keys and some money into a beaded evening bag, and flagged a taxi. I would be late, but maybe only fashionably so.

The taxi pulled up in front of an imposing 1930s building on a *quai* in the Seventh. I walked through a marble and mosaic entrance with double-height ceilings. When I got to the top floor, it was so quiet, I thought I might have the wrong address, but I rang the doorbell anyway. A blond woman with a streak of white hair and hammered gold jewelry answered the door. I was relieved when I saw she was wearing an ivory silk dress that showed off her bronzed skin. I wasn't overdressed.

"*Bonsoir, madame,*" I said. "*Olivier Vallant m'a invitée,*" I added. She gave me a cool smile and led me into an enormous living room packed with people. It was decorated with taupe leather furniture, abstract paintings, and large arrangements of gnarled twigs. She said something

I couldn't hear over the party chatter and walked away. As I searched the crowd for Olivier, I recognized a writer I'd seen on the talk show deep in conversation with a rock star who'd published a book of poetry. Then, my eyes connected with a familiar pair.

From across the room, Bernard Laveau frowned at me, his bushy eyebrows drawn together in two fierce slashes.

15

*Car à Paris presque tous les amants d'une fille
connue vivent en intimité.*
—ALEXANDRE DUMAS, FILS,
La Dame aux Camélias

Great. Just peachy. No sign of Olivier, and here was Bernard Laveau, barreling down the Aubusson carpet with a glass of champagne held high like a medieval weapon—that ball thing covered in spikes, attached to a chain. If ever there was a time to feel caught red-handed, this was it. I froze. My heels sank into the carpet pile.

"Alors, mademoiselle. Qu'est ce que vous faites là?" Monsieur Laveau asked. His voice was scathingly polite, barbed wire wrapped in a silk foulard. I tried not to flinch. For some reason, he thought I shouldn't be here. A waiter held out a tray of champagne flutes, and I armed myself with one.

"Quel plaisir de vous voir aussi, monsieur," I responded, trying to out-polite him. I gulped down half the champagne, trying to think. Olivier wasn't there, so Monsieur Laveau had no way of knowing he'd invited me. Unfortunately, there was no one else I knew. I searched the room

*For in Paris almost all the lovers of a well-known woman are friends.

wildly and made eye contact with a red-cheeked, middle-aged man in a rumpled linen suit. He stood with a small group of people by the large windows. I darted another glance at him. He gave me a perplexed look and went back to his conversation. I took another swig of champagne. Monsieur Laveau took hold of my elbow and wheeled me around.

"Do you have any idea how awkward this is?" he hissed. *"Vraiment, ça me déplait énormément,"* he said and proceeded to scold me, and none too discreetly. I could feel my face screwing up with tension.

"Comment vas-tu, ma chérie?" interrupted the man in the rumpled suit. He grasped my shoulders and kissed me on both cheeks, his razor stubble scraping my skin. He smelled of citrus and had the face of a sad Russian poet. I liked him immediately.

"Très, très bien, merci," I squeaked, nodding my head up and down.

"Et ta maman et ton papa? Oui? Sont-ils toujours—"

"A Los Angeles, oui," I interjected, nodding furiously.

"Tu me rassures. Ah, Bernard," the man said, turning. "You've met my young friend?" Monsieur Laveau looked discomfited, mumbled a gruff word of greeting, and retreated into the crowd, but not before giving me a final glare.

"Merci, monsieur," I said, relieved.

"Antoine," he corrected. "After all, we are old friends. Or rather, you must be the daughter of old friends I didn't know I had in California. Whose name is . . ."

"Anna," I said, smiling. "Thank you, Antoine. That was gallant of you."

"But bizarre, you must admit. Bernard Laveau is not the kind of man young women generally need rescuing from. And you looked so very distressed."

"Oh, that . . ." I tried to shrug it off.

"Surely you could give me an explanation? It would be most intriguing."

"Why?"

"Bernard used to be my editor. We had a disagreement and he's never forgiven me. Now, we meet at these literary parties"—Antoine waved a small, white hand—"and we ignore each other. Of course, he edits my wife, so we must be civil."

"I had no idea Monsieur Laveau was so . . . active," I said.

"You mean the dusty storefront? A kind of reverse snobbery, I suppose. One mustn't appear pretentious."

"How . . . nineteenth century," I said.

"*Si on veut. Plutôt intello gauche caviar,*" he said, using the French equivalent for "intellectual champagne socialist." "But it's an affectation. Bernard pretends to be retired, but he's still quite influential."

"You sound like someone who'd know. What kinds of books do you write?"

"Biographies. I am at present working on the life of Villiers de L'Isle-Adam."

"*Les Contes cruels?*"

"Very good. And how would you translate that?" he asked blandly.

"*Cruel Tales?*" I asked, puzzled. It was such an easy translation. "Am I missing something? How is it usually translated?" I asked.

"*Sardonic Tales,*" he said, with a curious little smile, a casual lift of the mouth, as if I'd said exactly what he'd expected me to say. As he lifted his champagne glass to his lips, his eyes darted almost involuntarily to Bernard. I'd walked right into it. Antoine was a sly old fox.

"You guessed," I said.

He shrugged. "I've known Bernard for years. He does not change his habits easily, and he has always been a cheapskate. It must be his Breton upbringing. So much less expensive to hire someone *au noir.*" Antoine gave me a concerned look, though it was hard to tell if it was genuine. "Surely you know you are not the first of his *traductrices?* Though you are, perhaps, the first to show up at one of these parties."

"Well, no, I mean, I hardly thought I was unique, but it did seem like an unusual situation . . ." I said, stumbling over my words.

"Ah yes, the secrecy, the weekly assignments, the gag order." He looked dreamy-eyed for a moment. "I like this expression, 'gag order.' It is delightfully fascistic. I remember when I first heard it, in a spy movie with Robert Redford. Always, I find it fascinating, this sexual fetishization of power."

"Not sure I follow," I said, watching him. His face pleated in amusement.

"Oh, the iconography of the phrase. It conjures up blindfolds, the S and M aficionado's mouth restraint with a rubber ball, black vinyl, latex. The friction between knowing something and not being able to speak it: it's the definition of suspense, a kinetic tension. What are you working on?" he asked. He had a style: outrageous provocation, followed by innocent-seeming inquiry. Slash and burn for the smart set.

"That was good," I said, admiringly.

"Was I close?"

"Let's just say I'm enjoying the friction between knowing something and choosing not to say anything about it."

His impish face crinkled again. "I'll get it out of you." He wagged a finger at me.

A short, beady-eyed woman in a burgundy dress and a jade necklace marched over to us. "Let me introduce you to my wife," he said. Victorine had wide cheekbones and a gravelly voice probably caused by chain-smoking Murattis. Flecks of ash dotted her dress, and she brushed them away with bony, blue-veined hands, the nails short and red. When I asked, she told me she wrote on semiotics, as well as the occasional novel.

"Like Kristeva?" I asked, trying to sound like I knew what I was talking about. She gave me a heavy-lidded, withering glance.

"Her biggest rival," Antoine explained sotto voce.

"I'm sorry, it was the only name I remembered," I explained.

Victorine sniffed. "We only come to these parties to gossip. Let's not talk about anything so boring," she said and waved over a couple, a book editor and her husband. Antoine handed me another glass of champagne as the conversation turned to Rémi Le Jaa. I leaned in to listen. Apparently, he hadn't published anything in years, and everyone had assumed he was either dead or dying a slow and sordid death in a distant country until one of the big publishing houses had announced a forthcoming book. When no one had any inside information, they moved on to one writer's messy divorce and subsequent face-lift, another's sale of movie rights, and yet another's dramatic exit off Laurent Ruquier's talk show the week before. It was like a movie party in L.A., but with better vocabulary. I wondered what was keeping Olivier. I reached into my purse for my cell phone, but it wasn't there. With a start, I realized it was in my other purse. The one that was back in the apartment.

I asked Madame de Saligny if I could use her phone. She showed me to a book-lined study. I sat at the desk and called my cell phone. By the time I realized I'd entered the wrong *code secret* three times—I'd used my L.A. cell phone pass code instead of the French one—the system had locked me out. I slammed the phone down. A woman walked in.

"Excusez-moi, je ne vous avais pas vue!" she apologized, smiling. She looked around fifty but was probably older, with sleek brown hair cut in a bob, pale, creamy skin, and wide green eyes lined in black. She wore a tailored green dress, showing off a slim, toned figure, with a fiery orange silk duster, *d'un chic fou*, open over it. She was stunning.

"Pas du tout," I said. "I was trying to call my friend, who seems to be missing in action," I explained.

"Comme c'est curieux!" she exclaimed. "At the last minute, I freed myself to come tonight, and my friend isn't here either!"

"Please," I stood up, indicating the phone. She glanced at my shoes.

"I nearly bought those! *Chez Lanvin, non?*" she asked. I nodded. "So pretty! I have such a weakness for shoes."

"Me, too. I got them on sale," I confided. There was something about her that made me want to tell her secrets, a feeling of instant *complicité*, that French word that means a delicious sense of being partners in crime without there being any actual crime.

"*Comme c'est étrange,*" she said, cocking her head to one side. "You remind me of me . . . oh! Such a long time ago!" She smiled but narrowed her eyes, studying me.

"Not so long ago, I'm sure," I said, blushing at the compliment. I left her alone to use the phone, wondering who she was, with her fabulous outfit and effortless charm.

The living room was hot and foggy with cigarette smoke. I helped myself to another glass of champagne. Olivier could have ten more minutes and a cheese puff, then I was leaving. Antoine and Victorine were still gossiping about people I didn't know and the cost of maintaining their eighteenth-century house in the Limousin. Prickly beads of sweat made their way down my back, but I didn't want to take off the jacket. Damn Olivier and his stupid invitation. I longed for my flannel pajamas. Maybe the DVD rental place was still open.

At a lull in the conversation, Victorine turned to me. "And how do you know Laure?" she asked, pointing her glass in the direction of our hostess.

"I don't. A friend of mine, who is reprehensibly late, invited me," I said. I swayed forward and grabbed a chair back to steady myself.

"Who is this unfortunate person?" she asked with a glazed, almost cross-eyed look.

"Olivier Vallant," I said. She gave a tinkling, somewhat malicious laugh.

"*Ne vous inquiétez pas, ma chère.* Estelle is here, so Olivier is bound to show up," she said, talking as if we were coconspirators. "*Monsieur le Ministre* is out of town."

"*Le Ministre?*" I asked.

"Romain Chesnier, our minister of *l'Education Nationale,*" she said. "*So* convenient to have a husband who travels," she added.

"Aha," I said, though I didn't follow. "Who's Estelle?" I asked. At this, Victorine looked even more pleased with herself. She waved her glass in the direction of the fireplace. The woman I'd talked to in the study sat, surrounded by admirers. As I watched, she crossed one long, thin leg over the other, a nonchalant flamingo.

"Who is she?" I asked. Victorine played with the jade beads at her neck.

"I thought you said you knew Olivier," she said, spider to fly.

"I do."

"Alors, voilà Estelle Bailleux, l'actrice. Son amie," I heard her say.

. . . .

"Friend" can mean many things in French, I repeated to myself in the *jaune de Sienne* marble guest bathroom. The same way it can mean many things in English: acquaintance, casual friend, old friend, friend friend. But spoken in that tone, with that look, it meant significant friend, as in romantic partner. I splashed water on my face.

When I looked up, I had black bags under my eyes. I looked like a raccoon. It wasn't waterproof mascara, which I'd forgotten, because I usually don't wear mascara. I was buzzed, and I looked like a raccoon. I rubbed my eyes with a linen guest towel. Now I was red-eyed, and there were black streaks on the towel. I dumped it in the sink and scrubbed it with my knuckles, splashing the front of my dress. I wrung out the towel and refolded it to hide the black stains.

I could hear the rumble and laughter of the party outside, but I couldn't leave the bathroom without an exit strategy. I couldn't talk to Monsieur Laveau, I didn't want to talk to a bunch of people I didn't know, never mind that I would probably never see them again, and I wasn't going to wait for Olivier to show up and introduce me to his "friend." The idea of shaking her hand and smiling insincerely while I ground my molars to a fine dust was too hideous. Someone knocked on the door.

"*Une minute,*" I called out. I reapplied my lipstick and stepped back to inspect my appearance. The wet part of my dress was a visibly darker black. I took off the jacket and held it in front of me.

"*Pardon, madame,*" Antoine said automatically as I came out. "Oh, it's you. We're off to dinner at Lipp. Before I forget," he said, fumbling in his wallet. "Here is my card. Call us, come to tea." He looked like he meant it.

"Thank you, that's nice of you," I said, putting the card in my purse.

"By the way, Olivier's here. He's looking for you."

"Good," I said, with a short smile. Antoine went into the bathroom. Let him look. I bolted.

The elevator was in use. Grasping the banister, I leaped down the stairs, nearly tripping on the carpet runner. Up above, the door opened and I heard Olivier's voice.

"*Mais elle est ici, je te jure, Olivier—*" Laure assured him, and the door closed.

I didn't listen for more. I sped down the rest of the stairs, feeling a little loopy making a thrilling escape from the clutches of an evil cocktail party, but I plowed on, impelled by a nameless euphoria, past the point of return. At the front door, I punched the buzzer and let myself out.

It was raining. Thick, fat drops that seemed to come from nowhere, which meant my chances of finding a cab were slim to none. Parisian taxis were like sugar: they melted in the rain. Sure enough, the stand across the street was deserted. The Seventh is one of those chic residential areas that seem to shut down at night. I had no idea where the nearest local café was, but I knew there was a big one across the river in the Eighth. I sprinted across the pont de l'Alma to Le Grand Corona.

They had California-style heat lamps, and there were several people sitting under the yellow awning. I got a seat in the back and smoothed my hair. A piece of plastic caning dug into my leg and snagged my stocking.

"*Un lait chaud,*" I said to the waiter. "*A la vanille, s'il vous plaît.*"

Beyond the intersection, the bridge curved up so that I couldn't see the street in front of the apartment I'd left, though I could make out the lights on the top floor. I scrunched down and felt along the back of my thigh, tracing the hole in the nylon.

Well, that was a narrow escape. My adrenaline evaporated, leaving behind an oppressive, sticky layer of disappointment. I hated disappointment. It was like nuclear waste, circling the globe on a barge with nowhere to go. When would I learn? When would I learn to stop getting ahead of myself? I shouldn't have assumed Olivier was available, just because he'd kissed me, just because . . . just because I wanted him to be.

I sat up as the waiter brought my hot milk. There was a thick layer of foam on top, and I stirred in two paper tubes of sugar. On childhood visits, my French grandmother had insisted I drink a big *bol* of it each morning. She made it with whole milk and a vanilla bean, and there were flecks of cream in it. It was too rich and too earthy for my low-fat-milk palate. I remember thinking I could smell the cow in it, cud and hay. It was vile, and the only way she could get me to finish it was by challenging me to guess whether she'd used the Quimper *bol* with the little boy or the little girl painted on the bottom.

Now she was gone, and here I was, drinking the hot milk I'd hated as a child. I wondered if certain things become second nature if you practice them enough, like raising one eyebrow, or calling someone "darling," or walking out on parties that make you uncomfortable. I wondered what happened to the little breakfast *bols*. I missed my grandmother, and I felt tears prick the backs of my eyes. I took a sip of the milk, but the frothy white sweetness blended badly with the salty taste in my mouth. I looked across the *place*, squinting as a figure crossed the street. It was Olivier, with his head bent against the rain. He walked directly toward the café.

I scrunched down farther in my chair. For a moment, I wondered if he hadn't seen me, if he'd just left the party and strolled toward the first random spot for a nightcap. That would have made more sense, because that story—the one where I was by myself, feeling sorry for myself in a café, on a park bench, in my car on the Santa Monica Freeway—that story, I knew. But this story, the one where the guy left the party to look for me? I didn't know it. I didn't know how it went, and I didn't know what to think.

He pulled up a chair and sat, looking grim. I folded my arms and glared back at him. We sat in silence for a moment. Two police cars raced down the *quai*, sirens blaring.

"Well, say something," I said, finally.

"*Non, toi.*" It was clipped. Yeah, he was pissed. Maybe I'd embarrassed him by leaving. Maybe it had been awkward. Maybe he wanted to tell me off.

Maybe I wanted to tell him off. This was the jerk who'd kept me waiting at that damn party for over an hour.

"I didn't think you were going to show up," I said.

"*J'ai laissé trois messages sur ton portable: pour te prévenir, pour faire mes excuses, pour te demander où tu étais,*" he said, explaining each message he'd left.

"I forgot my cell phone at home," I said.

"*Je suis désolé,*" he said, not sounding apologetic. "*Un calva,*" he said to the waiter. He looked back at me, his features softer but still not friendly. "*Quoi d'autre?*"

"Bernard wasn't very nice to me."

"*Il n'est jamais de bonne humeur. Tu le connais,*" he said, pointing out Bernard was rarely cordial. "*Pourquoi tu es partie comme ça?*" he asked. I folded the empty paper sugar tube into a small accordion. He touched my hand, and I snatched it away.

"Who's Estelle?" I asked. His face clouded for a moment.

"*Une grande actrice.* She's starring in the play I'm directing." His tone was short, factual. He lit a cigarette.

"She's very beautiful," I said.

"*Evidemment,*" he replied, implying I was stating the obvious.

"Victorine made it clear you were involved. I didn't feel the need to stay."

"C'est qui, Victorine?"

"One of the guests I was talking to," I said.

He exhaled a plume of smoke. *"C'est du passé,"* he said. *"Et puis, ça ne te concerne pas."* It's in the past, and it's none of your business. Usually, conversation between bilingual people ends up in one of the languages, but he refused to speak English, and I refused to speak French. It was a novel way of fighting.

"Are you mad at me?"

"Je ne te comprends pas."

"Yes, you do. You understand me perfectly well," I snapped.

"Je comprends l'anglais. Toi, je ne te comprends pas." He shook his head, aggravated. *"En plus, tu es partie juste au moment où je suis arrivé,"* he said. So he knew I'd taken off just after he'd arrived. I gnawed on the inside of my cheek.

It occurred to me that he might care what I thought. It also occurred to me, not for the first time, that I could be a pain in the ass. Somewhere in the back of my head, there was background noise. I heard "He's here, he's here, he's here" repeating, over and over. Actually, it was "He's here, you dolt," but never mind.

"You're here," I whispered. Timothy hadn't come after me when I'd left him in the middle of the night. But here was Olivier. The knife pleats in his trousers blurred.

"Comment?"

"You're here," I said, enunciating. When I looked up, two tears rolled down my face. He looked surprised. He stretched out a hand and pulled me to him. I leaned my head on his chest, holding on to the sides of his leather jacket.

"I'm sorry I was late," he said, switching into English. "Was it very awful?" I shook my head and made a muffled sound. I straightened up and blew my nose with the rough paper napkin under my hot milk. He gave me a tender look, and I smiled back at him. The air grew thicker between us, and I could feel my pulse beating in my throat. I leaned forward again, feeling like I was falling, and we kissed. He tasted of apple brandy and cigarettes, and his tongue was firm and gentle, sending a shooting thrill through me.

"*J'aime tes larmes,*" he said, caressing my face with his thumbs. I love your tears.

"That's a terrible thing to say," I muttered.

"They make your face more beautiful," he said. "Come on, I'll take you home."

16

Nothing is more perplexing to a man than
the mental process of a woman who reasons her emotions.
—EDITH WHARTON,
"Souls Belated"

The rain stopped, leaving the night air damp and velvety. We walked arm in arm up the avenue Montaigne. I tried to match my stride to his, but I had to take little half steps on the slick pavement to keep up. Jagged neon letters undulated backward in the shallow puddles. I felt dizzy, happy, and nervous, and I liked it.

Across the street, a woman sat underneath the bus shelter. She was dressed in black, with a beige raincoat draped over her shoulders, her face bathed in underwater blue-green from the illuminated print ad next to her. She seemed to be watching me, with a look that said: Even though you may not notice me, I am smiling at you with envy or nostalgia or solidarity or fondness for the happy, oblivious spectacle you are.

"Wait," I said. A small tingle went up my spine.

"Taxi!" Olivier called out, not hearing me, and waved at the driver. Up ahead, at the Plaza Athénée, a cab emptied itself of a trio of passengers. Olivier held the door open, and I slid in. Across the street, a night bus lumbered by, not stopping. After it passed, the bus shelter was empty. Olivier put his arm around me. I leaned into him and gave the driver my address.

"What were you looking at?" he asked.

"*Mon sosie,*" I murmured, using the French term for double. "Smiling at me from across the street."

"Your doppelgänger," he said.

"My twin."

"Your nemesis."

"*Peut-être. Mais je ne pense pas,*" I said. My ears popped as we drove into the tiled tunnel under the city center. Orange lights danced on grimy white ceramic. "Have you ever seen your double?" I asked. Boulevard Sébastopol to rue Réaumur.

"*Une fois,*" he murmured. When I looked at him, he kissed me. Rue du Temple to République. My dress rode up on the leather seat, and I tugged it down. He put his hand on mine. I closed my eyes and didn't open them until the taxi came to a stop. Just in case we hadn't gotten it, the driver cleared his throat.

"Would you like to come up?" I asked.

"Perhaps I should let you sleep?"

"No, I'm fine. Come up," I said, frowning. His question threw me. It wasn't even eleven. Was this politeness or reluctance?

We didn't speak in the cramped elevator. Inside the apartment, the minor awkwardness I felt took hold. He seemed too large for the space. I didn't know what to do with him. One of us was de trop, and I figured it had to be him.

"What can I get you?" I asked, resorting to hostess behavior. I held up a bottle of rum, a clear liqueur that looked like *poire William,* and a brand of Scotch I'd never heard of. Olivier stood formally in the living room. "Whiskey?" I suggested.

"*Oui, merci.* May I look around?"

"Yes. And take off your jacket," I said. He took it off and looked at the bookshelves. His fingers touched my hand as I handed him a glass, but I pulled away and stood in front of the stereo.

"What would you like to listen to?" I asked, feeling like one of the polite cartoon chipmunks: after you.

"Comme tu veux," he said. No, no, after you.

"Come on, help me out." I insist, after *you*, old chap.

"Du piano, alors."

I put on a Chopin CD and lowered the volume. He went to the desk and ran his fingers over my laptop. There was a draft of the translation next to it. He held up a page.

"The latest?"

"Yes," I said, watching him. "You can't read it."

"I can't?" He held the piece of paper above his head. I've always hated this game. It rubs me the wrong way: both the holding something out of reach and the reading—or pretending to read—of something private. I tend to be completely humorless about it.

"I mean it, Olivier." I plucked the page from his hand and shoved it in a folder. Crossing the room, I sat on the sofa. He looked surprised but sat next to me.

"Who lives here?" he asked, looking up at the ceiling moldings.

"No one. Usually, it's rented out to tourists. But it belongs to my aunt."

"And where is she?"

"Most of the time, San Francisco. She's lending it to me." I felt guilty for being brusque about the translation, but I didn't apologize. The piano music grated on my nerves, and the air was stuffy inside the apartment. He pressed a finger to my forehead, between my eyebrows. I blinked and pulled away.

"You're frowning," he said.

"I think too much." I shrugged.

"Don't," he said.

"I hate it when people tell me not to think. Like that's possible," I said. I tried to quell my annoyance, but it was there anyway. He took my hand, playing with my fingers.

"I was disappointed when you weren't there," he began. "Bernard gave me a very odd look—"

"He wasn't thrilled to see me," I interrupted. "Luckily, Antoine saved the day. It's hot in here." I got up to open the windows.

"Antoine?"

"Antoine Berlutti, Victorine's husband." I pulled the card out of my bag. "He came to my rescue."

Olivier didn't look at the card. "I had a small problem at the theater. I couldn't leave," he said.

"Fine. Whatever," I said. Did he think I wanted an explanation? Was I acting like I wanted one? Come to think of it, what kind of small problem takes over an hour to fix? I sat down again, not looking at him.

"Eh, oh! Je suis là," he reminded me. I nodded, biting my fingernail. I knew he was there; I just wasn't sure I wanted him to be. "Why did you come to Paris?" he asked.

"It's a long story."

"Tell me," he said. I took a sip of his drink. It burned my throat. I would never be a whiskey drinker.

"Un chagrin d'amour," I said.

He was quiet for a moment. "That's not a long story," he observed.

"I don't want to tell you a long story. I've been telling it for weeks, and it's worn me out." I could hear how unfriendly I sounded, but I couldn't help it. Anxiety made me prickly. I shrugged off the jacket.

"Why are you so far away?" he asked, looking at me.

"I don't know."

"Viens," he said, putting down his drink.

"Non, toi," I replied, batting the ball back over the net. Sometimes if you get a rally going, it almost feels like a game. He pushed up his sleeves and flipped through the Le Corbusier book on the coffee table.

"I think I will go," he said, closing the book.

"If you like," I answered.

He put on his jacket. I walked him to the door. It felt like the wrong way to end the evening, but since I couldn't make up my mind, this was how it was going to end. Except now that he was going, I didn't want him to.

"*Bon,*" he said.

My stomach knotted. "Olivier . . ." I said.

"*Oui?*" He looked at me coolly.

"*Je ne veux pas que tu partes.*" I don't want you to go. Even as I said them, the words felt experimental, like I was trying them out for the first time.

He leaned back against the door. "But you don't want me to stay, either," he said, looking puzzled. "You don't trust me around your translation, you don't want to tell me your story, you stay far away from me on the sofa . . ."

I winced; he was right. "I'm awkward," I explained. "I'm awkward and I'm nervous, and I think too much and then I tie myself up in knots and behave oddly," I said.

This didn't seem to clear things up. Maybe what made sense to me didn't make sense to him—or wasn't enough to convince him that I did, in fact, now want him to stay. He was going to leave, and it would be just like that scene in *Anna Karenina,* where the two characters who seem so right for each other go for a walk in the woods to pick mushrooms and then nothing happens and by the time they come back, the romance is over, squashed flat by the weight of missed opportunity.

Olivier grasped the door handle. Mushrooms! *Anna Karenina!*

I thought about the translation. Eve wouldn't have this problem. Eve would be clear about what she wanted. Eve would shut the fuck up and do something. I lurched forward and wrapped my arms around his neck.

"Please stay, Olivier," I said, my voice dropping an octave. I kissed his earlobe. "I don't want you to go," I murmured, dragging my tongue down the side of his neck. *"Reste avec moi,"* I whispered. Stay with me. I scraped my teeth lightly across his skin. This was fun. I could feel him wavering. He let go of the door handle but seemed to require more persuading.

"Olivier," I said, planting tiny kisses on his jaw.

"Oui?"

"J'aime ton nom sur mes lèvres," I said. I like your name on my lips. It was a line I'd borrowed from Eve. I unbuttoned his shirt and pressed my tongue to his chest. I alternated kisses and buttons. Then I tilted my head up and pulled his lower lip into my mouth. He hesitated a moment longer, but now it was because he was enjoying himself. He pushed me against the wall and kissed me back.

A poker buddy once told me, "The game begins before the game begins." I remembered I was wearing the killer underwear and grinned.

"Quoi?" he asked.

"Rien," I answered, not telling, still grinning.

I pushed his shirt and jacket off his shoulders. He felt around my dress for a zipper and, not finding one, tugged one side of the hem up to my waist as we kissed. I lifted my leg, wrapping it around his hip, and pressed into him, feeling him hard against me. He ran a hand along the back of my thigh, exploring the edge of the stocking, the bare flesh above it, and reached inside my panties.

I pulled him into the bedroom. He came up behind me and tugged my dress over my head. He undid the clasp of my bra and slid the straps off my arms. I liked being undressed. He stroked my breasts, bit the sides of my neck, then moved his hands down my stomach and inched off my underwear. My breath caught in my throat, and I hiccuped. I glanced at him in surprise, and then we both started laughing.

He fell backward onto the bed, pulling me on top of him. When the mood got intense again, I discovered he liked the lights on and kept his eyes open. Everything about him demanded I be fully engaged, and it seemed to raise the stakes. I was almost shocked when he held my face and moved inside me. It was like being in the last car of the roller coaster, at the top of the drop, hurtling forward at top speed.

....

I woke up a few times at night, alternately panicking as I felt him in the bed—*What are you doing? You barely know him!*—and grinning—*What are you doing? You barely know him!*

In the morning, he crept out of bed and got dressed. I pretended I was still asleep. He tiptoed down the hall, and I heard the front door click. A getaway! Not very gallant, I thought, but probably just as well. I'm bad at breakfast, let alone first ones; I'm barely civilized until I've had coffee, and even then, I feel raw and clumsy.

In the living room, his jacket was draped over the sofa; the door was propped slightly open. I glanced out the window and saw him walk into the *boulangerie* across the street. I made coffee and waited for him to return with a mounting sense of dread.

He came back with a baguette, croissants, and newspapers. He leaned over to kiss me at the same moment I lifted my coffee mug to my mouth, so he got my cheekbone instead of my lips. I made a big show of searching the cupboards for jam.

"Did you sleep well?" he asked my back, pouring himself a cup of coffee.

"No!" I snapped. He looked taken aback. "Did you?" I asked, softening my tone.

He shrugged and sat down. "I bought you the *Herald Tribune*," he said. "For the crossword puzzle."

"How did you know?" I asked, sounding suspicious. He bit into a croissant.

"The bathroom," he mumbled, his mouth full. I remembered the pile of crosswords between the toilet and the tub. I was being prickly again.

"*Olivier, le matin, je suis sauvage,*" I said, switching into French to explain that I wasn't a morning person. *Sauvage* doesn't just mean savage. It also means uncivilized, timid, shy, unsociable, rude, and/or barbarous.

"*Pas que les matins,*" he observed, splitting open a length of baguette. He pushed the newspaper over to me. I relaxed a fraction and settled down to read the front page. Olivier read *Libération*. I opened the paper. He didn't look up. I turned to the crossword puzzle.

"What are you doing this evening?" I asked.

"A rehearsal, but it's over by nine." He opened the jar of marmalade I'd unearthed in the pantry. "And you?"

"My friend Althea's birthday party. She's half-American, like me. An old, dear friend." I bit into my *tartine*. There was another silence. "Have you always liked marmalade? I'm conducting an informal survey. I believe it's an acquired taste," I said.

"Yes. I have liked it since I was a very small child," he said gravely.

With that, the rest of my tension dissipated. "Would you like to come to the party with me? It's in the Twentieth, a cute little house in Ménilmontant," I said.

"Or perhaps I can call you on your *portable* and meet you later, after my rehearsal? If you remember to take it," he said and ruffled my hair.

"You can do that," I said, beaming. I liked this. Birthday party *and* Olivier. Cookies *and* cream. Having cake *and* eating it: *le beurre et l'argent du beurre.* The hair ruffle made me feel tousled and sexy, like I should have been wearing his pajama top and nothing else. The faint taste of bitter oranges lingered on my lips after he left. Perhaps I could learn to like marmalade.

....

I scooped up the bra and panties off the bedroom floor and dropped them in a sink full of bubbly Woolite. I thought about my friend Marielle in New York, and her affair with a real estate attorney. He usually called her on Thursday afternoons before coming over after work. After the call, she would perch on the edge of her tub and shave her legs. It became such a ritual that the mere smell of mentholated shaving cream turned her on.

Mentholated shaving cream, lingerie. It wasn't about underwear per se—underwear qua underwear—but about the anticipation, the ephemeral idea the object elicits. People used to cast spells. Now we buy things and invest them with magic. I rinsed out the lingerie and left a message for Clara. I sat in front of the computer intending to look at the last six pages of the chapter, but I got to Googling, starting with Bernard and Editions Laveau.

It turned out Bernard had published several books under his own imprint in the last two years, among them a few *polars,* or thrillers, a biography of André Malraux, a new history of Napoleon's campaign in Egypt, and two novels. Next, I Googled Estelle, who turned out to be pretty famous. She'd started off in a long-running TV series in the eighties; had made the leap to film in a Rohmer movie that I'd actually seen, though she hadn't been the lead; and had subsequently been in dozens of French and Italian pictures. She'd served on the jury at Cannes a few years back and was frequently photographed with her husband, the popular, charismatic minister. In their wedding picture, Romain Chesnier was short and broad, with a pugilist's build, a mane of silver hair, and a large, broken nose. They looked good together.

I leaned back and stretched, then turned to the translation.

Later, that night, in our fourteenth-century Venetian hotel room, under a fresco of frolicking putti, we made love while Chopin played all night, the CD player stuck on repeat. . .

No, no, no. I backspaced over the paragraph, yawning. It's always hard to sleep that first night with someone. You're not used to each other; you roll over and there's a body in the space where you used to roll over. Arms fall asleep, body parts get smushed, you worry about drooling and morning breath and blobs of eye makeup congealing in the corners of your eyes. But there is also the pleasure of waking up with someone you like, someone you perhaps wake up before . . .

> *. . . for the pleasure of seeing her face as she stirs and opens her eyes. Eve didn't sleep like a child, innocent and bow-lipped. She slept like a mermaid, a sea creature on a busman's holiday, seducing men as she would dolphins and submarine deities. I ran my fingers along her back. Like a dancer, she had a beautiful curve to her spine—*

Ew. How did someone sleep like a mermaid? And "curve to her spine" sounded like something on a chiropractor's chart. I looked up the French word, *"cambrure."* I'd heard it used to describe the curve of a woman's back, usually right above the rear, as in *"une jolie cambrure."*

In the bilingual dictionary, I found *"camber,"* a word I didn't know, defined as "bend; arch; curve; instep." The English dictionary defined it as "1.a. A slightly arched surface, as of a road, a ship's deck, or an airfoil. 1.b. The condition of being so arched . . ." Not quite a *faux ami*: they meant the same thing but were used differently in each language.

Here again was a phrase—to describe a part of a woman's body— that didn't exist in English. I made a note in my journal, adding *"cambrure"* under *"la chute des reins."* There was something intriguing about the mere existence of these words and phrases, as if the subconscious personality of the French language was that of a fastidious geographer, who'd mapped and named every square inch of a woman's body. Was it a scientific attention or an obsessive one? Or both? Or was it like Eskimos having twenty-two different names for snow, even though I'd heard that was a linguistic fallacy? Still, it seemed to point to the development of a complex vocabulary for the thing you think about most: *le corps de la femme.*

I stared at the apartment across the street. A woman leaned over the balcony to shake out a tablecloth. I could make out mustard yellow walls so old they were fashionable again. Some of the cafés in the neighborhood had similar yellow paint, a vintage, shiny latex egg yellow, deepened by years of cigarette smoke and alcohol fumes. It had become trendy to leave them intact, with their air of 1959; *"tel quel,"* as is, described both the thing and its aesthetic.

I looked back at the screen, seeing the words but not reading them. I was useless. My lips were puffy and sore, my skin tender. Even when I wasn't thinking about Olivier, I was thinking about Olivier. I saved my work and turned off the computer.

17

Perhaps all romance is like that; not a contract between equal parties
but an explosion of dreams and desires that can find no outlet
in everyday life. Only a drama will do and
while the fireworks last the sky is a different colour.
—JEANETTE WINTERSON, *The Passion*

"*A* lors, *dis-moi tout,*" Clara demanded. I gave her a detailed account of my evening with Olivier, including my aberrant behavior, which she laughed at. We sat at Mariage Frères, the Seventeenth Arrondissement outpost of the venerable house of tea, done up in teak, rattan, and vintage maps in some designer's notion of luxurious colonial charm. It was a decorating theme I called Rangoon Racquet Club, after a similarly decorated but now defunct restaurant in Los Angeles my parents used to take me to.

"They make these very nicely," Clara said, taking a small bite of a delicate almond *tuile* biscuit. She ate with both a voluptuary's enjoyment and an ascetic's restraint, savoring food so profoundly it was as if she were gleaning information from it. Next to her, I felt ham-fisted and uncouth. "You look happy," she remarked. I blushed. "*Quoi? Tu rougis?*" she exclaimed.

"I think I'm a little embarrassed by how much I enjoyed myself."

I could feel my face grow hotter as I pictured his face, his mouth, his hands on my skin. I shivered. "I'm overwhelmed. It's too much. I need to pull myself back."

"*Quelquefois, la tendresse est douloureuse,*" she observed, a little sadly.

"Are you all right?" I asked.

"Of course. I just miss it. The delicious way it feels when you fall in love, how it turns you back into a hopeful child."

"I'm not in love," I protested. "That's way too big a word. Infatuated, maybe."

"*Que tu peut être chiante!*" she said, rolling her eyes as she called me a pain in the ass. "Your American overanalyzing everything. Or Puritanism. *En tout cas,* of course you're in love. It's a kind of love, anyway. 'Infatuation'—pah!" She looked impatient, which was one way to conceal discomfort.

"We'll see," I said. "I'm wondering if I should've taken things more slowly."

She swirled a spoonful of rock sugar crystals into her *thé au caramel.* "I think, *dans la vie, en général,* you should be romantic, even impetuous, about falling in love, and pragmatic about getting over it, and not *l'envers,*" she said. "This idea of caution, it's stupid. As if you can control it."

She played with her teacup. "I'll tell you a story, about when I lived in Spain. I was twenty, beautiful and arrogant—do you remember what being twenty was like? I was staying in Barcelona with friends of my parents. They had a son my age, Luis, and he fell in love with me. I had a boyfriend in Paris, and even though things weren't perfect with Julien, I didn't want to be with anyone else. I was cruel. I toyed with Luis. One night, we drove to the beach. It was just the two of us, and I could feel how much he loved me ... perhaps I was perverse; maybe I enjoyed making him suffer. I went back to Paris, but I had a secret inside, no one could touch it. I stayed with Julien because I had that secret." She looked down at her hands and twirled a ring around her finger.

"I ended it with Julien when I heard Luis was getting married. I regretted it for years, not seizing the opportunity with him. But when you're young, you think such things are common, frequent." She shook her head, her mouth twisting. "The truth is, I have never seen a man look at me the way that boy did." With a trace of anger, she added, "And no man ever will."

"Clara—" I protested, but she cut me off.

"No, it's true."

"I refuse to believe that isn't possible anymore!" I said firmly.

"You misunderstand. I don't think that love is impossible, just *that* kind of love. There are things that belong to a certain age, they are attached to certain moments, *c'est tout*. You can't relive them. And no one else can tell you what they mean." She tilted her head back, lifting her chin.

"I still think it's a sad story," I said. She sniffed and looked away. I wondered if I'd misunderstood her. Perhaps her careless attitude about her romantic life was a pose, a protective device.

"And you see? Of course it was love. This is a stupid word, 'infatuation,'" she said. "*Tu vois*, here's an answer to your constant questions about *le mot juste*. We may have fewer words in French, but they mean more. The context is everything."

"Clara, about that story . . ." I started, but she was done.

"Let's talk about something else." Her face shuttered. "Even if nothing comes of it, I think Olivier has erased Timothy," she noted.

"Good point," I said, nibbling on a lacy *tuile*.

"My mother says men always remember their loves, but for women, it takes only one man to make her forget everyone who came before."

"I wonder how men feel about that comment," I said, raising an eyebrow.

"*Bof.* For men, their former loves are like stamps or butterflies. They like to look at them and remember the chase, how they found them and added to the collection. For women, former loves are too often like train wrecks. Bad feelings linger long after they're done cataloging the damage."

"That's terrible!" I said. "Do you really think that?"

"I don't know. Perhaps I'm in a bad mood." She actually said *"de mauvais poil,"* of bad fur, like a cat rubbed the wrong way.

"You know," I said, changing the subject, "I did have this realization about lingerie—it's not frivolous in the slightest—"

"La frivolité est un état de révolte violent," she quoted.

"Who said that?" I asked.

"Je ne sais plus," she said, puffing her cheeks out in blowfish mock exasperation. *"Baudelaire, peut-être, ou Proust."*

"How can frivolity be a state of revolt? Let alone a violent one?" I asked. "I mean, by its nature, frivolity is trivial."

"Trivial compared to what?"

"Ordinary life, I guess—birth, death, love—the biggies."

"Précisément. It's a revolt against all these inevitable aspects of life," she said. She got up to take a call on her cell phone while I chomped down on the last almond *tuile.* This concept of frivolity seemed another particularly French idea, a contradictory puzzle that, to them, made perfect sense. I couldn't figure out if it was the vocabulary of the idea that startled me or the idea itself. The French always seem so practical, so logical, so able to explain everything rationally . . . except when they can't. In the realm of emotions, all that Cartesian logic goes out the window, and they leap to wild, euphoric, contradictory conclusions that they justify with poetic phrases. I couldn't tell if it was a profound, heartfelt examination of emotion or a sinuous exercise in rationalization via word arrangement.

Clara came back transformed, her face pink. "What time is Althea's party?"

"Eight. Aren't you coming?" I asked, guessing.

She shook her head. "His plane arrives at eight." Her up and down romance seemed to have taken a turn for the better. "I have a thousand things to do!"

She opened her bag and took out a small, gift-wrapped box. "Will you take Althea my present? With my apologies?" she asked. We cheek-kissed good-bye.

I went around the corner to buy Althea a large box of dark chocolate *pralinés* from her favorite *chocolatier.*

"C'est pour offrir?" the saleswoman asked. She had dyed blond hair and the overly but expertly made-up face of a beautician.

"Oui, merci," I said. She wrapped a ribbon around a dove gray box with a gold seal. She slid the box into a similarly emblazoned shopping bag and offered me a chocolate. I picked a dark chocolate *rocher,* a jumbo truffle with crunchy bits of nougat.

I inherited my sweet tooth from my mother. We have a similar weakness for chocolate, but her favorite candies are Jordan almonds, dragées. Years ago, I'd found a tiny boutique on the boulevard Haussmann, where they sold little else. The saleswoman always used the same dated paper, a rust-colored medley of autumn leaves, and wrapped the box with knife pleats, ribbon, and no tape.

I strolled down the boulevard now, passing the late-afternoon shoppers emerging from *les grands magasins,* and saw that the dragée store was still there. I thought about the cafés that hadn't changed since the fifties, clothing shops and umbrella stores that hadn't changed in decades, sometimes centuries. When I was a student, I bought my cigarettes from La Civette, where Casanova had bought his tobacco. I'd gone to a nightclub in a basement *cave* on the rue de la Huchette, where the band played swing music and the kids danced *le rock,* a kind of jitterbug. It turned out my father had hung out there as a college student as well.

Plus ça change.

....

I could hear the party before I rounded the corner. Walking into Althea's little house, I spotted Ivan first. A large, broad-shouldered man with thinning brown hair, blue eyes, and an air of benevolent preoccupation, he was sweaty and bristly with stubble when I kissed him hello. He directed me to the kitchen, where I found Althea, struggling to open a bottle of champagne, a sheen of sweat on her forehead. Her multicolored hair—now streaked with violet and blue—was held in place with a dozen plastic clips.

"Happy birthday!" I yelled over the music. I set the box of chocolates and Clara's gift on the counter.

Althea thrust the bottle into my hands. "It's good stuff, so if you can open it, you get the first glass," she said. She pressed the box of chocolates to her nose and inhaled, then hid them under the sink.

"Who's got such extravagant taste?" I asked, reading the vintage label. I threw a dishcloth over the cork, grasped it through the cloth, and twisted the bottle, not the cork, the way my French father had taught me when I was twelve.

"Patrick, my boss. He brought his rugby cronies," she said, rolling her eyes. "*Ça y est*. Their theme song," she explained, as the old House of Pain song "Jump Around" blasted through the speakers, accompanied by the thunder of people obeying the lyrics.

The cork wasn't budging. A wiry man with spiky brown hair and Elvis Costello glasses marched in. "*Non, non, non! Donne-moi la bouteille,*" he demanded, holding out his hand.

"*Oh, là, on t'a sonné, toi?*" I answered, just as rudely, and turned away so he couldn't grab the bottle. The cork eased up with a sigh, and I removed the dishcloth with a flourish.

"*Pas mal,*" he conceded. "Thea, you got any aspirin?" he asked.

"Yeah, hold on. This is Derek," she said. "He's harmless."

"Oi!" he shouted. "What she means to say is I'm an incredibly clever, dashing bloke the ladies can't get enough of," he said. "Ta," he added, taking two pills from Althea and downing them with a swig of champagne.

I poured myself a glass and walked into the living room, edging the mosh pit in the middle of the floor. At a table loaded with snacks and bottles of booze, I ran into Lucy, Althea's sister, carrying a stack of plates.

"Althea didn't tell me you were coming!" I exclaimed. She put the plates down and gave me a hug. She was a taller, more conservative version of Althea, with more freckles.

"Surprise visit for her birthday. Going back to London tomorrow," she explained. Lucy and I were old friends—I knew Althea through her—and though I didn't get to see her often, we kept in touch through e-mail and occasional phone calls. I fetched her a glass of champagne, and we caught up in a corner.

Someone cut the music and turned off the lights. As half the guests sang "Happy Birthday," the other half *"Joyeux Anniversaire,"* Ivan walked into the living room with a cake studded with candles. Althea stood on tiptoe to kiss him, then blew out the candles to the sounds of cheers and popping champagne corks. I ducked as one bozo tried to saber open a champagne bottle with a chef's knife, and helped Lucy serve cake.

"When are you coming to visit?" she asked. "Really, the Eurostar's not terribly expensive if you book ahead," she said. Her accent was becoming more English since her move to London last year. I heard it in the "really" and "terribly."

"Lu, Mum's on the phone!" Althea yelled. Lucy joined her on the call. In the dim light, I couldn't make out anyone else I knew. I walked into the garden.

There was a flashing message icon on my phone. It was Olivier, saying he was on his way. I sat down on a slightly damp wicker sofa and looked up at the sky.

"I can't find my wife anywhere," Derek said, sitting down next to me.

"Where was she last seen?" I asked.

"Reliving her college days playing DJ. God, I love that woman!" he yelled, causing a trio of smokers to turn and stare. Derek glared back.

"The French," he muttered, curling his lip. Seeing my surprised look, he added, "Keep your knickers on, I'm half frog. How long does aspirin take to kick in?"

"At least half an hour, maybe more. Maybe you should lie down?"

"I can't. There's someone shagging in Althea's bedroom."

"Althea won't like that," I remarked.

"Depends," he said.

"On?"

"Who's in there with her," he said. "Mad Hatter's tea party. I dub thee dormouse," he said and put his head in my lap.

18

He directed her attention to another question:
"When I speak to you in your language, what happens to mine?
Does my language continue to speak, but in silence?"
—ABDELKEBIR KHATIBI, *Love in Two Languages*

My phone rang, blaring with tinny majesty. I pushed Derek's head aside to answer it. It was Olivier.

"I'm looking for a parking spot right now," he said.

"When you get here, I'm in the garden," I said.

"A plus, ma chérie," he said. I liked being called *"ma chérie."* Much better than "my dear," which Timothy always pronounced ironically, as if it had quotation marks around it. Yes, I liked it *beaucoup*.

Derek caught the moon-doggie expression on my face and laughed. "You've got it bad, don't you?" Before I could answer, he waved to a wiry, pale-faced woman with a Louise Brooks haircut. "There's my wife! Eleni!" he called out. Derek introduced us as she made herself comfortable on his lap.

"Has he been boring you?" she asked.

"Just sleeping on my lap," I said.

"The housebreaking is taking a while," she said, pinching his cheek. "What do you do in Paris?" she asked.

"I'm doing some translation," I said. "A novel."

"Translation is total bullshit!" she announced. "I can say that, I'm a translator. Turkish, French, and English. Mostly legal documents now. I gave up on literature," she said. "Mostly because it never works."

"Come on," I said.

"No, I'm serious. All the really important stuff isn't translatable— the cultural framework, subtext, all the things that are unspoken but implied, even the poetry of language. I'm sorry," she said. "I'm really down on it right now."

"Tell her about the poetry," Derek said.

"No, it's too depressing," she said, but he nudged her. "Okay. I was translating this Turkish guy's poems," she began, rolling her eyes. "Terrible poems, utter crap; how he'd gotten them published, I don't know, but he wanted them translated into English. I spent weeks working on them, laboring over meter and rhyme. His American wife reads them and says, 'I always knew Omar was a genius, but I never knew just how good he was until I read him in English.'"

I laughed.

"See?" she said. "They were *bad*. Abysmal."

"But you made Mrs. Omar's day," Derek said.

They went inside to dance. Underneath a multicolored garland of outdoor lights shaped like Día de los Muertos skulls, Olivier stepped through the doorway into the garden. I sat still. I wanted to watch him find me.

There is a specific enjoyment in watching the face of someone you know in a crowd. It's not something you get to do often. You can gaze at the object of your affections when he's asleep, but that's different. This was like watching the relationship begin in a gesture: anticipating the moment when his face would change. He beamed when he saw me, and it was like opening a particularly good present all over again.

"Hello," he said, kissing me. "Where is the birthday girl?"

"Let's go find her." I led him into the house. Fewer people were dancing, most of the guests having retreated to the chairs and sofas to talk. The fog of cigarette smoke was as thick as the cartoon steam that leads the fox to Grandma's peach pie. I led him through the house, into the kitchen, and down the small hallway to the bedroom. I hesitated at the closed door, doing an about-face as I remembered Derek's comment. "I don't think we should bother them if they're in there."

"*Ah, d'accord,*" he said, looking amused.

"It's not me, for god's sake!" Althea said, barreling down the hall-way, clutching a bottle of champagne. She looked at us indignantly. "Come on! Ivan practically *lives* here! I don't need to screw him during my own birthday party!" She took a swig from the bottle and banged on the bedroom door with her fist.

"Well, then who's in there?" I asked.

"Patrick's Yugoslavian au pair. His kids went to a slumber party and she was moping around the house 'cause she didn't have anywhere to go, so he brought her, and now she's in there with one of the rugby boys. I can't get them out, Ivan keeps saying we'll sleep at his place, and Patrick thinks it's too funny to do anything about it." She gave an exasperated glare.

"It *is* pretty funny," I said, trying to smother my laughter. Althea wrinkled her nose, then grinned. "Doesn't it make you feel old, know-ing someone's au pair is getting laid in your bed?" she asked. "Jesus God!" She swayed and fixed her eyes on Olivier. "So, you're the dish. *Fais attention!* She's had her heart broken enough."

"Althea!" I exclaimed.

"Fuck, darling, you know it's the truth, and besides, it's my birthday and I'll say what I want to! *Allons, allons, vous-sortez déjà? Putain, j'en ai marre!*" she yelled, pounding the door again. Olivier and I retreated to the kitchen.

"Do you want anything to drink?" I asked, staring into the refrigerator.

"No."

"Have you eaten?"

"Yes." He leaned back against the stove. I closed the refrigerator.

"Do you want to stay?"

"No. *A moi,*" he said and tugged me toward him. "Do you want to stay?"

"No." I ran a finger over the small scar on his cheek.

"Do you want to leave right now?"

"Right this very minute."

. . . .

I got peckish at three in the morning and went to rifle through the pantry. Olivier followed me into the kitchen wearing an old silk dressing gown I'd stolen from my father when I was a teenager. It made him look like a refugee from a Rat Pack movie, Dean Martin's wicked French cousin. Especially when he poured himself a snifter of cognac.

"Do you know any Sinatra?" I asked, opening the fridge.

"No, I can't sing," he said and yawned. I hummed a few bars of "Fly Me to the Moon" and opened the freezer.

"Pay dirt!" I squealed, pulling out a box of Cornettos, movie-theater-style ice-cream drumsticks. Against his protests that eating in bed was a sloppy, uncivilized American habit, I took the ice-cream cone back to bed.

"Shall we go to a film tomorrow?" he asked. I peeled off the thin, foil wrapper.

"An old one," I said. "I love old movies." He cast me a sideways look.

"Hitchcock?" he asked. I nodded. "Wilder?" I nodded again, crunching nuts.

"Welles," I said. "And Sturges." I nibbled the chocolate coating off my cone.

"What about Steve McQueen?"

I gave him a funny look. "He never directed anything," I said. "But, sure. *Bullitt. The Thomas Crown Affair.*" He pulled my cone toward him and took a lick.

"*Guet-apens, La Grande évasion,*" he said. "My father loved *le cinéma,* especially anything with Steve McQueen," he said. "On Saturdays, we went to the movies, and he bought us ice creams like this. So, now, Gisèle, Sandrine, and I love McQueen. And ice cream." He gave me a lopsided smile.

I bit into the cone. "My father took me out for ice cream once."

"Only once?"

"It was after school, and these older boys were calling me 'stinky French girl,' and asking if I ate frogs' legs and snails, and if my house smelled like cheese. By the time my dad came to pick me up, I'd curled up in a little ball on the bench, clutching my schoolbag to my chest. He asked me what was wrong, and when I wouldn't tell him, he told me to stop crying and took me to Baskin-Robbins."

"How old were you?"

"I don't know. Nine or ten." I balled up the wrapper and tossed it into the waste-paper basket. I remembered that day. I was wearing a plaid skirt and Mary Janes, and I'd wished more than anything for jeans and sneakers so I could look like the other kids.

"Why didn't you tell him?"

"He wasn't that kind of father," I said. "He didn't know what to do with kids."

"*Pauvre petite chérie,*" Olivier said, stroking my face. I felt my eyes well up.

"Oh, *ça va,*" I said, pulling away to turn out the light. "It was a long time ago."

When I woke up, I stretched and rolled over, hugging the pillow. It smelled of Olivier. Lifting my head, I detected a whiff of freshly brewed coffee and the faint sound of France Inter on the radio. He padded into the bedroom with a large *bol.*

"Good morning, sleepyhead."

"Good morning," I said, amused.

"Isn't that what you say?"

"Just sounds funny, coming from you." I took the *bol*.

"No milk, just sugar," he said, looking pleased with himself.

"Very observant." I smiled.

"And you don't talk to me until you've finished drinking it, I know."
He wagged a finger at me and disappeared down the hallway.

. . . .

In the afternoon, we went to see *La dame du lac,* part of the Film Noir
festival at the Action Christine. A woman came up the aisle with a flash-
light, selling ice cream and candy bars from a wicker basket, like a cigarette girl from another era.

The movie was filmed as if Robert Montgomery, playing Philip Mar-
lowe, was the eye of the camera, a first-person film narrator. The other
actors talked directly into the lens when they addressed him, and Montgomery was visible only in rooms with mirrors. The effect was spooky
and jarring, like you were either in the movie or usurping the place of
someone who was.

Afterward, we walked along the small streets of the Fifth behind the
Panthéon to the place de la Contrescarpe. I pointed out the third-floor
apartment on the rue Tournefort where I'd lived as a student. We wound
down to the Jardin du Luxembourg, where it was the end of a long and
arduous play day for little Parisians and their parents. We sat at a café
facing the park, Le Rostand, watching children hang off adult hands,
swaying with punch-drunk kiddie fatigue.

I felt a little drunk with happiness myself. It was easy to be with Olivier, easy and fun. I couldn't have imagined him before I met him, and
yet here he was. I drank my *express*. Like the kids, I was exhausted, but
content. As if I'd made use of myself, instead of always holding something in reserve. Just as I was thinking these languid, pleasant thoughts,
Olivier put his cup down.

"That story you told me," he said. "You were embarrassed. Or angry. Why?"

"I don't know what you mean," I said, frowning at him, even though I did.

"About your father, the ice cream. *Allez, dis-moi.*" His eyes held mine, and even as I looked back at him, I could feel a part of myself trying to slip away, a thief tiptoeing out the back door.

"I think——" I stopped before I spoke the glib disclaimer on the tip of my tongue. Instead, I searched for an honest answer. "You're right, I was embarrassed. Because it started out light, an anecdote I was telling you, and halfway through, I realized it's a sad story—I mean, it makes me sad." I felt an old tension creep up my arms, bracing myself. "That my father and I couldn't connect, that I felt alone. I felt silly, telling you."

He gave me a lopsided smile and cupped my cheek and kissed me. "*Ah, bon.* I thought I'd offended you." I shook my head. He kissed me again. "I should go. I have to do some work."

"I should, too," I said, reluctantly.

After he drove me home, I sat on the sofa in the semidark, not wanting to turn on the lights. The streetlamp cast filigreed shadows on the floor through the lace curtains. The stillness felt dark and lush. I wrapped myself up in it, hugging my knees to my chest.

When it got so dark that I felt silly, I turned on the lights and booted up the computer.

"I lost my virginity at a masquerade ball," Eve told me when we returned to the hotel. "I was seventeen, dressed as Madame de Pompadour, and I didn't take off my mask." She sat on a tufted velvet stool at the dressing table and removed her earrings in front of an enormous gilt mirror.

"That's an idea," I said. "I can imagine you with a domino."

She looked amused. We stared at each other in the mirror, and I pulled up a chair behind her. I kissed the nape of her neck. She tilted her head back.

"In a way, you always wear a mask. I don't know what goes on inside your head," I said, speaking matter-of-factly into the soft skin below her ear. I undid the buttons of her blouse and pushed it off her shoulders. She watched me in the mirror, the blouse still fastened around her wrists. I unclasped her bra, exposing her breasts.

She was bare for me, bare in the mirror, and still I had the sense that I knew nothing. "You see," I said. "You're still an enigma."

"If you knew everything, there would be no mystery," she said, leaning her head back on my shoulder. I caressed her breasts, watching the nipples pucker and harden. From beneath half-open eyes, she watched me touch her in the mirror . . .

I could see the hotel room, picture the dressing table with the mirror, imagine the frescoes on the ceiling, the low light, the caresses . . . It felt different reading and translating the novel now that I actually had a . . . what? Lover? Boyfriend? Man I Was Seeing? Person I Could Imagine That Scene With? What was I going to call him?

French didn't offer any better alternatives. *"Mon amour"* used the "L" word I was shying away from, ditto for *"mon amoureux."* *"Mon copain"* was too casual, and could mean friend as well as boyfriend, and the same went for *"mon ami,"* which could also sound too established. *"Mon amant,"* my lover, sounded way too eighteenth-century and knowing in both languages. *"Mon fiancé"* was what Clara called her boyfriend, even though he was married and lived in another country.

He'd called me *"ma chérie"* on the phone. It was old-fashioned, warmer than "honey," not as cute as "sweetie," somewhere more in the neighborhood of "dear one." But it didn't give a name to what was happening, nor did I know what to call him.

I inched the fabric of her skirt up and trailed my hand along her inner thighs. Her stockings made a slithering, rustling noise. She raised her arms and clasped them behind my head, her fingers playing with the nape of my neck. Her head was heavy on my shoulder as she watched me . . .

I stopped. I suddenly felt like a voyeur. I sort of liked it.

I ran my fingers over the silk of her panties, tracing the shape of her through the damp fabric. Her eyes were smoky and dark, and she made little cat sounds. She turned and kissed the side of my neck. This time, I watched, as she undid my shirt buttons. Her head trailed down my torso, and I watched her descent in front of me and in the reflection in the mirror. She unzipped my trousers and freed my cock . . .

I cracked a window and went into the kitchen for some water. When I dunked ice cubes in my glass, they made a crackling sound. The French word was *"grincement"*: it meant creaking, grating, gnashing, and it sounded like it should exist in English: "grincing." It would be a good word for the squeaking sound ice makes when you crush it between your back teeth, the way it becomes almost chewy before it melts or breaks.

I traced my finger in the fog of condensation on the glass, thinking about the translation. Sometimes finding out what other people did in bed was intriguing; sometimes, it was grotesque. Other times, it seemed the way in which people talked about sex was far more sordid than anything they actually did.

I disliked the narrator less. In fact, I was even starting to like him. If the next scene was crass or ugly, my feelings could shift back again. I forced myself back to work.

"Blow job" in French is *"tailler une pipe,"* often abbreviated to *"une pipe,"* as in the request *"fais moi une pipe,"* make me a pipe. The literal translation means something like cleaning a pipe, though no one would translate it literally. Like no one translates reflexive verbs literally, let alone the idiomatic ones. It doesn't make sense. And yet, I can't resist: *"se rouler une pelle,"* the quasi-crass expression for a French kiss, translates into "to roll oneself a shovel," which almost makes sense. "Translation is bullshit," Eleni had said. I wondered what Monsieur Laveau thought.

Come to think of it, as I wasn't a professional translator, I didn't know whether reflexive verbs even exist in English. Probably not; they're too weird, especially the treacherous idiomatic pronominal verbs, which mean one thing with the reflexive pronoun and another without it. Like *"tromper"* means to deceive, but *"se tromper"* means to be mistaken. As if the insertion of the reflexive pronoun implies you are deceiving yourself.

Or maybe I was thinking about French in English, instead of thinking about French in French. Most of the time, I heard and spoke French like a French person. Sometimes I dreamed in French, sometimes I thought in French, and no matter where I was, when driving, I cursed in French. Maybe that came from hearing my father curse in the car when I was a kid, or maybe I liked *"putain"* and *"merde"* better than "fuck" and "goddamnit."

But my language hard drive had its own subjective, unpredictable filter, and sometimes I heard French as a foreigner, someone outside the language looking in, and I had to wrestle with whether words and phrases were fungible, even translate them into English. My grasp of French was trickier than I thought. I looked back at the text.

The narrator didn't use *"une pipe"* during the scene devoted to the act. In fact, as I translated, I noticed there were very few slang words at all. The narrator used *"la bite,"* which fell somewhere between the dictionary accuracy of "penis" and the crudity of "cock." It was actually a tender little scene of oral gratification. He wrote about the shape of her lips, the feel of her mouth, but also about running his fingers through her hair, the curve of her shoulders, a beauty spot he hadn't noticed, and how astonished and touched he was. Instead of being racy and raunchy, it was nearly *pudique*. I wrote it eight slightly different ways. I couldn't find a way to do it justice.

The phone rang. It was Althea, calling to thank me for the chocolates.

"Excellent party," I said. "Did you get that couple out of your bedroom?"

"They emerged around four. By that time, Ivan was making s'mores with dark chocolate and *petit-beurres* in the garden, but French *chamallos* don't melt the same way. I have goop all over my plastic lawn furniture. How's Mr. Handsome?" she asked.

"Good. Lovely, actually. He's sweet and likes old movies."

"Very nice."

"How do you translate *'pudeur'*?" I asked, changing the subject. "I know the dictionary says 'modest,' but that's not quite right."

"No, I agree. Like if you say *'Je suis assez pudique.'* It's not prudish, either. It's a kind of modesty about revealing too much," she said. " 'Reserve,' I'd say."

"That's it, thanks." Musing out loud, I added, "It's funny, the French aren't that repressed. I mean, even when they don't talk about it, you still get the feeling they're doing something. *Pudeur* implies reticence, not repression," I mused.

"On the other hand, Americans are rarely reticent," Althea observed. "Ivan just took the soufflé out of the oven. Gotta go."

I struggled with word choices until my eyes hurt from looking at the screen. The printer ejected pages striped with words, devoid of accents. I put my head down on the desk and doodled on a notepad. I thought about sex and writing, meaning and translation, and the things that were hard to come up with words for in any language. But underneath it all, I kept coming back to something that felt like melancholy. What was lingering at the edge of my thoughts that made me feel not quite sad, not quite gloomy? What was I missing? Maybe something in the chapter, or Sunday night blues. For the eight thousandth time that day, I thought about Olivier, and there it was: I missed him.

Maybe I was falling in love.

19

> *What makes literature interesting is that it does not survive*
> *its translation. The characters in a novel are made out of*
> *the sentences. That's what their substance is.*
> —JONATHAN MILLER

The week passed in a blur, despite the fact that it rained constantly, because I saw Olivier nearly every night. Even the nights he had rehearsal, he came over afterward. I didn't see the time go by, and I didn't seem to need food. I was on another planet, living on coffee, sex, and croissants, and the only real sleep I got was in the morning, after he left.

When I met Althea for lunch, she shook her head, pronouncing me "lost in Goofyland," which was as good a description as any. I barely looked at my e-mail.

On Friday morning, I could tell from the dim light peeking out from behind the curtains that it was gray outside. The *météo* predicted rain all day. I reread my final version of the translation and printed it out.

At the 96 bus stop, a girl in a parka did multiple-choice homework on the bench. My cell phone rang. It was Bunny, asking if I wanted to grab coffee at Le Flore.

"I'll meet you right after I drop off the translation," I said.

"Wait, I don't get to read it first?" he asked.

"I'll e-mail you a copy," I promised and hung up.

"*Excusez-moi, madame,*" the girl next to me said. "*Je vous ai entendue parler en anglais. Est-ce que je peux vous poser une question?*" She had heard me speaking in English and wanted to ask a question.

"*Bien sûr,*" I said, surprised at being addressed as "*Madame.*"

"*C'est quoi la différence entre* 'amidst' *et* 'between'*?*" she asked, pointing to her workbook. I frowned. I knew they were different, but for a moment, I couldn't think of how to explain it. I told her that "amidst" meant among many, whereas "between" implied between two things. I likened "amidst" to "*parmis,*" and "between" to "*entre,*" and hoped I was right. She thanked me but looked doubtful. Just because you speak a language doesn't mean you can teach it.

Nor does it mean you can translate it. I sat on the bus watching the rain spatter the windows, second-guessing myself about the chapter, even though it was too late to do anything about it. I distracted myself by coming up with things to do. Maybe Bunny was up for a movie. Or maybe we could poke around the used bookstores in the Fifth and Sixth. I yawned and rested my head against the glass.

. . . .

As usual, Monsieur Laveau was on the phone when I got to the bookstore. I poked my head in his office, and he put a hand over the mouthpiece.

"I'm sorry to inconvenience you, *mademoiselle,* but I don't have the next chapter for you. A mix-up with the courier service," he explained. "I will have to messenger the next chapter."

"Okay," I said. "Let me know. Meanwhile, here's last week's chapter." I handed him the original chapter and my translation. He resumed his conversation. I walked back into the rain.

Bunny was sitting on the patio when I got to Le Flore. *The Economist* lay open on the table, next to a double *crème.* I leaned over and kissed him on both cheeks.

"Hey, kid," he said in a wan voice. I took off my coat and hat and sat down.

"What's wrong?" I asked. He shook his head. "Something's wrong, I know it."

"It's my tooth," he said. "I need a root canal, and you know how much I hate my dentist." He sighed and bared his teeth at his reflection in a spoon. I ordered tea.

"Ever have a day when everything goes wrong from the moment you wake up and keeps getting worse?" he asked conversationally.

"Sure," I said.

He put the spoon down. "It's been like that every day for the past year," he said.

"Bunny!" I said. I half-laughed, thinking he was joking. He shook his head, sinking his chin into his neck. I put my hand on his arm. He shrugged it off.

"I'm not that guy, kid," he said, his eyes searching mine. "You think I'm some kind of warmhearted, wise adviser, but I'm not that guy. I'm not that guy you call Bunny that you're always so happy to see—"

"Yes, you are," I argued. "You are—"

"I want to be, but I'm not—"

"You are too!" I said, dogged.

"I'm a bitter old man, goddamnit!" he shouted, slamming his hand down on the table. His cup quaked in its saucer; the spoon fell to the floor. There was an excruciating silence as people swiveled around to look at us. I stared at him in shock: he'd never raised his voice at me before. The waiter placed a teapot and cup on the table. Bunny looked down at his hands, his mouth working.

"They want me to retire," he said, after a moment. "Golden parachute, the whole package, but they want me out," he said, looking down at the table.

"Oh, Bunny, I'm so sorry," I said. He loved working at the Acronym, his nickname for his division at UNESCO. "Isn't there anything you can do?"

"My lawyer's been working on it, but it doesn't look good." He canted his jaw over to one side and looked out through the glass. We sat in silence.

"Willya look at that?" he asked. I followed his gaze. A short, white-haired man in a navy blue coat embraced a tall, blond woman in a fur. "The Central European Love God in action. Always a beautiful dame on his arm. How does he do it?" he muttered to himself.

Years ago, Bunny had shown me a picture of one of his old girl-friends, an artist who lived in Vienna. In the photo, she had a kind face, with a gap-toothed grin and long black hair. When I handed it back to him, he'd stared at it, running the corner of the photo under his thumbnail.

Then he'd said, "You can get awfully far on memory and imagination," and the expression on his face had been both hopeful and crafty, like a child stealing a gum ball. Back then, I'd thought it a whimsical thing to say. There had been a lot of women in Bunny's life, and I could see how their memories might people his imagination. Now, it seemed profoundly sad.

He didn't stay long. After he left, I stared out the window, wondering what he'd meant about not being my Bunny and whether I'd done him some kind of disservice, burdened him with expectations.

The rain stopped, the sky brightening to an opaque white. I put my umbrella in my bag and went for a walk. Gray weather always meant sugar to me. Visions of fattening, decadent, expensive pastries danced in my head. I walked down the rue Bonaparte, window-shopping every boutique, even the expensive patisserie, with its desserts that looked like sculptures, especially the pink layered *macaron* and a chocolate-and-gold-leaf bombe. I texted Olivier on his cell phone, *"Un seul être vous manque et tout est dépeuplé."* I'd seen the quotation from Lamartine on a postcard, and I'd tried to figure out a decent translation—"You miss one person and the world is empty"—but nothing seemed to match the elegant desolation of the French word *"dépeuplé,"* literally, unpeopled.

I heard thunder. Suddenly, *il pleuvait des cordes*: it was raining ropes, the expression for cats and dogs, and the rain did look like silvery violin strings. It was the kind of weather that made me long for a Basil Rathbone Sherlock Holmes movie and, failing Olivier, who had a late rehearsal and wouldn't be over tonight, a cat to curl up with and watch it. I raced after the bus and jumped onboard. As it pulled away, I realized I hadn't gotten my check from Monsieur Laveau.

. . . .

Monsieur Laveau woke me out of a deep sleep at 9:01 in the morning, his voice oozing displeasure.

"Ecoutez, j'ai lu les pages que vous avez traduites, et je ne suis pas du tout content," he said, his tone emphasizing his unhappiness with my translation. *"Auriez-vous la gentillesse de passer me voir aujourd'hui?"* he asked, though it sounded like a command. I cleared my throat and asked him to tell me more, but he insisted I come to the bookstore to discuss it. *"Ce matin m'arrangera,"* he added.

"D'accord," I said, mystified.

"A tout à l'heure."

I couldn't figure out why Monsieur Laveau was so unhappy with my work. Sure, there were some word choice issues, but there were always word choice issues. Nor did I understand the note of glee I detected beneath the peremptory tones. Unless he was looking for an excuse to fire me and was thrilled to have one.

I walked out of the cold damp into Editions Laveau, where the heat was cranked up to waiting room in hell. Monsieur Laveau, on the phone again, waved at me to sit down. Already sweating, I balanced on the edge of the treacherous club chair, resisting the gravitational pull of its lumpy center.

"Oui, mais vous m'appelerez, d'accord? C'est promis? Bien. Allez, mon vieux," he said and hung up. *"Vous voulez un café?"* he asked me.

"Volontiers," I answered. As he fiddled with the coffee machine, I tried to make conversation. "I'm thinking of trying to read more in French. Read any good new fiction lately?"

He grunted and flipped a switch. The coffee machine gurgled.

"We are here," he said, handing me a small cup and saucer, "to discuss this latest translation, which I find completely inadequate. Evidently, you did not see fit to devote any amount of serious attention to the job at hand—"

"Wait a min—" I interrupted, trying to tell him how wrong he was.

"Laissez-moi terminer, mademoiselle," he said, cutting me off with an imperious hand. There was something downright unhealthy about how much he was enjoying himself. "This," he said, poking my pages with his index finger, "is sentimental fluff. I am surprised at you. It is like *un roman à l'eau de rose*—do you know this expression?" he asked.

"No, but I can guess," I said, betting that a novel written with rose water was saccharine and cloying.

"It is like a romantic schoolgirl writing in her diary," he explained, his mouth twisting as if he'd been force-fed the flowery pages. "I am most disappointed. I cannot give this to the author. I am torn between firing you immediately—"

"But—" I started again. My shoulder muscles were bunched up around my ears. I was being scolded like a bad child.

"Mademoiselle, je n'ai pas terminé," he reproached, as if I'd interrupted his soliloquy on the stage. He continued his harangue for another few minutes, essentially rephrasing the same point in increasingly elegant convolutions. I tried to tune him out.

"Mademoiselle, m'avez vous suivi?"

"*Oui, monsieur,*" I said, though I hadn't paid attention to his last few sentences.

"*Et alors?*" he asked.

This was the what-have-you-got-to-say-for-yourself portion of the day's entertainment. Looking at him, his bushy brows and bearish hands, fingertips pressed together, I had the weirdest feeling that all of this had nothing to do with me. I was a bit player in a complex, multiact drama that had begun long before I made my appearance as a mere plot device. In the script, I wouldn't even have a name: it would say "Enter Translator," then a few pages later, "Exit Translator." The thought took the edge off some of my anger, but not all of it. I gathered my arguments, pressing them into a hard, compact ball.

"First of all, I doubt you've read the French version of the chapter you gave me, or you wouldn't be giving me this lecture. You're either referring to a different incarnation of the chapter, or you're looking for something that is not in the text. It's true this chapter has a more romantic feeling than the previous ones, but that's because it's a romantic story—the characters are falling in love in Venice, for chrissake!" I gestured with my hands as I spoke. Bernard watched them wave about in the air, and I forced them into my lap.

"As to whether you're going to give me another chance, you should consider two things: the first is that I can read neither your mind nor the mind of the author, so I only translate what I see on the page. If there's a direction I need to be pointed in, then that is your job to tell me, not mine to guess. I suggest you clarify what you want from a translator before subjecting me to such a disagreeable *entretien*." I delivered my speech calmly, but I could feel my heart racing, and I was digging my nails into my palms.

"And the second?" he asked, his cheeks dimpling. Did he actually look amused?

"The second what?" I asked.

"You said you had two things to tell me."

I thought for a moment. "You owe me three hundred euros." Without a word, Bernard Laveau scribbled a check and handed it over with a regal gesture, as if he were paying off the troublesome third chambermaid on a large estate.

"*Merci,*" I said.

"*Je vous en prie, mademoiselle,*" he answered silkily. He picked up an envelope and slit it open. I shoved my arms into my coat and realized this might be my last visit to Editions Laveau.

"*Monsieur,*" I began. He looked up. "You don't like me," I stated.

"*Au contraire, mademoiselle. Vous m'amusez énormément.*" He chortled.

"*Ce n'est pas la même chose,*" I pointed out.

"You Americans, you always want smiles and reassurances—"

"It is generally the way one conveys whether you like someone or not," I snapped, bristling at "you Americans."

"No, it is the way in which you Americans communicate approbation. It is not, however, how we do it in France. I am not your pom-pom girl." I bit my lip to keep from laughing at the image of Bernard in a pleated miniskirt. He continued, "I am not going to tell you your work is good in the hope that such a lie will encourage you. You will either take intelligent criticism and work harder and or you will fail. *Un point, c'est tout,*" he said and leaned back in his chair, steepling his fingers.

I tapped my foot in annoyance. "You know, you're right. This is a French thing. We, *les Américains,*" I said, deciding to speak for my nation, "think you work better if you are given encouragement and accurate direction, whereas you think scathing criticism is the only way."

"I was not scathing," he said, studying his fingernails.

"You threatened to fire me! And it's not like I really care about how good a translator I am. It's not my life's work," I shot back. It wasn't true: I did care about the translation, but I was taking refuge in snottiness.

"Yes, but this book is someone else's life's work, and you will either do it justice, or I will find someone else," he said, leaning forward.

"Why are we even having this conversation? Why don't you just find someone else?" I asked, infuriated by the repeated threat.

"Because the other chapters were good."

I was silent.

"You look surprised," he said.

"I didn't know."

"I kept paying you," he said, as if this were sufficient proof.

"You could've told me," I said, reproachfully.

"*Mademoiselle,* do you think I don't have other egos to massage? The egos of writers? Is that not fatiguing enough?" He scowled at me. It's a good feint, exasperation, a variation on impatience, usually the first line of defense with the French.

"*Monsieur,* do you seriously think I worry about your level of fatigue?" I asked, with equal exasperation. The ensuing tense exchange of glares felt like our first real conversation. I searched his severe features for a sign. A smile at that moment would have won me over forever, but his face didn't change.

I plucked at a ragged bit of cuticle, peeling the skin back. Blood oozed out, lining the edge of my thumbnail in red. I made a fist around it and stood up. Monsieur Laveau held out a stack of pages across the desk.

"*Je ne comprends pas,*" I said, not taking them.

He shook them at me. "Rewrite it. It's too soft, too sweet. If you read it again, you'll see it's more subtle than purple. And though we are near the end—"

"We are? But they're just getting to know each other!" I said, taken aback.

"Though we are near the end," he repeated, as if I hadn't interrupted him, "I will not need it for two weeks. I am going out of town for a short trip."

"*Merci, monsieur.*" I put the pages in my bag.

"Je vous en prie, mademoiselle." Bernard walked me to the door, and for one startled second, I thought he was going to pat me on the shoulder, but he reached over and handed me my umbrella.

"A bientôt," he said.

20

You know what they call
a Quarter Pounder with cheese in Paris?
They got the metric system.
They wouldn't know what the fuck a Quarter Pounder is.
They call it a "royale with cheese."
—QUENTIN TARANTINO AND ROGER AVARY, *Pulp Fiction*

*I*climbed the stepladder in the kitchen and put the translated pages on top of the cupboard next to a dusty red ice bucket shaped like an apple. Of course, I had a pretty good memory of the old translation, not to mention a copy of it on my hard drive, so the gesture was purely symbolic, but I wanted to start from scratch, see if I could trick myself.

I reread the French chapter. At first, I couldn't concentrate. The words gamboled around the page, and I kept reading the same phrases over and over again, hearing them like annoying riffs from a bad song that was stuck in my head. I forced myself to focus: the narrator and Eve back at the hotel, the conversation about masks, the blow job. It all looked the same to me, and I heard the same English words in my head, familiar, obvious. Writing it differently would be a matter of nuance, not meaning. Less sweet, he'd said.

Eve's hair tumbled around her face. I couldn't see her expression as she made her way down my body . . .

Did "made her way down my body" sound stupid? Affected?

She unzipped my pants and pulled my cock—

I had used "cock" in the previous version. "Cock" was not a word you'd find in *"un roman à l'eau de rose,"* I thought self-righteously. What was Bernard talking about?

She wrapped her lips around—

Do lips wrap? I couldn't think. Was it possible to say "wrap your lips around a sandwich"? Did "she wrapped her lips around my penis" sound right? The languages blurred; I felt uncertain of my command of either one.

Althea called this the Franglais syndrome, when you can't speak either language, and when you do, the words feel awkward, borrowed, slightly wrong. Among the symptoms were forgetting how to spell words like "realize" *(réaliser)* and "sympathize" *(sympathiser)*, or confusing French and English slang, like saying you were going to the ATM to get liquid, forgetting that *"liquide"* meant cash but "liquid" did not.

The slang was more confusing considering there were a slew of English words that French had appropriated but given different meanings: *"cool,"* in French, meant laid-back and relaxed, not hip; *"space,"* an adjective, meant weird; and *"destroy,"* also an adjective, meant grungy-punk. There were even stranger ones: *"hard"* meant hard-core or gnarly; *"trash"* meant trashy, but in a punk, reprobate way; and *"roots,"* an adjective, described the neohippie youth culture trend of wearing baggy clothes and shunning designer labels.

Even entire phrases made their way over the ocean: "Spare me the gory details" became *"Epargne-moi les détails gore."* My current fave was *"partir en live,"* a hybrid construction. It meant when things go to hell, and was derived from the chaos that can ensue when a program is aired live on radio or TV.

I looked down at the text, seeing the word "cock" again. There was also the inevitable stupid factor. Obscene words in another language always seem tainted with school yard childishness, as if saying them makes you a foulmouthed tot. *"Suce-moi"* sounded idiotic to my ears, idiotic and embarrassing. It meant "suck me," but there was something about the double sibilance, or maybe it was the long "u," that made me want to snicker. Were vowels inherently ridiculous? Or smarmy and insidious? Dr. *Suce*. Dr. Seuss. Dr. Seuss-*moi*. *Suce*-ie and the Banshees. *Suce*-alito, California. I *suce*-spect I am *suce*-ceptible to *suce*-urrations.

Maybe it was the onomatopoeia aspect: "suck" sounded like the end of the act, the "ck" like the final pop when you remove a suction cup. *"Suce"* sounded like the act itself, as if to say it was to do it. The "s" sound insinuated itself into the ear like a hiss and lingered; it didn't have an ending.

I picked up a pair of manicure scissors and trimmed seven split ends, a nice time-*suce*. I was getting nowhere. I e-mailed my friend Marielle in New York. She spoke four languages fluently and her current boyfriend was French: "Does *'suce-moi'* make you squirm?" I wrote. I got an answer from her BlackBerry in minutes: "Ha! Know what's even worse? When Raoul says *'léche-moi les tétons'*! I hear 'lick my teats,' like he's a cow, and it makes me practically spit with laughter. Why do you ask?"

"Am trying to figure out why sex and slang words sound so lame in other languages. My internal four-year-old is running around the playground shouting bad words and screeching with laughter. I can't make her stop," I wrote back.

Maybe repeating the words over and over again would neutralize them. Maybe that would peel away the layers of association until I got to a core, a neutral agglomeration of letters.

Cock. Cock, cock, cock, cock. *Bite. Bite, bite, bite. Zizi. Zob. Cul.*

Ass, ass, ass, ass. *Chatte. Foufounette, foufoune, founette. Minette, mimi, moule. Minou, minou, minou.* Pussy, pussy, pussy, pussy galore, pussy ad nauseam. Cunt, cunt, cunt, cunt. . .

It didn't work. I couldn't make myself hear them any differently. The meanings stuck, stubborn and defiant; I couldn't peel them away, reduce them to sounds.

She wrapped her lips around my cock and pulled me into her mouth. I felt enclosed in a soft, tender prison.

"Suck me," I breathed, raking my fingers through her hair. The slickness of her mouth contrasted with the agile muscle of her tongue, as she explored me, learning the dimensions of my sex. She fondled my balls, teasing them into tight, swollen stones. I closed my eyes as she began moving up and down, letting myself drown in the sensation, feeling how simple and uncomplicated pleasure was, could be. I opened my eyes to watch her wide mouth curved around me, her swaying breasts, the nipples a dusky pink, the color of arousal.

She looked up, her green eyes glittering. With surprising strength, she pulled my hips closer. Her hair loosened and fell forward like a curtain, tickling my thighs. She reached underneath me and grasped my buttocks, toying with the tense, sensitive circle before delicately pushing a wet finger inside. I came with a shout . . .

Didn't seem purple to me. Nuh-uh. Not in tone, neither. I saved the new version and got up to examine the sorry state of the pantry. Three cans of kidney beans, one can of corn, *bœuf en gelée* (not mine), and a box of sugar cubes. In the fridge: four sprouting garlic cloves, reduced fat salad dressing, *fromage blanc,* and a bottle of champagne. Not much for Iron Chef to work with. I put on rain gear and went to the Galeries Lafayette Gourmet, the nearest designer supermarket.

I bounded down the aisles, flinging exotic products into my cart with reckless abandon: jasmine tea jelly, merlot jam, Italian white chocolate almond butter, rose-petal mustard, walnut bread. I found Dutch caramel waffle cookies, *stroopwafels*, that you place on a mug of hot tea to let the steam soften them; *tarama* with baby blinis and crème fraîche; and glacéed cherries and candied pears dipped in dark chocolate. I loved food shopping in general, but a gourmet supermarket was a kind of temple, a place I went when I wanted to be reminded how much I loved the French. I picked up a bag of artisanal muesli, tied with gingham ribbon and containing mulberries and macadamia nuts. My phone rang. It was Clara.

"What are you doing?" she asked.

"I'm conducting a sociological study at Galeries Lafayette Gourmet. I think the French are obsessed with bodily functions," I said. "I'm staring at a bag of muesli that has *'facilite le transit intestinal'* written on it in a red starburst."

"What do they put in the U.S.?"

"High fiber. It's succinct, it's nicely euphemistic, everyone knows what it means, and there's no need to mention intestines or facilitating travel therein," I said and tossed the bag in my cart. When I saw the eight-euro price tag, I put it back on the shelf. "Also, the whole *'crottin de chavignol'* thing," I continued. "In America, no one would ever call a food item 'a turd of something,' no matter how fragrant the cheese was."

"But no one thinks of it as a turd of cheese, it's just an expression for the shape," she protested.

"Look, you can't avoid the meaning just because you don't necessarily see it that way. Anything that's a turd in English is a turd. That it's a turd in French and also refers to one of my favorite cheeses does not take away from the fact that the description refers to a turd," I said, taking a childish glee in the repetition of the word.

"*Tu me fais chier,*" she remarked.

"See, and that's another thing. You don't say 'you're being a pain in the ass' or even 'you're being shitty' in French; instead, you say 'you are making me shit,'" I said.

"I know. I was adding to your theory. *Quod erat demonstrandum:* we are obsessed with shit," she said. "You have ruined my appetite," she added.

"Sorry." I passed a row of brightly colored syrups in glass bottles: fig, ginger, geranium, poppy, pink cotton candy.

"*Ne t'inquiète pas,* I'm on a diet. How is *le beau ténébreux?*" she asked, referring to Olivier as Mr. Tall, Dark, and Handsome.

"Addictive." I sighed. "I haven't seen him since yesterday morning and I'm pining away."

"*Oh, là, mais c'est grave!*" she exclaimed, laughing, and hung up.

I pushed my cart to the artful fruit stand and loaded up on *barquettes* of *physalis,* sweeter relatives of the *tomatillo* in Chinese lantern husks, and paper baskets of wild strawberries. A man in a black suit bumped his cart into mine. He apologized, glanced at my cart, and asked what I was going to do with the strawberries.

"Eat them," I answered. "Plain."

"*Quelle bonne idée,*" he said, taking a couple of baskets himself. "Would you like to eat them together?"

"No, thank you," I said. I wheeled over to the cheese counter and studied the display, blushing, absurdly flattered.

"*Alors, la belle dame, qu'est ce que je vous sers?*" asked the cheese man. I looked up with a start. Did I look different? Was there something going on that I didn't know about? I'd made no effort, and within five minutes, I'd been hit on and paid a compliment.

"*Un Saint-Félicien, un fougerus, et une rouelle de Tarn, s'il vous plaît,*" I said, giving him a quick smile. He wrapped up the cheeses and told me to come back soon. I noticed he wore a pink heart sticker on his apron.

By the checkout line, there was a red and pink sign decorated with hearts announcing that today was the first in a series of Saturday night singles' shopping nights, sponsored by Yahoo! Personals France.

. . . .

An exhausted Olivier came over after rehearsal. There were dark circles under his eyes and his jaw was blue with stubble. I made grilled cheese sandwiches with chèvre and walnut bread while he told me about having to fire the lighting designer.

"And you? How are you?" he asked.

"Bernard told me to redo this week's pages. According to him, they read like a Harlequin novel," I said.

"I find that very hard to believe," he said solemnly.

"Stop making fun." I poked his arm. "You try translating French porn."

"*Ah bon? C'est de la pornographie?*" he asked, surprised. Flashing me a wide, sharky grin, he leaned closer. "How pornographic?" he asked. He grabbed my feet. "Very pornographic?" he asked, tickling me. I shrieked, kicking and laughing until I wrenched free and caught my breath. He leaned toward me again, waggling his fingers.

"Stop it," I said, batting his hands away. "What do you know about it? You never told me." He sat up and rubbed his forehead.

"Not much. Bernard edits some interesting people. I met him for drinks a while ago to see if he might intercede with Rémi Le Jaa for me. Le Jaa is like you—*complètement sauvage*—but not just in the morning. He lives most of the year in an ashram in Kerala, doesn't do interviews, and has never allowed any of his books to be turned into films, but I thought if Bernard approached him for me, it might be possible."

"That would be a big deal?" I asked. I went into the kitchen and brought back two mugs of mint tea.

"To get the film rights to a book by Le Jaa? Not in Hollywood." Olivier shrugged. "Here, yes. Enormous. But it gets complicated: now *le tout Paris* knows that he is coming out with a new work, his first in eight years."

"Does that make it more difficult?" I asked. He tapped out a cigarette.

"I don't know. It focuses a lot of attention on him, *certes,* but it might make it easier to get financing . . ." He trailed off. "The curious thing is that Bernard let slip that he was eagerly awaiting a semiautobiographical *roman à clef,* and without actually saying anything, he implied that it was by Le Jaa."

"So you think I'm translating his book?" I asked, confused. "But I'm not a professional translator! If Le Jaa's new book is such a big deal, surely Bernard would find someone experienced and well-known to do the translation?" He shrugged.

I didn't know Rémi Le Jaa's work, though his name, like a recently learned word, kept popping up everywhere. How funny to think that my author might be famous and that his characters might be based on real people. "Strange name," I remarked. "What's his most famous book?"

"It's a pseudonym. He's only written a few. The one everyone knows is about a gay man living in Saigon before the war, *La Vie de bateau.*"

"Is he gay?" I asked. Olivier shrugged again. "Well, that would be interesting," I said. "The book I'm working on is the story of this guy's love affair with a woman named Eve. He meets her when he's still involved with his girlfriend, falls for her, takes her to Venice, et cetera. Laveau told me it was the author's retelling of his great love. He also told me I'm almost done." I tried to remember what else Monsieur Laveau had said about the author, but it wouldn't come to me. I sat back on the sofa and drank my tea, stretching out a hand to stroke Olivier's neck. He leaned forward to kiss me. He tasted of mint and smoke.

"Are you going to read me any of the pornographic novel?" he murmured.

"Maybe . . ." There couldn't be anything wrong with reading him one choice scene.

"I like very much to be read to."

"I could be convinced," I said, pretending to think about it. "It might require some effort on your part."

"Quel genre d'effort?" he asked. His hands were warm underneath my shirt.

"Continue, je te dirai."

21

J'avais envie de voir en vous cet amour.
—SERGE GAINSBOURG,
"La Javanaise"

*I*t's funny how quickly life can change, I mused one morning after Olivier left. All of a sudden, I was half of a couple, when I'd thought I never would be again. He kept a razor and a toothbrush in the bathroom, and I knew he'd tucked a spare pack of cigarettes in the desk drawer. He came over after rehearsal, we ate at home or at a neighborhood bistro, and then we'd make love and sleep. We had dinner plans with Althea and Ivan, and brunch plans with his sister Sandrine and her boyfriend. Sometimes, he'd sleep in, but most of the time, he woke up early to buy bread and the papers, we'd eat together, and then he'd leave midmorning.

I opened the *International Herald Tribune* and turned to the crossword puzzle. Sometimes Olivier wrote notes in it for me to find later. Today, there was a big heart drawn around the puzzle in blue ink. I glanced up at the book section and noticed a small blurb. It was a book review of a recent translation of Rémi Le Jaa's *La Vie de bateau*. The man was

---

*I wanted to see that love in you.

everywhere. I cleaned the mess on the coffee table and came across Antoine's card. *Tiens.* I picked up the phone.

"I was wondering if you were ever going to call us. Come for tea," Antoine said.

"I'd love to," I answered. "Thursday?" My cell phone rang, but I ignored it.

"I was going to suggest it. Victorine will be happy to see you again."

This seemed like an exaggeration, but I said, "How nice," as if I were flattered.

"She will want to pump you for information, but do not feel obliged," he warned. "We are in the Eighteenth, near Montmartre," he said and gave me the address.

I'd missed a call from Olivier, so I hit redial.

"Listen," he said, speaking in an urgent voice. "I've got something I must take care of— I'll talk to you in a couple of days."

"Are you okay?" I asked, concerned. "What's wro—"

"I'm fine, but this isn't a good time," he interrupted, his voice tense and unfriendly. "I can't talk. I'll call you later."

"Okay. I'm sorry," I said. I heard electronic bleeps and an intercom in the background before he hung up. It sounded like he was at the airport. I tucked the translation into my bag and put on my coat. It was wet and unseasonably cold for early October, but I walked over to the bookstore in a fog, oddly wounded. He's just busy, you caught him at a bad time, I kept repeating.

After a two-week absence, I pushed open the door of Editions Laveau and nearly tripped over a pair of semitransparent galoshes, the kind French grandmothers and my first-grade schoolteacher slid over shoes. A middle-aged woman in a turtleneck sat at Bernard's desk, correcting papers with a red pen.

"*Excusez-moi, madame,*" I said. "*Je cherche Monsieur Laveau.*" She looked up. There was a distinct family resemblance. She had his formidable brows, albeit trimmed and plucked into obedience. Her silver hair was cropped close to her head. His sister, I guessed, seeing the same pinkie ring with the family crest.

"*Non, il est à l'hôpital,*" she said and went back to her papers. Evidently, natural warmth and friendliness to strangers ran in the family.

"*Que s'est-il passé?*" I asked, concerned. She gave me an irritated look.

"*C'est un de ces amis. Un accident cardiaque. Il est allé lui rendre visite.*" I wondered which one of Bernard's friends was in the hospital. I hesitated a moment, tapping my fingers on a leather-bound *La Dame aux Camélias*, Dumas *fils*.

"*J'attends sa traductrice et puis je vais fermer,*" she warned, indicating that she was only waiting for his translator and not about to help any customers.

"*Eh bien, c'est moi,*" I said.

"Oh, you are the American girl?" she asked in a thick accent, frowning. "You do not speak French like an American." I tried not to roll my eyes. French people thought it was so rare that a nonnative spoke their language well that they tended to look deeply suspicious, seeking an explanation that either involved subterfuge or ill-gotten gains, like I'd mugged some unsuspecting French person and stolen her accent. I usually slid in my father's French nationality early on in the conversation and watched their faces clear.

"*Mon père est français,*" I explained with a brief, insincere smile.

"And where are you from?" she asked.

"*La Californie.*"

"*Quel beau pays!*" she said, gathering her papers and briefcase. "I drove up the coast with my second husband. Monterey, Big Sur . . ." she said, looking misty-eyed. "It was so beautiful, it made me forget how sad I was that I was going to divorce him."

I laughed, but she gave me a perplexed look: she hadn't meant to be funny. I handed her the translation.

"Bernard left this for you," she said and gave me a brown envelope. When I looked surprised, she added, "He said you would understand." Inside were two paper-clipped chapters, with a note that said, *"Continuez, svp."*

I thanked her and walked back into the rain, pleased that Laveau had entrusted me with two more chapters without even seeing my rewrite. I called Bunny, on the off chance that he was up for meeting me at Le Flore. His voice was thin and frail.

"What's wrong?" I asked.

"I just got back from the dentist, that's why I sound like this," he croaked. "I'm taking off this afternoon, motoring down to Avignon. I always thought I'd retire there, so I'm going to look around, maybe visit friends in Italy. I've got some buddies near Portofino, some New York pals further down the coast . . . . I need a change of pace."

"Are you sure you should be traveling?" I asked. "I mean, right now?"

"Lay off, Mom. It's only a root canal," he snarled.

"What are you not telling me?" I asked. There was a silence before he answered. When he spoke, his voice was flat, resigned.

"They forced me out. I got a nice package, but it's final. There was nothing my lawyer could do. I don't want to talk about it, I don't want to whine and moan. I just want to get out of town. I'm stopping at WHSmith for some books, then shooting straight down the Autoroute du Soleil."

"Oh, Bunny . . ." I sighed, sad for him and unable to think of anything comforting to say.

"Water under the bridge, kid. Hey, look, I'll be gone a couple of weeks, maybe more." His voice sounded breezier now, more animated.

"You can't go for too long. I might need your advice on the translation."

"Save me the good parts. That last one was a humdinger, and I'll want reading material when I return," he joked.

"I'll miss you," I said. "Be safe. Call the second you get back?"

"Promise."

I pocketed my phone and walked home. Bunny wasn't my only friend in Paris, but he was one of the dearest. He was an uncle, a father, and a best friend, the one I could make mistakes with who would always forgive me and was always there. It was hard not to feel bereft at the thought of his leaving town.

....

As I walked through the front door, the phone rang. It was Althea, reminding me to pick up dessert for dinner.

"Oh, right, tonight . . ." I said. Between Bunny and Olivier, I wasn't in much of a mood to be social.

"Tonight, dinner at my house. You said you'd bring dessert, or have you forgotten already?"

"No, no, I remember. Do I have to bake it or can I buy it?"

"We're in France, what kind of nutcase do you take me for? Get something from the place across the street. No strawberries. Ivan is allergic."

"Olivier can't make it. He's got stuff he has to deal with," I said, peering through the lace curtains down at the *boulangerie*. I could see a tart in the window: apple, maybe pear.

"No worries. I invited a few other people: Charles-Henri, Ivan's very *bece-bege* cousin, and his girlfriend, Justine, and an academic friend of theirs, *un prof à la fac*," she said. "I was going to invite Clara, but her man's in town, and they never leave the house when he's around."

"I didn't know."

"Yeah, I called to check. Anyway, eightish."

I went downstairs to buy dessert before someone else nabbed it. It was a simple *tarte aux pommes*, the apple slices layered and fanned like an Elizabethan lace ruff.

With an hour to kill before leaving for dinner, I glanced at the first new chapter, but I wasn't feeling industrious enough to get started on it. I checked my e-mail, then nosed around the Internet, wondering if there was a word for the French slang which abbreviates words by cutting off the last syllables, like Althea saying *"prof"* for "professor," and *"fac"* for *"faculté,"* or university. A lot of them ended in "o": *"ado"* for "adolescent," *"apéro"* for "aperitif," *"dico"* for "dictionary," *"météo"* for "meteorology." Some felt slangier than others: *"impec"* for "impeccable," *"resto"* for "restaurant," *"extra"* for "extraordinary."

I found it: the word was "apocope," a near palindrome, whose definition was a kind of metaplasm, or alteration of a word, by the omission of one or more sounds or letters or syllables at the end of the word. It was a Latin word, with a Greek root meaning to cut off, and it was the same word in French.

I put on my *imper* and remembered to take the tart out of the *frigo* before leaving the *appart*. I was the first to arrive at Althea's, promptly at eight. She greeted me in her bathrobe with wet hair.

"I'm totally behind! Can you help Ivan?" she asked.

I walked into the kitchen, in time to hear Ivan yell, "Motherfucking-*putain-de-merde-de-chat*! You come back here!"

Tobermory, Althea's fat calico cat, stomach to the ground, shot through my legs like a commando on mission, something long and brown dangling from his jaw.

"Damn cat made off with a piece of mushroom linguine," Ivan muttered, greeting me wearing a vintage "Kiss the Cook" apron. "You think it got cat hairs in there?" he asked, poking a pile of homemade pasta. Every surface of the kitchen was dusted in a fine layer of white flour. I smothered a giggle and handed him the tart box.

"Go ahead, laugh," he said. "Ooh, thanks. Drink?" he asked, pouring me a glass of white wine before I could answer.

"Tarte aux pommes. Can I help?" I hung up my coat and scarf.

He shook his head. "We're vegetarian tonight," he said, rolling his eyes. "Charles-Henri's friend—have you met my cousin?—doesn't eat meat, so it's pasta and vegetables." He opened the oven door to stir a pan of tomatoes and caramelized onions.

"Smells delicious," I said, sipping my wine.

"Good. Hey, would you set the table?" he asked, his face pink from the heat.

In the living room, Tobermory sat on Althea's linen tablecloth, cleaning one paw, not a shred of guilt on his plump pumpkin face. I scratched his head, wondering for the thousandth time where Olivier was.

....

At dinner, I sat next to Charles-Henri, Ivan's rich cousin. He lived with his girlfriend Justine, in the Sixteenth, in a *hôtel particulier* he'd inherited from his grandfather. He had pale skin, a wide forehead, and a thin, bony nose, and despite his pinched, aristocratic air, he was easy-going and quick to laugh. Justine resembled the Grace Kelly–like mother in the *Figaro Madame* comic strip, *Les Triplés*. Her straight blond hair was pulled back with a velvet Alice band, to show off the even, placid features of a Victorian debutante. By contrast, their friend Fred was curly-haired and rumpled, with wire-rimmed glasses, a Dudley Do-Right chin, and a hooded sweatshirt under his jacket. He taught French literature at one of the junior year abroad programs. Over the cheese course, he and Charles-Henri argued about an American writer.

"He's highly overrated," Fred said, cutting a slab of *comté*.

"You're wrong, he's an excellent writer," Charles-Henri protested. "His insights into human nature and psychology are quite profound."

"The language is beautiful," agreed Justine.

"I assure you, he doesn't read half as well in English," Fred said. "You like him because he's got a really good translator." At this, I looked up from my chèvre.

"Do you think a translation can make that big a difference?" Justine asked.

"If the original is mediocre and the translator is good, of course," Fred said. "Translation is totally misunderstood. It's a science *and* an art, but most people think all you have to do is find any bilingual moron and plug in the words. It's another matter entirely to convey the music, the pacing, the drama of literature in another tongue. When it works, it's magic, but when it doesn't, it can turn a classroom of smart kids off Baudelaire or Rimbaud like that." He snapped his fingers.

"Pretty high standards for your translation, huh?" Althea remarked, nodding at me. I flushed, "any bilingual moron" ringing in my ears. Everyone looked at me.

"I'm translating a novel," I said, not elaborating further.

"So you're up on your translation theory," Fred said, nodding. Althea brought the *tarte aux pommes* in.

"Well, no," I said, wrinkling my nose as I failed to remember anything resembling translation theory from my college days. Fred blinked in surprise. "I'm just translating a simple love story, written in a very basic style," I explained, unable to keep a note of apology out of my voice. "It doesn't require research," I said, looking around the table. "I use a few different dictionaries for the idiomatic expressions and some of the slang."

"It's that easy?" Justine asked, with a skeptical look.

"Well, some of the concepts are more French than I thought—it's as if the Frenchness sticks to them more, and it's harder to separate the meaning from the culture. Or maybe it's my Frenchness that's sticking to it, and because it's me, I can't see it . . ." I trailed off, sure I sounded incoherent. "Does that make any sense?"

"Give us an example," Althea said, putting a plate of *tarte* in front of me.

I thought for a moment. "Okay. How do you translate '*séduire*'? In English, 'to be seduced' has a connotation of corruption, an inkling of something against one's will or good intentions; '*être séduit*' is closer to being beguiled. '*Elle a un grand besoin de séduire*' doesn't mean she needs to seduce people but rather that she needs to be liked—and yet, while there is a notion of seduction that isn't sexual, it isn't nonsexual either. *'Légèreté'* means lightness, but in some contexts, it seems to describe an almost Zen-like state of serenity. How do you say 'lame,' or 'rude,' or 'confused' in French? Why is 'violence' in English so physical, whereas the French use it for emotions as well? Why do French people believe in love at first sight, and we think it's adolescent?"

"I don't think it's adolescent," Ivan said, blowing Althea a kiss.

"You translate a whole culture when you translate a novel," Charles-Henri declared. *"C'est normal.* You must give the flavor of the psychic landscape that produced the work in the first place, *non?* Otherwise, it's anachronistic." Justine stretched a languid arm out to play with the back of his neck.

"But if the ideas themselves are difficult to translate, how do you find the words?" Althea asked.

"You can't get caught up on trying to find a one-to-one correlation with each word. You have to understand the author's meaning and intention and translate based on those," Fred said. "That's the only smart way to do it."

"The problem is," I said, bristling at his sweeping pronouncement, "I don't know the author's intention—I don't even know how it ends. I get a chapter a week, and I don't know how many there are. I'm translating in the dark."

"That seems a half-assed way of going about things," Fred said, shaking his head.

"I get paid," I snapped and shoveled a piece of apple tart in my mouth.

"Who wants coffee, who wants tea?" Althea asked, getting up.

Fred leaned over. "You might enjoy reading what other translators have to say on the subject." He scribbled a couple of website addresses as well as his e-mail on a piece of paper. "Start here. Let me know if you need help—if you get in over your head."

"Thank you," I said politely, putting the paper in my pocket and vowing to shred it as soon as I got home. I got up to help Althea in the kitchen.

"What do you think?" she whispered, measuring out ground coffee.

"Kind of condescending." I stacked the plates in the washing machine.

"Really? I think he's cute," she said, loading the dishwasher. I shoved dessert forks in the cutlery basket. Althea gave me an inquisitive look.

"Sorry. Being patronized makes me surly," I explained.

"You're being overly sensitive."

"You say that as if it's a choice. It's not like I sit here and think, Oh, today, I'm with friends, let me be overly sensitive, whereas tomorrow I've got to deal with the plumber and the bank, so I'll be thick-skinned. It's just the way I am!" I exclaimed.

She put soap tablets in the machine and turned to me. "You've been quiet all evening. What's wrong?" she asked. I tossed a dish towel on the counter in frustration.

"I'm worried about Bunny. And . . . something's up with Olivier. Out of the blue, he was brusque on the phone and said something about not being reachable for a couple of days. Something he had to take care of. I don't know what it means, and I'm trying not to read anything into it."

"Which means you've already read ten thousand things into it and are driving yourself mad?" she asked.

"Yes," I sighed. "It's very annoying."

"I'm sorry about Bunny. But chin up about Olivier, I'm sure it's nothing," she said. She gave me a hug and sent me back in the dining room with the coffee cups and saucers.

. . . .

When I got home, there was a message from Olivier.

"Excuse-moi pour cet après-midi, mon ange. C'est compliqué, mais je t'expliquerai. Je t'embrasse."

His apology filled me with a warm-kitten sensation that everything was right with the world. Being called "my angel" helped. Of course, the next moment, I felt a spike of resentment that my mood was so susceptible. I went to bed.

22

Translation is entirely mysterious. Increasingly I have felt that
the art of writing is itself translating, or more like translating than
it is like anything else. What is the other text, the original?
I have no answer. I suppose it is the source, the deep sea where ideas swim,
and one catches them in nets of words and swings them shining into
the boat . . . where in this metaphor they die and
get canned and eaten in sandwiches.

—URSULA LE GUIN,
Dancing at the Edge of the World

I woke up with Fred's words ringing in my ears. I made coffee, turned on the computer, and surfed the Internet, cobbling together a Cliffs Notes version of translation theory. Clicking past the business-oriented sites and the reference sites, I focused on the academically oriented sites, with journals, book reviews, and forums on the nature and study of translation.

One academic journal, called *Palimpsestes,* was devoted solely to translation issues between French and English. There were articles with titles like "Reflections on the Transposition of Clichés and Stereotypes" and "Not-So-Dead Metaphors: Reinvigorating Dead Metaphors in *Moby Dick* and Its French Translations." An article on the difficulties of translating the Harlequin novel focused on the problem of preserving the tropes of the genre; another meditated on the complexities of adjective placement. Like most gold mines, it was totally overwhelming.

It was also riddled with an unfamiliar vocabulary, with terms like "source text," "target text," "discourse," "meta-contexts," and "honorifics," which referred to the various ways languages have of showing politeness, as in the French use of the second-person plural. I was entranced by *"chuchotage,"* a term used to describe the whispering of simultaneous interpretation into the client's ear. It came from *"chuchoter,"* French for "to whisper," but it sounded like something you did in bed. Maybe it was, if you spoke to your lover in a foreign language.

My favorite new word was "idiolect," defined as the "features of language variation characteristic of an individual speaker; [meaning] basically, everyone has a unique way of talking." On another website, I came across the concept of "deverbalizing," meaning "[to strip] away the words of the original document until we are left with only the representation of what the words describe" (Karla Déjean Le Féal, *"Pédagogie raisonée de la traduction,"* pp. 18–19). This notion suggested I ignore the words of the source text and privilege instead their meaning or feeling. Once free from the distraction of specific French words, I should be able to concentrate on finding the English words for the notions I'd isolated and understood. The author made translating seem like a scientific process, like curing olives or decaffeinating coffee.

I kept stumbling onto the word "palimpsest." From a college class, I remembered it referred to the ghostly shadows of erased words that remained, like clues, on Roman wax tablets and, later, on pricey recycled vellum back in the days before paper. Victor Hugo's *Notre-Dame de Paris,* written in the nineteenth century about the fifteenth century, was a palimpsest of a book, set in a palimpsest of a city. The metaphor was unending and perfect, an infinity mirror, and I thought of it whenever I saw other iterations of Paris: old street signs, carved into stone above the modern painted metal ones, or fading vintage advertisements on the sides of buildings. The idea of looking for the ghost of the original had stayed with me.

In translation, it is necessary to keep the ghost around as well, I thought now. Otherwise, you might stray too far from the original and start inventing things.

I got up to make toast and thought about an article I'd read in the *Los Angeles Times* about language and brain tumors. Through experimental surgery, scientists had determined that language isn't located in one section of the brain but spread out in nooks and crannies, like the melted butter in an English muffin commercial, with different areas for different languages. This means that if you had a stroke in one part of your brain and lost the ability to speak, the part of your brain that spoke another language might be able to retrain the damaged part to speak again.

As I'd been obsessed with brain tumors at the time, I'd found this reassuring. But now I wondered if bilingual people had different styles in each language, or if they spoke certain subjects or feelings better in one language than the other, or if they were funnier or wittier in one language or the other.

I ate breakfast, thinking about my new favorite word, "idiolects." If everyone had a particular way of speaking—and this didn't mean the voice-recognition spy technology of Hollywood movies but a style of slinging words together—could you recognize it, scientifically, and identify someone? Someone, say, who was writing a novel?

Did it follow that if everyone had a particular way of speaking, everyone also ascribed slightly different, personal meanings to the same words we all shared?

Maybe all language was translation, all words metaphors. Maybe we were always translating someone's words into our own personal concept of what we thought he or she said. It's amazing that we communicate at all. I pictured the brain as the universe, with neurons firing like comets and asteroids.

I turned to the translation.

Our last night in Venice, it began. Oh, right, they were still in Venice.

Our last night in Venice, we ate cuttlefish and squid-ink pasta in a trattoria in Cannaregio. We held hands across the table like adolescents, pretending to have intelligent conversation about Italian writers: Svevo, Calvino, Buzzati. Afterward, we walked around the canals, lured by the dark sky, an invitation to discover the sinuous city. Eve spotted the new moon, a blurry sliver in the night. She turned and kissed me.

"For luck," she said, her voice breathless, hinting of melancholy.

I felt it, too. Tomorrow, we would return to Paris, and the intrusions of the real world would not delay in finding us. Her hands wrapped around the back of my neck, and she pressed her face into my collar. I put my arms around her and rested my cheek against the top of her head. For a moment, nothing else mattered.

She looked up, tugging on my coat lapels. Her mouth found mine. I pulled her into an alcove. We kissed in the shadows, our bodies pressed against each other . . .

I got up for more coffee and peered outside. Right now, in late morning Paris, right this very moment, there were probably couples making out in alcoves, not to mention on balconies, park benches, street corners, sidewalks, while waiting for taxis, or sitting in the backseats of taxis. It was banal, commonplace, ordinary. Run-of-the-mill. *Quelconque.* I ran out of synonyms. I wondered where Olivier was.

We strolled along the deserted streets, prolonging the evening as we glimpsed bits of Venetian life. Beneath an open window, the sounds of a soccer game on television blared into the night; through an arched glass door, the night manager of a small hotel turned the pages of a newspaper and pushed his glasses up his nose; down a narrow alley, an old woman stepped onto a balcony, shook out a tablecloth, and closed her shutters. We passed a foursome of elderly German tourists, who pointed at stone carvings and Madonnas, repeating "Das ist schön" in admiring voices.

Then, no one. The city retired, and the cats took over. At the sound of our footsteps, they sprang away on agile feet, feline spies gone to warn their comrades . . .

Clunky; a little arch. I made a note and stretched. My back was sore.

It was then that I knew I'd fallen in love with her—while walking along a minor Venetian calle, whose name I didn't think to retain. The realization was as startling and luminous as a lighthouse beacon slicing through a sky of ink. The world as I knew it crumbled. I grasped her shoulders, filled with dread.

"What is it?" Eve asked. Her voice eased the constriction around my heart.

"Nothing," I answered, hoping she wouldn't see the fear in my eyes.

That night, we were nervous, careful around each other. I was clumsy. Eve was distant, aloof: even her hands were cold. But once we found our way back to each other, we were lost, swept up by a feverish ardor. Our lovemaking was heady, almost painful. A small, ragged cry escaped her lips, and I grabbed fistfuls of her hair.

I couldn't sleep. It felt as if there was someone watching us. I imagined the cherubs on the walls were conniving bookmakers, craftily setting the odds of our survival. You will pay for this interlude later, they seemed to say. I could hear them laughing. In the morning, I woke up knowing I'd dreamed I couldn't sleep.

Those few days we'd spent together existed in a bubble: a glass bubble, blown by a Murano craftsman; or a soap bubble, multihued,

impossible to hold, as ephemeral and specific as the scent of her per-
fume on my collar when she kissed the side of my neck outside the
Hotel Saturnia. I would not return to the same Paris I'd left.
Our story had changed. Everything was different.

I put the pages aside. I didn't want to read about their trip back to
Paris. All the signs were pointing to a bad ending. I wanted them to stay
in Venice, walking along the canals, eating weird seafood, and telling
each other stories. I wanted the rest of the novel to be that night, an endless night, a story that would stay put, fixed, in place, always on the edge
of something, never tipping into it.

You were supposed to outgrow "happily ever after"; it was a children's
phrase. But I wanted their story to end well. Was that too much to ask?

It was time for lunch. "Inspire me!" I commanded the fridge, but
the contents refused to oblige: shredded carrots, *fromage blanc*, a tube of
harissa; below, in the freezer, frozen vegetables and salmon steaks in a
sorrel sauce. On the ledge, the lovebird pigeons crooned their monotonous ballad.

The smell of food wafted up, seemingly through the floorboards:
roast chicken and buttery potatoes. I wondered who the cook was. Aside
from the concierge and her husband, the only people I'd ever seen in the
building were a Chinese family; a stocky man who was always carting
sporting gear around; and a grim, redheaded woman who wore flowing
capes and always seemed late for something.

I poured sugar into the *fromage blanc* and took it back to the desk.

We landed in Paris. Eve was distracted, as agitated as a little bird.
I'd never seen her like that. I was preoccupied by the intolerable idea
of returning to the apartment I shared with Daphne. Moreover, I sus-
pected she would subject me to a raffle of questions about my invented
business trip to Italy.

I massaged my earlobe as I stared at the screen. Something was off. I homed in on the word "raffle" and cracked open the French-English dictionary. I'd mistranslated *"une rafale,"* which meant a squall or a hail, as in a hail of bullets. Maybe "a volley of questions"? Would Daphne "pepper him with questions"?

Eve refused to let me take her home, insisting instead on a drink at La Closerie, though it was neither on my way home nor on hers. We sat at a small, round table.

She further surprised me by ordering a kir, a drink she claimed to dislike. This was a warning sign, and I watched as she drank half of it, grimacing.

"I can't see you for a while," she announced. She swallowed the other half of her drink. I could see the thin, ringed muscles working under the white skin of her neck.

"What does that mean?" I asked, keeping my tone light.

"I should have told you before, but I didn't want to discuss it," she said. "It is too tiresome." Her voice turned soft, placating, as if she were already trying to make something up to me.

"Eve—"

"Please don't argue, I hate it when you argue," she said, and asked the waiter to call her a taxi. This little piece of melodrama was beneath her. It was third-rate penny theater. Baffled, I waited for an explanation. She gave me a quick, almost frightened glance. How was it that she could make such an ominous declaration, then look at me as if I was her executioner?

Find a better equivalent for *"bourreau,"* I wrote in the margin. "Torturer"? It was associated with the devil, bedevilment, but perhaps too old-fashioned. "Oppressor," maybe. If I couldn't find a word, I'd have to use a phrase. "Tormentor"?

She pulled on her black leather gloves, struggling to fasten the button on the inside of each wrist. Her fingers slipped, missing the buttonhole once, twice, before pulling it through.

I knew her looks, her gestures. I knew the sly look that demanded I take her in my arms; I knew a one-shouldered shrug meant she was humoring me. She had a way of playing with her hair that sometimes meant melancholy, sometimes boredom. When had I started watching her so closely?

She hadn't buttoned her gloves once in Venice. Now, in that delicate gesture, I saw guilt. I thought of the man at Longchamp. I hadn't asked her about him. Now I knew why. This was no penny opera. No, it was a story as famous as it was common.

"Where are you meeting him?" I asked, conversationally. "Does he come to you, or do you go to him?" By her look of surprise, I knew I'd guessed correctly. I pulled out my wallet. "Go to your other lover, wherever he is. Give him my regards. Here's fifty francs for the taxi," I said, tossing a bill on the table. I spoke without thinking, as if I, too, were acting out a role I hadn't known had been written for me.

"I don't—" she started, then stopped. We exchanged a long, cold stare: we were two strangers now, taking refuge from each other, instead of in each other. She bent her head. Her eyes shone with unshed tears, but it didn't matter. I didn't believe them.

Ah, we were in French Movie Land. Everyone was being Very Dramatic. "It's our Latin sensibility," Pascal had explained once. After a Kieslowski film, Timothy had said, "All French movies are about sex, even when they're not about sex." I'd accused him of being reductive, but sometimes I thought he had a point.

I wrenched my attention back to the text. Why was the narrator being such a jerk? So what if she had another lover? Dude, it's not like you weren't still sleeping with Daphne! The notion of fidelity among people who were having affairs eluded me. If the narrator was still sleeping with the girlfriend, surely Eve had the right to sleep with someone else. Or were there ground rules I didn't know about?

I turned the page. There were only three sentences.

One moment, she was there.
Then she was gone.
I never saw her again.

I groaned and tossed the pages in the air. I went into the kitchen and found the Nutella, right where I'd hidden it, behind the canned kidney beans. Spoon in one hand, jar in the other, I went back to find out what happened to Eve in the next chapter. I suspected something bad was imminent: maybe she was going to die or throw herself off a bridge into the Seine. My cell phone twittered. A text message from Olivier read, "I'll b back soon. I miss u. Love, yr French lover." I laughed and wrote back: "Which French lover?" A minute later, he sent back "Steve McQueen, *bien sûr.*"

Daphne wasn't there when I returned to the apartment. I deposited my bags and went for a walk by the river to clear my head. The wind agitated the surface of the Seine, and I thought of the giant waves of Biarritz, where I'd spent summers with my grandparents after my mother died. My father lived there now, with his second wife, in the old stone house near the water. He liked Daphne; he was pleased I was finally building a life.

I stood on the Pont Neuf and looked out at the fading light. Cars zoomed by on the embankment. The wind whipped my skin and cut through my coat, and there was an unpleasant metallic taste in my mouth. At the place Dauphine, three small boys careened between trees and benches as they kicked an orange ball around the triangular square. Brightly lit restaurants beckoned, but the tables were empty. It was too early for dinner, too late for tea; it was, in fact, the hour of the

aperitif, the right time for a drink with your lover, if she hadn't just left
you, in a way that felt definitive.

I sat on a bench and shoved my hands in my pockets. Even though
thinking it felt like a curse, I knew she'd ended it between us. The
thought of never seeing her again was unfathomable. I wanted to be-
lieve I was merely imagining the worst, but that was a childish ploy
to allay my feelings. An ache manifested itself in my chest, to my sur-
prise, and I heaved forward. My head dropped into my hands . . .

I knew the *place*: I could picture it. I felt bad for Jean-Marc. As much
as it was a fine place for lovers, Paris for the heartbroken? Not so great.

I flipped open my phone and reread Olivier's messages, giggling like
a teenager.

23

Le verbe aimer est difficile à conjuguer:
son passé n'est pas simple,
son présent n'est qu'indicatif,
*et son futur est toujours conditionnel.**

JEAN COCTEAU

Eve vanished from my life.

I stewed in my anger, convinced I'd been right about her—she was an opportunist, a heartless manipulator who felt nothing for me. But when my anger wore off, and I still hadn't heard from her, I began to wonder what had happened. It didn't seem possible that she'd left me because of one ugly scene.

She didn't answer the phone. She didn't answer my letters. At night, I waited outside her building. The lights were never on. The concierge hadn't seen her.

On the landing, I accosted the cleaning lady, Madame de Sousa, a Portuguese woman of fifty in a tartan coat, toting a matching carrier

---

*The verb "to love" is difficult to conjugate: its past is never simple, its present is but indicative, and its future is always conditional.

with a black poodle inside. When I introduced myself as a friend, she smirked and told me she hadn't seen Madame in weeks. The poodle leaped out of its carrier and danced around my ankles.

I persisted, asking if there was any sign of Eve, dishes in the sink, for instance, or used towels in the bathroom. She raised a sharply penciled black brow.

"You are not the police?" she asked. I shook my head. "So, you are some sort of lunatic," she continued, "and me, I am supposed to help you? Ah, no!" She made a ferocious sound of disapproval, pulled her hat down, and marched away. The poodle trotted behind her. I watched as my only connection to Eve strode down the stairs.

"Please, madame, I'm not crazy, I'm not the police, I just need to see her—I'm very unhappy without her," I pleaded, chasing after her. Madame de Sousa looked me up and down, scrutinizing my appearance. "You are my only hope," I added.

"You poor man," she relented. "Your feelings are evident on your skin."

No, no, no. I can see your distress? Your sentiments are plainly visible to me? I can tell you are distressed? It's written on your face? I circled the expression I was having trouble with: "à fleur de peau," meant visible, obvious, apparent; literally, it meant "at the flower of the skin." It was used to describe a feeling so vivid you could see it on someone's face, as if the emotion had blossomed there. I'd always found it poetic, almost exquisitely so.

Perhaps it wasn't poetic in French. Maybe it was just an ordinary expression, a convention. But even some conventions had connotations. I rubbed my forehead, willing the words to speak to me. Was the expression pretty because it was pretty in French, or was it just pretty to me? Had the figure of speech become so common that its poetry had drained out of it? Or was it only pretty because, when I translated it into English, it seemed novel and pleasing?

Was I translating backward, reverse-engineering? I'd explained the expression "to nip something in the bud" to Clara once. She'd found it a lovely image, but it's not particularly lovely in English. In fact, finding it lovely seemed particularly French—the tragi-romantic death of the young bloom, as opposed to English, where it's merely a gardening metaphor. Not every figure of speech had a translation. Maybe I was searching for a kind of verbal refinement whose equivalent didn't exist in English.

My head hurt. Translating was getting more difficult, though I couldn't tell if it was because the author's voice had become more complex or because my translating skills, along with their limitations, were becoming clearer to me. Or maybe I was trying harder because I didn't dislike the narrator anymore.

Madame de Sousa confessed, "I don't know where she is. There is no sign of her."

"Since when?" I asked.

"Going on three weeks. Half of her clothes are gone. I picked up her dry cleaning, a dress and a coat, and put them in the closet, the bedroom armoire, not the one in the hall—she usually keeps coats and hats in that one," she said. I didn't interrupt her: I was hungry for any details concerning Eve, even the organization of her clothes.

"That's when I noticed the closet, but I don't know when she left," she said. "Sometimes, it goes on for months like this," she added. "Madame travels a lot. The accountant pays me—he sends checks."

Though it seemed desperate, I asked, "Can you give me his name?" Madame de Sousa pursed her lips and shook her head.

"She will contact you when she returns to Paris. If she cares to. But now, you should leave. It's not right for you to be here," she said.

"Please," I begged. "If I knew the name of her accountant, perhaps I could send her a letter there—it might get to her sooner," I said,

*scrambling for a reason. I held on to the banister, squeezing it as if my
grip could force the information out of her. Madame de Sousa pulled
on her gloves and scooped the poodle back into the carrier.*

*"Monsieur Richebourg, Cabinet Verlet-Stein," she said, and
walked away.*

*"Merci, madame," I called after her. Her heels clicked across
marble.*

Her accountant? He's going to track her down through her accountant? That was so lame. I scribbled "lame" in the margin.

I went downstairs for a baguette sandwich and sat on the sofa to eat
it, yet again bemoaning the lack of French words for "lame," "rude,"
and "confused," three words I happened to use a lot. There were various
phrases you could use to convey the same meaning, but no one-word
correlation. Lame was sometimes *"ringard,"* or tacky, *"nul,"* worth-
less, bad, or *"bidon,"* phony. "Rude" was either *"mal-élevé,"* raised by
wolves, more or less, *"un manque de politesse,"* which was only the absence of politeness, or *"désagréable,"* which wasn't accurate either, but if
delivered with the right tone of voice, it could be devastating.

I thought about how French had polite ways of insulting people. Only
in France could you actually say *"Je vous emmerde, madame."* In English,
saying "I suggest you go to Hell, madam," already far more polite than
the French phrase, was the stuff of drawing room comedy. We don't
usually observe form when insulting others, whereas in French, doing
so increases the injury. As for "confused," I tended to substitute *"je ne
comprends pas,"* I don't understand, but while that usually conveyed what
I meant, it wasn't an accurate translation.

I turned on the midday news. Romain Chesnier, the Minister for National Education and Research, was filmed leaving Lariboisière Hospital
days after a minor cardiac incident following a vacation in the country.
He was accompanied by his wife, the actress Estelle Bailleux. Wearing
dark glasses, she put up one gloved hand, either to hide her face or to

wave, I couldn't tell, as the cameras filmed them pulling away in the back of a chauffeur-driven car.

So that was who Bernard had gone to visit. It was the phrase his sister had used, "a cardiac incident." I took another bite of my *jambon-beurre*, the crisp baguette shredding my soft palate. A pigeon waddled along the window ledge.

And there it was. The thought was unbidden, unwelcome, snake-like and scaly, but coiled in my head nonetheless: perhaps those weren't airport sounds I'd heard on the phone; maybe Olivier had gone to the hospital as well.

························

Later, when he called and suggested a late dinner after his rehearsal at the theater, I wondered if he'd mention it.

I met him at La Cafétéria, a restaurant with fancy wallpaper and mood lighting. He sat at a table, smoking a cigarette and scribbling on a graph paper *carnet*.

"What are you writing?" I asked, leaning over to kiss him.

"Notes for the actors—things I must remember." He poured me a glass of wine. I draped my coat over the back of the chair. There were dark circles under his eyes.

"You look tired," I said, resting my chin on my hand.

"Quelques jours compliqués," he said.

"Do you want to tell me about it—the thing you needed to take care of?" I asked. He shrugged. "Is it the play? Or something else?" I asked. He gave me an odd look. "I mean, what with your actress's husband in the hospital," I said, watching him.

"That, yes," he said. He tapped his cigarette in the ashtray, not looking at me. I turned to study the chalkboard menu, but I didn't see the items written in French elementary school cursive; instead, I saw Olivier in a hospital corridor, his arm around the lovely Estelle as she cried on his shoulder and wiped—no, dabbed—her eyes with an embroidered lace handkerchief. I saw him there; I knew he'd been there, with her. There was nothing wrong with it, except that he hadn't told me and I knew. I took a long, slow sip of wine.

"I don't actually know anything about it," I remarked. He gave me a sharp look. "The play," I said. "I mean the play."

"It's in three acts, with three characters, but the same thing happens in each act. Because each act is told from a different character's point of view, they are totally different."

"Like *Rashomon?*"

"Un peu, oui."

"And what happens?"

"A husband and wife spend a weekend in the country with an old friend of hers, a man. During the weekend, the husband finds out that his wife and her old friend had an affair, before she was married. Even though it's been over for a long time, there is still a mysterious connection between the wife and her former lover, and it means something different to all three of them."

"And what does it mean?" I asked, wondering how close to home the play was.

"I can't tell you. It will ruin the surprise!" he exclaimed.

"Ah, so there's a surprise ending," I said.

He smiled and reached out to stroke my fingers. I looked down at his brown hand against my paler one.

"I will be curious to know what you think. You'll come to the opening?" he said.

I didn't answer right away; I was picturing his hand next to Estelle's.

"Yes." I smiled, not quite meeting his eyes. A plate of sautéed mushrooms appeared in front of me, shrunken ears in a fragrant butter and herb sauce.

After dinner, we went back to my place. I loaded a tray with two pale pink cups and saucers decorated with grayish white cranes. I'd read that cranes mated for life. If you ever saw a solitary adult crane, you could be sure it had lost its mate. I poured hot water over loose mint tisane and carried the tray into the living room. We sat on the sofa, and for the first time, I couldn't think of anything to say, probably because all normal conversation was being drowned out in my head by the clamor of all the things I couldn't bring myself to say. I put my feet up on the coffee table. He lit a cigarette.

"Would you like to go away this weekend?" he asked. "It's a holiday weekend, we won't rehearse. There's a place I love that I want to show you," he added.

"Sure," I said, looking up. "Where?"

"Normandy. A friend of mine has a house near Trouville. We could drive out on Friday afternoon."

"I'd like that," I answered. Olivier described the town, the beach nearby where he'd spent summers as a kid. We went to bed a short while later. Despite some awkward, fervent kissing, we didn't make love.

....

Olivier slept on his back, with one arm wrapped around me. I rested my head on his chest, listening to my breath with one ear, his heartbeat with the other. When I was little, I'd listen to my breath, the inhale and exhale, and watch my chest rise and fall. Thinking about it too much made it impossible to do naturally, and I'd panic, fearing I'd have to remember to breathe for the rest of my life, and what if I forgot? Unconscious, reflexive behavior, when observed, became fraught with difficulty.

I tried to breathe normally. It was impossible.

I thought about how hard it is to unlearn something you've been doing wrong all your life. Trying to stand up straight when you've always been a sloucher, for one. My third-grade teacher used to chastise me for not holding my pencil properly. "Look at that ugly callus on your middle finger," she'd said. Up until then, I'd liked my callus. I'd liked touching it, feeling its contours, the self-made bump of it, the indurate surface like orange peel. But after Miss Brendan pointed it out in class, I tried to bite it off, nibbling off bits of toughened skin. It didn't work. I still hold my pencil the same way.

I drummed my fingers on Olivier's chest. He didn't move. I wondered if he was pretending. Sometimes, I pretended to be asleep, mostly so I could find out what people would do around me. It usually just led to tiptoeing. In the rare cases when someone tried to wake me up, I'd have to pretend to wake up. It's always intriguing to watch actors do this on film. The ones who wake up too easily make me suspicious. Of course, the ones who do it well get no love either, because it seems like they're merely waking up. A siren wailed in the distance.

I eased out of bed and tiptoed into the living room. Olivier's pack of Camels sat on the coffee table. I hadn't smoked in years, but I lit one of his cigarettes. It was strong, and it burned my throat in a way I liked. The paper crackled as I inhaled, and the smoke hung in the room like a blue ghost. Smoking and sitting naked on the sofa made me feel like someone else.

Something was wrong. I didn't know what it was, but I couldn't shake it. Something about the translation, or something Olivier had said. Or something he hadn't said. He seemed a little bit far away, out of reach. The image of him at the hospital with Estelle flashed through my head again, but maybe I was being paranoid. I watched part of TF1's evening newscast on the computer, freezing the frame on the minister and Estelle leaving the hospital. She ducked her head and held up her hand. Hiding, not waving. There was no sign of Olivier, but then, there wouldn't be.

It was four a.m. and I was thinking too much. I took a sleeping pill and slid back into bed. Olivier mumbled something in his sleep. I tucked a pillow under my head and lay on my back, waiting for the narcotic, floaty feeling to kick in.

I pictured the drive home in Los Angeles. As I wound down the sinuous, moonlit road, a host of white moths shook themselves free from the trees and flew at the headlights. It was like being in a snow flurry.

I wound down the road again and dreamed about them. They were the thousand moths of memory, and each moth had the face of a Victorian angel, a pink-cheeked holiday caroler with Cupid's bow lips curved in an "O" of song. As they approached the windshield, their wings fluttered and released random memories. I saw images and heard bits of conversation and songs, as if a radio on scan were playing snippets of my childhood. It grew louder and louder, until the noise became a white, crashing static, and I fell asleep.

24

The Etruscans: For instance, the verb 'is.'
Marilyn: I didn't know 'is' was a verb.
The Etruscans: What did you think it was?
Marilyn: A light for the other verbs.
—ANNE CARSON, "Detail from
the Tomb of the Diver (Paestum 500–453 BC)"

*I*n the morning, Olivier whispered something in my ear and left. I lolled in bed, fuzzy from the sleeping pill and slightly headachy. Clara called to cancel our lunch: she'd sprained her ankle but told me not to worry, her mother was on her way in from Versailles and would take care of her. That left me practically all day to work on the translation before tea at Antoine and Victorine's.

Every time I thought about Olivier, a vague, worried sensation fluttered its wings and settled in my stomach, so I got to work on the translation in order to distract myself. I looked again at the chapter, wondering if I'd absorbed anything—like osmosis—from my amateurish foray into translation theory.

I skimmed through the pages: mostly plot-heavy, mostly about the narrator's attempts to get information about Eve from her accountant, who wouldn't talk. Well, duh.

Then he spent six pages rabbiting on about being sucked into a whirlpool of despair. Yeah, yeah, yeah; I was familiar with the whirlpool.
Was despair always this boring, or was it the way it was written? In des-
peration, the narrator called the friend he'd met Eve through, a writer
of detective novels. The friend sent him to a private detective near the
Gare du Nord.

I expected André Verbier to look like a hardened cop, but he was as
memorable as a tollbooth operator: dull gray skin and mouse-brown
hair in a shapeless suit. When he spoke, he revealed a row of jagged,
stained teeth, putting me in mind of a rodent.

He had no reaction to my story, other than to take notes.

"Do you handle cases like this often?" I asked. I looked at the
dusty blinds and the vinyl wallpaper, a pattern of blue and green bub-
bles outlined in silver foil. There was a brown water stain shaped like
India above the window.

"I specialize in finding women," he said with an inward smile. "I
am an expert."

"What makes you so successful?"

"I listen. People are always revealing information, whether they
know it or not," he said. I could tell he was waiting for me to ask him
what I'd revealed about myself. I refrained from doing so. He contin-
ued, "And then, I have been in the business for seventeen years, locat-
ing runaway teenagers, adulterous wives, suicidal girlfriends . . ."

"Why do women leave?" I asked. He looked at me with eyes the
color of shit.

"Because they are unhappy," he said.

It felt like a rebuke. Verbier made me feel small. It was odious to
be here, this office, the dingy neighborhood, his knowing air. I felt an
intense self-loathing, that I'd been reduced to this, hiring a detective
out of a trashy novel . . .

"Trashy novel" wasn't right. Too colloquial, and it didn't do *"roman de gare"* justice, considering there was a possible play on words: "train station novel," in this case, could refer to the genre as well as the location. Pulp novel? Dime-store novel?

"I will call you when I have news," Verbier said. When I shook it, his hand felt dry and firm, the opposite of how I'd thought it would.

I walked around the dirty neighborhood, riddled with garish cafés and storefronts selling prosthetic limbs. The thought of going back to the flat I still shared with Daphne was monstrous, and I was a monster for going home to her.

But Daphne was no fool. She'd probably sensed something. Perhaps she was as unhappy with me as I was with her, though I didn't care. My life had shrunk, reduced to the thought of seeing Eve again, if only once more.

During the two weeks I waited to hear from Verbier, I was cruel to Daphne. Perhaps the worst cruelty was that I did it without thinking. I was impervious to her manipulations. Though they had no effect, she tried every ploy in the book: being affectionate, being cold, attempting to make me jealous, ignoring me, watching me like a hawk. I came home to candlelit tables, elaborate meals, Daphne in various stages of undress. Or it was crying fits and angry scenes. After one final, semi-rehearsed speech, she announced her return to her apartment near the Jardin des Plantes and indicated that I should not contact her unless I came on bent, and preferably bloodied, knees.

I worked longer hours. Sometimes I stopped at a café near the place de Clichy for a drink. I was haunted not by the specter of my empty flat but rather by the darkened windows of Eve's apartment.

Verbier sent me a typed report peppered with explanatory notes.

"After many hours of research and a few well-placed payments (itemized in addendum A) I have ascertained that Eve Ribot, née Solange Ramzy, is living in Monte Carlo, at 39, avenue des Tilleuls,

in an apartment owned by Ericsson Holdings, Ltd. Eric Beaufort de Blois is CEO and majority owner of Ericsson Holdings, Ltd.

"Beaufort and his third wife, Bettina Beaufort de Blois, née Astiani, maintain separate residences. Madame Beaufort resides primarily in Saint-Jean-de-Luz. Beaufort and Madame Ribot are often seen together in public, even at the Red Cross Ball, which indicates their relationship is an open and accepted secret in Monte Carlo society . . ."

I threw the report aside. Just as I'd suspected, she was Beaufort's mistress. I'd guessed as much when I'd seen them together at Longchamp. I should've known, but I didn't want to know . . .

This was a letdown. I'd been hoping for something more interesting than another run-of-the-mill boy-meets-kept-girl story.

"Solange Ramzy was born in Alexandria in 1952, the daughter of Lisette Bouret, a French music teacher, and Ashraf Ramzy, a professor of Egyptian archaeology. The latter died of a heart attack when Solange was twelve. Her mother remarried a local jeweler, a widower with two adult daughters.

"At sixteen, Solange ran away to Cairo with a musician. After a month together, the musician left her for the daughter of a wealthy cigarette importer. Solange suffered through months of financial hardship, occasionally receiving handouts from her mother. She changed her name to Eve when she got a job as a singer at Le Lido, a seedy nightclub on the Pyramid road catering to Russian businessmen. She sang Edith Piaf and Nina Simone songs between belly dancer sets.

"Le Lido was known for its prostitutes, who encouraged clients to buy expensive bottles of watered-down whiskey. It is not known whether Eve exercised this trade.

"After two years in Cairo, Eve purchased a boat passage to France, but her plans were delayed when her mother and stepfather died in a

car crash on the Corniche. She returned to Alexandria for the funeral but chose to avoid a legal battle over the financial succession with her stepfather's children. Taking her mother's jewelry and fur coats, she boarded a cargo ship to Nice. [Note: charges for theft of jewelry and other personal belongings of Madame Lisette El-Nouri were filed and subsequently dropped.]

"Her whereabouts and activities between the time she arrived in Nice and the time she resurfaced in Paris, eight months later, are not known.

"Once in Paris, Eve lodged with a distant cousin of her mother's, Georgette Leclerc, a retired haute couture seamstress. She found employment as a house model at Nina Ricci and was able to rent maid's quarters near the Parc Monceau. She was now twenty. She studied dramatic arts at a private theater school.

"There were no significant romantic involvements until she met Fabien Ribot, a self-made nightclub owner. Twenty-three years her senior, he married Eve and then hired her to run L'Apparence, a private club on the rue Godot de Mauroy. Under her management, the former topless cabaret became a fashionable destination, attracting media figures and the international jet set. This is where Eve met Eric Beaufort de Blois, who was then married to his first wife, Vrouwtje Spoontje, a Dutch socialite.

"Financial mismanagement and, quite possibly, rumored drug use forced Ribot to sell his only successful asset, L'Apparence, to a food conglomerate, which transformed the nightclub into the flagship of its steak and fries chain. [Note: The property now houses an Irish bar and an adult video store.]

"In debt again two years later, Ribot took on two business partners, the Carvalho twins, brothers from Casamance. In August 1979, Ribot was stabbed in an alley off the avenue Foch. The police report states that his body was found by municipal street cleaners. The prevailing *theory was of a revenge killing, as he was found with 1700 francs in his wallet and two grams of cocaine. At the time, Eve Ribot was in the country with her cousin, Madame Leclerc. The murder remains unsolved.*

"Eve Ribot inherited an apartment in the Seventeenth Arrondissement, 18, rue Berzélius, which she still owns, and a small farmhouse in the Tarn. The Carvalho brothers took possession of Ribot's remaining nightclubs, Le Jazz Hot and Crazy Filles.

"Returning to fashion, Eve Ribot was hired to manage the Givenchy haute couture salon. Her acquaintance with Eric Beaufort de Blois was renewed when he married his second wife, Paula Ottinello, a patron of the fashion house. When Paula left him for a gigolo named Lars Braunschweig [Note: a pseudonym], Beaufort began divorce proceedings. During that time, he and Eve Ribot were frequently seen together.

"But Eve Ribot refused to marry Beaufort. He broke off the relationship and married his current wife. The marriage soured: it was rumored Beaufort de Blois found his wife in bed with her secretary, Madeleine Marchmont . . ."

Eve's life read like an Aaron Spelling miniseries written by Sidney Sheldon. The bio raised more questions than it answered: why did Eve leave Egypt? Did she ever work as a hooker? What was she doing during those eight months? Was she happy with Ribot? Why didn't she marry Beaufort?

I put down Verbier's report and poured another whiskey. I wanted to fly to Monte Carlo and confront her. But seeing her with Beaufort again was unthinkable. She'd chosen him over me.

I looked at the report again. I still didn't know why she'd left me, or if she'd felt anything for me. Did she feel obligated to Beaufort? Why?

What if he was dying? Maybe he had cancer, a congenital heart condi-
tion, or an inoperable tumor. These agreeable thoughts drifted through
my head, a narcotic of morbid hope. But as appealing as the notion
was, I couldn't assume she'd return to me after his death.

There was so much she hadn't told me: about her marriage, for one,
and to Ribot, a notorious mafioso. I remembered the murder, the news-
paper headlines. At the time, I'd been a research assistant, working on
my dissertation. Perhaps I'd been to L'Apparence, Ribot's nightclub.
I'd certainly heard of it, though at the time, there had been so many
clubs with names that began with "A": L'Atmosphère, L'Apocalypse
. . . even L'Apoplexie. How strange to think our paths might have
crossed all those years ago.

I drank whiskey after whiskey, wondering how long it would take
to pass out. Come, forgetfulness, unconsciousness, oblivion: I invite
you! I drank medicinally, counting the minutes, eager to get to where
nothing mattered. . .

I felt a small quiver of distaste. I knew what he was talking about,
which explained my reaction. I wanted to distance myself from his suffering. And yet, he had a right to feel miserable, I reminded myself: the
woman he loved had left him. If he wanted to get stinking drunk, he had
a right.

Maybe my distaste was also about how seductive suffering is, how
romantic pain is, how it seems to be an end in and of itself: self-enclosed,
exquisite, stuck. How stuck in it I could be. Had been.

I forced myself back to the desk. The narrator indulged in several
days of uninterrupted drinking, which took up seven pages of boring,
paranoid, intoxicated rants mixed in with genuine moments of despair.
I'd just about exhausted Mr. Roget's words for alcoholic stupor ("haze,"
"coma," "numbness," "daze," "unconsciousness," "glaze," "befuddle-
ment," "trance"), when Daphne reappeared.

The banging continued. I shouted obscenities at the door, but my un-
welcome visitor didn't stop pushing the bell. The shrill sound drove a
spike into my ears.

It was Daphne. She looked like a Madonna in blue. She gasped
when she saw me.

"There, you've seen me!" I roared. "Satisfied? Now get out!"

She shoved past me and marched inside, stopping at the array of
empty bottles, dirty plates, and glasses. A rank fog of cigarette smoke
hovered at eye level. She bent down to pick up a plate. I grabbed her
wrist.

"Get out! I don't want you here!" I shouted. She wrenched her
arm free.

"Look at yourself! You monster! You haven't shaved in days! You
stink of alcohol! Enough! It must stop!" she screamed, her face nearly
purple with rage.

She found a pair of rubber gloves in the kitchen and began clean-
ing. She washed dishes and glasses, emptied ashtrays, aired the rooms,
and made the bed with clean sheets. She ordered me into the bathroom
to wash and shave while she vacuumed. Cowed by her energy as much
as her anger, I went inside and filled the sink with water.

My hands trembled, and I cut myself twice before I threw the razor
aside. I sat on the edge of the tub and wept. Daphne pushed the door
open. "I'm going to run a bath," she said, as if to a child. "I'll help
you shave and wash your hair." I clutched her hand.

"I don't deserve you," I said. A pink flush crept up her neck. She'd
never leave me again.

"It's true, you don't deserve me. But you don't have me either,"
she said.

I added that last line. My fingers went on typing. Daphne didn't say it
in the original. All she said was *"C'est vrai, tu ne me mérites pas."* It was

an improvisation, though not a big stretch. In fact, it fit nicely with her new take-charge attitude.

I reread the words on the screen. If you added something that was in the spirit of the original, something that you felt expressed the original—even if it wasn't *in* the original—was it still translating? Or had it tipped over into writing, and by extension, in this case, taking liberties?

I stared at the sentence, reading it over and over until it stopped making sense, though I couldn't tell if it didn't make sense because it didn't make sense or because, if you stare at anything long enough, it stops making sense.

I pressed Delete and watched the letters disappear.

Then I pressed Undo Delete. Ctrl Z. Ctrl Y. Control zee. Control why.

What would Bernard think? What would the author think? I wondered if they'd even catch it. I wanted to leave it in to see if they noticed.

Daphne picked out a suit and tie, and helped me dress.

"There," she said. "You're presentable." She smoothed the lapels of my jacket.

"Jean-Marc," she said. "Your aunt called me when you didn't answer your phone. Your mother is very ill. She's dying."

Phooey! Just when he's scraping the bottom of the barrel, another crisis thwacks him upside the head. It was so predictable. It couldn't get worse.

I was wrong. I slogged through the next few pages. On the train to see his mother, Daphne kept throwing up and confessed she was pregnant. He proposed, his mother approved and promptly croaked, the young couple moved to Neuilly, and he became the editor of an aerospace industry trade magazine.

A year later, after the birth of our son, Tristan, we drove to Pau to visit my mother's grave. We stopped at a country inn on our way back. While Daphne and Tristan napped, I took a walk in the woods and found a clearing, a remote place I would never return to.

I removed Verbier's worn report from my pocket and set it on fire with a lighter Daphne had given me. I waited until there was nothing left but ashes.

It was twilight when I got back.

The chapter ended. That was it. I even looked in the envelope, to see if I'd missed a page, but that was it. A small sound caught in my throat, almost like panic, as I wondered if this was the end of the novel. If it was, I didn't like it. Maybe that's how real life unfolds, maybe events are swift, decisive, coincidental, pat, even slightly grotesque, but this reeked of the best worst ending, something hatched like a scheme, not an egg, and I didn't buy it.

Sure, sometimes you don't get closure. Sometimes people leave and don't say good-bye, and that's what Eve did. Sometimes there are no explanations. There was nothing inherently wrong with the narrator marrying Daphne, except he didn't love her. Then again, she'd put up with him and taken care of him when he was down—if she wanted him, she deserved him. But it happened too quickly, and he seemed numb at the end, even as he burned the report. Or maybe that was the point?

But none of this was my problem. My job was translating, not editing. I went back over my work, double-checking word choices, spell-checking, and making sure it read well. I hit Save and went for a stroll around the neighborhood.

On my way back up the street, I passed a new bookstore, with smart navy blue awnings. One window displayed a photo of Rémi Le Jaa and a reprint from a *Le Monde* article from 1989 titled "Le Phénomène Le Jaa." In the photo, he had straight black hair and wore little round glasses.

He looked almost Asian, except for the large, unmistakably Gallic nose. When I went inside, the harried bookseller told me that he'd sold his last remaining copy of *La Vie de bateau,* and that they'd also sold out his other books in anticipation of his impending new release.

I glanced at the fall books table, thumbing through new novels and wondering if my author was among them. No, I remembered now, Laveau had said he wrote on politics and sociology. I went over to a table marked *Nouveautés en actualité internationale,* but my cell phone rang. I went outside to answer it, but it was someone trying to sell me double-glazed windows. I walked home and changed into black pants and a smart red jacket for my afternoon tea.

At a neighborhood *fleuriste,* I bought a dozen *anémones* and carried the bouquet aloft as I followed Antoine's directions to their street behind the *butte.* As in my quartier, the buildings were all late-nineteenth-century *pierre de taille,* biscuit-colored Parisian limestone, but with more elaborate wrought iron and variations in the stone vermiculation. Some even had leaded glass windows and gold mosaics.

Antoine opened the door wearing a tweed jacket and a pink, open-necked shirt. He ushered me into a red and beige *salon* so jam-packed it seemed to sag inward under the weight of its contents. The walls were lined with floor-to-ceiling bookshelves, and every surface was loaded with more books, plus magazines, DVDs, scraps of paper, pens, objets d'art, even a banana peel, neatly folded, like a pair of spotted gloves, on the coffee table. A careless arrangement of red Chinese lantern flowers spilled over a vase on the marble mantel, obscuring the ornate mirror behind it.

"Merci," he said when I handed him the bouquet. He plunked it down on stack of dry cleaning on the piano. "Victorine forgot you were coming and went to the patisserie for something sweet," he added.

"She didn't have to go to the trouble," I said.

"Yes, she did. I have a terrible sweet tooth. *Asseyez-vous.*" He removed a stack of magazines and an umbrella from a chair and pointed to it. "Such a difficult week. We deserve a reward, no?" he asked. "For you, also?"

I nodded. "A friend of mine was forced into retirement, another friend sprained her ankle, and——" I stopped myself before I said anything about Olivier.

"And?" Antoine prodded.

"I couldn't sleep. Unidentified anxiety, probably. And you?" I asked.

"*On vieillit.* Every day I am reminded how fragile we are." He shrugged. The front door opened and slammed shut. *"Ah, voilà ma femme,"* he said and left the room.

When he didn't come back right away, I walked around a carved trunk to admire an old still life: an artful arrangement of a dead pheasant, cloudy-skinned grapes, translucent berries, walnut shells, a half-eaten loaf of bread, cheese, and a bottle of wine. Peering closer, I noticed three insects crawling over the food. The iridescent carapace of a scorpion was rendered in a metallic blue-violet; the sharp pincers on an earwig were done with a tiny brush. A malevolent, furry, red spider raised one delicate leg over a crumbling wedge of blue cheese.

"Do you like it?" Antoine asked, pushing a tea trolley into the *salon.*

"It's amazing. And repulsive. I'm not sure I could eat anything after looking at it," I said, brushing imaginary bugs from my arms. He chuckled.

"Victorine refused to have it in the dining room for that very reason. It's Italian, *ottocento,*" he said, waving at it. "Unsigned. I bought it at an auction house in Turin, years ago, even though it was an extravagance. So rare to find something that so closely echoes one's worldview, no?"

At a loss for words—his worldview was about decay? insects and rotting food?—I merely nodded. Victorine bustled in, her cheeks splotched red above a black turtleneck. She shook my hand and gave me a thin-lipped smile.

"Sit, sit, please. What's this?" she asked, pointing to my bouquet. *"Ah, c'est joli!"* she said, sounding as if she meant the opposite. She whisked the vase off the mantel and disappeared, leaving a trail of red blooms on the Persian carpet. She came back and plunked the anemones in the vase. "Do you take your Earl Grey with milk or *citron?*" Not listening for an answer, she turned to Antoine. *"Bon.* They didn't have a chocolate cake for you, *mon vieux,* so I got your *étouffe-chrétien,"* she said. I gave an involuntary laugh at the phrase, which literally meant a food that suffocated Christians but was often used for rich or dense cakes.

"Je suis épuisée!" She grimaced, falling into an armchair with theatrical exhaustion. "Why haven't you told me how you take your tea?" she demanded.

"Citron, s'il vous plaît," I answered. A white cat crawled out from underneath a tasseled ottoman, glanced around, and skulked away. Neither of them seemed to notice.

"An old friend of ours gave us a scare," she said conversationally. "At first, he thought it was a *crise de foie,* but then it turned out to be more serious. We were all at the hospital earlier this week. But surely Olivier told you?" she asked, slanting me a sideways look as she handed me a cup of milky tea.

I felt like the wedge of blue cheese. I glanced at Antoine, but he was cleaning his pipe. "Was it really a minor heart attack?" I asked, neatly sidestepping her question.

"The poor man!" she exclaimed, nodding. "Of course, Estelle has been a wreck. Thank goodness Olivier was there. She's always been able to lean on him." She crossed her legs and gave me a smile so insincere you could sharpen a knife on it. A crushed red lantern flower clung to her heel.

"Enfin, Victorine," Antoine said mildly. She tossed her head and cut into a raspberry cream cake. A dark red fruit coulis oozed out. I'd never been to such a dangerous tea: spiders and scorpions and bloody cake, oh my. Antoine banged his pipe against the mantel.

"*J'ai oublié les citrons*. Didn't you say lemon?" She gave my cup an angry look.

"Don't pay too much attention," Antoine murmured when she left the room. He patted my hand awkwardly, the way a man who doesn't like animals pats a friend's dog.

"What do you mean?" I asked, now on my guard with both of them.

"She's bored," he explained, looking guilty. When she came back with a plate of sliced lemons, he steered the conversation toward more anodyne subjects, and the afternoon took on a milder tenor. Without talking directly about the translation, I got them started on my new favorite topic: the difference between French and English.

"The pun, for instance, is respected in French. It is also more complicated; in English, it's a base form of wordplay. It is usually greeted with groans," Antoine said. "It explains why my American friends do not appreciate my sense of humor," he quipped.

"The French adore a kind of sculpted wordplay that Americans find baffling, as if they're being asked to admire an intricate tool which has no practical, modern use, like a hook for closing buttons on spats. But then the French place an aesthetic value on frivolity, finding art in something charming and meaningless and ephemeral, whereas Americans tend to find it trivial," I said, thinking about what Clara had said.

"'*Allons! Finissons-en, Charles attend!*'" Antoine said, quoting Louis XVIII's famous *calembour*, uttered on his deathbed about his successor, in which "Charles is waiting" was a homonym for "charlatan." He gave a crafty little smile and sucked his pipe. Victorine gave him a tired, indulgent look: she'd heard it too many times before.

"You see? We don't have *calembours* and *contrepétries*," I pointed out. "Even trying to explain them in English is hard: they're like sentence-long puns and complex, constructed spoonerisms," I said.

"*Ah, oui, le révérend Spooner,*" Victorine said, waving the cake knife in my direction. Dark red drops of coulis spattered the carpet.

"French has these complicated, contorted phrases that sound over-done and arch in English. And they all seem to be about very subtle, French sorts of situations," I said.

"What is a French situation?" Antoine asked, amused.

"My father likes the phrase *'astuce vaseuse dans un esprit marécageux.'* That's an elegant, if old-fashioned, way of describing a far-fetched, pseudo-clever, overly complicated allusion or observation. We just don't do that often enough in English to have a description for it." I thought for a moment. "We do have 'the elegant variation,' but we use it to de-scribe overwrought writing, specifically unnecessary synonyms."

"No one says *'astuce vaseuse'* anymore," Victorine pointed out.

"I know, but the idea seems more French to me, where turns of phrase and wit—*l'esprit*—count for something. In English, we'd just roll our eyes."

"Name another one," Antoine demanded.

" '*Passer pour un idiot aux yeux d'un imbécile est une volupté de fin gour-met,*' " I said. "That's Courteline, and we don't have this in English ei-ther. The notion that appearing—or pretending—to be an idiot in the eyes of an imbecile is some kind of refined pleasure? No, no, no," I said, shaking my head. "Maybe in England, but not in America. First off, no one in America thinks passing for an idiot is *ever* a pleasure—"

"But that's because you're so *premier degré,*" Victorine said. "Ev-erything means what it means. If you are precise, you're precise, if you're vague, you're vague. But we can be vague in such precise ways, and precise in vague ones. We like layers of meaning, subtlety, and contradiction."

"Sure. All the better to be malicious," I said. "Especially if it takes the person you're talking to a while to register any possible hidden or double meanings."

"You make us sound so cruel," she observed.

If the *chaussure* fits, I thought. "You have a more comfortable rela-tionship with cruelty, perhaps. After all, in French, to be *malicieux* can have a good connotation, like someone who has a delightfully pointed sense of humor: *malicieux et délicieux*," I said.

"But you have this as well—the wicked sense of humor," Antoine remarked.

"That's true," I admitted. "I hadn't thought of that." Victorine poked a finger in the teapot and took it into the kitchen. I put my plate back on the trolley. Antoine's pipe smoke made my head ache right between the eyebrows.

"We are not so different *à la base*," Antoine mused. "It is more a question of style, of the things we privilege more than you, and vice versa."

"Like?" I asked.

"You value approval more than we do. We privilege pride, this idea of 'saving face,' so important to the Japanese as well. You are more open, we are more reserved. We like riddles, you like answers. We are more interested in the game than the outcome," he said. The phone rang in another room.

"The game," I repeated, unsure what he meant.

"The game of social interaction," he clarified. "The discovery, layer by layer, of people. The unfolding of meaning. This is something we appreciate. It seems to me—but I am speaking in broad strokes and there are always exceptions—however, it seems to me Americans want to know who and what everything is, they want to fix it so it will stay put and they can move accordingly. Look at your politics," he said. "As de Gaulle said—and I am not usually one for quoting him—your country excels at attempting to impose simplistic solutions onto complex problems. But nothing is simple or fixed in life. People are surprising: vain, careless, flawed, contradictory, often blind, and full of foibles. This is diverting, confusing, maddening, and, of course, touching." He leaned back in his chair, pipe clamped between his teeth.

"I like that," I said, realizing I meant I liked him. A small clock on the side table chimed five with delicate pings.

Victorine came back in the room. "It is impossible to get off the phone with my sister," she said.

I stood up. "I should leave. Thank you for having me."

No sooner had I stepped outside into the brisk sun than the worried feeling came back to me. I walked up the street, replaying the earlier part of the afternoon in my head. I had to ask Olivier about Estelle. There was nothing wrong with him spending time with Estelle, but why hadn't he told me? There was something there that was confusing, even troubling.

They were *faux amis*: *"Confus"* meant embarrassed, uncomfortable. *"Troublant"* meant unclear, murky, vague. They meant different things in both languages, but right now, all four words worked.

25

*Le point commun entre tous les hommes
que j'ai aimés? Moi!**
—JEANNE MOREAU

I didn't ask Olivier about Estelle. The more I thought about it, the
more I thought I was being paranoid, and I wanted to protect him
from my paranoia. Or I wanted to protect myself by not revealing it.

He came over when I was watching the news. A journalist for a right-
wing newspaper defended his position, outlined in a column that morning, that Romain Chesnier should resign from his post as minister, given
his health problems. Olivier slouched down on the sofa next to me and
blew air out of his lips.

"How's he really doing?" I asked, pointing to the screen.

"Fine. Estelle says it's entirely political, all this talk about his health.
That's more stressful than his heart," he said. *"Quoi?"* he asked, looking at me.

"Nothing," I said. He grasped my arm and shook it gently.

"Il y a quelque chose," he said, insisting something was up. It was a
perfect opening, and I hesitated. The anxious creature in my stomach

---

*What all the men I've loved have in common? Me!

roused itself. I opened my mouth, then shut it. I couldn't do it. I didn't want to risk hearing something I might not like.

"I'm wondering how it's affecting your play," I said instead.

"It's distracting her, but she's a professional. Shall I make us some tea?"

....

On Friday, I tried to distract myself by cleaning the apartment and packing, but it was useless. Instead of happy excitement, I felt apprehension. I called Althea.

"Packed your *baise en ville*?" she cracked.

"I hate that expression," I said. "Only the French would call a weekend bag a 'fuck in town.' Besides, I'm going to the country." I filled her in on my worries and Victorine's comments.

"You're being a morose, broody cow," she said.

"Thanks. That's encouraging," I said. "I think you missed your calling. Crisis counselor. ICU nurse. No, kindergarten teacher. People are so soft on kids these days."

"Sweetie, stop being a pill. Can you tuck that part of you away? It's not fun to be with, either for you or for him. If there's something he needs to explain, let him."

I could always count on Althea to be bracing. I reread my translation, grimacing again as I got to the ending. I printed it out, scribbled a note, explaining my issues ("too quick, not believable, I don't know how he's feeling"), and stuck it to the last page. *Tant pis* if it pissed off Bernard or the author. I walked it over to Editions Laveau, hoping the exercise would take my mind off things. On my way down the rue des Archives, my phone rang. It was Bunny, calling from Italy.

"H-e-e-e-ey! I'm in the hills above Rapallo with Gigi and Matthew. The weather is gorgeous, and I'm sipping this foo-foo drink they make with lemons and almond liqueur. You'd like it," he said. I was relieved to hear how happy he sounded.

"We've got sun here, but it's only thirteen degrees," I said.

"I'm wearing shorts, sunglasses, and a Hawaiian shirt. Did I mention the sunsets are magnificent here?" He slurped loudly.

"You are a cruel, cruel man," I said.

"One of my better qualities. How are you?"

"Okay," I said. "When are you back?"

"Do I sound like I wanna leave? I'll talk to you later. Be good," he said and hung up. I trudged up the hill, picturing Bunny with a cocktail on a sunny terrace. He was probably asking the locals what the longest palindrome was in Italian. Or humming arias from obscure operas to waitresses half his age.

I remembered something he'd said a long time ago, when I'd known him only a couple of months. We'd been discussing my travel plans in a café in a boat on the Seine.

"Never go to Italy," he'd intoned in his wise and dolorous sage voice.

"But it's such a beautiful country!" I'd exclaimed.

"Never go to Italy," he'd repeated.

"Why, Bunny, why?" I'd asked, sensing a punch line, and happy to set him up.

"Because you'll never want to leave," he'd replied.

....

At Editions Laveau, Bernard and an elderly gentleman in a homburg and a double-breasted coat were deep in a discussion of medieval poetry. With a nod from Bernard, I walked past them and went into his office to wait for him. It was the first time I'd been in there alone, and I studied his bookshelves and the art on the walls, particularly a framed piece of parchment paper, written in elaborate brown calligraphy with oddly shaped accents. I was trying to decipher it when he came in.

"*C'est beau, n'est ce pas?*" he asked. "It is Latin, a legal document from the thirteenth century, something to do with property deeds, very boring. I found it at my favorite *antiquaire* in Blois." He measured out coffee and turned on the machine.

"What are all the accents?" I asked.

"Abbreviations," he said, beaming, as if the dear little things were precocious grandchildren. "Each one is a word."

"How curious," I said. He handed me a cup, passed me the sugar bowl, and calmly plucked a cube himself. There was a fat little silence as we drank our coffees.

"*Puis-je vous poser une question?*" I asked. "Why did you hire me? Is there something I should know?" I didn't know where the questions came from; they just tumbled out, and then it was too late to take them back.

"*Mais pourquoi vous me demandez ça?*" he asked, with a suspicious look.

"I'm not a professional translator—" I began. Bernard made an impatient, spluttering sound. "Let me finish. I'm not a professional translator. I know nothing about translation theory. Until this week, I didn't even know there were theories. I speak both languages well enough to know I'm doing a decent job, but I'm betting there are other people who could do better. Maybe they cost more, but I'm not so sure."

He didn't say anything. "There's also the matter of the secrecy, this chapter-by-chapter thing," I continued, putting my cup down. "If I knew the whole story, I'd have a better, global sense of it. But it started as erotica, now it's a doomed love story—who knows, it could turn into a mystery or tragedy or even science fiction—" I said.

Bernard exhaled a scornful gust of air.

"Or revert back to erotica," I said, persevering. "Not knowing is feeling my way through the dark. There are issues of tone to consider, shifts in vocabulary, but I don't know what it's laying the groundwork for, because *I don't know what happens*. That second chapter read like an ending! Is it?"

He shook his head in a noncommittal fashion, but before he could speak, I added, "Don't get me wrong, I like the work. I don't want to give it up. But I could do it better if I knew more. That's all." I sat back, anxious to hear his response.

Bernard turned his silver letter opener over in his hands. "You're right, of course," he began, giving me a sly look. I wondered if one of Sun Tzu's strategies was to agree with your opponent. "But as I have already explained, this is an unusual project, subject to constraints that may well impede its progress. But you have kept up, the author is satisfied, and as long as the arrangement suits all parties, it shall continue," he said. Pleased with himself, he put the letter opener down.

"That's it?" I asked. He tilted his head in assent. "At least can you tell me how it ends?" I asked, making a last attempt. He splayed his hands and bounced his fingertips against one another, pursing his lips.

"*Alors, là. Je ne sais pas,*" he said.

I gaped at him. He looked back, poker-faced over steepled fingers.

"What do you mean, you don't know?" I asked, queasy. Bernard toyed with his letter opener again. I sensed he was making a decision, though not about how much to tell me: about how much to leave out.

"*Enfin.* I don't know precisely. He's still writing it," he admitted.

"I'm translating a first draft?" I asked, outraged. I wasn't a professional translator, but I was a copywriter, and I knew it was ridiculous to translate a first draft.

"It's not a first draft, *voyons.* He's been working on it *depuis une éternité.* I've read it in its entirety. It is merely the last chapter that isn't finished, he is still refining it. Right now, there are four different endings. You've finished the first one. I don't know which one he will use. Perhaps he will use all four. You will understand when you read them." A faint smile hovered around his lips. It sounded good. But it felt like bullshit.

"A novel can't have four good endings," I snapped. He raised his eyebrows. "Okay," I said, waving my hands in the air, "maybe a post-modern novelist could get away with it, but your guy ain't that guy. There's nothing pomo about him. This thing needs one right ending, the thing that the story has been leading up to."

"You make rather grand pronouncements for someone who hasn't read the entire book. That is a limited way of thinking about stories. Perhaps there are four good endings to every novel! Perhaps the author merely chooses? Don't forget," he added, *"la bêtise consiste à vouloir conclure."* Stupidity consists of wanting to conclude. His face was impassive, his voice silky, but I could hear the worn groove in the vinyl, the snap and hiss of a line uttered a few too many times. Just because he could cite Flaubert's famous line didn't mean he wasn't dodging me.

I fidgeted, cracking my thumbs, noticing the deep lines down his cheeks and across his forehead. His whole demeanor seemed like a false front, a trick wall. If I was clever or stealthy enough, I might find a hollow catch that would make a door swing open, but I had to think fast. Any second, the cowbell would peal, or the phone would ring, and the moment would be lost.

"I'm not going to sit here and discuss theories of novel endings. That's just arguing for the sake of arguing," I said, but it was a feeble attempt.

He separated his hands and said *"ah,"* giving the "h" a glottal stop so sharp it backfired like a car. Combined with the amused look on his face, it meant "That's the way the cookie crumbles, cookie."

I tried another tack. "It's disappointing. I'd thought of it as a real novel, and now it sounds like a toy the writer tinkers with from time to time."

Bad move. Bernard drew himself up and took a haughty tone.

"Pourquoi vous dites ça? You insisted you were happy with our arrangement. You are not consistent, *mademoiselle,"* he chided. Hobgoblins, my mind raced, something about hobgoblins, consistency, little minds, but I couldn't think of the quotation fast enough to parry. It would probably come to me as soon as I left, *l'esprit de l'escalier* on the

sidewalk. "I must warn you, it is possible this work may not get published," he added, lobbing a new bombshell.

"Ever?" I asked.

"*Mademoiselle*, my client is a prolific writer—"

"You mean he's actually managed to finish *other* books?" I asked, sarcastic. Bernard was no longer amused. He clipped my check to an envelope.

"As you may have noticed, this is a personal work, drawing on his life and memories. It's not timely, so he's not as concerned with getting it out as he was with his latest—" Bernard stopped.

"His latest?" I prompted, but he'd caught himself.

"*Œuvre,*" he said. "Here is the next chapter, or second ending, if you will."

"*D'accord,*" I muttered and took the envelope.

"*Ne le prenez pas si mal,*" he said. But I was taking it badly, despite his warmer tone. In fact, I was peeved.

The wind delivered a crisp slap to my face as I stepped outside. At Saint-Germain, I turned left, walking past revamped cafés, with neon signs and techno music, past storefronts riotous with fall colors, even past Ben & Jerry's and the promise of Chubby Hubby. I didn't stop until I got to La Hune, the intellectual, smarty-pants bookstore wedged between the Café de Flore and Les Deux Magots.

Yeah, I wasn't supposed to know who the author was, but all the rules had changed. Besides, I was curious and I felt prescient, gut feelings on caffeine. For some strange reason that had nothing to do with reason, I thought I might be able to identify him through his style. After all, I knew about idiolects, didn't I?

I knew my writer was male, a famous intellectual, and I'd gotten the sense from Bernard that he'd published recently. I also suspected that he was not Rémi Le Jaa. I wondered whether Bernard was deliberately misleading Olivier, or whether that was just Olivier's fertile imagination.

To be sure, I went to fiction and skimmed the first few pages of Le

Jaa's *La Vie de bateau*. His style was spartan, the language elegant and minimalist, full of words I didn't know. No way was he Monsieur X. This was going to be easier than I thought.

I parked myself in front of Recent Arrivals and contemplated genres. I ruled out fiction. My author didn't know how to structure a novel, and apparently, he didn't know how to end one either. I sensed he was better at writing about real events, or maybe essays or analyses. And I remembered again: when I'd first met him, Bernard had said the author wrote about politics and sociology.

My eyes swept over the nonfiction table, a four-foot-wide, eight-foot-long ocean of titles. There was only one possible course of action: pick up each book written by a man, read the back cover, study any photographs, read the first page, and see if the style sounded familiar.

I tied my coat arms around my waist and began with a book on Mitterrand's political policy. I read the back cover: no author photo. I read the first page. No spark of recognition. Next were books on Sarkozy, Chirac, Dominique de Villepin, Jospin, Ségolène Royal, and half a dozen other French politicians. Nothing.

I moved to international politics: the "special relationship" between the United States and Britain, the relationship between France and America, the role of France in the twenty-first century, the European Union, the impact of immigration on the European Union, the impact of America on the European Union, the relationship between France and Algeria.

Still nothing. My back hurt from standing for almost an hour with locked knees. A young man corralled a wheeled, black stool, the kind that sinks to the floor when weighted, and sat on it to peruse the Sarkozy book. I was so jealous I wanted to bite him.

I soldiered on: numerous titles on Iraq, the first Gulf War and its implications for the current one, a new history of the Middle East, a history of the old histories of the Middle East, and a history of France's involvement in the Middle East. A swath of books on terrorism made my head spin. The salesclerk gave me the evil eye. I, in turn, bored holes into the back of the guy on the stool, but he hunched over his book, showing no sign of giving up his seat. A dull throbbing in my left temple threatened migraine, and so far, I'd come up with zilch. Outside on the sidewalk, a group of Japanese tourists stood around a street musician, who sang "It don't mean a thing, if it ain't got that swing."

With a heavy heart, I picked up a history of the Socialist party. The young man looked at his watch, tossed Sarkozy on the table, and left. I sank onto the stool and plowed through four more political party histories and a comparative study of the influence of labor unions. I was two-thirds of the way through the table when my cell phone rang; it was Olivier, and I went outside to talk.

"Salut, mon amour," he said. "Will you be ready by three?"

I looked at my watch. "Better make it four. I'll see you soon."

I went back inside. To my immense displeasure, the salesclerk who'd given me a dirty look was now using the black stool to shelve oversize art books. I tried to muster the stamina to keep going.

Twenty minutes later, I was done. Zip. No little hairs rose on the back of my neck, no drop in the air pressure, no red light accompanied by a honking submarine dive alarm to signal I'd found it. The only place tingling was my lower back, in knots from standing and reading. Either my gut instinct was busted or there was nothing here written by my author.

I looked over at the shelves and made a fainthearted foray in the direction of *Histoire Politique, Sociologie,* and *Essais,* but the sight of so many books, normally a pleasant thing, made me want to cry. There were hundreds of them, serious-looking, full of dense pages with intimidating vocabulary and complex concepts. I couldn't do it. I ducked into the métro and went home.

. . . .

At four, I closed the metal *volets* on the windows and went downstairs. The sun was peeking out of extravagant, fleshy, pink clouds, the sky as lush as a Rubens painting. Olivier pulled up in his blue Golf, and I got in.

"Off we go," I said sunnily. I was determined to be in a good mood. I was determined to be light. I was determined to keep my nasty suspicions from him. I would shove the goblins under the carpet, stomp down hard, and *chill*.

26

There is a crack in everything
That's how the light gets in
—LEONARD COHEN,
"Anthem"

Once we passed the suburbs and the *centres commerciaux*, the scenery changed to flat, green land, dotted with farmhouses and pictur-esque villages, with church steeples and the occasional castle or ruin. Olivier tried to tell me about rehearsal, but I didn't want to hear any-thing about Estelle, so I changed the topic. In a lame attempt to be play-ful, I asked him questions: the name of his first pet (Castor, a black cat), his favorite color (green), his favorite food (gnocchi with Gorgonzola tied with *baba au rhum*), and his Desert Island discs. I stopped when I realized my voice—high-pitched, airy, fake—made me sound like I was twelve and my questions weren't satisfying substitutes for the ones I really wanted to ask, like, What was Victorine implying? What's up with you and Estelle? Why didn't you tell me you were at the hospital with her?

"The house we are going to belongs to a childhood friend," Oliv-ier said. "It has been in his family for generations." The friend was a journalist, currently based in Bucharest. Olivier had the keys and came often, keeping an eye on the place.

"Did you grow up here?" I asked.

"No, but I spent summers nearby, learning to sail. My grandparents had a house near Cabourg. My grandfather sold it after my grandmother died, when I was at the Conservatoire."

"That must have been sad," I remarked. He gave a brief nod. I watched his face.

"*Quoi?*"

"Nothing. Just looking at you," I said. "There's so much I don't know." It came out like an accusation. He snorted.

"What's that supposed to mean?" I asked.

"*Et moi, donc?*" he asked, shooting me a dark look.

"Okay," I said, bristling. "Ask me anything."

"*Et merde!*" he cursed and exited the *autoroute*. "I missed the turnoff for the *départementale*," he explained. I turned on the radio. We listened to classical music in silence.

It was dusk when we arrived. Olivier drove the car onto a gravel path. The house was a two-floor Norman-style, with half-timber work and a thatched roof. There were apple trees and a lichen-stained stone table in the garden.

Using a heavy iron key, he opened the door and went to turn on the furnace. I looked around the living room, furnished with squashy canvas sofas, worn rugs over brown floor tiles, framed photographs, and piles of books. It looked lived-in and inviting. There was a stone fireplace with a large iron plaque inside, for reflecting heat.

Olivier picked up my bag and showed me the bedroom upstairs. It was decorated with faded red toile de Jouy under a low, beamed ceiling.

"Let's go for a walk while the house heats up," he suggested.

"Wait." I kissed him, but he pulled away.

"Come, I want to show you the village," he said, tugging my hand.

"Twilight" in French is one of my favorite words: *le crépuscule*. In

Los Angeles, the sun sets, and shortly afterward, it's night. Here, that in-between time can last for an hour. The darkness creeps up on you like an intuition, spreads silently like a stain.

We drove into town and walked along the boardwalk. The beach was wide and windy; my nose ran, and it was too loud to talk. When we got back to the car, the sky was royal blue, and the orange lights inside the houses reminded me of Magritte's *Empire of Light*. We passed a house with a goldfish bowl on the windowsill. A lanky black-and-white cat agitated the water with a paw as the goldfish swam around in a claustrophobic panic.

At dinner, our conversation was stilted and awkward. The weight of what I wasn't saying sucked the wind out of me. My back hurt from poring over all those books, and Olivier kept looking over my shoulder, seemingly more interested in talking to the waiter than to me. I got so fidgety, I smoked one of his cigarettes with coffee. It tasted like dirt.

When we got back, the house was still chilly. "I'll make a fire," Olivier said.

"Is there music?"

"In the study," he said, pointing to a doorway. I found the stereo next to a wooden wine case full of old jazz albums. I put a Duke Ellington album on the turntable. On the desk, there were framed photos of two little girls. I went back into the living room and sat on the sofa. He piled twigs over crumpled newspaper.

"Who are the little girls?" I asked.

"The younger one is my goddaughter." He put another log sideways over the first one and lit the newspaper.

"Do you see her often?"

"Not so much. I take her to the cinema from time to time."

"Let me guess: Steve McQueen?"

"*Bientôt.*" He smiled over his shoulder. "Right now, it's Disney and Miyazaki," he said. In front of the fire, with the music playing, I felt a warm rush go through me, something like happiness but fuller, almost achy. How stupid I'd been to get so stressed out. So what if he spent a couple of days at the hospital lending moral support to his old friend and leading lady? Surely I was big enough to understand that? I wrapped a light wool blanket around my shoulders. Being here with Olivier was simple, uncomplicated, a pleasure. I watched the light from the flames play on his profile, and thought about how much I liked him. If I put aside my neurotic tendency to overthink every situation, things would be fine. I had to tell him. Right away.

"You're a sweet man," I said. "Olivier," I began and stopped. "What did people call you as a kid? *Olive?*" I asked. He nodded, watching the fire. "I have a confession to make," I continued. He made an impatient gesture, as if to say it wasn't necessary. "No, this is important," I said. "I've been stressed for a few days, and then, at my tea with Antoine and Victorine, she made some stupid comments, implying something about you and Estelle. She was needling me, and I got paranoid and suspicious, and I think . . . I think I've been a bit tense. But it was stupid to let her affect me like that. I love being here with you."

I expected him to smile. No, I expected him to look relieved and say something like "That explains why you've been so strange." But he didn't. He dragged a hand down across his eyes, and squinted like he had a sudden headache.

"I need to tell you something," he said.

. . . .

My internal radio played a song from the eighties whose chorus went "Hindsight is twenty-twenty vision," each "twenty" a short, two-beat staccato. It's not true. Hindsight is a retroactive arrow that whistles through time to stab you in the back. I'd had all the clues, but I'd been blind anyway.

My first instinct was to laugh; it struck me as funny that I'd been through this before. The sense of déjà vu was inevitable, but I raced ahead. I knew the itinerary, could see it on the map, a southwest road

trip from hell: first stop, Shock, like Las Vegas on crack, everything neon and wonky; a long interlude in Anger and Humiliation, like being held hostage in an unair-conditioned diner in New Mexico; and then I would run out of gas and hole up in Miserable and Sorry for Myself, not a town but a rundown intersection with a motel and a buzzing vacancy sign. The rent was cheap and I was repeat business.

"Estelle and I," he said, "have a special friendship." *Spéciale* was one of the big-time sneaky semi–*faux amis*. It meant special, but in this context, particular, unusual. They'd been involved, romantically, on and off, for years. "I was madly in love with her for a long time," he said, shaking his head. Of course, he still loved her, but it was a different kind of love, he explained.

He said he'd thought about ending it when he met me, despite the fact that they were working together. But things had changed; she was going through a rough patch and she needed him. *"Ce n'est pas le moment,"* he said, caressing the knot of my fist. Now wasn't the time. He hoped I'd understand.

He spoke softly but clearly. I heard every word, every snap of the fire as it cast flickering shadows around the room. I was all ears, as if hearing everything would prevent the oncoming traffic that had already hit me. My arm muscles contracted. I was rigid with tension. But when I spoke, I was so composed, it was creepy.

"And you're telling me this why?" I asked.

"Because I wanted to be honest, too," he answered.

"Does she know about me?" I asked, remembering our chance meeting, her orange silk coat. Had she orchestrated it? "Were you *honest* with her?" I asked, verbally underlining the word. The nights he wasn't with me, was he with her?

"She guessed. She knows me very well," he said with a rueful smile. I think I hated him in that moment. I pulled my hand away.

"I'm sure she does," I said, nodding my head slowly, waiting for something, I didn't know what. For a rabbit to hop into the room, for

a Greek chorus to chant "We told you so," for something so surreal, it would make this feel normal. But nothing happened.

If he'd said something else, I thought later, I might have stayed. If he'd said he loved me, for example, and that he wanted to clear the air, make a clean break from Estelle, start over. Really, I might have stayed. Maybe.

"Why did we come here?" I asked. "I mean, it seems we could've ended this in Paris." He looked alarmed, opened his mouth to speak, but I continued. "Unless . . ." I said. He didn't say anything. "Unless . . . wait, you thought you could tell me this and we could . . . continue?" I asked. He made an awkward gesture with his hands, as if to offer me a large, invisible balloon.

I checked my watch. It was nine-thirty. I threw off the blanket and stood up.

"I'm getting my bag. Please call the train station and find out if there's a train back to Paris." There it was, that creepy composed voice again. I couldn't help it.

"I'll drive us back," he said in a tired voice.

"No." I shook my head.

"J'insiste," he said.

"Insist all you like. I'm not going with you, and I'm not fighting with you," I said.

"Why are you like this? Fight with me! Say something! *Merde!*" He hit a pile of books on the coffee table, sending them crashing to the floor. I was silent. *"Tu me punis, alors,"* he said. His tone was reproachful, and it pissed me off.

"Oh, no. No, no, no. I'm not punishing you, Olivier. I just don't want anything more to do with you," I said. He grabbed my arm, but I shook him off. I was not going to French Movie Land with him. He could do that with his *other* girlfriend, the movie star. I went upstairs.

I'm not going to cry, I'm not going to cry, I repeated over and over

again. *You should have seen this coming.* I avoided looking in the mirror. *You can cry on the train.*

"Can we talk about this?" he asked, when I came down with my bag.

"Why? So we can discuss you lying to me? So we can go over the times you've spent with her while we've been together? So we can talk about our feelings? So that—" Ooh, I thought, I have a friend in sarcasm.

"*Arrête.*"

"See? I don't want to do this, either. I've been to the circus before, Olivier. I know it's smoke and mirrors, I don't want to hang out with the clowns again, and I *don't do juggling.*" I wasn't sure I made sense, but it sounded good.

He drove me to the station. The round, illuminated clock in the tower echoed the shape of the full moon. Olivier went to the *guichet.* There was a half-hour wait at Lisieux, but I would make it to Paris by midnight.

"Stay. You don't have to go," he said, holding the ticket.

"Thank you," I said, plucking it from his hand.

"*Je t'appellerai.*"

I stood, studying him. There was a look on his face that reminded me of Timothy. It was a look I knew, one I could almost understand; a look that told me he was fallible and didn't want to lose me. It had caused me a certain amount of pain the last time around.

"Don't," I said. Forcing myself not to look back, I got on the train. It was just two cars long, with dingy brown vinyl seats. I sat by the window in an empty compartment.

Across the tracks, a woman in a belted coat stood on the platform. She checked her watch, then her cell phone. I watched her, wanting to be her. I wanted to be someone else, someone waiting for someone, not someone leaving.

I rested my head against the dark safety glass. It seeped an icy circle onto my scalp. An incomprehensible announcement blared through the PA system, and I made out the words *"destination Lisieux."* As my train pulled out of the station, the woman on the platform turned and opened her arms wide. A man at the top of the stairs walked into them like he was coming home.

That's when I started to cry.

27

Le bonheur est vide, le malheur est plein.
—VICTOR HUGO, *Tas de pierres*

*I*t would be a lie to say I cried all the way back to Paris because I didn't. The trip was nearly two hours long, and no one cries for two hours straight, though you might tell the story as if you did. I wept for a while, then I stared out the window. My eyes followed evenly spaced lights, going back and forth like a typewriter carriage, not seeing anything.

My lips were dry. I found lip balm in my bag and applied it, using my shadowy reflection in the glass as a mirror. It felt like a pose, as if I were being watched, though no one was there.

I remembered my first *crise de conscience*, though at the time, I lacked the vocabulary to name it. I was seven or eight, and seriously upset, for a reason that escapes me now. It probably had something to do with Barbie—wanting a Barbie, being refused a Barbie—or something else I'd desperately wanted. Maybe it was something I was convinced I'd be miserable without—a stuffed animal, permission to go to a slumber party, forgiveness for some minor transgression. I remember crying so hard my chest hurt, like after a day of playing in the pool.

*Happiness is empty, unhappiness is full.

But then part of my brain detached and watched the crying. Or noticed I was hungry. Or watched the cat bat at a fly on the window and heard the rippling sound of plate glass as it vibrated against the sash.

In that moment, I'd distrusted my tears. How could I be in so much pain if I could think about donuts? Could I truly be suffering if I remembered *Saturday Night Live* was on TV that night? Wasn't the honesty of emotions determined by their single-minded, all-encompassing focus?

Clearly, I was false. I was false, my grief was false, and I was a faker. The jeering voices of the playground, which shouted "Faker!" to anyone who overacted injury during dodgeball, applied to me.

It was years before I understood it was possible to remember to pick up the dry cleaning when it felt like your heart was breaking; to research and write on deadline even though your roommate wasn't talking to you; or to schedule a teeth-cleaning while nursing a righteous anger at the entire editorial department.

So, I cried on the train, but then I stopped and thought about crying. I cried tears of pure, hot rage as I pictured Estelle and Olivier together, and I cried sad tears, feeling stupid, ashamed, and sorry for myself. The sadness was centering, thick and familiar, and I wrapped myself in it like a shroud.

I'd used the last of my tissues when I noticed a little girl watching me. I could see her reflection in the window. About ten, she had long, wavy hair and big eyes behind thick glasses. She wore a Mickey Mouse sweatshirt with a plaid skirt, and sneakers with kneesocks. When I turned to look at her, she ran away.

I stared back at the window, bleary-eyed. The orange sodium-vapor lights of a highway flew past: tick, tick, tick.

"*Madame,*" a little voice said. She was back. With a solemn look, she held out a Carambar, fruit-flavored caramel.

"*Merci,*" I said, my voice catching. She watched as I unwrapped it and breathed in a pungent, artificial strawberry smell. It was hard and sugary, and chewing it sucked all the saliva out of my mouth. She fled with a squeak of her sneaker.

"Madame!" She came back and held out another Carambar. Chewing stale caramel didn't go with my tragic mood, but I didn't have the heart to refuse her.

"Comment tu t'appeles?" I asked.

"Félice," she answered and scampered away. She came back with a lemon Carambar and her brother. He was a smaller version of her, with brown pants and a green sweater, the same big eyes behind glasses. I felt like the human in a petting zoo; the nice children were feeding candy to the sad lady.

"Merci, Félice," I said, *"Mais—"*

"FELICE! VICTOR!" A loud, stressed paternal voice yelled. A man about my age, with a newborn in a BabyBjörn clamped like a limpet to his chest, shuffled into the compartment. He looked exhausted.

"Non, écoutez les enfants, vous laissez la dame tranquille et vous retournez tout de suite," he scolded gently, casting me a look that was half-apologetic, half-wary. *"Je suis désolé, madame."*

"Il n'y a pas de quoi, monsieur," I replied. *"Vos enfants sont très gentils."* He smiled at the compliment and took their hands.

"La dame pleurait, papa," Félice said, explaining that I'd been crying. Her father threw me a worried look. She turned around, and I waved good-bye. I bit down on the lemon candy, hoping I wouldn't lose any fillings. I thought about a time when a Carambar might well have made everything better, and it was a long time ago.

Maybe there was something fundamentally wrong with me. Perhaps in addition to being stupid and blind, I was destined to have men be unfaithful, like I was under a Sicilian curse. Better to never get involved with anyone again. I would become like my grandmother's eccentric friend, who went to live with the monks in Tibet after three failed marriages. I had a pleasant moment contemplating the purity of my future existence: the spirituality, the lack of material things, the bright, one-shouldered orange robe and shaved head. I imagined telling my sad story to an infinitely kind monk, who would reassure me that the reasons I came to Lhasa were unimportant.

I sat up in my seat. I was being a jerk.

Still, it made me wonder: perhaps it was time to go back to L.A. Or maybe place had nothing to do with it, and I was merely lugging psychic baggage from one city to another. When I'd left, Lindsay had accused me of running away. Maybe she was right.

All the times he was at the theater, was he really at the theater?

That time we met, at that cocktail party, did she know about me? Did her husband, the minister, know about Olivier? *I reminded her of her?*

What did Victorine know?

Bitch.

....

At Lisieux, I boarded the train with a teenager whose MP3 player was cranked up so loud I could hear lyrics and a craggy-faced woman who ate an apple with precise, vicious bites. No sooner had I found a seat in another empty compartment than my stomach spasmed. As the train pulled out, lurching from side to side, I listed over to the bathroom and threw up in the metal toilet bowl, which stank of urine and lemon-scented, industrial-strength cleaner.

I rinsed my mouth out with the tap water, marked *"non potable,"* and considered the various illnesses one could contract from impure water. Spitting to get rid of the taste of bile until I had no spit left, I wondered whether bile tastes the same to everyone, the way garbage smells the same way the world over.

I walked back through the near-empty train. Few people were headed back to Paris on a Friday night. Like so many other things that evening, it felt wrong, like the turn you make that gets you lost. Wrong the way everything the day of a car accident feels like an omen you couldn't see: the stubbed toe, the burned toast, the misplaced keys.

I thought about the night Olivier and I had driven home from Althea's birthday party. We'd parked on my street and made out in the car. We'd kissed on the sidewalk, in front of the *coiffeur*, in the elevator, laughing, delirious. He'd held my face and caressed my cheeks with his thumbs. *"Comme tu es belle,"* he'd said.

I pictured Estelle. The purring, husky voice, the wide eyes rimmed with sooty lashes. Smiling as she waited to use the phone. *Admiring my shoes.*

My head throbbed, a persistent hammer in my left temple. The train pulled into the Gare Saint-Lazare. I took the stairs up to the main hall, passing the empty Salle des Pas Perdus, the waiting room known as the Hall of Lost Footsteps. Lost because they led nowhere, those footsteps of people pacing, retracing the same pointless steps. I was taking me and my lost footsteps home, to a home that wasn't even mine.

I walked out with a small throng of cooler-than-thou French teenagers, couples on dates, and commuters with wheeled weekend bags. Everyone looked like they had a purpose, which is one way other people look when you're unhappy. I stood in line, waiting for a taxi.

Whenever a character walks around a city in a movie, there's always music playing. That's why I like portable music players, because you can choose your soundtrack. If you match the music to your mood, especially when traveling, you graft the song onto the city: David Bowie onto downtown Berlin, Sonic Youth or Cesaria Evora or Brahms onto the sidewalks of Aix-en-Provence. I had some tunes so affixed to certain streets in Paris that they floated into my head whenever I walked down them.

But I didn't have any music on me, so tonight my soundtrack was the screeching and honking of passing cars and, when I finally got a cab, Eastern European folk songs and a driver who sucked his teeth.

At home, there were two messages. I tried to suppress the hope that Olivier had called to say the impossible thing that would make everything fine, but it persisted, despite the fact that nothing could make it fine and I knew it wasn't Olivier.

The first one was from Tante Isabelle. "It's so last minute, sweetie, I'm sorry to do this, but I'm stopping by on my way to a conference in Geneva. Can you make yourself scarce? Don't worry about cleaning up. I'll be there with my friend on Saturday afternoon, and we'll be out by Monday."

The second was from Bernard Laveau. *"Ecoutez, j'aurais besoin de vous voir aussitôt que possible. C'est urgent. Veuillez me téléphoner ou venir me voir à la librairie."*

Great. I was homeless for three days, just when I needed to curl up in bed and die. On top of which, Bernard Laveau needed to talk to me ASAP. As if.

All I wanted was to be unconscious. I took a sleeping pill and crawled under the duvet. My body flattened into the sheets, and I relaxed as the muscles in my face loosened and slipped back toward my ears.

....

In the morning, I hauled myself out of bed and got to work. I needed the support and spare couches of my closest friends.

I couldn't ask Clara—not when she had a sprained ankle and her mother staying with her. I called Althea, who pronounced Olivier "a perfect shit" and promised a rollicking, drunken weekend with her, Ivan, and a good bottle of vodka. Pascal offered me the spare room and suggested selling the item about Olivier and Estelle to the gossip rag *Voici*. Then he invited me as his date to a dinner party at a fashion designer's apartment that evening.

"Allez, it will be fun," he coaxed. "Florian refuses to go and I need a date. There will be no straight men, only gay men, faggy haggies, and a famous lesbian, very glam. You can switch teams."

I made coffee and considered my options. Luckily, the flat wasn't too much of a sty. I remade the bed with fresh sheets. The phone rang. It was Lucy, Althea's sister.

"Right. I've just spoken to Thea, and I'm calling to tell you to get yourself on the Eurostar immediately," she commanded, not bothering with preliminaries. "I had brilliant plans for the weekend: Angus, this dreamy Scot I've been dating, was coming to London, but now his mum has broken her leg in a fit of passive-aggressiveness, and he's staying in Scotland to take care of her. I know she hates me; she calls me the 'Yank lassie.'" She let out a frustrated yelp.

"It's very nice of you, Lucy, but—"

"Not nice, selfish. I felt pathetic at the theater all alone last night. I won't have fabulous restaurant reservations go to waste! You must come," she urged. "It'll be fun."

"Um . . ." I stalled. What I really wanted was to mope at home and wallow in misery, but I couldn't do that with Tante Isabelle arriving in the next few hours.

"I'm looking at the computer—there are four trains that'll get you here in time for dinner. You can cry on my shoulder until you become a raving bore, then I'll tell you to shut up and make you listen to me whine. Deal?"

Just then, it felt right to get out of town, at least for a few days. I called Althea, Clara, and Pascal, and told them what I was up to. I called Laveau, but I got the machine, so I left a message telling him I was out of the country until Monday. I deliberately left my cell phone behind, picked up my still-packed weekend bag, bought a box of truffles from the *chocolatier*, and caught the bus for the Gare du Nord.

On the sidewalk outside the nineteenth-century train station, I found another witch doctor card. This one was blue and stamped with dirty sneaker tread marks. Maître Samadhi specialized in *"les problèmes de cœur"*; he could guarantee the return of my lover's affections by telepathy. The card was edged with crude drawings of a heart, a nose, an ear, and an eye. Magical realism cereal, I thought. Lucky Charms, breakfast spells for the heartbroken. I tucked it in my pocket.

I bought an expensive last-minute Eurostar ticket and, for the second time in less than twenty-four hours, boarded a train.

....

At St. Pancras, the bus driver, a ginger-haired man with muttonchop sideburns, called me "love." Parisian bus drivers don't use terms of endearment, let alone describe the highlights of the route. He pointed out Big Ben, Westminster Abbey, and the London Eye. A billboard for a snazzy red convertible read MEAN AND ROOFLESS.

Lucy lived in the Fulham Studios, a series of little houses originally built for artists located behind a wall on the Fulham Road. I followed a mossy walkway, decorated with lichen-stained urns and rusted garden furniture, to her door.

"You're here!" she exclaimed. She enfolded me in a tight bear hug and pulled me inside. "You're in the study. I've blown up an air mattress and moved all my work crap to the side," she said. She gave me a brief tour, pointing out the living room and kitchen, then her bedroom and bathroom on the second floor. The company where she worked as a senior financial investment manager paid the fortune in rent.

"Now," she said, giving me a beady stare, "you have two hours to tell me everything, then we're going to a mad trendy restaurant and we'll see what kind of trouble we can get into."

The late-afternoon sun streamed in through paned windows, and we sprawled on the sofa with tea and biscuits. Lucy listened and supplied tissues while I gave her a nutshell version of the Timothy story, then a more detailed account of the Olivier story.

"One right after the other," she said. "Gosh, that's rough!"

"Yeah," I said, but I sensed an opinion lurked beneath the sympathetic words. "Now tell me what you really think," I said, steeling myself. "I mean it."

"Let me ask you something," she began. "Did you ever talk about seeing each other exclusively?"

"Well, no. I just sort of assumed," I said. "Between the time we spent together and his play, it didn't occur to me— I mean, where would he find the time? Of course, that was dumb," I said, thinking of the evenings he'd spent at the theater.

"And you'd been seeing each other for, what, a few weeks?" she asked. I nodded. "Which is a relatively short period of time."

"True. But I thought we both felt the same way," I said.

Lucy gave me a kind look, like I'd made a very human mistake. "Well, it *is* abominable behavior on his part . . ."

"But?" I prodded, though I knew I wouldn't like what she'd say. Already I felt like a recalcitrant cow being dragged down a steep slope. I wanted to dig my heels in and snort, or at least moo in protest. If I wasn't the wronged party, I didn't know where—or even how—I was supposed to stand.

"What is it?" She looked at me over her cup. "You look so nervous! Like I'm the angel of doom."

"You think I overreacted. That the situation was relatively banal," I accused.

"I don't think you overreacted," she clarified. "But perhaps things aren't as irretrievably dire as you think. Look, you have a nice connection with him. He's in a tricky situation that predates you, and it's hard for him to extricate himself right now, but maybe it's worth hanging around to see if things get straightened out."

"But he's sleeping with her!" I blurted out.

"That's problematic." She bit into a biscuit.

"And he's not breaking up with her!" I added.

"I got that." This, with her mouth full.

"And—and—he lied! He hurt me! I feel bad! Humiliated, stupid, wronged! Betrayed!" These were very good reasons, damn it.

"Got that, too," she said, nodding her head. "If you want me to tell you he's a shit, I will. But there may be another way of looking at it," she said.

I folded my arms and burrowed deeper into the sofa. Lucy poured another cup of tea. I noticed the fine lines around her eyes, the worried furrow above her arched brows. I'd known her for over ten years. We'd met after college.

I looked down at my hands. I had a thin, maroon-brown scab on one knuckle. There was a pale, silvery scar the shape of an eyelash on the back of one hand where I'd scratched myself ten years ago, ripping the thin skin. The magazines said the back of your hand was as fragile as an eyelid: easily scarred and just as fine. I'd altered two of my fingerprints over the years: one from careless chopping with an expensive chef's knife, the other from overambitious use of a pair of jewelry pliers. The scar tissue underneath the pad of each finger would never go away. I had scarred hands, scarred fingers, a scarred heart, but I wasn't tossing them out the window.

"You think I shouldn't necessarily throw this away," I said in a low voice.

"It's a risk, but—yes," she said, her blue eyes clear and direct.

I looked out the window at the treetops, the pub chimney across the street, the second floor of a double-decker bus as it drove past. Down below, one of Lucy's neighbors watered his plants. The sunlight caught the water, shooting a spray of rainbow drops, and something like hope leaped in my chest and fell.

"No. It's been a lie from the start," I said. "You could be right, but I can't do this. I can't do this *again*."

She nodded as I spoke, and I wanted her to argue with me, to convince me I was wrong, because I wasn't sure I believed myself. But she didn't.

28

*Est-ce que l'âme des violoncelles est emportée dans
le cri d'une corde qui se brise?*
—AUGUSTE VILLIERS DE L'ISLE-ADAM, "Véra"

Lucy and I caught a taxi and rode into somewhere she described vaguely as "North Londonish." I was lost. None of the letters and numbers that designated London's regions and subdivisions made any sense.

"At least with arrondissements, you not only know where someone lives but what their zip code is," I said. "You know where to send mail, a thank-you card."

"The French are famous for food and logic, the British for gardens and eccentrics," she said and asked the driver to pull over so she could dash out to an ATM.

"Off we go then, love," said the cabdriver when she came back.

"It just happened again!" I hissed. She looked bewildered. "He called you 'love'! And went *willingly* to a cash machine!" I shook my head in awe. "I'm moving here."

---

*Does the soul of the cello disappear in the cry of a broken string?

We pulled up to a striped awning. A doorman dressed in a Nehru coat and turban opened a carved wood door. A square brass plaque read BHANGRA.

"Open says me," Lucy trilled and swanned in. She wore a slinky white dress, and I followed her, wearing a silk jacket and jeans, clutching her ancient green pashmina around me like a bath towel. A willowy blonde with a jeweled bindi between her eyes led us around a reflecting pool strewn with rose petals. A reclining gold Buddha lay at the other end. We went down candlelit stairs into a cavernous dining room.

Our "table" was a white bed covered with multicolored sari silk pillows. Underneath a tented ceiling hung with hammered brass lanterns was a sea of beds. Everyone ate and reclined at the same time.

"Someone," I said darkly, "has been peeking into my fantasies."

Lucy hopped onto the bed and ordered champagne. "You see why I wanted to bring Angus," she said.

"His loss is my Ganesha," I muttered, glancing at a stone statue of the elephant god. Bollywood remixes played on the sound system, and the smell of spices wafted through the air. "This place is trippy."

"Bhangra-la," Lucy said, kicking off her heels. A waiter in a pink kurta poured champagne into two jewel-encrusted flutes. "By the way, we don't order, they bring us food until we say stop. And I booked you a fortune-teller and me mehndi painting."

We clinked glasses, and I took a big gulp of icy champagne. Over crunchy pakoras, Lucy filled me in on her romance with "the handsome Scot," as she called him. A mehndi painter, a woman in a peacock blue sari, came over and applied a brown crust of intricate curlicue patterns around Lucy's ankle. Then she sprinkled lemon juice over it and propped Lucy's foot up on a terry-cloth stool to let it dry.

"Everyone drinks too much in England," I remarked over my third glass of champagne. Perfumed courses arrived on hammered brass plates: baby dosas, small cornucopias stuffed with cardamom and fennel spiced potatoes; samosas; coconut and tamarind rice; spinach with cheese; and fried puffy bread that looked like a flying saucer and came with a chickpea curry. Over pistachio ice cream, a rotund, middle-aged gentleman in a white suit and turban introduced himself as Sanjay, the fortune-teller.

"I hope you ate well?" he asked. He had almond-shaped eyes and a mustache.

"Very well, thank you," I said.

"Wretched excess," Lucy said. "You're reading *her* fortune," she added, pointing at me. "But you probably knew that." She laughed. He gave a polite smile. "You probably knew I would say *that*, too," she said, giggling. "Terrible thing about fortune-tellers," she whispered loudly. "You can't have a conversation with them—they always know what you're going to say." She nodded her head up and down knowingly. I swatted her arm.

He studied me for a long moment. "Please try to bring your mind into the room. Focus on being present but blank," he said and held his hand out for my palm.

I'm not good at making my mind blank. The only surefire way I know is to sleep. I have a contradictory streak, and being told to make my mind blank elicits a mulish laundry list of random thoughts. My mind raced through everything from Olivier to the fennel seed stuck in my molar to wondering if Lucy had any aspirin for my impending hangover. Sanjay studied my hand, then spoke.

"This is a symmetrical story. You have come from far away, and before that, from even farther. You have had two years of bad luck, which has been concentrated around an unsuccessful love life. There are two men. I will tell you who they are."

"Uh-oh," I joked, casting a glance at Lucy. She stared at Sanjay, glassy-eyed.

"Neither of them is right for you, though you have not closed the door on either one. I see they are both artists, and they have much in common.

"The first one is a charmer, a trickster, a magician. He dazzles you with sleight of hand, then disappears before the smoke has cleared. Your mistake is confusing a skilled display of artistry for substance—you have a tendency to do this, and it is something you must be wary of. You cannot hold on to him, not because he doesn't want to be held but because there isn't anything there for you to hold on to. He *is* the smoke."

He looked at my palm again. He spoke the way you would imagine a true seer would, if you believed in such a thing: not picking his words, merely a conduit for them.

"The other one holds on to a very old thread. The more he has held on, the more it has spun around him, until now, this thread he thought he could snip with ease has become a cocoon, though he may not know it or want to be free. You could help him. It would require effort and patience on your part, and in the end, the challenge may end up meaning more than the prize. A gamble."

His hands fluttered in the air.

"But all this is secondary. You must focus on your limitations, not another's. This is one source of your distress: locating their solutions in another. Why do you choose these men? What do you learn from these situations? You must look inward, past your deepest fears. Beyond them is the treasure of pure self, no less complicated but true. That is where you must start. It is where we all start. Begin there, and you will begin again. Do not rail against fate. Some things are meant to be."

He stood up. "Otherwise, health good. Less indulgence, perhaps. You must do something for your neck, and it would behoove you to practice meditation. It is very noisy in here," he said, tapping the center of his forehead. He bowed and left. Lucy and I gave each other spooked stares. My skin was taut with goose bumps.

"He's good," I said, rubbing the right side of my neck, where it was always stiff. Across the dimly lit restaurant, I saw a tall man with dark hair. His back was turned to me, but my pulse sped up. He turned around: it wasn't Olivier. It was someone else, and when he saw me, he glanced away. I had to talk to him, I had to tell him I wanted to see him. I had to tell him *right now*.

"Lucy, I need to borrow your phone," I said. She pulled her Black-Berry out of her evening bag. Clutching it in one hand, I wove through the restaurant, somehow managing not to trip over any of the low tables or woven rugs, and found a garden in the back. It was tented in red silk, and candles in ruby glass holders hung from the branches of a potted tree. It was like being inside a heart.

I misdialed the first time I tried. It took me a second to remember how to call France from the U.K. I tried again and it rang. I looked at my watch. It was only a little past eleven my time, past midnight for him.

"*Allô,*" he said, his voice congested and groggy.

"*Olivier, c'est moi. Ecoute, je t'appelle de Londres. J'ai envie de te voir, de te parler—*" The words tumbled out, clattering like dice. I want to see you, to talk to you.

"*Mais—*"

"*Non, laisse moi continuer.*" Let me finish, I insisted, pressing the device to my ear. "I'll be back Monday afternoon. Can I see you Monday night?" I hoped I wasn't slurring my speech, but I couldn't tell.

"*Je suis désolé, madame. Vous avez fait faux numéro.*" He hung up.

I stared at the screen. A wrong number? But it sounded like Olivier. I'd thought it was Olivier. I thought about redialing, but it was too late. Metal pans crashed inside the kitchen, followed by mad shouting in a foreign language. The moment was gone.

....

Lucy and I puttered around on Sunday, going to museums and an arty Japanese movie. On Monday afternoon, I took a half-empty train back to Paris. I tried to nap, but even with two empty seats, I couldn't get comfortable.

At home, a red "6" flashed on the machine. Three messages from Laveau, one from my mother, and one from Pascal, telling me I'd missed a spectacular party.

I stared at the wall, at a nineteenth-century etching of a dying horse. The last message was Tante Isabelle, sending her love and asking me to be home for the installation of the new washing machine she'd ordered.

In the desk drawer, I found a pack of Olivier's cigarettes. I wedged myself onto a corner of the balcony and smoked. Across the street, the line at the *boulangerie* stretched six deep onto the sidewalk.

I thought about the first time I'd met Timothy. I'd gone to a New Year's Eve party in Santa Barbara with a friend who didn't want to drive up alone. I'd been sitting on the deck when he came over to me. We ended up talking about books and film, but I'd assumed he was merely being friendly, despite how much fun I was having, as he'd brought a date.

Later, after midnight, when the party was in full swing, I slipped out and went for a walk on the beach. I walked and wished for Timothy, or someone like him. It was late, early morning on the first of the year, and I let myself wish.

And then he was there. I'd conjured him up out of thin air. I don't mean a ghost. I mean, one moment he was in the house, the next he was there, on the sand, not ten feet away, pants rolled up to midcalf, his head cocked to the wind.

I froze. I'd wished for him, and there he was. But instead of going toward him, I turned and walked away.

When I got back to the house, he'd left. We didn't see each other again until a chance meeting over a year later.

There's a corollary to never looking a gift horse in the mouth. Never walk away from a granted wish. Even if the granting of it stuns you. Even if it reveals something to you about your own wishes that you'd prefer not to know. Not to have known.

I've always been good at not getting what I want. Even when I get what I want.

29

I have said it before, I shall say it again:
it is the minor treacheries that weigh
most heavily on the heart.
—JOHN BANVILLE, *The Untouchable*

I caught the 96 bus, crowded with morning commuters, and arrived at Editions Laveau before it opened. A vellum-colored shade inside the door blocked my view. I paced on the sidewalk, longing for an *express* and a *tartine beurre* at a nearby café. I promised myself breakfast if Monsieur Laveau didn't show up by ten-fifteen. At ten-thirteen, as I was picturing a frothy *grand crème*, he came up the street, wearing a beige trench coat and his perennial frown.

"*Entrez, mademoiselle,*" he said, after unlocking the door.

"*Monsieur,*" I answered, by way of greeting. He indicated the club chair in his office, but I sat on a caned chair. He hung his coat on the door and dropped his worn leather satchel on the floor.

I looked on in happy anticipation as he made espresso. We'd almost become cozy. I smiled at him when he handed me a demitasse cup. He didn't smile back, but that was nothing new. He sat and placed his hands flat on the desk.

"*Alors, je vais aller droit au but,*" he began. At the grave tone in his voice, I stopped drinking my coffee. "It has come to my attention that you have some kind of intimate relation with one of my clients."

"I beg your pardon?" I asked, with *froideur*. My personal life, shambles or not, was none of his business. He hesitated a moment and shot his cuffs.

"This is most unpleasant for me, *mademoiselle*," he said. A muscle in his cheek twitched. Monsieur Laveau managed to look both distressed and contemptuous, as if he were girding himself for a repulsive task beneath his dignity, like removing a dead rat from a dinner at the Académie Française.

"You will recall that our project is highly confidential, and yet, you are consorting with an extremely interested party." In French, *"intéressé"* connotes "self-serving."

The conversation felt surreal. *"Consorting?"* I repeated, half-laughing. Just what century did he live in? Next, he'd accuse me of plotting to overthrow the king.

"I demand you take this matter seriously," he said.

"Putting aside the weirdness of you trying to dictate the company I keep, the only thing I take seriously is your insinuation that I would not keep a confidential matter confidential—" I started, but he cut me off.

"And yet, you described the plot of the novel to Olivier Vallant, who in turn repeated it, which is how I came to hear of it, and how my writer came to hear of it. Though the notion that you are translating Rémi Le Jaa, *alors là, c'est totalement absurde*," he said.

"But I thought you said—" I began, confused, remembering Olivier had told me that Bernard had hinted the author was Le Jaa.

"Enough!" he said, raising his voice. "You have put me in a difficult situation, professionally and with regard to my personal friendship with the writer," he said. "Even if I were to find another translator, the damage has already been done. *Mademoiselle, c'est grave!*" He thumped the desk for emphasis.

Seventeen kinds of embarrassment ripped through me. My face

flushed; I felt acid sting my stomach. I put the cup and saucer on the side table with a clatter. I didn't know where to look, and I felt the worst kind of stupid. What a very small world it was, when your former lover's lover was connected with half of literary Paris.

I thought back to what little I'd told Olivier about the translation. I couldn't remember saying anything specific.

Then I remembered. That night. I'd described the plot and read him a scene.

My hand flew to cover my mouth as my lower lip started to tremble. I didn't know what to say. Bernard drained his coffee in two neat sips.

"How? When?" I managed, my voice wobbly. He rested his elbows on the desk and put his fingertips together, his face granite above them.

"*C'était indirect, bien évidemment*. It came to my attention this week-end. A social occasion," he said with distaste. I winced. "*Eh oui,*" he added, tilting his head. In that gesture, I saw how aggravated he was. I pictured a dinner, a cocktail party, Estelle leaning toward Victorine, the whisper traveling as swiftly as a snake in the grass. *My dear, you'll never imagine what our dear Bernard is up to now. He's hired a translator for a mysterious new novel. Shall I tell you what it's about? Or who it's by?* I pressed clammy hands to my hot face. I saw Estelle in bed, her head on the pillow, Olivier's arms around her, and I heard his voice in her ear, her laugh, like shattering crystal—

"*Mademoiselle?*" Bernard's voice poked at me.

This seemed worse than finding out about Olivier and Estelle. Not just because it put an effective, definitive end to any ragged hope I might have harbored about mending things between us, but because it involved other people. I clenched my jaw. I would not cry in front of Monsieur Laveau.

"*Excusez-moi un instant.*" I stood, knocking over the side table, sending the cup and saucer, an ashtray, and two books to the floor.

"*Merde!*" I muttered, bending down to retrieve them. Monsieur Laveau came around the desk and grasped my arm at the elbow.

"Laissez, laissez, je m'en occupe," he said gently and took the china from my hand. My eyes welled up, and I darted into the little bathroom before he could see.

I turned on the faucet. A couple of tears squeezed out of my eyes, but I averted a complete breakdown. I thought about the French expression for uncontrollable weeping, *"pleurer comme une madeleine,"* and wondered how Proust's little lemon sponge cakes could sob. I had to remember to look that up.

A dusty window gave onto the courtyard. It started to rain, wetting a trio of children's toys: a red tricycle, a green plastic alligator, a pink hula hoop. I blew my nose on a wad of toilet paper, turned off the tap, and came out. There was a glass of water on the side table, and I drank it. Something vibrated in my ear, a small instrument thrumming under the ocean, a creature trying to kick free. I took a deep breath.

"Monsieur, in a moment of unthinking idiocy, I told"—I stopped. I couldn't say his name—"the person you mention a sketchy plot description, which I thought innocuous at the time, and a love scene. I see that was a horrible mistake, and you have my deepest apologies for it, and for the discomfort it caused you," I said, swallowing.

My speech didn't have the desired effect. I waited for Monsieur Laveau to lecture me, to shout, but he didn't. Instead, he deflated: even his chest seemed to cave in. For the first time, he seemed fragile, his wiry physique worn out.

"Je vois," he said blinking rapidly. "I'd hoped there was some other explanation." He looked over my shoulder, his eyes not meeting mine. He'd actually had faith in me; he'd imagined a mistake, perhaps, or a purloined chapter. But no, I'd let him down, embarrassed him. My toes curled in my sneakers.

"You must decide whether you'd like to continue our professional association," I said, my words formal and stilted. "But I can guarantee this will never happen again. It was a huge error, but one that will not be repeated." I clenched my hands in my lap.

He exhaled, puffing out his cheeks in the French blowfish manner that can mean exasperation, fatigue, impossibility, difficulty, or reluctance. In this case, it meant all of them. He turned his silver letter opener over in his hands. "What guarantee do I have?"

"Because I'm never going to talk to him again," I said, unable to keep the waspish tone out of my voice. "Our relationship ended—badly—on Friday." If this came as a surprise, he didn't show it. He swiveled away to look out the window. I watched, waiting for a reaction, but he merely looked sad and withdrawn, which was worse.

When he still didn't say anything, I picked up my bag. *"Je vais m'en aller, monsieur.* I'll assume that if you want to get in touch with me, you will." I stood up. "I'm sorry. I'm so sorry," I whispered and walked to the door on wobbly legs, wondering if this was going to be the last time I heard the cowbell.

. . . .

Ignoring the drizzle, I walked past cafés draped with Halloween decorations, and bought a pack of cigarettes and matches at a small *tabac.* I turned and walked down to Saint-Sulpice. The church, stained by the rain, looked heavy and forbidding in the gray light.

On the square, most of the Café du Marché's outdoor chairs were piled on top of one another and chained together, like victims of a giant furniture roundup. Under the awnings, a few loose chairs and tables huddled near two heat lamps for warmth, the setup for smokers. It felt like someplace I could hide. I sat down, ordered a large *double express,* and lit the first of many cigarettes.

The tears I cried felt bitter and brown, like oversteeped tea, and I wiped them away with a grimy, balled-up tissue I found in my pocket. I stewed in a caustic bath of embarrassment, shame, and disappointment. I felt terrible about Monsieur Laveau, and I railed against my own carelessness. What was worse, I knew Olivier hadn't told Estelle out of malice. He'd told her out of a casual disregard for me.

I could feel myself spiraling down into a familiar vortex of self-loathing. I smoked cigarette after cigarette, because it felt destructive and hurtful, staring at the passing buses in the damp air as the heat lamp burned my scalp. And I fell inward, like a brick off a building, further and further out of reach.

....

It was still raining when I left. I bought a flimsy umbrella and walked back to the Eleventh. My cell phone rang a couple of times, but I didn't answer.

At home, I took a quiche out of the freezer. I bent to put it in the oven and nearly fell over from the head rush. If a walk across Paris had that effect, I was seriously out of shape.

The phone rang, and my mother spoke into the answering machine like it was some kind of annoying flunky blocking access to her daughter. I picked up. She and my father were leaving for Hawaii, and she wanted to say hi before they left. I hadn't told them about Olivier and couldn't bring myself to do so now.

"Darling, are you sure you're all right?"

"Yes, just tired," I said, leaning against the refrigerator.

"Well, get some rest. I'll call when we get back. I e-mailed you the number in Maui, just in case." We said good-bye and hung up.

I sat on the kitchen floor, near the warm oven, and wrapped my arms around my knees, shivering. I slid my fingernails between the floorboards, digging up lint and crumbs. My eyes blurred; probably all that cigarette smoke. Maybe I was delirious. My head hurt; it felt hot against my hand.

I found a fancy digital thermometer in the bathroom. It beeped when it was ready, the display flashing Celsius and Fahrenheit. I had a fever of 102.

I changed into a T-shirt and pajama pants and padded into the kitchen when the oven timer rang. I stuck my hand in, trying to drag the quiche out with a dessert fork, then leaped back when I felt a searing pain, accompanied by a small sizzle. I'd burned the back of my hand on the electric coil. My skin turned red, and a transparent layer puffed up into a white crust. I fished ice cubes out of the freezer and held them to my hand while I ate a slice of quiche.

There was something in the medicine cabinet for *"brûlures,"* so I applied a thin gel to my hand, bound it in cotton gauze, and fell into bed.

I woke up fifteen hours later, my hand throbbing.

30

On croit que, lorsqu'une chose finit,
une autre recommence tout de suite.
*Non. Entre les deux, c'est la pagaille.**
—MARGUERITE DURAS

Something bad happened in the night. Someone spoke to me: a stranger, a tearful, accented woman's voice, telling me bad, horrible, irreversible things. I stared at the wall, racing through recent memory, trying to remember, but it was like trying to see around a corner.

My hand smarted. I peered under the bandage. The burned skin was goopy and red. It was hard to tell what was human goop and what was oily burn ointment, but it looked bad. I stood up, my damp T-shirt clinging to my back, and my legs shot out from underneath me. I fell back on the bed as the room spun. Little black shapes, like commas, darted soundlessly through my peripheral vision like warning punctuation. Not good, I thought, holding the walls for balance as I shuffled to the bathroom; not good, not good, not good. The thing I couldn't remember gnawed at me. What the hell was it? I stepped on something sharp

---

*We think that when one thing ends, another one begins right away. No. In between, it's chaos.

and yelped. It was a baguette crumb. In fact, there were bread crumbs all over the hallway. This was totally unacceptable. I tore open the hall closet and grabbed the broom. Too tall for the space, it was shoved in at an angle, stuck, the bristles bent over. I wrestled with it, gave one powerful yank, and knocked myself in the face with the wooden handle, missing my eye by half an inch.

"Putain de merde!" I yelled, clutching the tender bone of my eye socket. What next? Choking to death on leftover quiche? I sat on the floor, letting loose a torrent of frustrated tears.

The pigeons on the windowsill fluttered their wings and crooned avian love songs. They were probably billing and cooing and grooming each other. I wiped my nose on my sleeve. My face hurt. My hand throbbed. I was jealous of pigeons.

I put some ice in a towel and held it to my cheekbone. It was two in the afternoon, and I could barely wrap my brain around anything other than the fact that I was a wreck. And I'd forgotten something. Someone's birthday? Did I forget to pay a bill? I looked through my date book, but the page was blank. The nagging feeling didn't go away.

I looked up *"pleurer comme une Madeleine"* in the dictionary. It didn't refer to Proust's lemon cakes at all: the expression derived from Mary Magdalene, who'd cried at Christ's feet, and was spelled with a capital "M." This was what I got for being ignorant about religion. The danger of homonyms.

I put the dictionary down and grasped the desk as another wave of dizziness made the room spin. The answering machine light was blinking. I pressed the button.

"Message effacé," the automatic voice announced.

"Fuck! Fuck, fuck, fuck!" I yelled. Thanks to the miracle of digital answering machines, the message was gone, irretrievable. I punched the button again, but the awful digital voice repeated *"Vous n'avez pas de messages."* I wanted to rip it out of the wall: now I was sure whatever I needed to know had been on the answering machine. I raked a hand through my knotty hair, deliberately snapping individual strands. My eyes welled up with the pain.

I drank a glass of water that tasted like metal. Or my mouth tasted like metal and so did everything else. I swallowed three aspirin and went back to bed.

I knew how to take care of myself when I fell ill. I cosseted myself with comfort food and bad television. But the real battle was against the feeling that I'd never be well again. My thoughts drifted. The last time I saw Olivier, at the train station. Was that only days ago? Stop thinking about Olivier. Must exile Olivier from my mind. The last time I kissed Olivier. No, stop, I admonished myself. The last time I heard his voice. The last time Olivier and I made love—

I drifted off and dreamed I found Olivier on the beach, drawing in the sand with a piece of driftwood. His hair was messy, longer, and he looked almost gaunt. I held him, and savored the feeling of being held. In my dream, I gave myself permission to luxuriate in the memory; even so, it felt like something forbidden, something beautiful and careless, a bolt of red silk tossed down a flight of stairs.

I woke up, famished, at four in the afternoon. I seemed to be reverting to L.A. time. I reheated the rest of the quiche and ate it in the kitchen, listening to the ticking of the oven clock and making a list of things to do.

Change the burn bandage. Sweep up the bread crumbs. Take a bath, wash my hair. But then what? Beyond frying my eyes on TV until I fell asleep again?

Even when I was miserable about Timothy in Los Angeles, I still had to eat, sleep, work, pay bills, and guilt myself into going to yoga class. I followed a routine, and it kept me sane. Going through the motions, however mechanically, gave me a semblance of progress, at least movement through time.

Up to now, I'd had a similar—if pseudo—schedule, organized around regular work hours translating for Monsieur Laveau, long walks, hanging out with friends, and seeing Olivier. Funny how quickly I'd gotten used to it. But now? No more Olivier. Probably no more job. I lived in a borrowed apartment. I didn't have to be anywhere, anytime. My friends here had led regular lives before I came, and they'd continue to do so whether I stayed or left. I didn't intersect in any real-life way, and with no job, I'd have to go home pretty soon.

The piteous lowing of dying calves wafted up through the floorboards. The downstairs neighbor was practicing his clarinet. The upstairs neighbor closed his shutters, alternating shrieking hinges with slamming metal. All around me people went through motions and actions with purpose, with rhythm. I'd come to a standstill. I was stuck in place, treading water, while the rest of the world swam by.

....

The fever persisted, giving me body aches and a dull headache that wouldn't ease up. And I got no respite, because whenever I did sleep, I had nightmares, about fires and accidents, sirens and ambulances wailing through the night. A woman sobbing, repeating the same unintelligible phrase. Aspirin and sleeping pills didn't help. My eye developed a yellow-plum halo.

The washing machine deliveryman and his teenage assistant removed the old model and replaced it with a stainless-steel number while I sat on the sofa in Tante Isabelle's *robe de chambre,* catatonic in front of the world's most boring detective, *Inspecteur Derrick,* a German series dubbed into French, and the news, which kept showing the same aerial shots of a tunnel on the A8 between Ventimiglia and Nice, the scene of a massive car pileup over the weekend.

I didn't hear from Monsieur Laveau, and I didn't hear from Olivier, and it was hard to tell which felt worse. I missed Olivier and hated myself for it, because that was easier than hating him. I fantasized about him breaking up with Estelle and begging me to take him back. Like that was going to happen. I knew that if I wanted Olivier back, I would have to accept the Estelle situation, which I considered at least five or six times a day before hating myself for that, too.

As for Monsieur Laveau, the thought that I'd disappointed him made me miserable. I'd enjoyed our antagonistic relationship as well as the translating work. I'd grown attached to him, the way you grow fond of an eccentric relative or neighbor, particularly once he or she dies or moves away. I felt a pang every time I thought of his bushy eyebrows and forbidding stare over our shared espressos. I couldn't even bring myself to read the second ending, the one I'd gotten last Friday, which seemed like a century ago. I wondered if I should mail it back to him.

And I dreaded sleep. My nightmares morphed into claustrophobic horrorscapes of being trapped in a large metal box, hammered in on all sides, or less specific but equally violent scenes of explosions and natural disasters. After three days of this, I felt brittle and frail, as if the only thing holding me up was a scaffolding of twigs.

31

*Hashish. One imitates certain things
one knows from paintings: prison,
the Bridge of Sighs, stairs like the train of a dress.*
—WALTER BENJAMIN, *The Arcades Project*

Pascal and Florian stopped by to check in on me on their way to an art opening. Pascal handed me a goody bag filled with beauty products, and Florian brought two cartons of Picard Surgelés sorbets and herbal tea. Pascal took one look at me and stepped back.

"*T'as pas bonne mine,*" he said, shaking his head.

"*Ben, évidemment,*" I replied, exasperated. "I've just spent four days in bed, I bruised my face, and I haven't gotten a decent night's sleep. You'd look like shit, too." He gave me a puzzled look and sat down to page through a *Vanity Fair* Tante Isabelle had left behind. I forget the French think that they're being helpful when they criticize you. Saying nothing, or telling me I looked fine when I didn't would be the equivalent of blowing smoke up my skirt, which is tantamount to hypocrisy. Of course, hypocrisy has its place in France, as it does anywhere else, but between friends it's a crime.

"Ginger tea, with lemon and honey," Florian said, prescribing treatment. "Every hour on the hour. At night, you can put something medicinal in it, like this." He picked up a bottle of rum from the liquor trolley. I nodded, resting my head on the sofa arm.

"I brought you *de l'herbe,*" he added. "So you can sleep."

I blinked at him. "You brought me pot?" I asked.

"Oui," he said, inhaling the word in that peculiar French manner that can mean resignation, vexation, fatigue, or nothing at all. Pronounced that way, it doesn't resemble a word so much as a sound effect, the short flight of a swift paper airplane: *fweeh.* "Be careful," he said, removing a cigarette case from his jacket pocket, "this is very strong stuff." He took out two neatly rolled joints and placed them on the coffee table.

After they left, I ate a bowl of *soupe au pistou* and watched TV. I smoked half a joint. It was past ten, though it seemed later. My limbs felt sluggish, my arms too heavy for my shoulders. The dull throbbing in my head increased, a jungle tom-tom, and I went to the window to press my forehead to the cool glass.

Down below, the orange streetlights cast dramatic tree shadows that seemed to bend and climb like spiders over asphalt and sidewalk. I studied the wrought-iron balconies of the buildings across the street, fascinated by their seemingly infinite, lacy designs. Was there a book on wrought-iron balcony designs? Was there a union for wrought-iron forgers? Were there people who invented patterns all day? Did the patterns have names, like Elisir and Arpeggio? I was more than a little stoned.

Down the street, a tall, stooped man in a trench coat walked underneath the trees.

"Bunny!" I whispered, craning my head. He went around a corner and disappeared. I stumbled, steadying myself with a fold of curtain. I turned off the lights in the kitchen and living room, calculating the fastest route to bed. I could almost taste the exquisite pleasure of my head sinking into the pillow.

I pulled on a fresh T-shirt and pajama bottoms and stretched, grasping the top of the doorframe. A couple of bones in my spine cracked, and my fingertips came back coated in gray dust. I wanted to press myself into a hard, flat surface, roll myself out like clay. I sat on the floor and uncurled my back, yoga-style. I fell on the floor with a thud.

A series of contractions started in my face, as if all my features decided to twitch in concert. My lower lip trembled. The contractions moved to my throat, shoulders, and arms. My stomach tightened, then my inner thighs. Uncontrollable impulses shot down my legs. My kneecaps contracted and released like cap guns. I felt tight knots, like cramps, in my calves, shins, the arches of my feet.

It stopped. I was aware of a tingling in my body, as if the muscles were humming, ready to pounce, but not on my command. I wondered what it meant to have muscles that were usually voluntary respond involuntarily.

It started again, this time in my feet.

The contractions were stronger, more specific. Each muscle gathered itself into a knot, then released like a blast of hot water, pins and needles and sparks. My heels drummed on the floor as my calves, tight as baseballs, contracted and released. It felt like my body was climbing up inside itself of its own volition. I broke into a sweat.

I saw myself from the ceiling, flopping around on the floor like a fish on dry land. My quadriceps tightened, my hamstrings like bows, buttocks like fists. Goose bumps swept over my skin. I ricocheted between panic, fear, and a misplaced fascination about what was happening.

The contractions continued up my body, clenching and unclenching. My fingers curled into my palms. Shooting convulsions wrapped around my neck, tightening like a noose. The spasms crept, like little paws, up my face. It'll be okay, I tried to whisper. My breath caught in my throat, and I coughed, choking on my own spit.

It stopped. I lay still, waiting. The contractions didn't come back. I stayed on the floor, a blind rabbit listening for a fox: my mind the blind rabbit, my body the fox.

I'd had all kinds of nightmares as a child, but the worst were when

I'd wake up paralyzed with fear, unable to move or speak, and I'd have to talk myself down. It came back to me like an old habit, the gentle cajoling of an internal voice that spoke to an unyielding body until it relented. *It's all right, pick yourself up, shhh, everything is fine.*

The phone rang; the machine answered. No one spoke. I sat up, my limbs trembling, numb with the kind of cold that makes you think you'll never be warm again. I squinted at the clock. Who calls at midnight and doesn't leave a message? I pulled on a wool sweater, a pair of wool socks, and a thick terry bathrobe.

My stomach hurt with a hollow, precise ache, as if I could trace its outline with a felt-tip pen. I heated milk in a saucepan, stirring in vanilla and sugar with hands that looked blue. I sat at the table with a mug. My eyes smarted, and the buzzing of the overhead light seemed to crowbar into my ears.

I put my head down and slumped over the kitchen table, pressing my forehead into my forearm. In the dark angle of my elbow, I shuddered. That was scary, I admitted to my arm. I'd been afraid and alone. I peered underneath the bandage at my injured hand. The edges of the wound seemed puckered and hard. Gangrene, probably.

I needed sleep. Restful, uninterrupted sleep would cure me. I smeared on fresh burn ointment and pressed the bandage back into place. I climbed into bed in the sweater, socks, and bathrobe, wondering what the fuck was in the pot.

32

What good is insight? It only makes things worse.
—RAYMOND CARVER

French/English Word Game (toggle back and forth):
  "Siege" in English to "siège" in French (identical spelling), to
  "chair" in English (identical meaning), to
  "(la) chair" in French (identical spelling), to
  "flesh" in English (identical meaning), to
  "(une) fléche" in French (identical pronunciation), to
  "arrow" in English (identical meaning), to
  "héro" in French (pronunciation starts to fudge here), to
  "hero" in English (identical spelling and meaning) . . . and then
it falls apart, because I can't think of a homonym except for "gyro"
and I can't do anything with

Hungover and fuzzy from the pot, I sipped lemon-ginger tea and read the scrap of paper I'd found on the kitchen floor. The list, scrawled in a handwriting that sort of looked like mine, but was more likely mine on drugs, reminded me of a Lewis Carroll word puzzle where you had to transform one word into another, for instance, "love" to "hate," by moving one letter at a time. The trick was to do it in as few steps as possible, but each letter shift had to create a legitimate word. This list seemed to be an attempt to build some kind of French-English word chain, based on meaning and sound.

I looked at it again. What was disturbing was the fact that I couldn't remember writing it in the first place. Was there some kind of hallucinogen in the pot? Would I have flashbacks? Or was it merely an idiopathic reaction?

I love the word "idiopathic."

I called Pascal and Florian to ask them about it, but they weren't answering. I checked my temperature. I still felt weak, but I'd slept peacefully and I couldn't take being cooped up in the apartment anymore.

I pulled opened a drawer, looking for a bra. There it was, my expensive lingerie. I'd worn it exactly twice. The first time, with Olivier—that first time. A second time, also with Olivier. It hadn't stayed on long, but wearing it had made me feel, for lack of a better term, gift-wrapped. I'd hand-washed it, as Clara had told me to.

I fingered the taupe silk: it was unbearably soft, so delicate it made the backs of my teeth hurt. I crushed the panties in my fist and breathed in the smell: Woolite, with a top note of lavender, from the sachet in the drawer.

It was only underwear, after all, not the repository of memories. How stupid was it to spend a small fortune on it and only wear it twice? I pulled on the panties, fastened the bra and tugged on the straps. I layered on warm clothes, tucked my music player in my pocket, and caught the 96 bus. I figured I'd sit in the Jardin du Luxembourg, then treat myself at the gelateria on the rue de Buci.

I sat by the window on the bus and leaned my head against the glass until the rattling over cobblestones made my ears itch. I got out at Odéon and felt a pang as I looked up the street toward the rue de Condé and Editions Laveau. My vision blurred as I stared into the middle distance between the statue of Danton and me. It was a moment of unguarded confusion, as if I'd left a door open, and a feeling, as unpleasant and familiar as a bad habit, crept across the threshold of my thoughts: the sense that I was guilty of coasting, or worse, escaping.

Once in the park, I could tell venturing this far from home had been overly ambitious: it was cold, and my legs were shaky from the short walk. I plunked myself down on a green chair, by a bed of limp yellow flowers. Just then, my player shut down; I'd forgotten to recharge it. A couple of joggers went by; an old couple walked arm in arm, in matching beige *imperméables* and brown hats. An airplane bisected the sky.

I wondered if I'd overstayed my Paris welcome. Perhaps I should've only stayed long enough to lick my wounds, not develop new ones. On the other hand, I did have the right to be here, and I didn't want to leave. Did that justify my staying? If I never heard from Monsieur Laveau again, would I look for another job? Come to think of it, who was I, if I wasn't *doing* something? Was my sense of identity based only on doing things—reading, eating, working, walking, seeing friends, going to movies or museums, et cetera? Even now, I was sitting in a park, making resolutions. How did I want to define my life?

I gnawed at a ragged skin flap around my thumbnail until I could peel it off like wallpaper. I got it between my bottom and top front teeth and worried it into small pieces. Some people just eat raspberries. I have to split the seedy bits in half before swallowing them.

Across the *allée*, a man sat facing me. He had wispy, light brown hair and one of those jutting jaws that make me think of determined farm animals. He walked over.

"*Je peux m'asseoir?*" he asked, pointing to the chair next to mine.

"I beg your pardon?" I asked.

"You were looking at me, I was looking at you," he said, as if it were obvious.

"I wasn't looking at you, I was staring into space," I protested.

"A woman alone is always waiting for someone," he purred, with a knowing look. "Why not make a new friend?" It wasn't just what he said but the unctuous way he said it, as if we were playing a game, as if what I said didn't matter. Wracked by a wave of nausea, I hoisted myself out of my chair.

"*Monsieur, vous faites erreur,*" I said and walked toward the exit. At the tall gates, with iron spears shaped like arrows, I felt a pebble in my sneaker. I bent down to undo my shoelace. My vision blurred, and I fell over, scraping my knee and both palms on the concrete. A teenage boy reached down and helped me to my feet.

"*Mademoiselle? Ça va aller?*" he asked. My eyes welled up at his kindness.

"*Merci, ça va,*" I said and limped into the métro station. I opened my palms: they were scratched, the abrasions black with dirt.

I got home and drew a bath, dialing Bunny's number while waiting for the tub to fill. His voice wasn't on the machine, but I left a message anyway. "Are you still in Italy? I don't know if you're checking messages, but would you please please please call me? I miss you." My voice caught in my throat and I hiccuped. I pulled off the lingerie. My period was early; there was a dark red stain on the crotch where I'd bled into the silk. "Fuck, fuck, fuck," I muttered, dumping the panties into a sink filled with cold water. I draped the bra on the window handle and climbed into the tub, cursing again as the hot water stung my hands and knee.

I sat in the tub until the water grew lukewarm, then went to bed. What I wanted most in the world, in that very moment, was to collapse into a deep sleep, the kind that would fix everything.

....

Under the fluorescent light above the mirror, my face looked bloated and haggard. I didn't look like myself, though perhaps no one does at three in the morning, after an intense crying jag. It was a preview of what I would look like in thirty years, if I never used moisturizer again and went to work in a coal mine. I couldn't remember what I'd been crying about, just that I woke up sobbing, beset by an unidentified sense of loss. I splashed water on my face and slunk back to bed, falling into a restless sleep.

In the morning, I made coffee for the first time in days. The phone rang, but I'd turned the volume on the answering machine down too low to hear the caller. I remembered snippets of my dream: horrible images of an explosion, plus the shrieking of twisting metal, sirens, a voice I didn't know, cacophony. I wondered how long I'd keep dreaming the same nightmare.

I used to have a recurring dream. It took place in a house I'd never seen in real life. It had a stone fireplace in the living room, with a ledge I liked to sit on, and a rickety, screened-in porch, with a back wall lined with books and a desk facing the ocean. The house was raised, on stilts, to accommodate the tide, and I imagined it was somewhere in Georgia or South Carolina, places I'd never been.

Over time, my dreams had furnished it. A circular staircase led to a bedroom under a pitched roof. The sheets were printed with extravagant cabbage roses, not my taste, but I got used to it. In one dream, I'd thrown a party: there was a fire in the fireplace, music, lots of people, noise. I could draw the house's architectural plans, except I didn't know where the bathroom and kitchen were.

I'd grown fond of it; it was cozy and ramshackle. But one night, I dreamed someone broke in. It was night, too dark to see, but I knew my way around, and despite the crash of waves breaking on the sand, I could hear creaking sounds. I crept onto the porch, and someone wrapped a cloth around my neck and tried to strangle me. I woke up, the way they say you do, because you can't die in your dreams. I never dreamed of the house again. Now I wondered if something awful had to happen to me in my recurring nightmare for it to stop.

I went into the living room to listen to my message.

"*Bonjour, mademoiselle. Ici Bernard Laveau. Auriez-vous la gentillesse de passer me voir ce matin, de préférence avant treize heures. J'ai un nouveau chapitre à vous confier . . ."* Monsieur Laveau had a new chapter for me! I'd almost given up hope. I played the message again to make sure those were really his stentorian tones, summoning me with that familiar, politely veiled condescension. A new chapter! I was forgiven!

....

As I walked up the rue de Condé, I shivered, despite the layers I'd piled on: a hint of winter hung in the late October air like a premonition. But the chill couldn't dampen my mood: I wanted to throw my hat in the air, skip across sidewalks, even smile at strangers, an activity usually associated with Americans and the developmentally challenged.

I pushed the bookstore door open and shook it, so the cowbell would clang repeatedly. Monsieur Laveau called out, *"Un instant, je vous prie."*

As usual, he was on the phone. I cleared a stack of books off a chair and sat by the door. Bernard raised his voice.

"Ecoute, j'ai fait de mon mieux! L'autre traductrice n'est pas disponible, et celle dont on a parlé voyage en Amerique Latine, alors que veux-tu? Soit on utilise celle-là, soit tu te débrouilles, mon vieux, parce que moi, je n'en peux plus!"

My elation went flat, a needle to a carnival balloon. Bernard was talking about me. He was on the phone with the author, and I wasn't his first choice of translator. Not even his second. The first one wasn't available; the other one was in South America. Moreover, he was fed up with trying to find someone. I was the *solution de secours,* the emergency exit, the last resort.

My fingertips felt cold, as if all my blood had drained into my shoes. I stared down at my feet. I wanted to disappear.

I thought about sneaking out, but the office door swung open. Bernard sported a recent haircut, his silver hair trimmed close to his head, but the bushy eyebrows were as splendidly arachnid as ever. He wore a blue shirt under a gray V-neck sweater.

"Entrez, mademoiselle. Merci d'être venue," he said, gesturing for me to come in. His voice was polite, almost warm, but I didn't waste any time.

"Ecoutez, monsieur, j'ai entendu votre conversation." My voice trembling despite myself, I confessed that I'd overheard him.

"Oui?" he asked, as if to say, so what?

I glared at him and said, "Maybe you should wait until one of your *other* translators becomes available." He straightened out a pile of books on the table. "While I'm not a professional translator, I had thought I was doing a decent job. But now I find out I'm your third choice and your writer doesn't like my work. Well, I prefer not to be foisted on anyone, *monsieur,"* I said reproachfully.

He leaned against the doorframe and crossed his arms, narrowing his eyes at me as if he were trying to remember what ill wind had blown me through the door.

"I don't know if your mother warned you about eavesdropping," he said conversationally, "but one of the obvious dangers is that you might misinterpret what you overhear." A two-syllable "uh-oh" tolled in my head. I caught a pea-size chunk of my lower lip between my teeth.

"I was on the phone with a client of mine," he continued, eyes gleaming, "a writer of supernatural thrillers set in the American South. Because he speaks French adequately, and also because his main character is a *Louisiana Creole* and employs both the *Creole* language and slang," he said, his voice escalating in volume as I flinched, "he is *extremely demanding* when it comes to the translation of his books into *French!"*

Pausing to let the words sink in, he removed a linen handkerchief from his pocket and blew his nose. My neck disappeared into my shoulders.

"Now," he added silkily, folding the handkerchief, his voice resuming its normal pitch, "as I believe I have already mentioned to you, it is enough work for me to massage the temperamental egos of my writers without having to do the same for my translators. For the second time, would you do me the supreme kindness of stepping into my office?" He smiled, revealing a row of small, square, ivory teeth.

It was the first time I'd seen Bernard smile, at least at me. I walked into his office and sat. Though I'd been chastised like a snotty-nosed twelve-year-old, I felt a thrill at being lumped in the category of one of "his" translators. Until that moment, I hadn't known exactly how much I'd been thirsting for a reason to stay in Paris, and here was Bernard handing me one, ready-made, prêt-à-porter: I was a translator.

He poured me a cup of fragrant espresso. "A special blend. A friend of mine brought it back from Milan," he explained.

"Merci," I said in a small voice.

The phone rang, and he sank down in his chair to answer it, glaring at me in mock severity. I grinned into the coffee cup, the heat tickling my nose.

"Ah, c'est toi. Oui. Je suis avec elle en ce moment, cher ami," he said, giving me a pointed look. This time, it really was my author. I pantomimed getting up, gesturing toward the door, but Bernard waved at me to stay put. *"Sans faute, sans faute. Evidemment. A plus tard,"* he said and hung up.

"That was Monsieur X!" I exclaimed.

"Si vous voulez," he said. He lifted his cup to his lips.

"He does exist!" I said. "I was starting to wonder if you'd made him up," I joked.

"C'est quoi, 'made him up'?" he asked, the bushy eyebrows drawing together.

"To invent," I explained.

He leaned back in his chair, his gaze cold. *"Mais voyons, mademoiselle,* if I had invented him, whose work would you be translating?" he asked.

"Well, maybe you wrote it, or . . ." I trailed off. Bernard was not amused. "Never mind." I said, slouching down on the chair. Playtime was over. He handed me an envelope. I reached for it, but he didn't let go.

"Inside, you will find another ending, and you will recall you owe me the translation of the second one—"

"I haven't started that one. I didn't know whether I should," I said, interrupting him. "But I'll get right on it."

He nodded. "So you will owe me two chapters," he said, "and you will find also a confidentiality agreement and a standard contract, which you will sign and return to me, as well as information about *droits d'auteur,* or author's rights. In addition, I want your word that you will not discuss this work with anyone. *Ever.*" His voice was solemn. He let go of the envelope and leaned back, steepling his fingers together.

"You have it, of course. But I'm never to talk about it? Even after it's published?" I asked. He gave a long-suffering sigh.

"*Mais non, mademoiselle.* If it gets published, *then* you may discuss it. And *if* it gets published in English, you will, *bien sûr,* receive credit in *very small print* beneath the author's name, or his pseudonym. *If* we sell the English-language rights, your rights will also include, as you will see from the contract, a bonus compensation plus royalties. *If,*" he repeated, shaking a finger at me.

"Royalties? I get royalties?" I grinned.

"*Il ne faut pas vendre la peau de l'ours avant de l'avoir tué,*" he said, the French equivalent of not counting chickens, except it was about selling a bearskin before you kill the bear. "*Vous ne buvez pas votre café?*"

"*Si, si.*" I picked up the cup and downed the coffee in two gulps. He looked at me expectantly. "*Molto buono,*" I said.

He nodded. "You'll see, there's a shift in the writing. Let me see your work by Friday midday, as I am going to the country." He stood. I was discharged.

"*A bientôt, mademoiselle.*"

"*A bientôt, monsieur, et merci encore,*" I said. I stood there for a moment, hesitant, wanting to tell him how grateful I felt, but I didn't know quite what to say. He gave me a questioning look, then nodded, understanding. I squelched an urge to kiss him on the cheek and instead gave him a jaunty salute.

He glanced at my hand. *"Qu'est ce qui s'est passé?"* he asked, pointing to the bandage.

"A bad burn," I answered. "But it's healing."

....

I walked out, realizing our relationship had changed. I'd felt it in the playfulness in our exchange. It was like a dance, a minuet, where I constantly trod on his toes. Behind his amused, impatient, stern manner of putting me in my place, I could tell that not only had he forgiven me but he liked me. The French didn't bother instructing people they didn't care about: knowledge was a gift you bestowed on people you liked. If the French were indifferent to you, they let you labor in ignorance. If they disliked you, they delighted in your lack of knowledge.

Therefore, Bernard's condescension, chastisement, and lecturing meant he liked me. The conclusion was so delightful that I grinned at a young woman pushing a navy blue pram. She glared at me.

I cut down to the rue Jacob and window-shopped the antiques stores. I examined storefronts displaying ormolu sconces, nineteenth-century furniture, brass carriage lamps, gravures of maps, oil paintings of jowly burghers, fraying tapestries, and my favorite, stacks of ironed, monogrammed, and *ajouré*d tablecloths, napkins, and bed linens.

The sun made stealth appearances through breaks in the clouds. I crossed back over the Seine on the Pont du Carrousel and into the Tuileries. Although it was a crisp day, Parisians strolled through the garden and sat on the benches, soaking up a bit of sun.

Up ahead, I could see the large round fountain at the end of the garden, its jets turned off. Green enamel metal chairs were arranged around it in random fashion. I'd sat there before with Bunny, usually around this time of day, after lunch at one of his haunts. The Austrian brunch place and the soufflé restaurant were nearby, off the rue de Ravioli.

I wondered where he was. I wanted to tell him about Monsieur Laveau, how I'd nearly lost my job. As I got closer to the fountain, the sunlight shimmered on the surface, and I squinted against the starbursts of light. A large figure in a khaki trench coat, jeans, and sneakers sat on a chair under a tree, his head balanced on his fist like Rodin's thinker. My toe stubbed a large pebble and sent it skidding over the gravel.

It looked like Bunny, but it couldn't be Bunny. Bunny would've called to tell me he was back in town, to make plans, to eat an *onglet* with *frites* at Le Petit Victor Hugo in the Sixteenth or that Indian place he called Banana. Bunny would've called when he got back, to complain about European drivers, the lack of good food on the road, the lamentable state of Top 40 radio. So, it couldn't be Bunny. But the man seated on the green enamel chair looked just like him. I walked toward him in the bright midday light.

33

*Dans le domaine des sentiments,
le réel ne se distingue pas de l'imaginaire.**
—ANDRÉ GIDE, *Les Faux-Monnayeurs*

*I*recognized the giant sneakers. There was a plastic WHSmith shopping bag on the ground next to him. I stopped a couple of feet away.

"It's you, isn't it?" I asked rhetorically, because now I was sure. Pale skin, thin gray-brown hair, age spots on his cheeks and hands.

He looked up. "He-e-e-y," he said, as if surprised out of a reverie. "You found me."

"When d'you get back?" I asked. He dusted off the chair next to him, and I sat. He looked tired, the bags under his eyes thick and droopy.

"I don't know. Couple of days, I guess." He looked across the park.

"Did you get my message?"

"Will ya look at that kid?" he asked, his eyes lighting up. I followed his gaze across the fountain to a toddler, speeding toward the water with a large stuffed animal. His mother gave chase, catching him just in time to prevent the ignoble dunking of Babar, king of the elephants, complete with a green three-piece suit and a yellow crown.

---

*In the realm of the sentiments, the real is no different from the imaginary.

"Bunny," I said. He tore his eyes away and looked at me.

"Yeah, yeah, the one where you sound like a refugee. I can't deal with hysterical women," he said, screwing up his eyes against the sun.

"I wasn't hysterical! I missed you!" I protested, irked.

"Cool it, I'm kidding. I got back last night. I was going to call later. I just had to get my head together, pick up a few books. Incredible food, but not a decent bookstore on the whole coast."

"But you read Italian," I said.

"Just because I *read* Italian doesn't mean I *wanna* read in Italian. When I'm on vacation, I want a thriller in my native tongue. Ed McBain. Or Vonnegut," he growled.

"What's wrong? Are you in a bad mood?" I asked. Something wasn't right, as if he were out of sorts, not entirely there. He picked a twig off the ground.

"Takes a while to get used to 'Ris again," he said. "Not sure I want to stay."

"Would you really move to Avignon?" I watched as he drew lines in the hard-packed sand. A gust of wind blew dust up, and he tossed the stick away.

"Maybe. It's small, but I want somewhere warm. I'm tired of cold," he said, pulling his coat around him. "Winter here is dark and gloomy." His mouth set in a line.

"How about Dalloyau, for an *opéra*? My treat," I said.

A tired smile flitted across his face, but he said, "Nah. It's too far."

"There's one on the Faubourg Saint-Honoré," I said.

He shook his head. "The doc says I have to watch my cholesterol, and I didn't in Italy," he explained. "Besides, my back is killing me. It's an eleven-hour drive from Genoa. I had to take the métro here. I hate the métro." He leaned forward, his face tight. For a moment, it looked like he might cry.

"Bunny." I reached a hand toward him, but he sat back. "What's wrong?"

"I'm fine, kid. I'll get used to things again. You?"

"Fine," I answered, though my voice rose at the end of the word, making it sound like a question. He leaned over and kissed me on the cheek. It felt like a shock of cold air, his lips were so cold. "I'm gonna go. I have to descend the hell of the Sixteenth back to Boulogne. See you."

I watched him lumber up the slanted walk toward the Concorde station. At the top, he paused and raised his right hand to wave without turning around. He looked like a mirage, his coat flapping in the wind before he disappeared behind the stone balustrade.

I sat in the park, letting the wind blow my hair around. Bunny's sad mood seeped into me. It had to be hard, being squeezed out of your job. At least Italy had been a distraction. But here, in the city where he'd lived and worked for the past twenty years . . .

I walked toward Ravioli and took the métro home. I was thrilled to have my job back, and not one but two chapters due in days.

At home, I sat on the sofa and looked at both chapters. Each one was twenty pages long and, I suspected, in a smaller font than the earlier ones. Bernard was one sneaky bastard, I laughed to myself. I stretched out and read the second ending. It began where the previous one had, with the narrator waiting for the detective's report.

During the two weeks I waited to hear from Verbier, my relationship with Daphne disintegrated. We barely spoke to each other. Returning home from work one evening, I found a taxi driver putting her suitcase in the trunk. Daphne sat waiting for me, her set of keys on the table. It was astonishing how little it affected me.

She lit a cigarette. "I didn't know you smoked," I said, pouring myself a whiskey.

"There are many things you don't know," she said coolly, straightening a pleat in her skirt. "I don't know who she is, and I don't care. I'm leaving you for Mathieu."

"He didn't tell me he was getting a divorce," I remarked, trying to picture them together. Mathieu and I had done our military service together. I'd been a witness at his wedding. Daphne put out her cigarette, slapped me once, very hard, picked up her handbag and gloves, and left.

Afterward, it was the silence I noticed. It was the only thing that bothered me.

Aha. So, Daphne the Veal could take care of herself. Good for her.

I spent more time at the office, immersing myself in work. But I couldn't stop thinking about Eve, especially after Verbier's report arrived in the mail.

"After numerous hours of research, it has been determined that Madame Eve Denoël, née Marguerite Rashwan, is currently living in Biarritz, at 6, allée des Libellules. She is often seen in the company of Monsieur Eric Beaufort de Blois, chairman of Ericsson Holdings, Ltd., and a widower. He also maintains a residence in Biarritz, the Villa du Soleil, which overlooks the sea . . ."

It was as I'd suspected, when I'd seen them at Longchamp: she was Beaufort's mistress. Why had I disregarded it? I'd been a fool to think it didn't matter.

"Marguerite was born and raised in Lausanne, Switzerland, the daughter of Lisette Cabourg, a French socialite, and Raouf Rashwan, a retired Egyptian diplomat, former ambassador to France and the United Nations.

"When her father died of lung cancer, Marguerite was sent to Miss Pym's School in Gloucestershire. Her mother moved to Geneva and remarried twice. The first was to a British banker, Ian Rathmines; he died skiing in Crans-Montana in a freak avalanche. A year later, Madame Rashwan-Rathmines married Fletcher Flanagan, a retired pulmonary surgeon and fellow member of the Alpine Birding Club.

"At eighteen, Marguerite left England with her boyfriend, Ricky Taher, a student at Cambridge and scion of a prominent Cairene family. They lived together briefly in Cairo but split up when Taher's family pressured him into marrying a distant cousin.

"Marguerite enrolled in classes at the American University and moved in with an American student, James Rochester. With various friends, they formed a jazz music band; James played piano and Marguerite sang. They played once a week for the expatriate crowd at the Hôtel Méridien. Marguerite changed her name to Eve.

"Rochester, addicted to hashish and prescription drugs, was prone to violent mood swings. While still living with him, Eve began an affair with a Russian petroleum engineer. James attempted suicide, leaping from their third-floor balcony and breaking a leg as well as injuring a donkey tethered in the street below. Eve returned to Geneva, remaining there until her mother's death from leukemia.

"She donated a portion of her inheritance to cancer research, then spent a year abroad before moving to Paris. She bought an apartment and studied theater. During this time she became involved with Laurent Weissman, a documentary filmmaker for TF1.

"At the Cannes Film Festival, Eve struck up a friendship with Eric Beaufort de Blois, a French industrialist fifteen years her senior, an acquaintance of her stepfather. Beaufort was married to the fashion designer Alix de Cruz. It was also at this time that Eve discovered Weissman's numerous infidelities. She left him shortly thereafter.

"She accepted a job in public relations for the house of Alix de Cruz, and a friendship developed between the two women. A year later, Eve married de Cruz's brother, Jean Denoël, legal counsel and chief financial officer of the fashion house."

Ending number two was nearly the same story but slightly tweaked, a parallel universe.

"In an uncanny case of history repeating, Jean Denoël disappeared in a heli-skiing accident in the Bugaboos. Search-and-rescue teams failed to find his body.

"Eve retreated to Switzerland. Coaxed back to Paris by Alix de Cruz, she resumed work at the fashion house six months later. When Alix de Cruz overdosed on painkillers, Beaufort closed the fashion house (under two preexisting contracts, the brand name Alix de Cruz continues, licensed to an eyewear company and a textile manufacturer, for a line of cotton sheets). Beaufort devoted himself to his hobby, breeding racehorses. Eve Denoël became a frequent visitor to his farm in Normandy . . ."

I put the report down. My fury with Eve was replaced by an acute sense of disappointment. She had a long history with Beaufort. I was a minor deviation on a predetermined path they walked together.

Ew. Really clunky metaphor. I made a note to tinker with it later.

I couldn't understand how I could have fallen so deeply for a woman who was so involved with someone else. The thought occupied me for days. I had no insight as to why, but I had to be pragmatic. There was no choice but to let go. And yet, I couldn't.

"I want a detailed description of Eve Denoël's daily activities in Biarritz," I told Verbier on the phone. "Where she eats, who she visits, where she gets her hair done."

I would go to Biarritz.

Uh-oh. I suspected my narrator was about to get his ass kicked.

Less than five days later, I booked a hotel and a ticket on Air Inter.

I pressed Save. My stomach rumbled, and I went into the kitchen to hunt down dinner. Finding a frozen herbed *merlan* steak, I put it in a pan and set the timer. I made a mental note to check the Web for its mercury levels and, while I was at it, what kind of fish it was. My French fluency had alarming limits: I knew the fish I liked in English (yellowtail, black cod), I knew the fish I liked in French *(bar, loup de mer, cabillaud, rouget)*, but I didn't know how to translate them, aside from the obvious ones: *saumon, truite, thon.* Maybe one ate different fish in different countries, given the different oceans. Or maybe there weren't enough neural pathways in my brain connecting the two languages. My dabbling in translation theory had kick-started all sorts of questions.

If the fish were different because they lived in different oceans, were people different in each language? In English, I sounded more monotonous, and I didn't need to open my mouth much to speak it. French, on the other hand, required precise contortions of the lips, use of the back of the palate for the "r's," and an almost musical scale for emphasis and exclamations. If I was tired, my French pronunciation of *"concert"* sounded like *"cancer."*

Sometimes, my English-language brain smirked at the theatrical way my voice rose and fell in French. An explanation on the Internet said French was a "syllable-timed" language, meaning each syllable was of the same duration, versus English, which was a "stress-timed" language, meaning that, depending on the word, each syllable might have a different length but that the time between the syllables remained consistent. I sounded out words, trying to figure out what this meant, but I didn't get it.

In the next few pages, the narrator went down to Biarritz and stalked Eve. This led to one quasicomical but somewhat pathetic scene where he knocked over a display of stocking-covered plastic legs fanned out like a peacock tail in the hosiery section of the Printemps department store before confronting her at her apartment.

"What are you doing here?" Eve shouted, dropping her shopping bags. "You gave me such a shock, you cretin! What's happened to you? You look terrible."

In all my fantasies, these were not the first words she spoke to me.

I chuckled. Every once in a while, Monsieur X had a sense of humor.

I followed her inside her apartment. It was a sunny place, painted white and furnished with ugly modern furniture the color of goose shit.

I backspaced. *Caca d'oie* is not a color in English. I changed it to "dung brown."

"You look terrible," she repeated, but smiling this time. "But I'm so happy to see you." She folded me in her arms.

"How could you disappear like that?" I asked her hair, confused.

"I told you I was going away," she said, pulling away from me.

"You neglected to tell me whether you were coming back," I pointed out.

"Of course I was coming back. I live in Paris." She turned to put various food items in the refrigerator and in cupboards. I reached out a hand to stop her. Startled, she dropped a jar of jam on my foot.

Ignoring the pain, I said, "You're living here! In his apartment! Going to restaurants with him! Why would I think you were coming back?" I asked.

She recoiled. "You've been spying on me?"

"I was going mad," I said, grasping her shoulders. She shook herself free . . .

The narrator and Eve yelled at each other for a couple of pages, the fighting escalating. He called her a heartless kept woman; she called him a dirty spy. She broke things, then broke down, sobbing. He tried to comfort her; she pushed him away. He broke down and kicked the furniture. Did people really fight like this?

Eve's eyes flashed with fury. "This is my apartment," she said, pointing to herself. "It has belonged to me since my husband died," she said. "Eric has been like a father to me, his wife was my closest friend. Your suspicions are repugnant," she hissed.

We looked at each other across the white floor. My anger dwindled away. I believed her. I believed her, and I saw her as if for the first time, vulnerable, hurt, angry, but above all, the woman I loved.

"Eve," I began, moving toward her. "I was going mad, wondering if you'd come back," I said. She didn't say anything. I took another step.

"I came here to beg you to come back—" I stopped as one pear-shaped tear rolled down her cheek. "I love you, Eve. Why did you leave?" I asked.

"Venice frightened me. I didn't want to care for someone so deeply," she said. "But now you're here . . ."

I waited, holding my breath. If she asked me to leave, I would banish myself from her life.

"I love you, too," she said.

I didn't like this ending much, either. It was almost sweet, but it was too thin to have any real impact. I saved my work and called Clara to ask how her ankle was doing.

"It's better. A lovely shade of green," she said. "Do you want to come over? My mother bought out the Italian *traiteur* and rented *Quand Harry Rencontre Sally* yet again."

"No, but thanks," I said, laughing at her exasperated tone. "Tell me, what's it called in French when a film ends happily but in a way you don't believe?" I asked.

"An American ending," she said.

. . . .

I looked at the screen again, but my eyes smarted. Instead, I fixed myself a dinner tray with the fish and its gooey herbed sauce, vegetables, and a glass of white wine, and carried my rectangular tableau of early-twenty-first-century solitary angst, complete with white paper napkin, into the living room.

On the television, I surfed past *Star Academy*, and the live-action movie of the comic book *Astérix et Obélix*, set in ancient Gaul. Another channel was showing a program about irrigation techniques in the Pyrenees, complete with close-ups of black tubing and pressure valves. I thought about ponying up for cable. On M6, attractive mutants kitted out in customized leathers gritted their teeth, flared their nostrils, and accelerated menacingly on motorcycles: an American TV show.

The only acceptable option was the movie on Arte, the PBS-like French-German channel: a German drama about a mild-mannered scientist who falls in love with an art dealer, only to find out she's the daughter of the hit man who killed his father. It looked watchable. I took my tray into the kitchen.

When I came back, Olivier was on-screen. I froze in the doorway. Much younger, he had long hair and razor stubble. He wore a paint-splattered T-shirt and jeans, and he played the painter boyfriend of the art dealer. Over dated synth pop, he posed in front of an abstract canvas trying to look intense, a hand-rolled cigarette drooping from the corner of his mouth.

He wasn't convincing. Not the slightest bit. He was awkward and mannered, and I felt a rush of tenderness for this puppy version of him—overeager, cocky, unformed. When the camera zoomed in for a close-up as he tried to convey tormented artistic genius—*in German*—I laughed. When the art dealer girlfriend stopped by, he dropped his paintbrush in a jar and gave her a knowing, wolfish grin.

My indulgent mood snapped. I knew that smile. I knew it intimately. Tense, muscles rigid, I watched the rest of the movie. When he wasn't on-screen, I got impatient, wanting a fast-forward button. I took an intense hatred to the actress who played his girlfriend, a freckled redhead who, by any other standards, would have been an appealing heroine. I liked her better when she told Olivier she was leaving him. He broke down and cried.

I'd never seen him cry. Watching him now, I felt an odd combination of nausea and pleasure, at once voyeuristic and unsettling. It didn't occur to me that he was acting. I thought I was looking through a window, able to see what he looked like when he was really hurting.

After the credits rolled, I got into bed in my clothes. In my head, I played an endless cinema of loss, remembering a hundred moments that had slipped through my fingers like sand: Olivier with me in the kitchen, at the movies, in restaurants, cafés, in bed.

I curled up in the dark, insulated by my own misery. I felt still and small. Even my breathing seemed diminished, as if I needed less air. As if I'd folded myself into a small space, the way I sometimes folded paper into halves, then quarters, eighths, sixteenths, thirty-seconds, until the paper was a tough, tiny Chiclet.

....

All I wanted was to sleep. No, scratch that: all I wanted was to be unconscious.

I dreamed I was alone on the rocky beach of a river. People paddled by in kayaks and yelled out to me. I plugged my ears and sang "la la la la" at them. The pebbles beneath my feet began speaking, and as I ran away, they shrieked at me.

I woke early, to walls that were a pale blue, as thin as eggshell, and wiped the sweat off my face with the bedsheet. It was an odd dream, but strange things happen in dreams. In the past, I'd dreamed that I was a bar of soap, that Edward G. Robinson was both a French bulldog and my long-lost uncle, and that flying was a matter of breathing properly and bobbing, like being perfectly weighted when diving.

I shivered and changed into a dry T-shirt and sweats. My skin still felt clammy. Maybe I was having a flu relapse. Clara had given me the name of her internist, and I searched for it now, sifting through the small mountain of miscellaneous notes, receipts, postcards, and business cards I kept on the marble mantel. I pulled a dark red card out of the pile. It was an addition to my collection of African witch-doctor cards. This one was for Professeur Moro. I skimmed the text, reading, *"Protection contre tous les mauvais esprits."* Maybe a bad spirit was giving me the bad dreams.

It was getting lighter and noisier outside, but I put on an airplane eye mask I kept on the bedside table and stuffed orange foam earplugs in my ears.

This time, I dreamed of the childhood summer weekends I'd spent at the beach in Ventura with my best friend and her family. We used to play on the man-made jetty, an accident of concrete cylinders shaped like giant plumbing pipes, and collect hermit crabs from the tide pools.

It was cruel what we did, collecting the hermit crabs in a plastic bucket with an inch or two of seawater. I couldn't remember if we dumped them back into the ocean or if we forgot about them, our new pets, and left them to rot and die in the bucket.

Not remembering doesn't mean it didn't happen, came the thought, distant, faint. I rolled over and pulled the duvet over my head. When a jackhammer began tearing up the sidewalk, I gave up. I took a shower, made coffee, and turned on the computer to start work on the third ending.

34

Et les mouettes se délectent de nos anecdotes.*
—ALAIN BASHUNG,
"J'écume"

Midday, I took a break and went to the organic market to buy Clara her favorite pears and a box of chocolate truffles and then hopped on the bus to her apartment. She greeted me at the door, still hobbling but in good spirits.

I followed her into her spotless white kitchen. I chopped herbs while she beat eggs for an omelet.

"How do you like yours? *Baveuse?*" she asked, adding the herbs. She poured the mixture into the pan and shook it back and forth over the flame.

I made a face. "That's such a gross word," I said.

"What, *baveuse?* It's just runny."

"It means runny, but it's the actual word for 'drooly,'" I said. "*Bave* is drool."

She rolled her eyes. "You're spending too much time translating."

---

*And the seagulls delight in our anecdotes.

"Maybe. But it's kind of keeping me sane," I said. "Clara, can I ask you something? How do you stand it? With your friend, I mean?" She served the omelet onto two plates. I breathed in herbs and butter.

"What do you want me to say?" She tossed aside a dish towel and sat next to me. "Yes, of course, there are times when I am inconsolable, when I can't stand it anymore, and I think of ending it. But other times . . . if he left his wife, I'm not sure I'd want him."

"Really?" This was a surprise.

"The qualities that I like in him are a lover's qualities. He is attentive, always happy to see me. I get the best of him. I'm not so sure I would like him so much if I had to look at his dirty laundry or argue about housework."

"I hadn't thought of that," I said. I hadn't gotten to the laundry or housework stage with Olivier. I took a bite of the omelet. "This is delicious," I said.

"And what would I do in Antwerp?" She made a face. "His company is there. Antwerp! It's nice for a weekend, but to live? *Ah, non! Je suis Parisienne, moi!*"

. . . .

When I came home, Daphne was packing her bags.

"What are you doing?" I asked stupidly.

"Jean-Marc, you don't love me anymore," she said, folding a yellow sweater. She placed it in a suitcase on the bed, her face hidden behind her blond hair.

"That's not true," I said, moving toward her.

"Yes, it is. Otherwise, you wouldn't treat me this way." She shut the suitcase. Floral-printed silk dangled out the side. I recognized the pattern of one of her dresses.

"Don't be silly," I cajoled. I swept her hair off her shoulder and bent to kiss her.

"I can't believe you!" She whirled around, her face an ugly shade

of red, a bruised fruit. "Don't touch me!" she shouted. I backed out of the room.

A foreign sensation—perhaps it was panic—edged into my thoughts. Daphne pulled the hard plastic suitcase behind her on a leash. It rolled awkwardly, sinking in the carpet pile. I didn't help her. She gave the room one last look.

I touched her arm, slid my hand down to her wrist. I didn't know what to say, so I said the obvious. "Don't go."

"That's my problem, you know," she said sadly. "I always believe you, even when you say things you don't believe yourself. 'Don't go,'" she mocked. "You don't mean it—you don't want to eat dinner alone, that's all."

"That's not true." But I said it because I had to say it, even though she was right. She gave me a pitying look. "What can I do to change your mind?" I asked, studying her face, the skin sprinkled with summer freckles. We would have had pretty children.

She wheeled the suitcase into the elevator. Her face was impassive; she was already a stranger to me. I watched, helpless, as she disappeared from my life.

This was the second variation to dispatch Daphne, I noticed.

I immersed myself in work. I hated coming home. Daphne's words rang in my ears. It was true: I didn't like eating alone. It made me feel shabby.

I scribbled a note: is "shabby" right? Maybe "lame" or "stupid" or "like an idiot" would be better. The sentence was *"Je me sentais con."*

When Verbier's report arrived in the mail, I tore it open.

"My research has determined that Madame Eve Dessès, née Hoda

'Francine' Abdi, is presently in London, in a suite at Claridge's Hotel in Mayfair—

This was the third version of Eve, with yet another name.

"—reserved in the name of Eric Beaufort, of Beaufort Communications, Ltd."
    So, she had gone to him. I hadn't been wrong.
    "Beaufort is separated from his second wife, Elizabeth Burrows, owner of the public relations firm EZ Burrows & Associates. When in London, Beaufort stays at Claridge's, where his longtime mistress, Madame Dessès, usually accompanies him. Beaufort dines with his wife once a week at Cipriani . . ."
    I poured myself a shot of whiskey, and drank it . . .

I paused, hands hovering above the keyboard, confounded. To drink something down in one gulp in French was to swallow it *"cul sec,"* literally "dry ass," another variation on words derived from *"cul."* "Chug-a-lug" didn't quite capture it. It was the Franglais syndrome again: I couldn't remember the expression in English. I wrote "I downed a shot of whiskey."

"Eve Dessès, née Hoda 'Francine' Abdi, was born and raised in Cairo, the only daughter of an Egyptian silversmith and his Syrian wife. After her father died of a brain aneurysm when Francine was thirteen, her mother remarried and sent Francine to a French Catholic boarding school, Notre-Dame de la Sainte-Espérance. She ran away from the school numerous times.
    "At seventeen, she ran away again. She was found months later in Alexandria, where she was working as a dancer in a French cancan revue. There, she'd become involved with a notorious gambler,

Ali Marwan. When the news reached Cairo, her mother collapsed and had to be hospitalized. Her brothers went to Alexandria and brought her home. She lived under virtual house arrest for the next two years.

"Her brothers attempted to marry her off to a middle-aged Syrian, owner of a textile factory in Damascus, but two weeks before the wedding, Francine stole her passport and flew to Athens, where she changed her name to Eve Abdi. At first, she worked as a belly dancer in a Lebanese restaurant, then she became the star of a cabaret show at the luxury Twelve Nymphs Resort. She was rumored to be the girlfriend of a shipping magnate and fled the country after receiving death threats from his wife.

"She turned up in Paris, renting a studio apartment near Château Rouge and working as a dancer at the Crazy Horse. Her boyfriends at the time included a professional soccer player, a Nigerian restaurant owner, and her landlord.

"A knee injury put an end to her dancing career. She worked at various jobs, including translation of Arabic newspapers and literature, and a stint as a salesgirl at the Samaritaine department store. A small role in a soft-porn film by the Italian filmmaker Alessandro Diavoli made her a minor cult celebrity and introduced her to the film's backer, Gilbert Dessès. A Moroccan immigrant who'd amassed a fortune in import-export, Dessès had become a film producer (though he is credited as a writer on the film Una Notte a Parigi, *1974). He was seventeen years her senior and married to a French writer, Véronique Boutros.*

"Obtaining a divorce, Dessès married Eve Abdi, but the marriage was not a success. Neighbors complained of screaming and suspected physical abuse, and the police were called to the apartment twice. Eve began divorce proceedings, but before the divorce became final, Dessès died in a private plane crash in the Dolomites."

People keep dying in this woman's life. Often in snow.

"Eve Dessès inherited the Dessès estate. She became an ardent advo-cate for women's rights in the Arab world, chairing fund-raisers and giving interviews. Over the next few years, she became involved with an American investment banker, P. Stanley Carruthers; a French pub-lisher, Bertrand L'Huissier; and a French journalist, Alexi Barthès-Levinsky. Her comfortable life in Paris came to a halt with the pub-lication of Véronique Boutros's roman à clef, The Many Lives of a Femme Fatale. *The scandalous bestseller depicted the amorous ad-ventures of a ruthless woman who seduced and discarded men at will. While Eve Dessès was never actually named as the character in the book, it was widely assumed the two were one and the same.*

"The Many Lives of a Femme Fatale *is no longer in print.*

"Eve left Paris for London, where she made the acquaintance of Constantine Ziyad, a Greco-Iraqi horse trainer for a Saudi Arabian prince. Through him, she met Eric Beaufort . . ."

Stunned, I read Verbier's report, unable to imagine this was the woman I knew.

"She has maintained a relationship with Beaufort for the last four years. They meet in London, as well as in Paris. The relationship is not exclusive. Beaufort's other girlfriends include a Russian model and a Milanese makeup artist. While in London, Eve Dessès has also been seen in the company of Trent Blackburn, an American sculptor."

I threw the report on the table.

I'd thought I was in love with her. Now I didn't know who I'd been in love with. I could make no sense of anything.

Interesting that he felt so shocked. Just because there were other people in her life? Because her life was more exotic or scandalous than he'd expected?

One single thought haunted me: this information wasn't enough. I had to see Eve again, find out the truth about us. I bought an airplane ticket to London. Whether it was to win her back or perform an exorcism, I would let fate decide.

I drummed my fingers on the table. This version seemed just as flimsy, albeit in a different way, as the other two. It was as if they were all sketches, cartoonish, opera buffa rather than sweeping sagas. So far, I couldn't tell whether this was intentional or an error in tone. Perhaps it was my error—this was where translating got iffy.

Or maybe they were supposed to be flimsy, like transparencies or thin coats of lacquer, meant to be layered on top of one another.

I thought back over the previous versions and made a chart: in the first version, he marries Daphne in some kind of vaguely Oedipal fantasy in which Daphne mothers him just as his own mother dies. He eventually forgets about Eve and burns the report.

In the second version, the Fear of Intimacy version, he and Daphne break up, Eve runs away, he stalks her, she turns out not to be Beaufort's mistress, and they get back together after she confesses her feelings for him had overwhelmed her.

The third version was shaping up to be the Femme Fatale story, what with her history as a dancer, her many lovers, and the scabrous novel. It had elements of *Camille*, and I was already anticipating someone dying and the obligatory deathbed scene: tears, confessions, swooning violins, a trip to a cemetery under gloomy skies . . . or it could veer into film noir, something with gangsters, guns, and nightclubs.

I leaned back, making the chair creak, trying to picture Eve, what she looked like, what she wore. On childhood visits to Paris, I used to beg my grandmother to buy me French fashion magazines, claiming they would improve my vocabulary. My favorite was *Vogue*, with its thick, glossy paper and risqué photos. One photo stayed with me, a black-and-white Guy Bourdin, which I saw again many years later, at an exhibit at the Jeu de Paume. It was of a woman in a flowing, printed chiffon dress, which fell off one shoulder and revealed her entire right breast. She was photographed from above, and her eyes were closed, her lips dark and shiny. I was twelve, and the photograph represented everything that was glamorous and mysterious to me about being a woman. That was Eve, I decided: sexy, a little undone, lost in another world.

The clock said 12:34. I wondered if Bunny was up for a late lunch. Though his answering machine beeped, there was still no message. "Hey, it's me. Are you around? Call me," I said. I went to the kitchen and rifled through the cupboards. Definitely bare.

I left another message. "I'm thinking Café Beaubourg. Maybe an exhibit afterward," I said. "Please come if you're free."

I walked through the Marais to the café by the Pompidou. There was no sign of Bunny, but a banner on the museum advertised a new exhibit on Surrealism. I ordered a quiche and a green salad, wolfing them down while reading the paper. Afterward, I spotted Bunny's head outside, towering over a crowd gathered around a fire juggler.

"You got my message," I said, walking up to him. He grimaced.

"I could barely hear you. That machine is a stupid piece of shit. Probably assembled by some exploited ten-year-old in Guangzhou after he ate a rancid fried turnip cake, poor kid, which explains why it is a piece of *merde* and I had to throw it out the window," he fumed. He turned back to the juggler, his eyes following the flames.

"That's a lot of anger you're carrying around there, big fella," I remarked.

"Insomnia," he explained. "Let's go for a walk."

"I had a strange dream," I said, falling into step next to him.

"What was it about?" he asked. We stopped on the corner of the rue du Temple to watch a parade of clowns in rainbow suits zoom by on scooters. One clown with a pink Afro and extralong shoes grinned and tooted his horn at us. Bunny laughed and waved back, the worn, tired look erased from his face.

"Bunny, promise you won't go to Italy again," I said instead, my tone urgent. He exhaled. It sounded like a gust of wind over the ocean.

"I'm not going anywhere for a while, kid."

....

I checked into a small hotel in Chelsea and followed Eve around London. My own impulses puzzled me. Here I was, hunting her like a predator.

She frequented an exercise spa near Sloane Square. She ate in an Italian restaurant on Beauchamp Place. Her dentist was on Bond Street. I followed her to a bookstore in Hampstead.

It seemed like the right moment to approach her, but through the window, I saw her greet a man in dirty jeans and cowboy boots the way I'd hoped she'd greet me, by flinging her arms around his neck. He whirled her around as other shoppers shot them disapproving looks. They walked out, arm in arm, oblivious to the world. I turned away to face a pyramid display of Kingsley Amis books.

I got drunk in a nearby pub and crawled back to the hotel. Still drunk, I called the Claridge and demanded Eve. At first, they claimed not to know who she was. "Please tell Beaufort's mistress that her former lover is here from Paris and demands to speak to her," I said and gave them the name of my hotel.

A banging on the door woke me up at two in the morning.

"What the hell are you doing here?" Eve asked when I opened the door. She brushed past me into the room.

"I could ask you the same question," I said. I could smell her perfume. Her pink coat was open over a silky black evening dress. A pulse beat in her neck. She didn't seem like the same person who'd come with me to Venice. This person stared at me—

I looked up *"dévisagé"* in the dictionary. I knew it meant to stare at someone, but it was a particular kind of stare, something hard, insolent, calculating, even intimidating. The word seemed to imply a stare that had an almost physical impact on its object, but the dictionary merely said "to stare." None of the synonyms in the thesaurus—"to pierce," "to pore over," "to scrutinize," "to peer at," "to study"—felt right. Maybe I was reading too much into the French word. And yet, certain stares are shocking, and we don't have a word for that in English. I made a note to ask Clara.

—with shrewd cat's eyes that glittered in the low light, and I was no longer sure who was the predator.

She shrugged out of the coat, letting it drop on the floor. She leaned her arms back on the dresser. She gave a delicate shrug, and a strap of her dress slipped off her shoulder, revealing the hollow above her collarbone. "So, now that you're here . . ." she whispered, reeling me in. I bent forward to kiss her, and she stopped me.

"This won't change anything," she murmured. "I won't change." She looked up at me through half-closed lids. I undid the row of buttons at the back of her dress and pressed my face to her neck.

"I know," I said. She unzipped my trousers.

She never has.

That wasn't right, either. The sentence was *"Elle est restée fidèle à elle-même,"* literally, "She has remained faithful to herself," or "She has remained faithful to who she is," which was clunky, and I wasn't sure it even meant anything in English. Did "She never has" convey all that it needed to?

That was the third ending. They had a way of sneaking up on me, these endings. I reread the chapter to see if I'd misread something, but I hadn't. I shut down the computer and stood up to stretch.

I stood in front of the mirror above the mantel and put my hand inside my T-shirt, slowly running my fingers over my collarbone, feeling its contours, the dip above and below it. I pulled the neck down farther and looked at my breasts. In the dim light, my face, the woman in the photograph, Eve, they all blurred together.

....

I slept soundly and deeply, and woke up refreshed and energetic. In the shower, I spied a bottle of Tante Isabelle's body oil. I patted myself dry and massaged the citrus-scented oil into my skin. It took a while to sink in, so I kept rubbing, not sure whether this was self-indulgent luxury or a lot of hard work, but afterward, my skin felt slippery and velvety at the same time.

But when I got dressed, my jeans stuck to my legs instead of sliding over them. Body oil was for women who had the time or patience to recline on lounge chairs in gauzy caftans. My T-shirt clung to my arms. I felt like roast duck.

I pulled the *trotinette* up the hill to the African market. A woman in a print dress and matching head wrap leaned over furry, bone white oblongs of dried fish, a small tot tucked into a fabric sling at her back. By the Belleville métro, a man passed out cards. I took one and read:

"Rapid, Efficient, Guaranteed Results. Professor Sissé Diasebakou, Grand Seer, Medium, Clairvoyant. He will succeed where others have failed. Exceptional gifts. Thirty years of experience. Ease of payment. Telepathic, he will see your destiny with empathy and beneficial manner. Resolve all your problems, family difficulties, return of affection, physical problems, professional success, luck in games, protection, driver's license, etc. Come, and chance will smile on you. The result will be positive! Payment after results."

I tucked it in my pocket and loaded up on fruit and vegetables.

35

You are more and more authentic the more you look like
someone you dreamed of being.
— PEDRO ALMODÓVAR, *All About My Mother*

*I*fastened the narrow straps of my kitten-heeled Mary Janes and looked
at myself in the mirror. I shimmied from side to side, admiring my
legs. It was only the second time I'd worn a skirt in recent weeks, and
I'd pulled on lace-patterned stockings. On top, I wore a pale pink mo-
hair *cache-cœur,* a wrap top. Usually I wore it over a T-shirt, but today
I'd slipped it over a lacy camisole I'd forgotten I owned. I'd twisted my
hair up and put on makeup, even lipstick and mascara. I looked soigné,
well taken care of.

On my way to Laveau's, I took a circuitous route, rounding the back
of the Picasso Museum. I stopped in front of a North African patisserie,
displaying patterned ceramic plates piled high with sesame-seed balls,
fried dough wings dusted with sugar, and trays of baklava, cut into loz-
enges and glistening with syrup.

The neighborhood felt hushed, deserted, as if everyone had already
left town for La Toussaint, the first of November holiday weekend. I
stopped in front of a window arranged to look like a dressing room,

where an old-fashioned mannequin with a Joan Crawford pout wore a vintage black evening coat with jet buttons over a pleated chiffon dress. A trio of shoes sat on a mirrored dressing table: Pucci-print slippers, peep-toe platforms, and white go-go boots. The door read SUMIKO ISHI-GAWA, ANCIENNES COLLECTIONS ET VINTAGE. I went inside.

"Bonjour," I called out to a short, slender woman I assumed was Sumiko. She wore cropped tweed pants with purple kneesocks and gold stilettos, an orange V-neck over a poet's blouse with lace cuffs, and a fur pelt with an animal head. Only two types of women could get away with that kind of outfit: card-carrying fashionisti and the deranged.

I asked about the coat. It was Balenciaga, late fifties, she said and shook her head.

"C'est trop petit pour vous," she said. I tried not to feel like a big galoot. *"Qu'est ce que vous cherchez?"* she asked.

"Je ne sais pas," I said, philosophically. It was true; I didn't know what I was looking for, though walking into a boutique does seem like an invitation for something to find you.

"Attendez, j'ai peut-être quelque chose . . ." she said and dashed behind a curtain.

My mother had taught me not to go into shops in Paris unless I was serious about buying. The French did not try things on for fun, and French saleswomen could tell if you were wasting their time. Things had changed somewhat, but not entirely, and I'd just made a tactical error. It was one thing to admire the clothes, but once she started picking them out for me, I'd feel obliged to try them on, or worse, buy, and this place—the tag on the Balenciaga coat read 1200 euros—was out of my price range.

"J'ai trouvé trois choses," she said, emerging from the back with three items. The first was a sleeveless trapeze Courrèges dress in lemon yellow, perfect with the white go-go boots if I ever wanted to be Nancy Sinatra for Halloween. Next, she held up a lovely navy blue organza dress with beaded buttons and a poufy skirt, but years of high school

uniforms had given me a nonnegotiable aversion to navy blue. Finally, she pulled out a pale pink wool coatdress, with small rhinestone buttons and wide, turned-back cuffs. I blinked. I may have squealed. One word came to mind: *mine*.

It was handmade, with no designer label and a silk lining printed with pink tulips. I slid out of my trench and tried it on. It fit snugly, cinching in at the waist and flaring slightly at the hips. I could wear it closed, as a dress, or open over my outfit.

"Vous êtes magique," I said.

Sumiko cocked her head to one side, satisfied. I looked at the price tag. *"Merci, mais c'est trop cher,"* I said, forcing the words out. I handed it back with genuine regret.

"Je vous fais une reduction," she said. She tapped some numbers on a red and white Hello Kitty calculator and showed me the figure. She'd subtracted thirty percent. I thought about it long and hard, about ten seconds, and took out my credit card. She pulled out tissue paper to pack the coat in a box, but I told her I'd wear it.

I left feeling like Audrey Hepburn, Grace Kelly, and Ava Gardner rolled into one. I'd eat lentils and pasta, skip the gourmet supermarket. It was almost noon when I rattled the cowbell and waltzed into the bookstore.

Monsieur Laveau was dusting a set of books with a sable brush.

"Antoine's author," I remarked, reading the name Villiers de L'Isle-Adam over his shoulder.

"First editions. I found them for him," he explained.

"I thought you didn't like each other."

"Idle gossip." He waved a dismissive hand in the air. *"Asseyez vous, mademoiselle,"* he said, tilting his head like a benevolent king. There was a new armchair in front of his desk, a handsome bergère upholstered in worn brown leather. He busied himself with the coffee machine.

"C'est nouveau!" I exclaimed, sitting down. *"Et confortable!"*

"On m'a dit que l'ancien était d'un confort moyenâgeux," he said. I

smiled at his use of the word *"moyenâgeux"* for the old chair. Literally "Middle Ages–ish," it was a synonym for "medieval," but less literal and more playful. He turned and handed me a cup of coffee, glancing down at my legs.

"What do you think he's doing with all these endings?" I asked.

"Hein?" Bernard said, uncharacteristically, still looking at my legs. I suppressed a smile and tilted my head to twirl my pearl earring, shivering as my cold fingers fondled my earlobe. The onomatopoeic French word for "what?" or "huh," *"hein"* was almost always used as an interrogative and seemed to have three vowel sounds shoved in it. Along with *"ben,"* the French sound that could mean well, so, or um, they were the language tic twins: *Hein* was an overweight, Teutonic college boy with a pale mustache, and *Ben*, his nerdy sidekick, was all elbows and knees.

"Is there a purpose behind the multiple endings? As opposed to, say, a wimpy lack of decision-making skills?" I asked.

"I'm not familiar with the word 'wimpy,' but I believe I understand your meaning, *mademoiselle*," he said with asperity. "I do not believe he has any difficulty making decisions," he said, a familiar reproving note in his voice.

"I still don't see why I had to get them in such a piecemeal fashion," I said.

"Age has only increased my friend's monumental stubbornness," he said. I squinted at him. *"Va chercher,"* he said, shrugging, and I heard "Go figure." It was a nearly seamless translation.

"Will you really never tell me who he is?" I asked. He frowned at me, not saying anything. "Okay, fine," I said. I stood up and smiled, changing the subject. "What do you think of my new coat?" I asked. He came over to me and examined the turned-back cuff of one sleeve and the hand-stitched silk lining. He walked around me and smoothed out the shoulders, then tugged the sleeves down. I could smell his cologne, something cool and green.

"My mother always took me along to the dressmaker. I have an excellent eye for women's clothing," he explained. It was the first time he'd revealed any personal information. "It is very different for you, *non?* It changes you. *Je vous trouve très élégante, mademoiselle. Félicitations,*" he added approvingly. He was right: it was different for me: it was dressy and elegant in a way I sometimes aspired to be but too rarely made the effort for. He sat and drank his coffee.

"Do you have special plans for the weekend?" he asked. A compliment and now a personal question? We were almost pals.

"Nothing in particular. And you? You're off to the country?"

His mouth twitched ruefully. "*Hélas,* I had to cancel my plans. I must stay in town for the theater."

Ah. The theater. We made eye contact, then he looked away, realizing what he'd brought up. I pretended not to notice, and he pretended it was convincing.

I pointed at an envelope. "Is that my check? With the chapter?" He nodded and handed them to me. "This is the last ending," I said. "I'm nearly done, *n'est-ce pas?*"

"*C'est vrai,*" he said, tilting his head as if he were considering something.

"How funny, I thought it was going to last forever," I said lightly.

"*Eventuellement,* I might have other work for you," he said, pawing through the stack of manuscripts on his desk. "A thriller that might sell to the Americans; would that interest you?"

"Yes, definitely. Thank you for considering me." I got to my feet.

"*C'est normal.*" He walked me to the door.

"Well, *bon week-end, alors.*"

"*Vous aussi, mademoiselle.*" An impish impulse made me lean over and give him a peck on the cheek. As I left, the cowbell pealed in surprise.

....

A bright autumn sun beat down on the pavement. I tripped along the street, feeling pretty as I caught a few admiring glances. I crossed the

Pont des Arts, intending to treat myself to some window-shopping in the Palais Royal. By the time I got there, I could feel a hot, sore blister developing on my little toe. How did Frenchwomen do it? Limping into the garden for a place to rest, I saw Bunny, seated in a green enamel chair, a WHSmith bag on the ground beside him. A crowd of pigeons fought over a piece of bread nearby.

"Fancy seeing you! Why are you feeding pigeons?" I asked, sitting next to him.

"Flying rats." He scowled. "I have a technique: distract them with a showy chunk. While they're fighting over it, I break off these little pieces and put them near me, where the sparrows are protected." He pointed beneath him with a doting smile: three little sparrows pecked at crumbs on the ground.

A squabbling scrum of pigeons squawked as one daring player made off with a fluffy piece of *mie*. Bunny sneered as the pigeons chased the scoundrel en masse.

"Idiots," he muttered. I slouched down in my seat, listening to the breeze rustle through the trees. Bunny sighed and crossed his legs at the ankles.

"What'd you get at Smith?" I asked, looking down at the bag.

"Couple of old Le Carrés I probably already have. *The New Yorker* and *The Economist*," he said.

"You can read it online, you know."

"I like paper. I like the feel of it, the sound of it, dog-eared pages, ink. I like holding what I'm reading," he said, miming holding a newspaper. I looped my wool scarf around my neck.

"I'm going. I want to beat the wage slave traffic home," he said and stood. "By the way, you're looking very, ah, womanly. It's nice." I smiled, about to thank him, but he'd already left.

I sat in the park awhile, unable to keep myself from thinking about Olivier's play. But then another thought edged into my head, as I remembered what little Bernard had said about his friend, the stubborn author. There had to be a way to figure out who he was. I pulled out my cell phone and called Antoine.

"*Ah, chère amie!* We were wondering where you'd disappeared to," he said.

"Still here. How's the biography going? I just came from Bernard's. He has first editions for you."

"Excellent news, I thank you. My book is done: I've sent it off to my editor. I was hoping to celebrate at our place in Normandy, but we've got to stay in town."

"Let me guess. You're going to the opening of *Un Week-end à la campagne*," I said, trying not to sound bitter. They'd all be there— Bernard, Antoine, Victorine, the whole literary crowd gathered around their glamorous friend Estelle and her *cicisbeo*, her *cavalier servant*, her admiring protégé and swain. Inamorato. Paramour.

"Indeed. Will we see you there?"

"Conflicting plans, alas," I lied. "You'll have to tell me about it," I said.

"*Bien sûr,*" he said. "Will you come for tea?" he asked.

I said yes, and before he could hang up, I slipped in a question. "Antoine, is Bernard associated with any imprint other than Editions Laveau?"

"Very interesting question. Will you tell me why you ask?"

"Absolutely not," I said.

He laughed. "I'll leave you to your intrigues. Look at Les Editions Pas de Mule. Bernard has a long-standing agreement with them."

"Thank you, Antoine."

"Don't think I'll forget it, dear lady."

"I'm sure you won't," I said.

....

I walked down to Les Halles, in the mood for a movie. There was bound to be something I wanted to see at the twenty-three-screen multiplex.

I bought a bag of banana marshmallows and a ticket for a critically acclaimed film about a sock manufacturer.

It was a slow, quiet movie, with several subtle, touching moments among the three middle-aged characters, and beautifully photographed scenes of a rundown beach resort. But you had to be in the right mood, because at least two people in the theater fell asleep. I know because they sat in front of me and one of them snored.

Afterward, as I walked toward the métro at Rambuteau, I saw a bright orange poster on a round kiosk across the street.

A theater poster under glass, it was lit from within and over two meters tall. Walking closer, I saw Estelle's name in black block letters on the orange background. Then the title, in the same size, UN WEEK-END A LA CAMPAGNE. Below that, the names of her costars. I let my eyes wander farther, down to Olivier's name.

There it was, in the same font. A sharp pain pierced my side, a runner's stitch made with a thin needle. At times like this, I wish I were a practicing Buddhist, so that I could murmur something like "This poster is not real" while conjuring up the sound of babbling brooks, but then I would also have to say "I am not real," which I find problematic.

I sighed. I would have to read the reviews. Maybe even see it, especially if it was good. Even more if it was bad. Definitely if it was bad.

Or not. I could turn a blind eye, avoid pumpkin orange posters. It wasn't like you couldn't spot them from afar. It wasn't that bad. I'd been through this before, and it had been worse with Timothy, in Los Angeles. Reminders of him everywhere. This was nothing. I'd be fine. Fine.

I piled reassuring thought upon reassuring thought, but they were weightless and flimsy. At home, there were no messages on the machine. In the back room of my brain, I thought about Olivier's play. I changed into pajamas and sat through a documentary on volcanoes, seeing it but not seeing it. I left it on, merely to hear the sound of voices. I was back in my elevatorlike existence, between floors, out of sorts, neither part of the city nor not part of it. I was ungrounded, a sad little boat that had slipped its knots and drifted away on the undertow, seduced by the bottomless black sea.

....

I couldn't breathe. I was suffocating. I thrashed around in bed, kicked my feet, and flung the covers aside. "Enough!" I said.

It was five; the morning traffic was just beginning. A truck drove by, making the windows buzz. I padded over to the window in my sweaty pajamas and pressed my forehead to the cold glass; the city beyond it was still dark.

I felt fragile and bruised, shaken by another violent dream and awake with the wired, ready-to-get-on-a-plane feeling you don't go back to sleep from. I hauled myself into the shower, trying to wash the images from my head. Under the water, I saw a tall white column billowing smoke and shedding ashes like an oddly shaped volcano. I remembered the TV show from the night before. I was so suggestible these days.

It was time to leave. Living in Paris wasn't good for me anymore. I was sinking into morbid depression. The nightmares felt malevolent, a sign of imminent decline.

I ate cornflakes out of a bowl, one by one, like miniature potato chips, and jotted down a list of things to do, a game plan for returning to L.A. First, I'd get in touch with George, my old boss, in case he'd jumped into a new job and could throw me some work. Then I'd need to e-mail my tenant and tell him the sublet was ending.

I poured myself a cup of coffee. Tell Tante Isabelle. Finish the translation and get my last check from Monsieur Laveau. Say good-bye. I burst into tears.

I missed Olivier. I didn't have a real job or a real reason for staying. Outside, it was gray. It was probably sunny in California. I thought about my desk, my work rituals, deliveries from Juan, my FedEx guy, editorial meetings. I remembered work as a refuge, a cure, the thing that put things in perspective and distracted me. The French call overthinking your problems *du nombrilisme*. Belly button–ism.

I needed to make work work for me. Unwieldy on a T-shirt, but it summed matters up. I turned on the computer and waited for it to boot up. I thought about how I'd become more efficient at breaking up sinuous, multi-claused French sentences into shorter English ones. I wondered whether I was doing the author a disservice: he wrote complicated, meandering sentences. That was his style. It wasn't an amazing style, and he wasn't writing great literature, but he did have a style, and here I was, turning it into something else, repackaging it so it read well in English. Maybe the truest translation would be as convoluted and flowery as the original. Or retain a measure of convolutedness and floweriness.

On the other hand, I could count on Monsieur Laveau to tell me if he didn't like my work. I had to assume he read English well enough to judge. I pulled out the pages. A note fell from the envelope and fluttered to the floor.

It was a long, thin piece of paper, like a bookmark but with perforations on the top. Written with a fountain pen in a congested, shaky scrawl, it said: *"Mon cher Bernard, voici le dernier chapitre . . ."*

It was a note from Monsieur X, telling Bernard this was the last chapter.

"Les traductions me plaisent, plus ou moins, mais je n'ai plus envie de le faire publier."

That was odd. He didn't want to publish it any longer? Then why was I translating it?

"On en reparlera. Amitiés . . ."

It was signed with a scribbled flourish. An initial, or initials, I couldn't read; possibly two initials superimposed one on top of the other, but totally indecipherable. S.G.? G.S.? E.S.? E.G.? G.E.? G.G.? Maybe a stylized F, or C, or an extravagant L.

I groaned in frustration. Rereading it, I smarted a bit about "The translations please me, more or less," but why didn't he want to publish it any longer? It was maddening: in my hand, I held a note to Bernard from Monsieur X. A note in his handwriting. With his initials. Which I couldn't read. It was both frustrating and strangely intimate, as bizarre and useless as owning, say, a pair of his socks.

This was the last chapter. He didn't want to publish it anymore.

D.S.? Z.S.?

Initials bounced around my head like crazy, gumball-dispenser rubber balls. I doodled on the envelope, trying to copy the scribbled initials to see if I could make sense of them. Then it came to me, like a whisper: initials. I opened my file of last week's translation and combed through the names, making a list.

"A small role in a soft-porn film by the Italian filmmaker Alessandro Diavoli made her a minor cult celebrity and introduced her to the film's financial backer, Gilbert Dessès."

A.D. G.D. I continued looking.

"He was seventeen years her senior and married to a French writer, Véronique Boutros . . . Over the next few years, she became involved with an American investment banker, P. Stanley Carruthers; a French publisher, Bertrand L'Huissier; and a French journalist, Alexi Barthès-Levinsky."

V.B., P.C. or P.S.C. or S.C., B.L. or B.L.H., sort of. A.B. or A.B.L. Hah! Double hah! Even triple hah!

There it was: B.L. He was even a French publisher. Hello, Bernard Laveau. And A.B., a French journalist, as in Antoine Berlutti. He wasn't a journalist, but writer was close enough. That left Véronique Boutros as

Victorine Berlutti. Coincidence, or was I onto something? Could it be a roman à clef about people I actually knew?

I scrolled through my computer files of the previous two endings, looking for corroboration on the other characters' initials. None of them matched up with anyone I knew. Maybe it was just this chapter. I looked at the initials again. B.L., A.B., V.B. It had to be them: it wasn't just the initials; the careers matched up as well.

Maybe Antoine was the author. He'd just finished a book, after all. When I'd met him, he'd claimed he and Bernard weren't friendly, but Bernard had found him the Villiers de L'Isle-Adam first editions. What were they up to? Was that why he'd befriended me? Why he always asked about the translation? Could he be that devious?

I Googled Victorine again. Her biography showed she'd been married once before, to an Austrian playwright, but his initials didn't match. Her bibliography contained nothing remotely resembling the title *The Many Lives of a Femme Fatale*. Rats. I scrolled through a list of her articles. There was one entitled *La séduction et les mots*, but it wasn't available online. While I was at it, I checked Amazon.fr and Fnac.com, but as I suspected, *The Many Lives of a Femme Fatale* was not a real book.

The author could be Antoine. Or, come to think of it, Victorine. I needed to get ahold of something each of them had written and compare their writing styles. I wasn't ruling Bernard out, either, even though he'd scoffed at me when I'd suggested it.

Or the initials were coincidence.

That left me with Les Editions Pas de Mule, which I Googled. The publishing company was located on the rue du Pas de la Mule, off the place des Vosges. It was a play on words: *"Pas de la Mule"* meant the steps or paces of a mule, but without the article, it meant "no mule." They didn't have much of a website, but their book list showed they specialized in political nonfiction. None of the authors' names meant anything to me. Monsieur X could be here, but I had no way of finding him. I needed a list of the people Bernard edited, or at least a list of his friends, but short of stealing his address book, I didn't see how to get one. I gnawed my thumbnail. I was almost onto something, but it was a slippery eel of a feeling. I needed another clue.

36

Il ne faut pas laisser les intellectuels jouer avec des allumettes. *
—JACQUES PRÉVERT, "Il ne faut pas..."

A few days later, I took a long walk to Antoine and Victorine's in Montmartre. I rang the doorbell, and Antoine opened it with a warm smile.

"Alors, chère amie, comment ça va?" he asked, taking my coat. He looked dapper in a camel hair jacket over a red striped shirt. *"Victorine!"* he shouted. *"Anna est là!"* He ushered me into the *salon*. "Would you like tea? Or shall we push *l'heure de l'apéro?"* he asked with a mischievous grin.

"Qu'est ce que vous me proposez?" I asked, smiling back.

"Un petit whiskey?" he suggested. *"Du Xérès? Un Lillet?"*

"Un Lillet, je veux bien essayer," I said. I'd never tried the old-fashioned aperitif. Antoine served it with lemon rind in a thin crystal glass etched with flowers. He poured himself a finger of whiskey and held it up to the light.

"Laphroaig. A gift from my publisher," he explained. *"Tchin."* The Lillet was sweet, not unpleasantly medicinal, one of those French drinks

*One should not let intellectuals play with matches.

whose ingredients were impossible to divine: probably a blend of vegetable roots or mountain herbs.

"I like this," I said. He held out a dish of salted nuts. I took one and bit into a rancid almond. I looked around for a paper napkin to spit it into, but there were only little linen cocktail squares on the table. I grimaced and swallowed. He didn't notice.

"So, what did you do this past weekend?" I asked, shamelessly transparent.

"We went to the theater," he said, squinting at me. "But I'm so dull! Of course you know. Your friend Olivier's play," he exclaimed.

"I'm so sorry I missed it," I said blandly. "I'm sure it was wonderful," I prodded.

"Estelle is magnificent on film, but she hasn't been on the stage in years, and *les mauvaises langues* would have been happy to see her fail," he said, looking at me. Then he gave a start and looked away, as if he realized that looking at me at that precise moment might be indelicate. I tried to keep my face impassive, because even though I was one of the "bad tongues" who might have been pleased to hear she'd fallen flat on her face, I didn't want it to show. While I wouldn't have wished catastrophic failure on Olivier's play, a kind of middling mediocrity would have been just dandy.

"But no," he continued. "She was excellent. Her costars, too. Well-directed, if I can pretend to such discernment. The play, *alors là*"—he raised a hand—"it has flaws, lacks intellectual rigor. But it makes up for it in emotion. A satisfying experience."

"I'm so glad," I said, which was a blatant untruth. "I'm not sure I'll go. Olivier and I had a falling-out, you see," I said casually.

He nodded and clamped a pipe between his teeth. There was a wealth of information between us: what he knew, what I knew. I looked at my glass. The lemon rind had curled into an O. I went over to the oil painting.

"I'd remembered it as repulsive," I mused, "but it doesn't look at all repulsive to me now. After the feast, the insects appear . . . the dead pheasant, the half-eaten bread, the cheese—it's life, isn't it?" It came out dull, a platitude.

"You could see it that way," he said. Victorine strode in, wearing an olive green twin set and a rope of pearls. She grasped my shoulders and kissed me on both cheeks.

"How are you, dear girl?" she asked in a hearty tone.

"Fine, th-thank you," I stuttered, surprised by her friendliness.

"We were just talking about Anna's translating work," Antoine said, matching my earlier lie with one of his own.

"Yes?" she asked, pouring herself a small whiskey. "I enjoyed our last conversation. Tell me, have you always been a translator?"

"No, I wrote PR copy," I said.

"It is not so different," Antoine remarked. "In both cases, you are putting someone else's words into another form." He looked at Victorine.

"Yes, but you remain invisible," she said with a thoughtful look. "Tell me, I know so little about you. What was your childhood like?" She leaned forward, all ears. An *apéro* with Mr. and Mrs. Freud.

"Fine. Average," I said. "I grew up in L.A., but I was sent away a lot, to France, in the summer. Mostly to stay with my grandmother, which is how I learned French."

"Was she a *grand-mère gâteau,* or a strict, severe type?" she asked.

"Both," I said. "And capricious. Not predictable at all," I said, thinking back.

"Ah, so you had to be careful. Do you feel more French or American?"

People often asked me this question. There was no easy answer. "I feel both. Most of the time, I feel at home in both places, but sometimes I feel French in the U.S., and American in France. I guess like most people with mixed backgrounds."

"Hence your fluidity in two cultures, two languages," she said. "You had to learn to fit in, adapt quickly, a chameleon—"

This was sort of true, and I opened my mouth to agree, but Antoine jumped in.

"But also the need to remain in the shadows, not conspicuous, already a spy—"

"The question of identity, always shifting, never defined—" she said.

"At home everywhere and nowhere—" he added.

"Always on the outside, looking in—" she countered.

"Not rea—" I tried to say, but they were off, riffing back and forth.

"She marries a Frenchman, a soldier, who dies in North Africa—"

"Naturally, she volunteers for service—"

"Before her tragic end at Ravensbrück!" Victorine said. Baffled, I looked at them. "But I don't know if she keeps the child," she added. "It might be too tragic."

"*A toi de décider,*" Antoine said, lighting his pipe. The white cat I'd seen the last time crawled out from under the sofa and leaped into my lap.

"*Non, Grisbi!*" Victorine scooped the cat up in her arms and left the room.

"She is writing a movie script based on a World War Two spy who was half-English, half-French," Antoine explained, pouring himself another drink. "She's probably abandoned us for her desk."

"It looked like you were having fun," I offered.

"She is my best critic, and I hers, I like to think," he said. "But what about you? Tell me, how is your translation? What's the story again?" he asked, as if he'd known and had forgotten. I said nothing. "*Bon.* What can you tell me?" he asked, smiling.

"Aside from telling you the author is anonymous and I've no clue who he is, nothing," I said. "I'm sworn to secrecy. I've signed papers."

Antoine rubbed his chin. The cloying, sweet pipe smoke filled the room. "So, when you asked me who Bernard edits, it was because . . ."

"Idle curiosity." I shrugged. "I know so little about him."

"I know what you're up to, my dear," he said, waving his pipe at me.

"*Enfin*. Bernard knows so many people. You may be translating someone he does not edit at all. But tell me, I thought he'd acquired a new manuscript by Le Jaa?"

I shrugged. "He may have, but I doubt it's this one."

"You're sure?" He looked disappointed.

"Positive. It's a totally different style," I said, shaking my head. "What's more, I doubt Bernard would give a new Le Jaa to a novice translator."

"Ah, well," he said philosophically. "Perhaps it will remain a mystery." He leafed through a book on the mantel. Now that I'd made it clear I wasn't translating Le Jaa's book, he didn't seem as interested in talking to me. By contrast, this did make it seem less likely that either he or Victorine was the author of my book.

"But if I were to try to figure out who my author is . . ." I said.

"I just thought of something *my* author wrote," he said. "He believed the imagination was more beautiful than real life." He ran his fingers over a leather book. "'Science will not suffice. Sooner or later you will end by coming to your knees . . . Before the darkness!'" he quoted, pointing his index finger in the air like a Roman orator.

"The darkness," I repeated. They were both a little strange today, the married writers. I stood up to go. At the door, I could hear Victorine typing as a tinny transistor radio blared classical music. I kissed Antoine good-bye and went down the stairs.

Outside, it was brisk and sunny. I walked around Montmartre. It didn't change, Montmartre: still the same bad art, souvenir shops, crowds, and inevitably, someone strumming "Hotel California" in front of the Sacré-Cœur. I sat on the steps and looked out at the view, which reminded me of the view from a Japanese restaurant in the Hollywood Hills, the same orientation. I picked out Notre Dame, Saint-Eustache, Beaubourg, the Eiffel Tower, and the Grand Palais before heading down the hill to the métro.

. . . .

When I think back on that time, it startles me to realize just how fool-ish I was, how little I knew. In my arrogant, ignorant youth, I thought I knew the world. I assumed life was a mystery; that once solved, it would work like a well-oiled machine: predictable, ordinary. Until I met Eve, nothing had challenged these precepts.

I revisited that last scene between us countless times, each time coming up with yet another speech, another formula to make her stay.

Verbier's information was trite and inconsequential. He was a ter-rible private detective, though I spent a small fortune on his services before I discovered it. From what I could glean from his inane reports, I concluded that Eve had left me for reasons I could spend the rest of my life trying to discover.

Daphne and I parted ways. She completed her dissertation, became a sought-after political consultant, married a lawyer, and produced four children in rapid succession, one of whom became my godson. I directed my energy into my work. My career became the driving force in my life.

A series of articles I'd written on the looming economic crisis and the potential role of alternative sources of energy caught the eye of Monsieur K——, who appointed me his economic adviser when he be-came an important figure in the Mitterrand government.

I married my secretary, Magda Szabo, a Hungarian émigré six years my senior. We were, if not happy, comfortable. Magda could not have children, so we considered adoption, but after many disappoint-ments, we gave up. She became involved with fund-raising for an or-phanage in Budapest, traveling to that city several times for extended visits. We divorced when she told me she'd fallen in love with a UN aid worker.

I missed her company, but while there was no one significant in my life, I was not often alone.

Then, one day, as if released from the most banal of curses, I found Eve again.

This chapter read like a confession, an autobiography.

Eve had been living in London and had become well-known, even famous.

That was coy. "For what???" I scribbled in pencil in the margin.

I was invited to dinner at the house of an old friend, Christopher, a Labour MP who happened to be a friend of her brother's. Dinner for twenty-four at a house in St. John's Wood, surrounded by landscape watercolors and Arts and Crafts woodwork. Eve provided the glamour, resplendent in blue-violet silk, her glossy hair cut short.

She'd aged, of course, but her face was more beautiful, full of expression, the lines around her eyes indicating she'd laughed a great deal over the years. She'd suffered as well; I could see that, too.

She greeted me like an old friend, smoothing away any awkwardness there might have been. We spoke briefly before she was whisked away by an Italian writer. At dinner, we were seated at opposite ends of the table. During a lengthy discussion I had with our hostess on the difference between the French and British systems of education, our eyes searched each other out across a linen-white sea of china and candelabra.

She left after coffee, claiming an early morning engagement. As she said good-bye, she squeezed my hand. It was the tiniest pressure, a pulse, but to me, as clear as if she'd said, "Find me." I stepped backward into an imagined past, like a cherished idea, the old fantasy that it was possible to find someone again.

The chapter ended. There were no more pages. This was taking the experimental ending thing a little far, I fumed. I'd been hoping for at least one decent ending. Was that too much to ask? I debated writing another note to express my dissatisfaction, but Monsieur X hadn't responded to my previous one, so I was guessing he didn't care what I thought.

In the morning, I reread the translation and spell-checked it, but there wasn't much to look for—it was only four pages long. I printed it out and called Bernard to tell him I'd be by later.

"*Entendu. A plus tard,*" he said, shorter than usual, and hung up. I called Bunny, wondering if he was up for coffee at Le Flore, but the answering machine didn't pick up. I wondered if he'd ever buy a new one. It was only when I was on the bus that it occurred to me there might be an explanation for the chapter: a mistake, or missing pages. I walked into the bookstore at one, as Bernard was getting into his overcoat.

"*Je suis très pressé, mademoiselle,*" he said as soon as he saw me. Never get between a Frenchman and lunch.

"This will take two minutes," I said. He puffed out his cheeks in exasperation.

"Could you double-check that I have all the pages? Four pages seems a little short for Monsieur X," I said. He frowned and looked at the chapter.

"*Mais non, mais non,* of course this isn't all of it. Why didn't you call?" he asked. I shrugged. "I can have them for you this afternoon. Will you come back?"

"At three?" I asked, thinking I could catch a movie in the neighborhood.

"*Plutôt seize heures. Et maintenant,* I'm already late," he said.

"I'll walk out with you," I said. He gave me a suspicious look and tucked his cognac leather portfolio under his arm. I waited while he locked the door. He shook my hand, making it clear I wasn't to walk with him, and strode away.

"*A plus tard,*" I called out. He shook an irascible hand in the air, like he was shooing away a fly.

I was near three multiplexes, plus the revival houses in the Fifth. There were also several cafés nearby. I contemplated my options, watching Bernard's retreating back. If he could get the missing pages this afternoon, maybe he was lunching with the author.

I darted down the street, following him. He walked down the rue de Condé and veered into a café with orange awnings called Les Editeurs.

I knew the place. The food was good, and, as befitted the name, the walls were lined with books. Clara and I had sat there once and flipped through a comic book of rebuses. She'd explained the expression *"tiré par les cheveux."* Literally, it meant pulled by the hairs, but it really meant overworked or far-fetched, "like a joke that requires too much information to be funny," she'd said. "Or this book."

I stopped to think. If Laveau and Monsieur X were eating on the ground floor, in the café, my excuse would be that I'd stopped in for an innocent *express*. But they could be in the upstairs restaurant, which posed a problem: if I went up there and Bernard saw me, he'd know I was stalking him. I stood to the side and scanned the clientele in the café. No sign of him; he had to be upstairs. I could pretend I was looking for the ladies' room, but I knew it was in the basement . . . though I could pretend I didn't know that. Or I could have coffee downstairs and wait for them to come out. But if Bernard and his lunch date didn't leave together, my waiting for them would be useless.

I paced up and down the sidewalk, losing my nerve. Who was to say I'd even recognize the author? I wouldn't be able to identify him unless he was really famous. Bernard certainly wouldn't introduce us. Maybe I could ask the maître d' who Bernard was eating with. I fumbled in my pocket. How much did one tip for information?

This was getting too complicated. Best to pretend I was looking for an imaginary friend who just happened to be free for an impromptu lunch at this very restaurant. That would be my cover. I went inside.

A quick but thorough sweep of the café confirmed that Bernard was not seated there, not even in the back. I climbed the narrow circular staircase to the upper dining floor, which was divided into two rooms. In the first, there were four tables of couples and one table of six, four women, two men. No Bernard.

In the other room, I glimpsed white hair and ducked behind a rubber tree. He sat facing me, talking to someone half-hidden by another potted tree. I poked my head out. The formidable eyebrows slammed together as he leaned his head out, trying to see around the tree. I half-crouched, shrinking back. Their waiter opened a bottle of wine, and Bernard's companion put an elbow on the back of his chair, like he was going to turn around. A waiter stopped in front of me. I straightened up.

"Vous cherchez quelqu'un?" he asked. Bernard looked right at me.

"Uh, non, enfin . . . je voulais voir . . . euh . . ." I mumbled. The jig was up. Exit, stage left, but it was blocked by a group of elderly men trudging up the narrow circular staircase.

I stole another glance behind me just as Bernard's date turned around. It was Olivier. He looked stricken, as if the sight of me wounded him, or maybe that was how I felt about seeing him, but I didn't wait. The last man barely cleared the stairs, and I squeezed past him, ignoring his taken-aback *"Mais, enfin!"*

I ran down the boulevard Saint-Germain, trying to outrun embarrassment itself. Olivier. Having lunch. With Bernard. And they'd caught me spying.

Drops spattered my head. I looked up, half-expecting to see spiteful pigeons, but it was only rain. I went inside Saint-Germain-des Prés.

It was cool and dark in the church. I sat on a wooden pew, my heart pounding. A thin woman in a purple coat knelt and crossed herself, whispering as she hurried past.

Bernard and Olivier. They were friends, it was true. Friendly. Acquaintances, at least. How crazy to assume Bernard was lunching with my author. I'd been so stupid, and I'd thought myself so clever. I took out a tissue and wiped my forehead. I was a first-class twit. Bernard would be supremely irked.

A few people sat in front of me, and a couple of tourists strolled up the aisles, reading from guidebooks. Spotting the back of a tall, familiar head seven rows up, I nearly laughed with relief. Because of his height, Bunny was always easy to pick out in a crowd. I slid next to him, nudging him with my shoulder.

"What's a lapsed Catholic boy like you doing in a place like this?" I asked.

"*Mais—*" said a gaunt man with sunken cheeks, looking at me askance.

"*Excusez-moi, monsieur,*" I whispered and got up, my face burning. That was twice I'd embarrassed myself today. *Jamais deux sans trois,* the French say. Never two without three. I dropped a euro in the donation box and lit a taper. Please make this day get better, I thought, wishing hard, like a child in front of a birthday cake.

Later, seated under a tropical fresco, complete with parrots and peacocks, in Ladurée's Left Bank *salon de thé,* I lost myself in rapt admiration of the twelve-euro plate of eight silver-dollar-size *macaron* cookies before me: orange blossom, caramel *à la fleur de sel,* rose, chestnut, strawberry, vanilla, chocolate, and pistachio.

The waitress showed an elderly American couple to the table next to mine. She was Asian, with short black hair and a dark green pantsuit over a turtleneck. He was African-American, with a neat, gray beard and a tweed jacket over jeans.

"Look at what she's having," the woman said softly, tilting her head toward me. I made short work of the chestnut *macaron.*

"What did we have yesterday?" he asked, looking at the menu. "The chocolate thing, with the layers, the coffee?"

"An opera." She shook a pill out of a bottle. His mouth turned down.

"No, I want that thing you used to buy at the bakery in Park Slope. A napoleon," he said, scanning the menu again. "El, there are no napoleons here," he complained.

Unable to resist being Information Lady, I leaned over. "Excuse me," I said. "In France, they call a napoleon a *mille feuille*." They looked at me warily. "It means a thousand leaves, like layers. Here, they make three different kinds: the classic, with rum; another with raspberry jam; and a *praliné* version. They used to have a licorice-caramel flavor, the mere idea of which upsets me," I said, giving a shudder. "But they took it off the menu."

He nodded and said, "*Meal foy,*" attempting to pronounce it.

"Close enough," I said. He smiled and leaned over to introduce himself.

It was their first trip to Paris. For almost an hour, I didn't think about Bernard or Olivier as David and Ellie and I chatted. He was a retired professor of music history at NYU; she was a lawyer. They'd traveled extensively in Africa and Asia, but it was their first trip to France, and so far, they'd seen the Louvre, the Musée d'Orsay, the Musée Picasso, and the Musée du Quai Branly.

The waitress placed a *café crème* in front of Ellie and a *mille feuille au rhum* in front of David. "I'm guessing the trick is eating them," he said, looking at the layers of *pâte feuilletée* and *crème patissière* in mock despair. I ate a rose *macaron*.

"And what do you do here?" Ellie asked.

"I'm doing some freelance translating, but that's going to end soon," I said and changed the subject. "What else are you planning to see?" I asked.

"We're going to an experimental art piece in Bobigny with some friends. It's a combination of dance, poetry, and opera. I can't wait," Ellie said, clapping her hands together. I tried to hide my look of surprise, but David saw it.

"What's that about?" he asked.

"I think it's wonderful that you're going to see experimental art," I said.

"Because we're old?" he asked.

"That's not what I meant!" I protested, but I blushed, because he'd caught me. I couldn't see my parents going to a dicey suburb at night, let alone to see anything with the phrase "experimental art" in it. David reached across the table to hold Ellie's hand.

"People think that beauty is what is pleasing to the eye," he mused, talking to me but looking at her. "It's not. Beauty is seeing without bias."

His words stuck with me after they left. I pushed *macaron* crumbs around my plate, wondering if I knew how to see without bias. I tried to figure out if it meant convincing my parents to go to experimental art pieces or not judging them for not going to experimental art pieces; or maybe it meant not having any preconceived notions about experimental art or its audience until I saw a piece myself. Or maybe it meant trying to have an open mind all the time, and not just when it was easy, like with nice strangers in a *salon de thé*.

I walked back to the bookstore. I thought about calling Bernard and inventing an excuse not to face him, but I couldn't do it: somewhat to my regret, I had a backbone.

I stepped aside to let a messenger with a helmet exit, and walked in, sounding the cowbell of shame. Bernard sat at his desk, studying figures in a ledger. He didn't look up. Not taking off my coat, I sat down.

"Monsieur, je me sens ridicule—" I began, but he held up a finger to stop me and totted up numbers on a calculator. I sat like a truant. The desk clock ticked "tsk, tsk." When he finished and looked up, I took it as my cue to speak.

"When you said you'd have the pages this afternoon, I thought you might be having lunch with Monsieur X," I explained. "I know, dumb conclusion, but I couldn't resist the thought of seeing him. When I saw"— I stopped. Pronouncing Olivier's name evoked the memory of the last time his name had come up between us—"who you were eating with," I continued, "I realized how foolish I'd been."

"C'est tout?" he asked, his face expressionless. I nodded. *"Bon,"* he said, but I heard it as "Scram." He handed me a manila envelope. Instead of accompanying me to the door, or even saying good-bye, he turned back to his ledger.

Bernard was angry.

I left, pulling the door open as slowly as I could and closing it gently behind me. The cowbell didn't sound at all.

37

I asked him
For one more moment of the dream,
which gave me peace.
—CZESLAW MILOSZ, "Guardian Angel"

When I got home, there was a message from Olivier. The sound of his voice was so unexpected, so profoundly weird, that I thought it was a wrong number. Or that I was imagining things. When I was thirteen, I'd fallen in love with a pair of suede boots I'd seen in a fashion magazine. I'd wanted them so much, I'd dreamed I'd gotten them, and I'd checked my closet in the morning to see if they were there.

The machine clicked and replayed the message. I looked up at the ornate corner moldings, the marquetry pattern along the edge of the desk, the marble elephant on the bookshelf. I was cataloging details, as if doing so could make time slow down, so I could catch up. I pressed Play again. My finger left a smeared print on the black plastic.

It really was Olivier, and his voice was like something I could hide in. "It was a shock to see you, *un choc fou*. I can't stop thinking about you. Nothing has changed for me. *Tu me manques. J'ai envie de te voir.*"

I sat on the floor, boneless, and played it again.

By the fourth time, I had a minor sobbing fit, crying not the way you do when you're sad but the way you do after you've narrowly missed being hit by a car or a falling boulder: a trembling, hyperventilating kind of crying that you would label hysterical if you passed someone on the street crying that way. By the fifth or sixth time, the words ran together, ink in rain, sound smeared with language.

I curled into a ball, pressing my cheek to the cool wood floor while I listened to his voice. Even as I did it, I had an image of myself lying on the floor, listening to his voice wash over me, and it was sort of glorious, like opera, except I kept having to reach up to press Play, as the answering machine didn't have a repeat function.

Olivier missed me. I thought about that weird French construction that still confuses me: not "I miss you," but "You are missing to me." Because that's how I hear it, it's somehow more direct and poignant at the same time, though the French don't hear it that way. To them, the construction is just another convention; they say *"Tu me manques"* and hear "I miss you." But I always felt a kind of melancholy in the form, as if missing someone wasn't an action but rather an awareness, the observation of a loss. Also, the fact that the French switches the direct object and the subject throws me. I understand it, but it's always foreign: I can't get inside the French to see out of it.

I was missing to him. He missed me. It wasn't just the construction that was foreign but the sentiment, too. My own sense of loss had occupied all the space in my head that had anything to do with Olivier. Now I had to consider that he was suffering in some way. I remembered the look on his face in the restaurant, then pictured him sad, then sadder, then very sad, like Pierrot with white face paint and black tears.

I reached up for the phone and called Althea.

"What's up?" she asked.

"I saw Olivier today—by mistake," I added when she groaned. "Then he left me a message on my machine, saying he misses me," I said.

"Too bad for him. He should sort out his life," Althea said. "Uh-oh, are you going to brood about this?" I didn't answer, because while I wouldn't have used the word "brood," I was considering mulling, dwelling, maybe some light agonizing. "You are, you broody cow!" she exclaimed. "Listen, come to this thing Fred invited us to—"

"What thing?"

"An art opening at some posh gallery. Meet us there at seven—"

"Can I dress up?"

"Yes, we'll go out for dinner after. It'll be fun."

I lolled on the floor awhile longer. I blew away a dust bunny and pretended to debate calling him back, but I knew I would. I was just luxuriating in the question of when.

....

There was already a small crowd on the rue de Seine when I got there. I was wearing my pink coat over a black dress and high heels and feeling very French. Althea wasn't there yet, so I looked at the art, a collection of black-and-white portraits that had been painted over with bright tribal patterns. Fred was talking to a skinny, waiflike woman on the sidewalk. I overheard a snippet of their conversation.

"*Entre moi et la Havane, c'est une histoire d'amour,*" she said, her voice throaty. She exhaled a plume of cigarette smoke and pouted. He murmured something I didn't catch. "I lived with artists in Cuba. I went into the worst ghettos to buy grass, man," she said. She pooched her lips out like she was blowing on a cup of tea. He grimaced.

The word that came to mind was *poufiasse,* somewhat stronger than "bimbo," with elements of "poser" and "twit," though *pétasse,* a rather rude word for "tart," would've been just fine as well.

I walked over to them and kissed Fred on both cheeks. He was wearing a turtleneck and jeans, and he smelled of citrus. "Fred! How lovely to see you! I've been meaning to call and tell you how helpful your translation theory advice was," I gushed. The waif narrowed her eyes at me. "Hello," I said. "Are you one of Fred's students?"

"Anna, this is Muriel," Fred said.

I smiled at her and took his hand. "Do you mind if I borrow him for a moment?" Not waiting for an answer, I pulled him inside. I helped myself to two glasses of wine and handed him one.

"Cheers," he said, clinking my glass. "What was that all about?" he asked.

"You looked like you needed rescuing," I said. "And I need practice flirting."

"You're doing just fine," he said. His eyes crinkled in amusement. "In fact, you look like the cat that ate the canary."

"I could be," I said, looking at him over my wineglass. Althea and Ivan joined us, along with Charles-Henri and Justine, and two other couples, and we went down the street looking at other galleries, drinking more glasses of art gallery wine. We ended up at a tapas place in the Fifth, at a large corner table.

After we'd ordered, Ivan stood up and cleared his throat. "Everyone, I have an announcement to make. Althea has agreed to marry me, reckless woman that she is, and I'm officially moving in so we can live in sin until the big day!" There was cheering and clapping. I looked over at Althea and smiled, and she smiled back, looking flushed and happy. Someone called out, "When?"

"We're thinking late summer," Althea said, looking at Ivan.

"In Provence, in the garden at Charles-Henri's house," Ivan added.

"I'm paying for the champagne," Charles-Henri announced, to more applause.

I went over to congratulate them, and there was a round of kissing and hugging before everyone sat down again. I glanced across the table, seeing Ivan and Althea holding hands. I thought about how their two worlds intersected, and how that intersection was full of secrets and stories that knit their lives together.

I had a secret, too. And I was going to call him back.

Althea came over and sat next to me. "You'll come, won't you?" she asked.

"To the wedding? All of us gloriously drunk and celebrating you and Ivan in the lap of luxury? I wouldn't miss it," I said. "I'm so happy for you."

"Thank you," she said. "How are you doing about Olivier?" she asked.

"I was just about to call him," I admitted.

She gave me a careful, even look. "I can lecture you until your ears bleed, but only one question counts: What do you want?" she asked. I gave an involuntary shudder, like a cat shaking water from its paw.

"The things I want, I won't get. Olivier without Estelle. An Olivier who hadn't lied to me," I said. "Or maybe I just want a proper ending."

"Sweetie, you know you deserve to be with someone who can give you more," she said. "That said, and I'm not judging you, sometimes we take what we can get." She kissed my cheek.

I went outside and called him. It was late, and I knew the play would be over.

"*Viens. Je t'attends,*" I said. I'm waiting for you.

. . . .

At home, I perched on the sofa, nervous, my heart beating wildly. I thought about taking a shower and changing. I thought about putting on music, something appropriate, or heavy-handed, or symbolic. I thought about opening a bottle of wine. I thought about all the other times he'd come over, and I thought about snipping, once and for all, the invisible spider silk thread between us.

I thought all of those things, and I did none of them. Thinking them was a distraction, a scrim to disguise myself from myself, a pointless ploy because I did know what I wanted. I also knew that when you made a deal with the devil, you wrote your own draft, and mine said "One more night."

In the bathroom, I took a good look in the mirror. I wanted to make sure I knew what I looked like. Under the harsh, white light, I memorized what I saw, and the face that looked back at me was determined and old enough to know what I was doing: *majeure et vaccinée*, past the age of consent and I'd had all my shots.

....

I put my fingers on his lips. They were soft, damp, a little chapped. I pressed my face to his neck, breathing in the scent of him, musk and skin, a whiff of tobacco, a trace of aftershave, something new I couldn't identify. I raked my fingers through his hair, feeling its length and thickness, the shape of his skull.

He put his arms around me, but I didn't want to be held, not just yet. I pulled back. He moved to kiss me, and I turned my head. I pushed him against the wall and sniffed him like an animal. I pressed my face into his neck, his chest, his arms. When he groaned, I put my hand over his mouth, feeling the heat of his breath against my palm.

I undressed him in the bedroom. I slid his coat off his shoulders and unbuttoned his shirt, slipping my fingers between the buttons to touch the skin underneath. I pulled his shirt off and traced his shoulder with my tongue. I unbuckled his belt and unzipped his jeans, reaching my hands inside to hold his hips. When I slid my hand inside his pants to grasp his cock, I heard his sharp intake of breath. I pushed him back on the bed.

And then I was thirsty. I went to the kitchen and drank a glass of water. I felt powerful, hungry. I poured another glass of water and walked back to the bedroom. He lay flat on his back, his arms outstretched on either side. I gazed at him, prone on my bed: his profile, the matte, olive skin, the curved angles of his muscles, the line of his hip, the soft, curly hair on his chest and legs. I was no painter, but I wanted a canvas and palette, I wanted to paint him there, naked, waiting for me.

I put the glass down on the bedside table. I pulled off my dress, unclasped my bra, stepped out of my underwear, and felt goose bumps prickle across my skin. Still I watched him, letting the tension cloud the air, making it difficult to breathe.

By unspoken agreement, everything was on my terms. He waited for me to approach him, and I took my time because I'd never been here before. I'd always been where Olivier was. I'd been the naked object in bed, while someone else watched. Timothy had watched me. I could see where he'd gotten off.

It was almost like being with someone else, and though I didn't know if it was because I was really seeing him for the first time or because I felt like a different person, I finally understood what it was to own my desire, instead of being swept up in someone else's.

I climbed on top of him, sliding my limbs over his, and kissed him. I pressed his shoulders down with my hands and explored his mouth with my tongue. He pulled my hips down. He slid his hands around my back, around my waist, up to my breasts. His hands were warm, but I shivered. He wound his hands in my hair, pulling me closer.

I reached down between my legs and grasped his cock, guiding it inside me. I leaned into him, moving against him, barely hearing the sounds we made in the dark.

....

I woke up in the night. Olivier slept with his cheek pressed to the nape of my neck, his arm like a safety belt across my waist. I slid out of bed. In the bathroom mirror, my lips were puffy and my hair was a Medusa-like tangle, but I still looked like me. I heard the sheets rustle. A trapezoid of light appeared on the hall floor when he turned on the lamp.

"Tu as soif?" I called out.

"Oui," he said. I brought him a glass of water. He sat up to drink, and the shiny glint of his watch, still on his wrist, caught my eye.

"You are frowning," he said. "I don't like to see you frown." He pressed his thumb between my eyebrows.

"How do you say 'frown' in French?" I asked. "I've forgotten."

"*Je ne te dirai pas,*" he said. When he leaned forward to kiss me, his lips were cold and wet, like a boy's.

It would be light in a couple of hours, but right now, it was still dark, and Olivier was still here. We made love again. Afterward, I listened to him sleep, feeling twinges, flutters in my body that would translate to soreness in the morning. When I closed my eyes, random images flashed through my head: the crazy carpet patterns you see when you rub your eyes, the faces of strangers, grassy hills, fanged monsters, old-fashioned glass jars of milk that shattered on pale green tile floors. Spasms of the imagination.

Olivier's eyebrows were thick and dark, the eyelashes short and curved. In sleep, his nose looked bigger and beakier. A sigh escaped from me, a tender little sound. I slid my leg between his, feeling the soft curls of his hair against my skin.

My attempt at an exorcism was slipping away from me.

"Don't be here in the morning," I whispered.

....

When I woke up, I could hear him rooting around in the kitchen. There would be *viennoiseries* on the table, France Inter on the radio, a pack of cigarettes next to *Libération* and the *International Herald Tribune*. These were things I knew.

I sat up. Other things I knew included the fact that he was still involved with Estelle and nothing had changed. I'd known it last night, but it hadn't mattered last night; last night had been about last night.

It wasn't such a bad thing, if you wanted to share your lover with a married actress nearly fifteen years his senior. I stretched, pointing and flexing my toes. In the space of one night, he'd become a lover, not a boyfriend, not a man I was seeing or dating, not *"mon amoureux."*

I heard him singing "L.A. Woman" in the shower. Some women

could do it. Clara did. I probably could, if I wanted to, but I didn't want to. Not because I had old-fashioned, bourgeois ideas about love, though I probably did, but because I wanted more.

I shoved my arms into my bathrobe and went into the kitchen. My internal voice, like a panicky parrot, squawked, "What are you doing? What are you doing?"

"I'm having breakfast, like a civilized person, with the man who spent the night," I muttered. "I'm drinking coffee with my lover and the specter of his married girlfriend. In the clichéd, if accurate, if odious, pop-psychobabble of my generation, I'm breaking bread with someone who is not available," I continued. Olivier came in.

"*A qui tu parles?*" he asked, tilting his head to shake water from his ear.

"*Personne. Je suis folle,*" I said, because talking to myself did feel a little crazy.

"*Ah bon? Je ne savais pas,*" he said, coming over to kiss me. I pulled away, leaning back against the sink. "*Qu'est ce qu'il y a?*" he asked.

"This doesn't work for me, Olivier." I swept my hand in the direction of the kitchen table. The sight of two croissants and four little *cannelés*, caramelized vanilla cakes, on a plate, made my stomach hurt.

"*Le petit déj?*" he asked, mystified.

"No, not breakfast. You being here."

"But you invited me," he said, amused, as if we were playing.

"I know." I was going to have to do better than this. I cupped his cheek. "You're with someone else," I said. He stiffened. "That's what doesn't work for me."

"You know that doesn't matter," he said, with a touch of anger.

I had a dizzying sense of déjà vu, déjà vu repeating, a tautology curving back on itself, and I knew he'd used that line before, not just on me, on someone else, and I'd heard it before, not just from him. It was one thing to make a decision in the dark; faced with Olivier, in the flesh, in front of me, it was harder. I was susceptible, I could be seduced by words; they could inflate and expand, become so big that I couldn't see around them, but I had to see around them.

"It matters to me," I said. "I wanted last night," I said, trying to explain. "I wanted a proper good-bye. That's what last night was about—"

"*Tu as tort,*" he interrupted, telling me I was wrong and grasping my shoulders. "*Je t'aime,*" he said softly. "*Le reste, ce n'est pas important.*" I love you. The rest isn't important.

There they were, the big guns, but it was too late. I stepped back and said, "*Si,*" thinking only the French would have a specific kind of yes you use to contradict someone. "It is to me," I added.

"Why are you doing this?" he asked, folding his arms across his chest.

"Because I have to," I said, even as the sirens wailed from the rocks. Why can't you have this? The man just said he loves you! Isn't that better than nothing? You'll regret it! One day, it'll be over with Estelle— she's getting up there in years, the old bat. If you push him away now, it will be *over*!

"*Mais tu es complètement ridicule!* This is American extremism!" he exclaimed. "All or nothing, black or white! It's childish! Destructive!"

Yes, I nodded. From his point of view, it was true. But not ending it now, while it might have been a vote of confidence for Olivier, was a bet against me, and I was holding out for me.

After he left, I could still see him, an afterimage on my retina. I saw him leaning against the wall, arms folded, and saw him walking toward me. I heard his voice, felt his cheek against mine, the softness of his lips. He was on my skin, the smell of sex and sweat. I sniffed my arms, my hair, inhaling deeply, trying to memorize it. But as evocative as scent was, I knew you couldn't conjure it up in your memory. It didn't replay, the way a song did. The only way to have it back was to have it back.

I took a long, hot shower and washed my hair. Then I stripped the bed and gathered the towels and threw them in the shiny new washing machine. I threw out the croissants and all but one *cannelé,* which I ate. I drank a cup of coffee and smoked one of his cigarettes, then I threw those out, too.

38

Le monde, chère Agnès, est une étrange chose.[*]
—MOLIÈRE, *L'Ecole des femmes*

I had nightmares every night. Which was odd, because during the day, I was fine. I was sad about Olivier, but it was ordinary, dull sadness, the kind you recover from, not bottomless despair, and already it seemed distant. But at night, I saw the same thing, over and over: a crash, followed by billowing clouds of black smoke. Someone crying or screaming. I'd wake up in a sweat around four, then sleep again until seven.

After three nights of this, I woke up determined to do something different, shake up my routine. I decided to get out of my neighborhood and go to a museum. I picked a group show at the Musée d'Art Moderne.

I had most of the show, sculptures and videos of ten artists from around the world, to myself. In one room, I crawled into a hollowed-out, upside-down Volkswagen Bug, suspended by steel cables from the ceiling. Inside, there was a blanket and pillows, and a sped-up video of

*The world, dear Agnes, is a strange affair.

the Eiffel Tower in front of the Palais de Chaillot played on the TV installed in the rear window. The sky went from day to sunset to night in a matter of seconds, then started over again.

It was like being in a postapocalyptic baby carriage. I fell asleep, waking up only when the museum guard nudged my shoulder. It was the best sleep I'd had in days.

I went home and continued work on the last chapter.

I went back to my hotel that evening savoring the possibility that lay before me. I'd longed for her even after I'd taught myself to forget longing. I stepped onto the balcony and looked out over Hyde Park at night, thinking back, remembering the detective I'd hired to find her, as if the knowledge would bring her back to me. Life, the years, in their own time, had done the work. I was filled with the wildly incongruous sense of being alive again.

As it turned out, she found me. Her voice on the phone was so familiar, yet richer, burnished. We still knew each other. Some people change their essence over time. Friends you once loved you can no longer find common ground with, the only thing between you an increasing sense of misplaced nostalgia. Others change over time, becoming more who they are, more how you knew them, distilled, as it were, into purer forms of themselves. So it was with her.

We arranged to meet in Venice, in two weeks' time.

Time passed like honey: thick, slow, but infinitely sweet. I wasn't sure the day would actually come. I crossed streets certain I would be run over by a bus; I drove, convinced that my car would crash; I even boarded a plane convinced it would drop out of the sky. Pitched between a nervous, joyful anticipation and the vicissitudes of ordinary life, I hovered between two versions of my own existence. I would have lived to see my life come full circle. To see the one woman I'd loved and lost come back to me.

I put the pages down. Yeah, it was one of the oldest stories in the book—finding your old sweetheart later in life—but I had to admit, it worked for me.

There is no romantic like an old romantic.

There we were, the two of us, in the same city, together. In a hotel, which was not the same hotel but which might as well have been the same hotel, we sat on faded damask furniture and talked, as if nothing had changed, though everything had changed: the thing and its opposite, existing together, a hallucination of time explained by physics, a chiaroscuro of shadowy contradictions, illuminated by memory and desire.

(Love, yes, in its hibernal form.)

As if things hadn't changed, as if we hadn't changed, as if only the stories had changed and we had merely to catch each other up, fill in the blanks, make the most minute of corrections. After all, we'd always told each other stories.

How to resolve the problem of *histoire*, which means both story and history?

There was a sense of continuity between us, history stopped and started again. As if our story was a book, carelessly set down on a summer's day, only to be picked up and read, years later, in late autumn. The memory of that earlier season, with its sharp, green impetuosity, lingered briefly, then dissipated.

Her voice had deepened with age and the cigarettes she'd given up. The lines around her eyes and mouth were a testament to all the years she'd smiled without me. They only made her more beautiful. She would laugh at me for that, but I wouldn't mind. How precious it is, the sound of her laughter.

I stared out the window, absentmindedly tracing the shape of my own lips with my finger, imagining them on the bed in Venice, wondering what it would be like to find someone again all those years later. For a moment, I let myself sit on that bed in Venice with Olivier. I pictured us older, imagined myself wiser and yet unpretentious, as if I wore the mantle of a well-lived life as casually as the fetching dress I saw myself in.

I edited the image: maybe a silk shirt with flowing sleeves. Narrow black skirt, sheer stockings, and a different perfume, one that came out of an old-fashioned, cut-glass bottle . . . Suddenly, Olivier wasn't in it anymore. I'd let my mind wander, and I was with someone else in Venice, a man I loved, like a presence I could imagine but not quite see.

On the street, a garbage truck shrieked to a halt. Hydraulic arms shrieked as they lifted and emptied the green recycling bin. The unmistakable sound of shattering wine bottles put an end to my reverie. Still, even after it faded from my mind, I felt a pang of nostalgia for my pretty little scene.

I flopped back on the couch with the chapter, staring up at the ceiling molding as the garbage truck groaned down the street. He wasn't a bad guy, my author. "My" author, I thought wryly; I liked him now—or, he'd become someone I liked. Someone who could look at the woman he'd loved years before, and love her more.

She told me about her lovers, her travels, her marriage and divorce. I told her about mine. We talked about our careers, the ambitions we'd fulfilled, the ones we'd regretted, the ones we'd left behind.

There we were, in the most romantic city in the world, and we chose to barricade ourselves in our hotel room, ordering room service and drinking Barolo. She still had an endearing penchant for sweets and disposed of the Toblerone chocolates in the minibar.

I untied my shoelaces. She'd long since kicked off her shoes, tuck-

ing her feet underneath her. Now we both lay down on the enormous bed, yet another island in the liquid city.

"Do you remember that place we met?" she asked. "What was the name of it?"

I could see it, the restaurant with the yellow walls, the long table, but the name wouldn't come to me. "I don't remember," I confessed.

"Ah, memory," she said ruefully. She turned, sliding a pillow underneath her head. Her hair fell to one side. "We could have stayed in London or Paris for this," she remarked with an impish smile.

"Yes," I agreed. As if to refute us, a water taxi sped by on the canal below, throwing sparkling lights on the ceiling. "But I'm happy we're here," I said. A moment passed. She toyed with my cuff link.

"They have a phrase for it in the Venetian dialect, the lights playing on the ceiling," she mused.

"What is it?" I asked.

"I've forgotten," she said, working the cuff link free. She bent down, pressing her cheek to my wrist. We fell asleep in our clothes, holding hands like children.

I don't require much sleep anymore. I wake at dawn. Sometimes I read, sometimes I write. I stood at the window. There was mist on the horizon, obscuring everything but the dome of Santa Maria della Salute. I thought about waking Eve so she could see it, but she lay asleep, a faint frown on her forehead, as if she were impatient in a dream, and all I wanted to do was memorize her face. She smiled, her eyes still closed.

"And if I returned to Paris?" she asked.

"Nothing would make me happier," I murmured.

"It won't be easy . . . I have certain obligations, certain attachments," she said.

"I make no demands," I said. An idea of us thickened from a mist of imagination and took form.

. . . .

In the late afternoon, I went for a walk through the Marais down to the Seine to catch the sunset. On the way back, I stopped in a *boulangerie* to buy my favorite licorice candy, shiny, slightly oily black tubes stuffed with sugar paste. They were stale, just the way I liked them: tough and chewy.

On the rue des Archives, a hard chunk of licorice caught in my teeth, and I stopped to pry it free from a molar with my fingernail. In front of a store I must have passed a hundred times but never noticed, I looked at the windows, displaying various old magazines: a sixties *Vogue* with Twiggy in striped kneesocks, a *Paris Match* with Marilyn Monroe and Arthur Miller, and a yellowing *Paris Soir* newspaper about the war in Algeria. The shop was full of old periodicals, a reference treasure trove for pop culture historians as well as fashion and design people.

I pocketed my bag of licorice and went inside. Mountainous piles of magazines, some so old the edges of the paper were tobacco brown, made up a haphazard maze. The air was thick with a fug of cigarette smoke, and I heard two male voices argue heatedly about the recent insider trading scandal.

I saw them when I rounded a tower of milk crates. The owner, seated behind a table, tapped his ash out in a Cinzano ashtray. Beneath him, a Yorkshire terrier sat on a chewed-up fleece cushion. The other man wore a suit. I muttered a hasty *"Bonjour."*

I wandered through the chaotic piles of publications, trying to determine the logic, if any, of the organization. Every conceivable French magazine was there: political journals, fashion magazines, sports, interior decorating, music, gardening, crafts, and knitting. Remembering Clara's birthday was coming up, I stopped in front of a table of fashion magazines. Maybe she'd enjoy an *Elle* from the year she was born.

It was amazing how the articles in women's magazines hadn't changed much in thirty-odd years: "How to Dress for That New Job," "How to Tell If He's the One," "Interview with Sylvie Vartan." Even-featured girls and women posed stiffly, smiling up from yellowing paper. They were touching, those models, trapped in a dated archness, a bygone vision of femininity—especially the ones from the fifties, with their headbands and vacuum cleaners and recipes for *béchamel* and *mousse au chocolat*.

I found an issue of French *Vogue* from August 1975. Perfect for Clara. I tucked it under my arm.

Nails tapped on varnished wood. The Yorkie came around the corner and barked, a high-pitched yap followed by a pint-sized growl. I tried not to laugh.

"Venez, César!" the owner called, addressing his dog in the formal second-person plural. The little dog gave me another yap and clattered away.

As I straightened up, I saw a hoard of *Figaro Madame* magazines in a box beneath the table. I picked one off the top: from 1989, with Iman on the cover, stunning in a white linen dress and dangling, gold earrings. When I'd lived in Paris as a student, my grandmother used to save me the fashion magazine from her Sunday *Le Figaro*.

I flipped through the pages, looking at the fashions of the late eighties: huge shoulder pads, *Flashdance* off-the-shoulder sweaters, and Anaïs Anaïs, a perfume I used to wear. I remembered the department store bombings, the student riots, the year the Seine flooded, making the *quai* highways unusable, and later, when I studied in Paris, the seminar I took with a famous French political scientist who smoked a pipe in class—and the curly-haired philosophy student I fell in and out of love with, who had a face like an Italian cherub and worshiped the Ramones.

I flipped past a photograph of a woman with familiar, exotic features and pink frosted lipstick, and then turned back without thinking. There it was, proof the brain is faster than the eye: an article titled "Estelle Bailleux: sa vie, ses amours."

My once rival. My nemesis, if I wasn't being too grandiose or present-tense. I had to read it.

In 1988, she'd completed a successful run of *Private Lives* in the West End and had made a film with Alain Resnais. Recently divorced, she'd started a new relationship with a man she described as *"l'homme de ma vie."*

It's such a romantic expression from the English-language point of view: "the man of my life," the "of" and "my" implying a whole life, the single most important man of your life. The French equivalent of "the one," or "my soul mate," but lacking the pop-culture shorthand of the former and the gooey romantic aspect of the latter. The expression is simple, concise, and direct.

I turned to a two-page spread of Estelle wearing a pink gown embroidered on the back with two black squiggles of sequins shaped like the curvy openings on violins. Meters of duchesse satin flowed out behind her. The dress was Christian Lacroix; the choker of diamonds and rubies at her neck was Mauboussin. Seeing her at roughly my age, in a getup worthy of the court of Louis XIV, I found it hard not to feel outclassed.

I devoured the interview, looking for information about her personal life, but it was mostly about her new film, her passion for the theater, and her country house. She refused to name her mysterious new man, saying only that he was recently divorced and that they'd known each other for years.

I kept hoping I'd stumble across some lurid morsel of information, but the interview was full of the usual platitudes.

"Avez-vous besoin d'aide?" a voice called out, asking if I needed help.

"Non, merci, monsieur," I called out, feeling like I'd been caught with pornography. On the last page, the interviewer, determined to worm another snippet of information about her personal life, asked how she knew her new love was Mr. Right.

Estelle replied that, now that she was in her thirties, she understood her previous relationships had been shallow. "It is true," she mused, "that you do things differently when you get a little older. You waste less time, but you are more cautious—you've learned enough not to expect the world."

She went on to confess that the first time they'd spent a weekend together, she'd had a terrible nightmare. To comfort her, he'd told her about a summer he spent as a child with some relatives in Brittany who owned a small farm. He'd never been away from home, he barely knew his relatives, and in the middle of his first night there, a large spider had crawled on his face.

In his sleep, he'd slapped it, flattening the spider to his cheekbone. The sound had woken him, and he'd fled in a panic to the kitchen, running into his eldest cousin, a young woman who'd snuck in after a late night. She'd cleaned his face and made him hot milk.

" 'To this day,' he'd said, 'the smell of hot milk and vanilla brings back that night, a roaring country fire, the kind of comfort you could get as a child.'

"When he told me that," Estelle said, "this successful, dynamic man, when he shared this story, I knew I loved him."

I gripped the magazine, my fingertips sweaty on the glossy cover.

Hot milk and vanilla. A spider, squashed on his cheekbone. I knew this story.

I reread the paragraph.

Cette femme merveilleuse. The woman who'd made the hot milk and vanilla was *cette femme merveilleuse.* I don't know why I knew that, but I did. It rang a bell. Not in a hackneyed, figure of speech kind of way but in a distinct, familiar way: a cowbell.

I would need to look at my computer files to confirm it, but I knew. It was an early chapter, the one about his childhood friend, the kid with the hot mom, staying at their country house, waking up with the insect on his head. My author.

I knew who my author was. He was married to Estelle.

As calmly as I could, I walked to the table where the owner sat. Without a word, I handed him the *Figaro Madame* and the *Vogue*. The Yorkie yapped at me again.

"Ça suffit! Couchez!" he said to the dog and coughed, making a honking sound, thick with phlegm. I vowed never to smoke again.

"Vous avez trouvé ce qu'il vous fallait?" he asked.

"Parfaitement, monsieur," I said. He charged me only eight euros for the *Figaro Madame*. Dirt cheap.

I walked to the Italian place for a cone of *stracciatella* and crossed over to the place des Vosges to savor my discovery on a bench in the late-afternoon sun.

My author was Monsieur le Ministre, Romain Chesnier. Eve was Estelle. It was probably the minister's second marriage, as I was betting he'd previously been married to a woman very much like Daphne, but that would be easy enough to verify.

Funny how Olivier didn't show up in the book. The minister had to know about him, especially if he'd gone to the hospital to be with Estelle in her hour of need. Unless he was the sculptor in London in the third ending, a very minor role indeed.

Did Estelle know what her husband was writing about? They were already a celebrity couple. *Quel scandale* if anyone ever found out!

I wondered why Chesnier had written it, why there were four different endings, and why he didn't want to publish it anymore. Had something happened, aside from the "minor cardiac incident"? Cold feet? Was he afraid its subject was so obvious that people would recognize him even if he published anonymously or under a pseudonym?

Then again, maybe it wouldn't be a scandal. Literature was a big deal in France—it would probably be a feather in his cap: aging politician publishes sensational, thinly veiled account of his love life with glamorous actress. He'd get invited onto all the literary and pop-culture shows. I could picture Estelle in the audience, beaming in Prada or vintage Saint Laurent. Media picnic! The press would try to get him to say it was the story of his life with her, he'd avoid answering in that eel-like, evasive way of politicians—which in France always includes repeating the interviewer's full name *("Je vous dirais, Michel Denisot")*—and everyone would assume it was rooted in fact.

Which it probably was. Though the best word for it, I thought, licking a dribble of melted ice cream from my thumb, was "juicy." I pictured the look on Bernard's face when I told him I knew. He'd be so very, very annoyed, and I knew what very annoyed looked like on him, I'd seen it often enough. "Hah!" I said out loud, as if I'd been clever instead of freakishly lucky.

The downside was that I couldn't actually share my secret with anyone aside from Bernard. I could hardly tell Olivier. No doubt Antoine and Victorine would relish knowing, but I wouldn't betray Monsieur X to them. My friends might find it interesting, but I couldn't see any of them getting excited about it.

Except Bunny. Of course, Bunny. Bunny always loved a scoop; even surly retirement couldn't take the newspaperman out of him. I finished off the cone. The sun cast long shadows across the seventeenth-century square.

On the lawn, a man in baggy pants and a sweatshirt counted out steps, practicing some kind of balletic martial art. I watched as he balanced on one leg, leaped through the air, and landed in a warrior stance. He was lithe and sinuous as he repeated the routine.

"He's good," Bunny murmured, leaning over the back of the bench.

"I was just thinking about you!" I exclaimed.

"Shh," he said, walking around to sit next to me. He dropped his WHSmith bag on the ground, stretched his legs out, and folded his arms across his chest, his eyes focused on the dancer in the distance.

The setting sun backlit the dancer's dreadlocks, giving him a fuzzy, golden halo. He dove, rotating fluidly in the air, and landed in a somersault. Two couples, crossing through the park, also stopped to watch. He continued dancing after the light faded, until the streetlamps came on around the square. Then he gathered his jacket and backpack and left.

"*Fermeture du jardin,*" someone called out. Park closing. "*Nous fermons, mademoiselle,*" intoned a uniformed park guard behind me. Bunny and I walked out.

"What are you doing this far east?" I asked.

"I hadn't been to the place des Vosges in a while. I miss the old square," he said, looking at the red-brick façades, lit by streetlights. We turned onto the rue de Turenne.

"Listen, have I got a scoop for you!" I said, gleefully pulling out the magazine.

"She is one fine-looking creature," he remarked, gazing at Estelle in the pink gown. "I mean," he corrected, catching the black look I gave him, "for an old bat."

"Whatever," I said. "But isn't it wild? I'm translating Romain Chesnier's life story! *Le Ministre de l'Education Nationale!* Amazing, no?"

"Hold on! No one says it's autobiographical," Bunny cautioned.

"But it has to be!" I put the magazine back in my bag. "Remember what Bernard said? How it was the story of his great love?"

"Yeah, but maybe this was some other guy she was in love with back then," he suggested, then shook his head. "Nah, they're a famous couple. Been together for years. Still," he added, "Laveau could be misleading you, and you could be jumping to conclusions. It's still *fiction*, remember? That means he made it up. Besides, how great can the love story be if his wife has your guy on the side?" he asked.

"He's not my guy," I muttered. Bunny peered into an art gallery. "Maybe he's writing it for Estelle," I suggested. He made a rude sucking sound, pushing air through his teeth. "Like a declaration, a testament to all they've been through. A present," I said.

"Give me a break," he said. He pointed at an oil painting of a barbed-wire fence. "Do people pay money for that?"

"C'mon, Bunny," I pleaded.

He thought for a moment, his mouth working. "Maybe," he said. "But you can't know for sure, you have to prove it."

"I can't prove it!" I wailed. A French couple in front of us, carrying groceries and a baguette, turned around, startled. "I just know," I said. "I have a hunch."

"Well, I ain't gonna argue with a hunch." He gave me an indulgent smile. "Funny, I always thought Chesnier was a sour old windbag. Never read any of his books on ancient Gaul. Who knew, eh?" We stopped in front of the République métro entrance. "Here's where I leave you," he said and went down the stairs.

I walked the rest of the way home thinking about Eve and the author, Estelle and the minister, the four of them, the two of them, Olivier a footnote.

I was a footnote, too, in a way; a footnote to a footnote. How funny that Olivier had wanted to turn the novel into a film; how funny that Laveau had deliberately misled him. Once you knew why, it made sense. How funny, too, that I'd ended up translating it, and that my nemesis turned out to be my heroine. Good old Bernard. Wile E. Bernard. *"Ce sacré Bernard,"* Olivier had called him. He didn't know how right he was.

39

You are now out of your text.
—WILLIAM SHAKESPEARE, *Twelfth Night*

I spent the next morning checking and double-checking the transla-tion. Maybe he didn't want to publish it anymore, but I wanted it to be as close to perfect as possible. I printed out a rough draft, read it aloud, made a few more corrections, and set it aside.

I called Editions Laveau and left a message, saying I would swing by later. I didn't mention I knew who the author was; I was no longer sure I would. Bernard wouldn't congratulate me on my intrepid sleuthing, and I didn't want to piss him off.

I Googled Romain Chesnier. He and Estelle had gotten married two months after the *Figaro Madame* article, and sure enough, he'd been married before, to an Italian news reporter. In his younger days, he'd been handsome, but from the recent photos I'd seen and the brief TV news clip, I knew he'd put on a paunch, and his eyes seemed to sink behind his glasses. I read that his father, a prominent businessman, had died of a heart attack, so heart disease ran in the family.

He'd written a half dozen books on ancient Gaul, including a for-ward to an anniversary edition of the Astérix and Obélix comic books, but none of them were published by Les Editions Pas de Mule. His most famous book, *Vercingétorix à Alésia*, had been translated into twelve languages. Like nearly every other French politician, he'd been to ENA, the Ecole Nationale d'Administration, France's elite school for senior civil servants, but he'd also read history at Cambridge.

I looked at the rough draft one more time, made one correction, and hit Print. As the pages spewed out, I kept seeing Chesnier's face. Before, the author had been a shadowy presence, lurking somewhere beyond my reach but vibrant, a radio station transmitting a voice I could hear but not see. Now that I knew what he looked like, it was hard to picture him as my author. He was just an identity pasted onto a page, a passport photo superimposed on my text.

I put the translation in my bag, next to the *Figaro Madame*. I showered and searched my closet for something stylish but *sobre*. I ended up in black, as if handing in the last chapter meant I was going to a funeral.

When I got to the bookstore, there was a young, pixielike woman with light brown hair sitting behind his desk, chewing on a pencil as she studied an old book.

"Il n'est pas là, monsieur Laveau?" I asked.

She looked up. *"Il sera de retour dans quelques minutes, madame,"* she said. I tried not to flinch. To Bernard, I was always *"mademoiselle."* It felt as if I'd aged overnight.

"Ah, bon," I said. *"Parce que j'ai amené une traduction . . ."* I explained, pointing to the envelope in my hand. She smiled, revealing a gap in her front teeth.

"You are the translator?" she asked in accented English. "My uncle told me you would come. He will arrive very soon. Would you like a coffee?"

"No, thank you," I said firmly. I would drink my *café* with Bernard.

"Are you sure? It's very good," she said. "Very high-tech," she added. Turning, I saw the old espresso machine was gone. In its place was a playful yellow contraption with chrome knobs and buttons, an appliance from the Teletubbies' kitchen. "Please let me make you one," she said. I nodded and sat down.

"What are you reading?" I asked, glancing at the desk.

"Traité d'anatomie et de physiologie," she said. "It's an antique book. The illustrations are quite wonderful." I glanced at the open page. It showed an intricately crosshatched diagram of the foot muscles. She placed a cup of coffee in front of me.

"I am at the Ecole des Beaux Arts," she explained. "We are studying *la morphologie,* so my uncle found me some books."

"You're an artist," I stated, trying to picture Bernard as a doting uncle, picking out books for his niece.

"One day, I think. Yes." She nodded happily. *"Ah, le voilà!"* she exclaimed as Bernard came in. *"Ils sont géniaux,"* she said, pointing to the pile of books. She bounded up to him and kissed him on both cheeks. *"Je te remercie."* His face softened, his eyes dancing with pleasure. It was a look I hadn't seen before, and I felt a twinge of envy.

"Elodie, tu nous laisses deux minutes?" he asked. She left, closing the door.

"Alors, mademoiselle," he said, turning to me. "You have the final chapter! Let me write your check," he said. He sat heavily, not removing his coat, and took his checkbook from the desk.

"Uh, Bernard . . . since it's the last chapter, I was sort of hoping," I began. He didn't look up. "I was hoping we could go to lunch, or something."

His hairline moved back as he raised his eyebrows in surprise. *"Je suis désolé, mademoiselle.* I am having lunch with my niece," he said apologetically. "But perhaps you would care to join us?" he added. The offer was phrased with just enough enthusiasm that I couldn't tell whether it was genuine or excellent manners. I was too embarrassed by his look of surprise to accept.

"No, no, I wouldn't dream of imposing. But perhaps you'll be available another day," I ventured. I had manners, too. I knew enough to say this, even though "another day" sounded a lot like a euphemism for "never."

"*Mais bien sûr,*" he said. "It would be my pleasure. I will be in touch about future developments," he said, cocking a significant eyebrow. I stood up.

"*Ce fut un plaisir, monsieur.*" It has been a pleasure. I held out my hand.

"*Et pour moi, mademoiselle,*" he said, shaking my hand, his lips twitching with a small smile, either at my solemn tone or my use of the simple past. I turned and left the office, walking as if I were on liquid sand, striding away from the ocean while the water receded, not sure whether I was going forward or backward as I moved through the bookstore and out the door, ringing the cowbell for what was, perhaps, the last time.

I put distance between me and Editions Laveau, me and Bernard, me and the translation, the author, the minister, Estelle, Olivier, everything, away from me. I walked east, not slowing until I got to the end of Saint-Germain, as the pink-gold light of the setting sun faded.

Later, in the métro, I overshot my stop. I got out at the Gare du Nord. As I trudged down a long, tiled hallway, I saw a man in a gray suit distributing pale blue cards with shiny navy letters. I picked one off the floor for my collection and read: "*Maître Seydi, marabout Africain.*" The card promised results in less than twenty-four hours, with a specialty in deliverance from all manner of ghosts, evil spirits, and bad dreams. CAUCHEMARS was printed in bold, all caps.

He came over to me. "You don't need that, *mademoiselle.*" I looked up at him. Tall, with tired, brown eyes, he smiled and reached for the card, but I held on to it. Something in my face must have startled him, because his expression changed. "If you do need help, my brother is a very wise man. *Il n'est pas comme les autres,*" he said. His gaze was gentle, despite formidable raised scars on his cheeks, and I didn't want to stop looking at him. "Tell him Souaré sent you. You won't have to wait."

I walked home along the canals, watching the wind whip the water against the concrete banks. A seagull squawked, circling overhead. I picked my way over the uneven cobblestones and sat on a bench. Under a darkening sky, I stared at the water, bending the blue card back and forth between my fingers.

I made an appointment for the next day.

40

*So that no one may forget how fine it would be if, for each sea
that awaits us, there were a river, for us. And someone—
a father, a lover, someone—capable of taking us by the hand and
finding that river—imagining it, inventing it—and placing us on
its flow with the buoyancy of a single word, adieu.*
—ALESSANDRO BARICCO, *Ocean Sea*

The next day, I met Bunny in the Parc des Buttes Chaumont. Up on a
sunny hill not far from the folly, with a sweeping view of the city. I
told him about my nightmares and my appointment with Maître Seydi.

"A witch doctor? Are you kidding me?" He folded his arms across
his chest and glared at me. The cold wind whistled through the air.
"Mumbo jumbo," he said, his mouth twisting. "Though I suppose it explains why you've been acting so strange lately."

"I have not been acting strange!" I protested. He slid me a sideways
look.

"And you think this *marabout* can cure you?"

I tilted my head and looked at him. "It's worth a shot."

He was silent for a moment. "You want me to walk with you?" he
asked. I nodded. He picked up his WHSmith bag, and we walked toward the avenue de Laumière.

At number thirty-nine, I punched in the building code and pushed the door open. Bunny stood, stubbing the sidewalk with the tip of his running shoe.

"I'm not coming in," he said.

"Fine," I said, exasperated. He squinted, looking down the street.

"I may not be here when you come out," he added.

"What do you mean, you might not be here? Why can't you wait for me there?" I asked, pointing to the café on the corner, Le Carambolage.

"I don't know, I have stuff to do," he said, wrinkling his nose with a cross look.

"But—"

"I don't know this neighborhood, and who knows how long you'll be. Plus, I'm tired and it's cold," he said, playing his trump card. I couldn't argue with that, and he knew it. I looked at his face, the wrinkled skin and watery eyes.

"You'll be okay, kid. You know where to find me," he said. "You always do." He bent his head to whisper in my ear. "You'll be okay."

. . . .

I climbed four flights of stairs to Maître Seydi's apartment, wondering what I would find. What if it was mumbo jumbo or voodoo? Or dangerous? I paced the landing, scenes of zombie movies flashing before my eyes, but then the fragrant aroma of onions and garlic sautéing in butter wafted through the air, and it reassured me.

Maître Seydi opened the door. He was a small, slight man, whose meticulously pressed olive green suit looked baggy, as if he'd lost some weight, perhaps due to illness. His cheeks sagged as well, but unlike his brother's, they weren't scarred. He had short gray hair, wore mirrored aviator sunglasses, and spoke French with a singsongy accent.

"*Bienvenue chez nous, mademoiselle,*" he said, opening his arms wide in welcome. Was I supposed to hug him?

"*Merci, maître,*" I said.

He took my arm above the elbow. *"Venez, venez,"* he said, pulling me into a small room. It was painted yellow, the paint peeling at the baseboards, with ikat-covered chairs surrounding a round table. A vase filled with wilting yellow roses sat on the table. An Elgar suite played in the background, a piece I knew.

"S'il vous plaît," he said, pointing to a chair. He pinched the pleats in his pants and sat next to me. He asked me a series of questions, about my background, my marital status, profession, and health. Then he got up and turned off the music. When he sat down again, he stretched out his hand. I placed mine in it. It was warm and dry.

"Alors, parlez-moi de votre problème," he said. As I told him about my bad dreams, the disasters and claustrophobia, he nodded and made small clicking noises.

"You say car crashes, explosions?" he asked. I nodded. "Yes?"

"Yes," I said. "Sometimes a woman's voice, weeping, maybe Italian or Spanish."

"Every night?"

"No, but a lot of nights *quand-même,*" I said.

"You're lucky you found me," he said matter-of-factly. He squeezed my hand. I let out a sigh of relief. "Of course you are not crazy," he said, reading my thoughts. "Someone is trying to tell you something. How long has this been going on?"

"Oh, I don't know. Weeks."

He whistled. "Weeks! It is a long time to sleep with such dreams."

"I got used to it, I guess."

"This is because you are unmarried and have no children," he declared, shaking his head. My faith in Maître Seydi took a nosedive. I made a noncommittal hum.

"Don't pretend to agree with me!" he rebuked, shaking my hand. "I am trying to understand. You did not come here to tell me stories!" He looked fierce as he furrowed his forehead, his mouth grim below the motorcycle cop shades.

Des histoires. I had lots of stories. Eve's story, Monsieur X's story, which was also Monsieur le Ministre's story. I was, in fact, surrounded by story.

"Sometimes, the world is too much to bear," he said. "This pain, it can take up residence in the hidden part of your mind, your dreams."

"Huh?" I didn't follow. He grimaced, two dimples appearing by his mouth.

"Your skin, it is a membrane that protects your body from disease. In a similar way, your being must protect itself. It must filter, reason, understand, feel, of course, but with perspective, moderation."

I blinked.

"But now, it must stop! You must make it stop," he said and, turning to face me, gripped my hands. "Concentrate," he said.

A distant memory came to me: holding a friend's hands in second grade, two little girls spinning around on the playground.

"Il faut surmonter la souffrance, pas vivre dans son ombre," he said. You must surmount suffering, not live in its shadow. "Close your eyes."

"I don't understand," I said.

"Stop thinking so much," he snapped.

I shut my eyes. The room spun, and for a moment, as if from far off, I heard a couple of piano notes and a rustle of wind, as if they were coming from a TV next door.

"Breathe!" Maître Seydi barked, startling me. My eyes flew open and I sucked in air, not knowing I'd been holding it. "Again," he said. I closed my eyes again, but now all I could think about was the shape of his fingers, the odd intimacy of holding hands with a stranger. I opened one eye to peek at him.

"No, no. You are not serious," he said, his mouth curling. He let go of my hands and leaned back. He was sweating, and something told me he was working harder at this than I was. He shook his head. "Come back another time."

"But—"

"You must concentrate, then move out of the way. I cannot do everything. *Ce n'est pas sérieux.*" He waved his hand in the air, as if to sweep me away, and pulled a cell phone out of his jacket pocket. His gravity was bracing. I didn't want to give up; I didn't want him to give up on me.

"Maître," I said, "the first time, I remembered something from my childhood, and I heard laughter. This is strange for me, but I want to try again." To my surprise, my voice cracked.

I couldn't tell what was going on behind the mirrored glasses, but he tucked the phone away and held out his hands. I placed mine in them. I closed my eyes and took a deep breath, picturing myself asleep. He tightened his grip, and, like the slow dance of a merry-go-round, the room began to spin again.

It was dark, but in the distance, I saw something small and bright, like an illuminated scene in a snow globe. The snow globe grew larger, until I saw myself, younger this time, maybe five or six, wearing a pinafore and white shoes, hiding in the corner of a garden. I was clutching a small stuffed animal, its long, floppy, torn ear in one hand, and crying my little heart out. I walked closer.

She looked up at me, her face swollen and red. I reached down and drew her into my arms. There was an ache in the air, the sweetest, saddest piano music mixed with the scent of roses, the smell of freshly mowed lawn, and me and my little childhood self. It echoed inside me, that aching, sweet sadness, fitting itself to me like a lover.

I don't know how long I sat with her, with me, her hand tucked into mine. The wind kicked up. She stood and wiped her face. The sun was setting, and up above, the sky was turning a deeper blue. I felt minuscule and frozen, as if I were watching the world from inside a glass marble which got smaller and smaller. I started to panic, but I heard a familiar voice, and I pulled myself on it, a rope in a storm.

"You'll be okay, kid."

. . . .

My eyes snapped open. Only Maître Seydi's grip kept me from toppling over. For the second time in my life, I saw stars, only this time they looked like silent insects, doing cartwheels through my peripheral vision before they disappeared.

I didn't speak as I got my bearings. My face was wet, and I blew my nose. I noticed a tall wood sculpture in the corner of the room, a white cane beside it. Maître Seydi removed his sunglasses and rubbed the bridge of his nose. His eyes were a pale, milky blue, and I saw he was blind. He cleaned his glasses with a white linen handkerchief, a gesture that seemed both absurd and touching, and put them back on.

"I didn't know. How sad she was," I said in a small voice.

He pulled a cigarette from a silver case and lit it with a matching lighter. It felt like he was watching me from behind those glasses. When he exhaled through his nose, the two escaping plumes of smoke made me think of a dragon. One thin, blue stream of smoke curled itself into a question mark, hung in the air between us, and dissipated.

My mouth was suddenly dry, and my eyes stung. Maître Seydi cleared his throat.

"But you know, there's nothing I can do about your ghost, *ma petite*." He said it in the kindest voice, so gently I almost didn't understand. "The tall one, your rabbit friend."

....

My legs wobbled beneath me as I went down the four flights of stairs. Outside, it was bright and sunny. The sidewalks seemed to sparkle with bits of glass and broken jewelry. I was a little unsteady, but I walked through the unfamiliar neighborhood, passing a *traiteur* advertising fresh *terrine de lapin*. I walked all the way to Père Lachaise, entering the cemetery behind a group of American college students looking for Jim Morrison's grave.

I meandered down the dappled alleys, amazed, as always, by the variety of names, headstones, sculptures, and urns. I continued up the hill to the columbarium beyond the narrow, white smokestack rising above the cemetery heights. I walked down the stone steps to the second floor and made a left, my feet taking me, the rest of me just following. Inside, the air was cold and moist. I stopped when I found it: a small, shiny onyx square with bright gilt letters. There, in the dark, I sighed, and knelt my forehead against Bunny's name.

....

I found a spot with a view under some rustling trees. In front of me, Paris stretched out under a blue sky with cotton-candy clouds. There'd been a phone call, weeks ago, in the middle of the night, the one I didn't want to hear, the strange woman's voice, the woman who'd gotten my number out of his book, telling me about Bunny's car crash on the Italian *auto- strada*. It had been so easy to press the wrong button in the morning.

I leaned back on the bench and watched a pair of magpies swoop and chase each other. Sparrows pecked at the ground. I would miss visiting him in the park. Any park.

It was a long good-bye. The light changed, my hands got cold in their gloves, and my nose ran. When my toes began to go numb, I walked out of the cemetery and found a taxi at the gate. I climbed in and checked my cell phone. I listened to Bernard Laveau tell me he thought I'd enjoy translating a nineteenth-century murder mystery, and would I come by on Monday morning. The driver, a chatty sort, caught my eye in the rearview mirror. He told me he was an engineer, but he'd been laid off. Then he asked what I did for a living.

"*Je suis traductrice.*" I told him I was a translator as I watched Paris go by: people sitting in cafés, standing in line at the *boulangerie,* walking home with plastic bags from Monoprix . . . couples and children, singles with groceries, and little old ladies with little old dogs.

"*Quelles langues?*" Which languages?

"*De français en anglais,*" I said and relaxed back in the seat.

"Aha! I have a tricky one!" he announced, switching into English.

"No one ever knows this. I've been known to offer a free fare to any-one who can tell me," he said, though I noticed he didn't offer it now. "How do you translate *'Nous ne sommes pas encore sortis de l'auberge'?*" he asked.

"We're not out of the woods yet," I said.

"Ah!" Excited, he turned to look at me at the red light. "You are the first one who has been able to answer me. You must be very good," he said.

"Pas mal," I said. "Not bad at all."

I looked at my reflection in the glass and smiled. In French, "not bad" meant pretty good. We drove west, and the new crescent moon, like a sliver of my heart, hung as if suspended in the early evening Parisian sky.

Acknowledgments

I would like to extend heartfelt thanks to the following:

Friends and early readers: Marjorie Gellhorn Sa'adah, Gail Vida Hamburg, Maria Grasso, Amy Waddell, Rebecca Turner, Lisa McErlean, and David Ulin. Also, to the every other Wednesday writing group, where this book first took shape.

Jeanne Robson and everyone in years of Tuesday nights.

Friends from whom I borrowed bits and pieces: Natalie Milani, Pascal Reveau, Cynthia Coleman-Sparke, Drea Maier, Leyla Kahla, Sophie Poux, and Elizabeth Brahy.

To everyone at HarperCollins, especially my wonderful editor, Jeanette Perez, for her kindness, keen intelligence, and incisive comments, as well as Carrie Kania, Cal Morgan, Jennifer Hart, Nicole Reardon, Mary Beth Constant, Alberto Rojas, and Rachel Chubinsky.

At Sterling Lord Literistic, Inc.: special thanks to the great Robert Guinsler, for his guidance, wisdom, faith, and humor.

To my teachers at Bennington.

My family and friends, in both Los Angeles and Paris: Fifi and Alain Marsot, to whom this book is dedicated; Vanessa Marsot; Thésy Marsot; Jean-Pascal Naudet for my writing retreats at Les Tilleuls; the Gang at Avenue L and Eighth Street; and ROF for the enchanted summer.

Nancy Mitford fans will recognize the story of the Venetian house and the French grandmother from *The Pursuit of Love*, from which it is shamelessly borrowed.

The City of Paris, the landscape of my dreams.

And to the memory of Roy Koch, the *Oberbefehlshasen*.